TREASURE HUNT IN TIE TOWN

TREASURE HUNT IN TIE TOWN

V.J. ROSE

WOLFPACK
PUBLISHING
— EST 2013 —

Published in the United States by Wolfpack Publishing, Las Vegas.

Wolfpack Publishing
6032 Wheat Penny Avenue
Las Vegas, NV 89122

wolfpackpublishing.com

Paperback ISBN: 978-1-64119-365-8
Ebook ISBN: 978-1-64119-364-1

Library of Congress Control Number: 2018953468

Cover image by Walter McClintock, 1909, Beinecke Rare Book and Manuscript Library, Yale University

TREASURE HUNT IN TIE TOWN

ONE

"YOU'RE CUTTING INTO THAT FROG TOO DEEP, DUD," Ponder said, sitting on a stump, spitting tobacco.

Dud Washburn looked up. "I think I know what I'm doing," he said. Every time he looked at his uncle, he saw his future. Lean as a razorback, with piercing blue eyes sunk deep into his head, Ponder's white hair and moustache had once been the same light color of brown as his own. Shaking his head, Dud bent back down to his task. From the corner of his eye, he caught sight of Old Tom standing up and sniffing the air.

Dud believed the big orange dog possessed an eccentric talent identical to the oddball general he was named after. Every sense common to canines—sight, smell, intuition—seemed to be heightened in Old Tom, as the soldier sense had been heightened in General Jackson. Unfortunately, other people viewed Old Tom as some had perceived Old Stonewall—as a gangling nuisance. Old Tom commenced barking, and Dud looked up.

A rider on a mule leading a horse approached the

ranch. Old Tom recognized the slender, dark-skinned man holding one shoulder up like a bird with a broken wing, and his barking soon stopped, and his tail began to wag.

"It's Chicken Wing," Ponder said unnecessarily. "What's he doing with that grulla and carrying that tote sack for? He still owe you money?"

Since Chicken Wing perpetually borrowed money, paid him back and then borrowed more, Dud did not bother to answer. He ignored Chicken Wing for a moment and continued to follow the yellow pus line. Digging with his small knife deeper into the hoof, he strained as the gelding shifted his weight, putting even more pressure on his back.

Chicken Wing got down from his mule, unhooked the sack from his saddle horn and walked forward with it. "Mr. Dud, Mr. Ponder, how you be doing?" he said with a toothsome grin that showed miles of white teeth and dark blue gums.

"Howdy, Chicken Wing," Dud said.

"That's a mighty fine-looking horse you got there, Chicken Wing," Ponder commented.

"I had an old Mexican come by my place," Chicken Wing explained. "He'd been on the run and was plumb wore out. His ticker gave out on him during the night." He opened the bag he had brought along. "He left the horse and this here box. I thought the horse and the box might even us up on the money I owe you, Mr. Dud. That poor old Mexican ain't got no use for it now."

Dud found the pus pocket and let it drain. Setting the hoof down, he stood up, feeling his back creak and inwardly cursing the arthritis that had begun to plague him. With stiff legs, he walked over and taking the ornately carved box, opened the lid and found it empty.

"I know how powerful fond you are of your sister and her little girls," Chicken Wing said, trying to put as much persuasion in his voice as possible. "I thought they might enjoy that pretty little box."

Dud grunted. He tossed the box, little more than a useless trinket, to Ponder and began to examine the gelding. The teeth were all right, not too long. He crouched down, running his hand down a straight leg.

Ponder eyed the box. "Why would a Mexican on the run bother with toting this thing around?" he muttered.

Dud paid him no mind. He calculated the amount of the loan against the value of the horse. Standing up, he nodded. "Fair enough, Chicken Wing," he said. "We're even."

Chicken Wing let out a sigh of relief. The amount of money he had owed this time had been no small amount. He reached in the bucket of water and brought up a rag. "I'll finish cleaning out that hoof for you, Mr. Dud. I still got one good arm left."

Dud nodded, standing aside. Chicken Wing got more done with one arm in a shorter length of time than most of his cowhands. Dud pushed back the brim of his Stetson and wiped his forehead. They were nearing the end of summer, and the hot days showed no signs of abating. While he and Ponder watched, beads of sweat broke out on Chicken Wing's face as he worked.

"You missing any cattle, Mr. Dud?" Chicken Wing asked with his head down.

"No more than usual, why?" Dud asked.

"Word's getting around that people are missing a few

head here and there, and that some folks on the south side of the border are missing more than a few."

"First I heard of it," Dud said.

Chicken Wing finished with the hoof and threw the rag back in the bucket. "Started when Mr. Reid moved in here. I know he's a friend of yours, but I'm not going to tolerate none of that on my place," he said.

"Ev Reid?" Dud said. "He's more of an acquaintance than a friend. He is just somebody my older brothers used to run with before the war."

Ponder gave an agitated spit. "I told you, Dud, I told you when that bastard moved in here he was trouble."

"Uncle Ponder," Dud said, "why don't you go boil us a pot of coffee?"

Ponder got up on shaking legs and made a snort of disgust.

"You better watch out, Mr. Ponder," Chicken Wing said in a teasing tone. "One of these days, Mr. Dud is going to find a woman who can cook, and you're going to be out of a job."

"Pfuff," Ponder said. "If it depends on that, my job is as secure as a sixteen-year-old virgin's on her first night of work in a whorehouse."

Chicken Wing grinned and watched Ponder walk slowly to the house, carrying the box.

He turned to Dud. "Mr. Ponder's going downhill fast, isn't he?"

"Ever since this last wife died," Dud agreed. The week before, Ponder had left a skillet of hot grease on the cook-stove and narrowly missed burning down the kitchen.

As Dud led his new horse to the corral, Chicken Wing looked around the place with open admiration. Big barns, well-built corrals, the roomy rock house with its deep galleries, all evoked uncomplicated esteem in Chicken Wing's eyes. For a brief moment, Dud wished his ex-wife had viewed it the same way. Chicken Wing turned back to him.

"How are your nephews, Boyd and Jesse, doing?" he asked. "They married and settled down yet?"

"No," Dud said, closing the corral gate. "There aren't any unattached females out there where they live."

Chicken Wing grinned. "They better watch out or they're going to end up like you and Mr. Ponder."

That evening, more visitors came. Dud stood on the gallery, watching the two riders approach. As they neared, he saw hard, deep lines on their faces that made them appear older than they probably were. That and their white skin told him one thing—they had just got out of prison. Despite that, they wore looks of faint surprise, like country boys who had been dealt a stiff blow they could not handle. Grateful for the unexpected company, they gave Dud no cause for concern.

"Get down, get down," Dud said. "Have you had supper?"

"No sir, we have not," the taller one said. "We would surely appreciate something to eat."

"Well, come on back to the kitchen; I was just about to rustle up some grub for myself."

With hats in hands, they followed him into the house, looking with wide eyes at the sparse, but expensive, furnishings. They were small, slightly built men, and by their voices, Dud knew they were not Texans. He could not place them immediately—they spoke in soft accents, but not the drawl of the Deep South.

Dud put a pot of coffee on to boil. "It's going to have to be steak and potatoes, boys, because that's all I know how to cook," he warned. They said that would be fine, and with a nod he acknowledged the gratitude in their eyes. After peeling several potatoes and slipping them in grease to fry, he dug out a few steaks Ponder had fried earlier and preserved in lard. Throwing them on the griddle, he asked the men if they had run into any bad weather. They answered a courteous "no sir" but did not elaborate.

They sat in silence and try as he might, Dud could not draw much conversation out of them. Realizing they must be half-starved and would probably eat everything in sight, Dud went to the kitchen door and hollered down the hall.

"Uncle Ponder! If you want something to eat, come and get it."

He put the food on the table and sat down. After a while, Ponder tottered in. He eyed the men and got a plate. After taking his place at the table and filling his plate, he looked at them and said, "You men just get out of the pen?"

They blinked hard, and Dud let out a sigh. It was against the rules of civility in Texas to ask a man where he was from, where he was going or how much land or cattle he owned, but now that Ponder had gotten older, he did not give a hang about rules anymore. Perhaps it was because the question was so blunt and unexpected that they answered.

"Yes, sir," the smaller one said. With no prompting from Dud and little from Ponder, they spilled their story. They were brothers from Missouri and had been incarcerated at Huntsville.

"We were trying to get in the cattle business in Texas," the taller one explained. "We went in partners with a man from Southeast Texas who said he knew of some good cattle we could buy. He told us we could drive them to Abilene, fatten them up along the way and make a killing. We borrowed money from a bank in Corpus and started driving the cattle."

His brother took up the story. "Our partner said he had to leave for a day or two to say goodbye to his sweetheart. The next day we were stopped and told the cattle had been stolen."

Dud nodded his head. The partner disappeared, along with the man they bought the cattle from. The bill of sale meant nothing.

"The judge told us he tended to believe our story, but the cattle were stolen, and we had to pay the price for our gullibility. He let us off with five years." He stopped and looked at his brother.

"From what little we could pick up here and there, we think the original owner of the cattle was in on it, and the man we went in partners with and the man who pretended to be the owner worked for him," his brother said.

"And you think that man has a ranch around these parts now?" Dud divined.

They nodded, but refused to divulge his identity. "We want to see him first. It might not be the same man, and we don't want to blacken anybody's name in the meantime."

"Can't you describe him to me?" Dud pressed.

They refused to let go of any more information, however. Instead, they talked about returning to

Missouri and their family as soon as they got their
money back.

"Go back home right now," Ponder advised. "Your
folks are probably worried about you."

"We never told them. We didn't write," they explained
in turn. "We thought it would be better for them not
to know."

"Then that's all the more reason to let them know
you're all right."

They would not be persuaded, just as they would not
reveal the name of the man they were after.

"Let's just say you better keep a close watch on your
cattle, mister."

The brothers left at dawn the next morning. Dud
thought the Missouri boys stubborn and more than a little
foolish, but he had to admit they knew horseflesh. They
zeroed in on Chicken Wing's Mexican grulla and immediately asked to buy him.

"No," Dud said, still a little peeved at them for being so
secretive. "I believe I'll keep him."

They got on their horses to leave. "We're much obliged
to you, mister."

"I wish I could change your mind," Dud said. "I got a
bad feeling about what you're going into."

The next day, Dud's foreman went into town for mail
and supplies. When he returned, he had two dead bodies
in the wagon. Dud did not even have to turn them over to
know who they were.

"Where'd you find them?" he asked.

"By the side of the road," the foreman said. "Looks like
they were bushwhacked by robbers. Nothing left on
them." He pulled a small tintype from his pocket and

handed it to Dud. "Found this in the grass, lying near the bodies."

The tintype showed a small girl of about eleven or twelve with large, expressive eyes, by the resemblance, probably a sister. Thick bangs covered her forehead, her light hair pulled loosely back. The little face wore such an expression of trust and happiness that Dud felt a knot come in his throat. He quickly stuck the tintype in his vest pocket.

Ponder came out and looked at the bodies. "You warned them." He turned to Dud. "Well? You think Ev Reid is involved some kind of way?"

Dud shook his head. "I don't have proof of anything. They were just two boys out of prison with a wild tale who may or may not have been killed by road agents." He stared at the bodies of the young men, wishing they had not been so obstinate. He shook his head again and told his foreman. "Get some shovels. We'll bury them on the hill, and I'll say a few words over them."

"I'll fetch the Bible," Ponder said.

The box Chicken Wing gave him stayed on the corner of Dud's desk for three days, along with small mounds of correspondence, newspapers, circulars, and receipts. Ponder's and his housekeeping tended to be haphazard, but Dud finally sat down late one afternoon to go through the pile, pushing the box out of the way.

The massive desk sat in a large room that served as office, entrance, hallway and parlor. Thick rock walls kept the house cool in the summer. An oversized fireplace on one end of the room and a box stove on the other that Dud had ordered from the Sears & Roebuck catalog kept it warm enough in the winter. While Dud sorted through paperwork, Ponder sat on the other side of the desk, occasionally spitting into an empty peach can.

The front door opened and their foreman walked in, a grizzled man of six feet of solid muscle. It struck Dud again that everyone on his ranch, including the help, was getting old.

"You sure you don't want to go to the dance, boss? I don't mind staying here."

"No," Dud said, shaking his head. "You men go ahead. I had the runs this morning. No telling what Ponder's been feeding me." He turned to Ponder. "Ponder. Ponder! Do you want to go?"

Ponder shook his head. "No, don't feel like it."

Dud exchanged glances with the foreman. There was a time they could not have kept Ponder from a dance. The foreman gave a shake of his head, shooting Dud another sad look before leaving.

"Ev Reid is up to no good in this part of the country," Ponder said when the door shut. "Any man who uses two bottles of hair oil a week is not to be trusted."

"Well, you ought to be considered completely trustworthy then," Dud said, picking up a receipt for fourteen rolls of barbwire. "Because you ain't got enough hair left to grease."

"Just laugh, just laugh," Ponder said. "I'm telling you, he's the one behind this rustling, and it wouldn't surprise me one bit to find out he killed those Missouri boys."

Dud thought for a minute, picturing Ev as he riffled the papers. A big man, beginning to show signs of running to fat, Ev had always been somewhat of a lady's man. Black wavy hair, a big smile with flashing white teeth, he wore dark suits with string ties that were more reminiscent of a gambler than a rancher. It had surprised Dud when Ev had moved to their remote area of the state west of San Antonio. "All we've heard is gossip," he said finally. "Remember, Ev was friends with Milford and Rayford."

Agitated, Ponder stood up. "I don't care if he was friends with your brothers before the war," he said. "And besides, Rayford and Milford cooled that friendship before they left."

"Uncle Ponder, We're not missing so much as a jackrabbit off this ranch," Dud said. "There is nothing I can do."

Ponder gave a frustrated wave of his hand, accidentally knocking Chicken Wing's box off the desk and sending it flying across the room. It skidded across the mesquite floor and hit the wall, flinging the lid open. Old Tom, who had been sleeping in the corner, looked up. He stood and walking to it, began to sniff it with interest. Dud rose and went over, picking it up. To his surprise, something else had also popped open. It appeared to be a secret drawer, and looking inside, Dud spied a folded piece of paper. Taking the box back to the desk, Dud withdrew the contents and spread it out in front of him.

"Well, I'll be damned," he muttered with a short laugh.

"Why? What is it?" Ponder demanded, and when Dud did not immediately answer, he came around the desk to see for himself.

Dud smoothed the paper, moving a little so Ponder could see. On it, someone had drawn a crude map of the state. In the center and slightly up and to the right, a heart was drawn where three rivers or streams came together. Near the streams were three little arrows that took Dud several seconds to realize were intended to indicate mountains or hills. They were labeled in Spanish: *Huellas de los itanakaala*. In the lower left-hand corner, three lines had been written in a shaky hand: *Cuando tres corrientes se unen, Donde los espíritus vagan, Cuando el torro está muerto.*

Ponder could speak fluent Spanish, but not read it. "What's it say, Dud?" he asked.

Dud ran his fingers over the three lines and read: "Where three streams come together, Where spirits wander, Where the dead bull lies."

"What's wrote by those little hills?" asked Ponder, who had recognized them immediately for what they were.

"*Huellas de los itanakaala*. It means trail of the something, but I don't know what '*itanakaala*' means," he admitted.

"Sounds like an Indian word," Ponder said. "What the hell is this thing anyway?"

Dud grinned. "It's a treasure map, Uncle Ponder. Old Chicken Wing inherited a treasure map." He laughed, and putting the map in an envelope, he stuck it in his shirt pocket.

The next day, Dud saddled the Mexican horse. Before he could get on, his foreman stopped him.

"There ain't no use in you going out to Chicken Wing's," he said. "Word came this morning that somebody went out there yesterday and found him in the yard with his neck broke. Looks like his old mule threw him. Funny thing is, it looked like Chicken Wing's old cabin had been gone through, but with his housekeeping, it's hard to tell."

Dud felt his stomach sink and his throat tighten. He pulled the map partially out of his pocket and looked down at it. He swallowed and stuffed it back in.

TWO

"I am not going," Ponder said, pounding his fist on the desk for emphasis. "You are just using this as an excuse to visit every whorehouse you can find between here and Dallas." He leaned back in the chair, crossed his arms and heaved his chest.

Dud picked up a pistol and checked to see if it was loaded. Satisfied, he opened a drawer and taking out boxes of shells, stuffed them in his saddlebags. He left the saddlebags on the desk and went to the gun cabinet to fetch his rifle.

"What did I say?" he demanded, opening the cabinet door. "Besides looking for treasure, we'll be looking for wives for Boyd and Jesse. It's too late for me and you, but not for them."

"I know what you said, but I also know what you'll do," Ponder said, shaking his finger at Dud. "I know how you are about women, Dud. I don't want to be a cold, wet blanket in a long line of places with hot sheets and sin." He added one more time, "I am not going. You don't listen

13

to a dang word I say, anyway. If you had, you would have found a decent woman to live with a long time ago instead of wasting your life on whores."

"Fine!" Dud said in a flash of anger. "Stay here and rot then."

Before he left, Dud confided his suspicions to his foreman, warning him to be on the lookout for trouble. "And watch out for Ponder, would you?" he added. "But don't let him know it."

His foreman laughed. "Boss, I've knowed Ponder just as long as I've knowed you. You don't have to tell me a thing."

Along with his dog, a buckskin mare, the little Mexican grulla, and a hardheaded mule, Dud met Ev Reid on his way out of town.

"Dud! Dudford Washburn! Nice to see you again," Ev said, smiling broadly. "What's this I hear about you leaving town?"

Dud gave him a quick glance. "My brother-in-law has been down in his back," Dud said. "I thought I might go there and help out a bit. Maybe make a trip to San Antonio."

Ev gave him a wink. "San Antonio, eh? Ponder's staying home, is he?" he said with a chuckle. "Say, how is your sister doing? My, she always was a pretty girl."

"She's all right," Dud said. His sister was forty and had six children, but she still received admiring glances from men.

"Those were the days, weren't they, Dud?" Ev said. "When we were all back in Goliad."

Dud did not bother to answer, and Ev ignored his

silence. "Did you hear about poor old Chicken Wing? Pitched right off his mule."

Dud nodded while Ev gave a sad shake of his head. "But speaking of old times, Dud, do you recollect Mary Powell from San Antonio? Back before the war?"

"Sure," Dud answered, surprised. Who would not remember her? She had been the belle of San Antonio, seventeen with dark hair and wide, slanted eyes. Men had drooled at her feet, including himself and all his brothers. Two prominent Bexar County attorneys had gotten in a duel over her, and countless bar fights ensued every time she favored one man over another. His older brother Rayford and Ev had been in the running, but she had barely noticed him, just a gangly teenager at the time. "I heard she'd got married after the war and moved to Dallas," he said.

"She's been married and widowed twice. You know, Dud, she recently moved back to the San Antonio area. If you get up that way, you ought to go see her," Ev said, naming the small town she lived in. "As a matter of fact, I ran across her in San Antonio, and she asked me about you."

Dud gave a snort. "I can't believe that," he said.

"Oh yes, she did. Asked me all about you and what you'd been up to," Ev said. He suddenly gave a small frown of remembrance and uncharacteristically blurted, "I don't understand why women like you so much, Dud. I never thought you were much to look at myself."

Dud grunted again. Despite what Ev said, he might as well have been invisible for all the attention Mary paid him.

"I thought you were sweet on her, Ev," he said.

Ev wiped away his scowl, trying again to be smooth and agreeable. "Oh, that boat sailed a long time ago. She's just a friend now. You really ought to go see her, Dud, if you get up that way."

"Maybe I will," Dud said.

Two days later, around suppertime, he topped a hill and looked down on his sister's ranch. Clarissa, his oldest niece, stood at a clothesline, hanging sheets. She looked up and recognized him. "Mama! Mama! Come quick. It's Uncle Dud!"

Dud smiled, grateful that even though she was fourteen, Clarissa continued to wear her blonde hair in pigtails and could still get excited by a visit from her old uncle. The other three girls bounded out of the house, paused on the gallery, squealed in delight and joined their sister in the race to greet him, their little dresses and aprons flapping in the breeze.

"Uncle Dud! Uncle Dud!" they called, gathering around him as he got off his horse. Dud picked up the youngest, dark-haired Gracie, and gave her a hug, while Clarissa hugged him. Brigit and next-to-youngest Katie had attached themselves to his legs.

"How's my girls?" Dud asked.

"Fine, Uncle Dud," they said in unison.

Dud's sister came out onto the gallery wiping her hands on a dishcloth. A smile spread across her face, and she waved the cloth. "Dud!" she called. "We're so glad to see you."

Before her mother reached them to stop her, Gracie whispered in Dud's ear, "Did you bring us something, Uncle Dud?"

"Well of course I did, sugar," he said. "I brought you

16

some chewing tobacco because I know that's what little girls like."

The girls broke into a fit of giggles and were about to protest when his sister arrived. "Girls, girls! Don't choke Uncle Dud to death hugging him so tight."

Dud gave Gracie a kiss on the cheek and put her down. His sister embraced him while the girls petted Old Tom, who wiggled in delight.

"You're looking well, Sister," Dud said. Her dark blonde hair held a little gray around the ears, but her cheeks looked rosy and fresh while her eyes danced.

"You are too, Dud," she said, smiling at him. Her eyes took him in. "Dud! For goodness sake's, when are you going to buy some new clothes?"

Dud grinned. "Sister, I don't ever see anybody."

"Oh you," his sister said. "Really, Dud, you've got the money."

Dud handed the reins to the two oldest girls. "Don't try to unload anything heavy, girls," he warned. "Just water the animals and give them a little feed. I'll be out directly to tend to them."

While the older girls led the horses and the mule to the barn, the rest followed him to the house. Dud looked up and saw Old Tom searching for a bone he had buried on their last visit. The dog went for the flowerbeds in front and began to dig.

"Did you get lonesome for us, Dud?" his sister asked. "Where's Uncle Ponder? Didn't he want to come?"

Before he could answer, she spied the dog.

"Stop, you wretch!" she yelled, and began to run toward the house. "Get out of there!" She grabbed a broom from the corner of the gallery and proceeded to whack Old Tom with it in soft blows. Ignoring the broom, he kept digging until he found his bone and then trotted happily away.

"For goodness sake's, Dud," she said, giving up on Old Tom and turning back. "You've taught that dog a dozen tricks; can't you teach him to stop digging?"

Dud laughed. "Oh, a dog's just got to be a dog sometimes, Sister."

They stepped onto the gallery and went into the house. Although his brother-in-law could afford to build a new one, his sister was a sentimental woman and refused to part with their old cabin, so he added on to it and expanded walls as children came. As they entered the large main room, Dud could see vittles bubbling in pots on the stove. He walked past the long dining table and threw himself down heavily in an easy chair in the back section that served as a family room and parlor.

"Dud, is your arthritis bothering you?" his sister asked.

"Oh, just a little when I first get up in the morning," he answered, stretching his legs and getting comfortable.

"Now, Dud," she fussed. "Don't start that drinking just because you have a few aches and pains. I don't want you to end up like poor old Uncle Finn, drunk every day and worrying and embarrassing poor Mama to no end. Soak some willow bark in water and drink a little of that if you have to."

Dud nodded as he had a hundred times before. If Uncle Finn had accomplished only one thing in his miserable life, it was to be held up as a model of what not to be by his teetotaling sister. "I could sure use a cup of coffee," he said to get her off track.

"Of course," she said, fretting because she had not offered before.

The two oldest girls came into the house carrying a few of his things. They gave their mother a hopeful look, and she said sharply, "Candy after supper, girls."

Dud grinned and said with an air of exaggeration, "My hair is so full of dust. I sure wish I had someone who would brush my hair for me."

Clarissa spoke immediately. "I'll brush your hair for you, Uncle Dud."

"Me too," Brigit hollered and began racing in front of Clarissa to reach the hairbrush first.

"Girls," their mother reprimanded as she poured his coffee.

Gracie and Katie watched him with solemn, waiting eyes. He winked at them. "My feet are powerful achy. If I just knew two little girls who would take off my boots, I'd be so happy. Why, I bet I'd bring them double candy the next time I came to see them."

Grins covered their faces. "We'll do it for you, Uncle Dud," they said in unison.

Using his toes, he pushed against his boots while they pulled. "Ah, that feels better," he said. His sister brought his coffee while Clarissa and Brigit appeared with the hairbrush.

"You are incorrigible, Dud," his sister laughed. As the girls took turns brushing his thinning brown hair, Dud and his sister began to talk. In a while, they heard the sound of boots hitting the gallery boards.

His brother-in-law and two nephews entered the house, his brother-in-law's deep raspy voice exclaiming as he walked into the living area.

"I should have known that if a man came into my house and started bewitching my womenfolk, it would be Dud Washburn." His brother-in-law grinned and seated himself in the opposite chair. While his sister looked much the same, Dud thought his brother-in-law looked older, his dark curly hair a little more grizzled than he remembered from the last visit.

Boyd, tall and muscular, and Jesse, shorter than Boyd and slender, both said, "Hello, Uncle Dud," and happily shook hands.

Dud spoke to them and then turned his attention back to his brother-in-law. "Well, somebody has to do something to liven up the dreary lives that you make these poor womenfolk lead."

His brother-in-law, a large bear of a man, snorted. "Do you know what I came home and found your sister doing yesterday, Dud? Sitting on the floor having a tea party with Gracie and Katie—like she didn't have a thing else to do in this world."

"She's got to do something to ease the mental pain of putting up with you, old man," Dud countered. "My word, I'm surprised I haven't had to put her in the nut house by now."

His sister burst into laughter. "Stop it, you two. A stranger walking in would never dream you've been best friends for twenty-five years."

She put her hands on the backs of the two oldest girls. "Girls," she said. "Wash your hands and help me put supper on the table. Gracie, Katie, take your papa's boots off for him, and then you two wash your hands and set the table."

A chorus of "yes ma'am" issued forth, and Dud rose to

wash his own hands and face. While he and the rest of the men washed, they talked about the weather and the condition of their cattle. Once at the table, while his brother-in-law and nephews ate in continuous motion with few words, Dud told his sister of seeing Ev Reid before leaving town and all the other gossipy little things he could think of that he thought she might like to hear.

In the meantime, he threw speculative glances at his nephews. They were good-looking young men, but not so regularly featured they could be called "pretty boys." Both had brown hair with noticeable waves. Boyd had big muscles and thighs that strained against the fabric of his pants. His eyebrows were straight, and his lips were fuller than most men's, but not so much to be overpowering. Both boys had light blue eyes and strong, straight noses. Jesse's eyes were rounder, his face thinner. Boyd had an uncomplicated and straightforward personality, while Jesse's quiet demeanor hid a propensity for elaborate and witty practical jokes.

Dud, sensing the time was right, began to tell the story of Chicken Wing's box. As he talked, his nephews raised their heads and slowed their forks.

"A treasure map," his sister exclaimed. "Of all the…."

Dud answered their questions and promised to show them the map after supper. "That's the main reason I'm here, Sister," he said. Taking the plunge, he added, "I want Boyd and Jesse to go with me to find it."

"What?!" she said, almost in a screech, her eyes wide in shock. "Heavens no! They don't need to be gallivanting all over the state on a fool's errand when their papa needs them here."

Boyd and Jesse shook their heads with mouths open,

so thrilled at the prospect of a treasure hunt they could not speak. Their mother continued to pooh-pooh the idea.

"I declare, Dud. That treasure isn't there anymore—if it ever was there. Of all the foolish things!"

Tears welled in her eyes as she turned from the boys to Dud and back again. That they wanted to go was so obvious it further upset her, and she unleashed her anger on Dud. "Dud, you're just bored. That's all it is. You are just bored stiff. You miss all those old cattle drives and all that excitement of going new places and seeing new things. There is no treasure! It's just a hoax."

In frustration, she blurted out, "You just want an excuse to lay your head on the bosoms of some old barroom floozies!"

THREE

THE GIRLS GASPED, AND DUD'S SISTER COVERED HER FACE with her hands in shame, bowing her head low, fighting to stop a burst of tears.

"Children," his brother-in-law said. "You've had enough to eat. Go outside, your mother and I want to talk to Uncle Dud alone. You, too, Boyd and Jesse."

They got up from the table, reluctant to leave, but they filed out the front door. Dud could hear their footsteps going off the gallery and several seconds later heard the sounds of breathing coming from the opened window behind him. A small body thumped against the wall of the house, and the sound of a sharp whispered word floated in. Boyd, or perhaps Jesse, issued a soft "Shhh."

When they had settled into place, Dud put his hand on his sister's arm. "I know my life has not turned out the way you hoped, Sister. And perhaps that's why I don't want to see Boyd's and Jesse's turn out the same way."

She removed her hands, raised her head, and sniffed. "What do you mean?"

"There is another reason why I want Boyd and Jesse to go on this treasure hunt with me," he explained. "Now you know for various reasons there isn't a decent girl of marriageable age within a hundred mile radius of this ranch. Boyd and Jesse are at the age when a man needs a wife, Sister."

He leaned back in his chair and looked at her squarely. "While we are hunting for treasure, we are also going to be on the lookout for some good women for Boyd and Jesse."

His sister's eyes flashed. "No, no, no! They are too young. Boyd is only twenty-two, and Jesse is only twenty."

"Boyd is almost twenty-three, and Jesse is almost twenty-one," Dud pointed out.

"That's too young," his sister said. "You wait and look for that treasure next year or the next. If it's really there, it's not going anywhere."

While they argued back and forth, his brother-in-law rose from the table and went into the kitchen. He brought back a pie and set it in front of him. After cutting a large slice, he commenced eating with his bushy head bent down over the plate.

After dreaming up more impossible reasons why they should not leave home, Dud's sister reverted back to her original argument. "Their father needs them here!"

"Sister," Dud said.

By mutual consent, they turned to Dud's brother-in-law. Without lifting his head from the pie, he said, "They can go." He raised his eyes. "They deserve a chance to find the same happiness I've had."

A blank look came over Dud's sister's face as she stared at her husband. She shut her mouth, blinked her eyes once and turned to Dud. "When do you plan on leaving?"

"Day after tomorrow," Dud answered. "I'm not as young as I used to be, and I want one day of rest. Boyd and Jesse will need to get their things together."

His sister rose from her chair. "That doesn't give me much time," she murmured. "Girls," she called as she began to pick up utensils. "Come in and help me with the dishes. You can visit with your Uncle Dud this evening, but tomorrow we have to get up early and get busy cooking and washing things for Boyd and Jesse. They're going on a treasure hunt."

Cries of "Whoopee!" came in through the window, and the children rushed back into the house.

"Sister," Dud pleaded. "Don't wear yourself out cooking for us. We can't take that much, and we'll make out on the trail."

"Don't tell me what to do, Dudford Washburn," his sister said, pausing with a plate in her hand. "I know what a lousy cook you are, and if my baby boys are going to leave with you to go tramping around the countryside, they are at least going with full stomachs and more to take along baked by their mama."

"Yes, ma'am," Dud said, and his brother-in-law laughed.

After the girls cleared the table, Dud removed the treasure map from the inside pocket of his vest and spread it out. The family crowded around him to look.

"Read what it says, Dud," his sister asked, and he began to translate for them.

"Where three streams come together
Where spirits wander

Where the dead bull lies"

"What in the world can that mean?" his sister asked. "A cemetery by a river? Nobody would put a cemetery close to three rivers. Just think of the flooding."

"I don't know what it means," Dud answered. "I've wrestled with it and figured our best bet would be to start where three rivers converge."

"What about the words written by these mountains, Uncle Dud?" Boyd asked, pointing to the figure of hills.

Dud read them in Spanish first. *"Huellas de los itanakaala.* It means trail of the something, but I don't know what *'itanakaala'* means. Ponder thinks it is an Indian word."

He turned to his brother-in-law. "We need those maps you borrowed."

"I loaned them to a neighbor going to Dallas," he replied. "I told you that's the reason I wanted them."

"I don't remember you saying that."

"Well, I did. Where you think this could be?"

Dud looked back down at the map. "The only three rivers I know of that come together in Central Texas are the Lampasas, the Nolan, and the Leon, flowing into Little River.

"We can get a new Texas map in San Antonio," he said, "and go from there." He added confidently, "There ought to be plenty of maps in San Antonio for sale."

They debated for some time over the identity of the rivers and the secret of the riddles, but without a map, they were hamstrung. They finally gave up and sat down in the family room. While the adults talked, the children played with Old Tom. Dud had trained the dog to sit, stay, be quiet, crouch down, and crawl on command. The older girls pretended they were Indians while the younger ones crept along the floor with Old Tom in stealthy pursuit. The youngest girl grew tired of playing and climbed into Dud's lap.

"Old Tom has fleas," Gracie said. "He has a lot of fleas."

Dud smiled down at her. "I know. Old Tom has more fleas than a coyote has howls."

Clarissa and the other girls stopped playing and sat on the floor beside him.

"How many howls does a coyote have, Uncle Dud?" freckle-faced Katie asked.

"I'm not sure," Dud answered. "But every time I hear a coyote howl, I think, oops, another flea just jumped on Old Tom."

They giggled and Brigit pleaded, "Tell us the story about the first time you saw our papa, Uncle Dud, please."

"Oh children," his sister said. "Uncle Dud doesn't want to tell you that old story again."

"Yes, he does, Mama," Brigit said. "Uncle Dud loves to talk. Papa always says it's a fight between Uncle Dud and Uncle Ponder to see who can gab the most. Isn't that right, Papa?"

His brother-in-law nodded his head like a wise old sage while the others laughed. Dud made a show of grimacing at him and began the story.

"Your mother was the prettiest little gal in five counties," he began.

"Last time you said it was four," Katie pointed out.

"Don't interrupt, Katie," her mother admonished.

"Well, I remembered another one," Dud said, beginning again. "Me and my older brothers were used to having fellows coming around courting her. Some of them came from as far away as Austin and Bastrop.

"Now we didn't want just any old fellow marrying our favorite baby sister. Now our older sister was a different matter. We would have paid the first one that come along a twenty-dollar gold piece to take her."

"Dud!" his sister admonished.

"What was wrong with her, Uncle Dud?" Clarissa asked. "Was she mean? Was she ugly?"

"Was she mean?" Dud said. "Was she ugly? She was meaner than Satan's wife and with no hands could eat a biscuit out of a jar."

"Dud! She was not," his sister said. "She was just a little bossy, and you shouldn't speak ill of the dead."

"A little bossy?" Dud said. "A little bossy like General Santa Anna of the Mexican army."

"I'm not like her, am I, Uncle Dud?" Clarissa asked anxiously.

"Of course not, sweetheart," Dud assured her. "You girls are like angels compared to that unlucky woman, God rest her soul. Our poor old pappy used to look at her and your mama and say he sure wished they could mix their personalities together a little instead of being so different. Because you know, girls, your mama was always easily led, and we were sure worried she would take up with the wrong man."

"Dud, I was not!"

He ignored her and began the story again. "So anyway, my older brothers and I devised this scheme to weed out the wheat from the chaff, so to speak. When a fellow came calling on your mama, we put him to work. That way we could see what kind of man he was."

"What do you mean, Uncle Dud?" Brigit asked.

"Well, if he shirked work, putting the heavier load on another man, or if he said he did something when he didn't, or if he got mad and ill-tempered with people or animals too often, then we knew he was too da..., er, dang sorry for our sister.

"Anyhow, your pa came riding up one day, and we told him before we would let him court our sister he had to help us round up some cattle. He gave us all a dirty look and started to cuss us out, but just then your mama stepped out onto the gallery and smiled at him, so I guess he figured it was worth it."

"And Pa outworked you all!" Katie shouted. "Didn't he, Uncle Dud? Didn't he?"

"Worked like a dog worrying a bone and made us all look like sissy-boys," Dud agreed. "And then the funny thing happened. Our neighbor came over and said, 'What are you boys doing? That man ain't no ordinary cowhand. He owns one of the best ranches in DeWitt County.'"

The girls laughed. Brigit said, "I guess you all felt pretty silly, didn't you, Uncle Dud?"

"Oh, we just laughed," Dud answered. "We knew the joke was on us. But we plotted our revenge. We were going to make him take our older sister in to live with him and your ma when they got married. But then the war came along and saved him."

"No it didn't," his brother-in-law said, rising from his chair. "You got your revenge. I'm still stuck with you, old man," he said with a grin. "Come on everybody, it's time to bed down. Boyd, Jesse, make sure Dud has a bed to himself. All this lying has probably worn him out."

The next day, Dud stayed out of the kitchen while his

sister prepared enough food to feed Grant's army. Taking pity on the girls, she finally sent them down to the creek to bathe Old Tom. Boyd and Jesse were so excited; they were like tongue-tied schoolboys going to their first dance. Dud's brother-in-law went about in the same deliberate, calm way he had always done, but he stopped his work every so often to look at the boys. The air that evening crackled with excitement until Gracie began to cry, and then suddenly the girls were all bawling, hugging and kissing Boyd and Jesse until their father sent everyone to bed.

The next morning, Dud left the breakfast table and went to the barn. The horses were saddled, the packs ready on the back of the mule. As he checked the cinches, he heard a quiet sound behind him. Turning, he saw Clarissa walking out of the shadows.

"Uncle Dud," she said, her lips trembling. "May I talk to you for a minute?"

"Why sure, little bit," Dud answered. "What's on your mind?"

She advanced with her head down. It came to him with a pang that she would not be a child much longer. When she reached him, he said, "Come on now, out with it."

Suddenly she wrapped her arms around him, burying her face in his forearms, and began to sob.

"There now, there now," he said, patting her head. "What is it?'

She raised her face and stood back, wiping her eyes with her fingers. "Uncle Dud," she stuttered. "I know you're going to try to help Boyd and Jesse find wives. But what about me, Uncle Dud? Papa isn't going to let me marry any of the boys who live south of us. He says they're trashy. Our ranch hands are too old. The rest of the neighbors only have babies, or girls, or else no children at all."

She began to sob again. "You wouldn't want me to end up a dried-up old prune, would you, Uncle Dud? And what about Brigit and Katie and even Gracie?"

At first he could not think of what to say except, "Hush now; stop that crying."

As he thought about it, he realized Clarissa made a valid point. "All right," he said. "I'll

see what I can do. What kind of fellow are you looking for anyway?"

"Oh thank you, Uncle Dud, thank you!" Clarissa said, hugging him. She looked up with bright eyes. "I want a boy with dark hair like my papa—a brave boy with dark snapping eyes."

"All right, all right," Dud said with a laugh as Clarissa drew back and smiled. "I'm not making any promises, and you're too young right now anyway, but I'll see if I can't at least put someone in your vicinity when the time comes."

"And Brigit and Katie and Gracie too?" she asked anxiously.

"Yes, yes," Dud agreed.

Clarissa smiled again and gave him her thanks. "I'll say my prayers for you and Boyd and Jesse every day," she promised. She added with a grin, "Every time I hear a coyote howl, I'll think, 'oops, time to say a prayer for Uncle Dud.'"

"You do that, little bit," Dud said, smiling back.

She left, almost skipping to the house in a happy trot. Dud looked down at Old Tom. "I don't know who appointed me matchmaker for the whole dang bunch," he told the dog. "You can find your own woman."

Before they left, Dud's sister also took him aside.

"Dud, don't you let my boys bring home bad women," she warned, shaking her finger. "I don't want them marrying tarted-up, jaded saloon girls who are going to be running around behind their backs the minute they get bored with ranch life."

He nodded his head. "Yes, Sister. Yes, Sister," he said.

"Well, Dud, I know how you are about women. And you be careful," she added. "If anyone gets wind of what you and the boys are looking for, there'll be trouble."

"Yes, Sister," he repeated, nodding again.

She stood looking at him. "Dud...," she said, stopping. He knew she was thinking about his disastrous marriage. The woman he married had not been a saloon girl, but she had detested ranch life with all her being, and then she detested him.

"Sister," he said. "I promise I will take good care of the boys. I always have."

"I know you have, Dud," she said, giving him a hug.

Although Boyd and Jesse had been away from home on yearly cattle drives starting when they were just tykes to only a few years previous, this trip signaled something different. As they made their farewells, the girls and their mother wiped tears from their eyes while Dud's brother-in-law stood looking happy and wistful at the same time, as if wishing he could go too.

FOUR

THEY DID NOT FOLLOW THE MAIN HIGHWAY TO SAN Antonio; they knew every settler on that road. Instead, Dud led the boys through the back ways, riding on little used trails he barely remembered. Boyd and Jesse agreed with this maneuver, but worried about Dud's casual treatment of the map.

"Don't you think you ought to try to hide it somewhere besides your inside vest pocket, Uncle Dud?" Jesse asked.

"If anybody knows about the map," Dud answered, "they would torture me or one of you to get it anyway, so might as well make it easy for them. Anybody who waylaid us would probably kill us and what good would it do us then? Might as well leave off being too crafty."

Both boys could see this made sense. With the crying and kissing goodbye, they had started out later than expected, and they did not come across any farm or ranch houses that day. At first, Dud congratulated himself on making good time until he remembered there was no hurry, so he slowed down. Bedding down under the stars that night, Old Tom gave a contented sigh. Dud slept lighter than normal, and during the night when Old Tom was in his deepest sleep, he awakened and stayed awake for a while, but did not hear or see anything unusual.

The next afternoon, they still had not crossed paths with anyone. However, toward the end of the day, they found a small log cabin in a clearing. Dogs barked and ran to greet them. An old man with a beard that reached his waist came out onto the gallery.

"Get down, get down," he said, pleased to have visitors. He hollered at his dogs. "Shut up, you mangy hounds!"

An old woman with a knot of gray hair came out, wiping her hands on her apron. "Lands sakes!" she cried. "We haven't had company in a month of Sundays. Come on in, you're just in time for supper."

Dud gave them a smile, a little disappointed that the first people they came across did not appear to have an eligible female on the place, but at least they were pleasant and happy to receive them.

The cabin, although sparse of furniture, had the scrubbed look of a rag happy housewife. They asked the blessing over nothing more than cornbread and buttermilk, but the cornbread tasted delicious and Dud complimented his hostess.

"Oh, go on with you," she said, pushing a gnarled hand in his direction and smiling unselfconsciously with a mouth missing teeth. "Here, sonny, have another piece."

Dud grinned and replied, "Don't mind if I do. I haven't tasted cornbread this good since my mama died, God rest her soul."

She twittered, and Dud smiled again. He could have eaten more and knew Boyd and Jesse could have dug into every bit of food the old couple had in their house, but their mama and papa had raised them right, and they restrained themselves even without a warning look from him.

After talking until the moon shone high in the night, telling all the news they could think of, they slept on the gallery, even though their hosts offered them the floor inside the cabin. Before daybreak, Dud shook the stiffness out of his legs, moaning as usual about his arthritis. He went to Boyd and Jesse, kicking them lightly with his boot.

"Get up, you lazy outfits," he said.

Boyd sat up and rubbed the sleep from his eyes. "Dang, Uncle Dud. You're going to give me and Jesse the rheumatism, too, if you keep making us get up so early." Nevertheless, he and Jesse got up, stretching with grins on their faces.

They offered to do the milking, and while Jesse handled the ornery cow, who did not much appreciate strange hands, no matter how kind and gentle, Boyd and Dud chopped kindling and brought firewood into the house. They breakfasted on fried salt pork, gravy, and more cornbread before leaving.

"Ya'll come back, hear," the old man and woman called as they waved goodbye.

Dud regretted the lack of daughters, and for a while, it looked as if they were not going to find anybody on the trail, male or female, for some time.

Late in the afternoon, Old Tom stopped and raised his head, sniffing the air around him. They could not smell anything in the late summer air except dried grass and horse droppings. Old Tom, however, began to bark and run, and his bark was answered by a melody of dogs yapping in the distance. After sniffing the ground in circles, he headed down a faint trail.

Turning to his nephews, Dud said, "We might as well check it out."

They struggled through the brush, limbs whipping against their arms and legs while they tried to keep from getting hit in the face by low lying branches. They had gone only a short way when they came upon a clearing, and with one look, Dud wanted to turn around and leave.

In the clearing sat a shack surrounded by garbage. Tin cans, broken plows, every sort of junk imaginable lay in the yard. Just as Dud was about to wheel his horse around, three people came out of the cabin onto a ramshackle gallery.

"Get down, get down, strangers," said an old man in ragged overalls. "Shut up, dogs!"

An obese woman beside him added, "Get down and water your horses. We sure are glad for the company." She and the old man plopped down in rickety chairs, spreading their legs and spitting tobacco between their bare feet.

The third occupant of the gallery said nothing. Instead, she twisted her long blonde hair around a finger, her full young bosom heaving in pleasure at the sight of Boyd and Jesse. Dud could see immediately that she did not have a stitch of underclothes on over her bodacious curves. Her tattered dress revealed trim ankles, rounded calves, and dirty feet.

As he got off his mare, Dud glanced at Boyd and Jesse. Jesse's eyes looked about ready to pop out of his head, and Boyd's tongue lolled at the edge of his mouth. With misgivings, Dud watered his horse and went to the gallery. The fat woman smiled at him, her dirty blonde hair tied back in a sloppy bun, her face an exploded and wrinkled version of her daughter's. All three of them had tobacco juice running out the corners of their mouths.

Dud introduced himself and his nephews as pleasantly as he could. The boys stood silent, staring at the girl who batted her eyelashes at them while grinning slyly. Dud thought Boyd would rub his mouth raw licking his lips.

While Boyd and Jesse eyed their daughter, the couple eyed Old Tom. "That sure is a big dog," the old man said. The woman grinned. "Powerful lot of meat on that dog."

Old Tom put his head down and slunk behind Dud. "Thank you," Dud said with reserve.

"Whelp, ya'll are just in time for supper," the old woman said, heaving herself up. "Come on in the house." They spat their tobacco onto the ground beside the gallery.

Dud dreaded going inside, and when he entered, he saw his fears were correct—it was just as bad a mess as the outside. The old woman swept dirty dishes aside with a soiled arm, knocking bones and scraps off the table that the dogs immediately set upon. The old man shooed them noisily out of the house.

"We're having leftover fried squirrel," the old woman announced. "Sit down and snatch what you can before my fork gets it," she cackled.

Dud, with Jesse and Boyd by his side, sat on rough

benches across from the old man and woman. The girl sat across the table from Boyd and Jesse, still not speaking but lustily sucking on bones while staring openly at them. Not bothering with plates or utensils, their hosts grabbed the food the old woman placed on the table and ate noisily, throwing the bones on the floor when they finished with them. Jesse sat in shocked silence, while Boyd stared at the girl with love struck eyes. He and Jesse kept giving slight jumps at the table. Dud pretended to accidentally drop a piece of meat on the floor, and when he retrieved it, he saw a shapely foot rubbing against Boyd's leg, then moving over to Jesse's. He sat up and gulped nervously.

The old man and old woman, despite mouths full of squirrel and cornbread, wanted to keep up a running stream of conversation, and as a guest, Dud tried to oblige them. Jesse joined in occasionally, but he had a hard time keeping his eyes off the girl's overflowing mammary glands. Boyd, never removing his eyes from her, put food in his mouth mechanically, once missing it and poking himself in the chin with a bone. Even then, he only blinked.

The cornbread was as dry as sawdust and just as tasteless, the squirrel greasy. The squirrel reminded Dud of something, and as he pushed it around in his mouth, he realized what it was. He had not had it since the war.

He swallowed what he could, and when the others finally finished, the old man leaned back, put his thumbs in his suspenders and let out a tremendous belch. The old woman grinned and said, "Daughter, why don't you take one of these young fellers out to the barn and show him that new shovel we found last time the creek flooded."

While the old man nodded his head in approval, the

girl stared at Boyd and Jesse. "Why Ma," she said. "I'd like to take both of them to the barn."

The old woman grinned salaciously, "Oh, these young'uns, they will have their fun."

Dud stood up. "We have to go," he announced hurriedly.

Jesse stared at him while Boyd, round-eyed, cried, "What?"

"We have to leave," Dud said, the words tumbling out of him in a rush. "I'm a wanted man. The sheriff is after me, and I don't want to stay here and get caught."

Jesse stared at him in surprise while Boyd gaped in horror. "But Uncle Dud!"

The other people looked at him with avid interest. "Wanted?" the old man said, his face lighting up. "Is there a bounty on you?" the old woman asked hopefully.

"No, no," Dud answered. "I killed the sheriff's dog. I'm ashamed to tell this, but his dog and my dog got into a fight, and when I saw my dog was losing, well, I couldn't help myself, I shot the other dog. I know it wasn't manly of me, but I couldn't help it. Anyway, he can't put out a warrant on me or a bounty, but he wants to kill me."

He looked at Boyd and Jesse. "We have to leave," he said, pulling up on Jesse's arm. He went around the table and jerked Boyd to his feet.

"But Uncle Dud," Boyd said, almost crying. "Can't we stay for just a little while?" He looked at the buxom daughter. "Can't we stay for just thirty minutes?"

"No," Dud said. "We have to leave right now." Not wanting to be indebted to them for anything, he reached in his pocket and pulled out a fifty cent piece. "I know you folks are too good and refined to accept money for this food," he said, placing the coin on the table. The three looked at it greedily. "But I'd be so obliged to you if you wouldn't tell the sheriff we'd been here, that I'll be glad to give you this as a token of my thanks."

They looked at Dud with purposely innocent faces, shaking their heads. "Oh, we won't tell," they agreed.

Dud shoved Boyd and Jesse out the door as fast as he could. "Come on, Old Tom," he hollered. "Move it, boy." He got on his horse swifter than he had in twenty years, waving a quick goodbye to the three people on the gallery, who stared at them with happy and somewhat puzzled grins.

Although Boyd got on his horse and went with Jesse and him, he was visibly distraught to the point of tears. "Why did we have to leave?" he kept saying. "Why, Uncle Dud? Why? I think I'm in love."

"You're in something, but it's not love, boy," Dud answered. "I promised your mama I'd take care of you, and by golly, if wind of what happened at that table ever got to her ears, I'd never hear the end of it. Those people were trash; can't you see it, boy?"

"But she was so pretty, Uncle Dud," Boyd moaned.

"Hell yes, and so was her mama twenty years ago," Dud retorted. "Do you know what we were eating? Rats, that's what. Those weren't fried squirrels; they were fried rats."

Jesse looked away, making a grimace, but Boyd said, "I don't care! We could have stayed for a little while!"

"Look, boy," Dud said patiently. "We could have, but I'll be danged if five years from now, I wanted to ride by this place again accidentally and run across a child in that nasty yard that looked like you. Or Jesse," he added pointedly. "And besides that, I think they wanted to eat Old Tom."

That seemed to get to Boyd, and he calmed down, although he grumbled in a low tone off and on for the rest of the evening about Dud ruining his life. Dud did his own grumbling.

"No maps, no decent women, nothing!" Dud complained under his breath. "And I'm starting to sound just like Ponder!"

Although Dud pretended to debate whether or not to go to the town where Mary Powell lived and look her up, he knew in his heart he would. The sun shone down on them warmly when they drew near the small community, with just a hint of a gentle breeze swaying the green grass. The village looked and smelled clean in the distance, and as they got closer, they passed a neat white frame house on the edge of town. A large tree, heavy with leaves, shaded the front lawn, and nearby a narrow creek rolled lazily, giving the scene an almost idyllic appearance. The door to the house opened, and a woman walked onto the gallery, shading her eyes against the setting sun.

In an instant, she was running from the gallery toward them, her white dress billowing around her ankles. "Dud! Dud Washburn! Is that you?" she cried.

He stopped and got off his horse, holding the reins awkwardly in his hands. There was no awkwardness about Mary. She hugged his neck and kissed his cheek.

"It's me, Mary," she said, smiling broadly.

"I would have known you anywhere, Mary," Dud said. "It's good to see you again."

The pretty slender girl had ripened into a beautiful curvaceous woman. The same glossy dark hair and widely spaced dark eyes greeted him. Her lips, though somewhat thinner, stretched across her face showing the same beautiful smile. Boyd and Jesse had dismounted, and Dud introduced them.

"Oh, they look just like your older brothers, Dud," Mary said, clutching their arms and kissing their cheeks lightly. "The Washburn boys weren't the most handsome of men, but they always had that special something." She turned back to Dud. "What are you doing here, Dud?"

"We're just passing through, Mary," he said. "We're on our way to San Antonio, and then we're headed for...," he was so overwhelmed by Mary's warm welcome, he could not remember where they were headed. He began again. "We're heading north on a cattle and land buying trip—looking for some good investments."

"Dud, you must stay with me," Mary said. "I have this big house; there's plenty of room, and we have so much catching up to do."

He looked at the house and back at Mary. His brain did not seem to be working right. It took him a few seconds to get back on track. "Thank you, Mary," he said, "but we'll bunk at the hotel, out of your hair." He wanted to take her up on her offer, but he had to consider Boyd and Jesse. They would need to look around town at the eligible women, and they might feel constricted staying under the watchful eye of another female.

"Oh Dud," Mary said, looking disappointed, and she tried again to convince him to stay with her, but he stood firm.

"Well then, you must eat supper with me every evening while you're here," Mary said. "I insist."

"Mary," he said with a laugh, "we don't plan to be here that long."

"Nonsense, Dudford Washburn," she said. "Now that we finally meet again after all these years, you must stay and visit with me for a while." She smiled so pleasingly, Dud felt his head nodding.

FIVE

At six o'clock, as Mary instructed, the three men stepped onto her gallery. Mary had the door open even before they knocked. Her family had been well-to-do in San Antonio; her first husband had been a banker, and her house had the solid respectability of the upper middle class. The walls were white, the floors bare wood, but the little furniture she had was of the best quality, buffed and waxed to a shine. The house was fresh and clean looking, but devoid of knickknacks. Mary led them into the dining room where a small gray-haired woman huddled in a chair at the head of the table.

"Mother," Mary said, speaking loudly. "This is Dud Washburn. Do you remember the Washburn boys, Mother?"

The old lady smiled and nodded her head, wearing the blank pleasant look older people often had when they could no longer hear.

"And this is my son, Randall," Mary said, indicating a

44

quiet, but sturdy boy of about ten. He nodded his head at the introductions, but would not look them in the eyes.

Boyd and Jesse sat across from Dud while Mary sat by his side. She kept up a steady stream of conversation, laughing and joking about old times, occasionally putting her hand on Dud's thigh, giving it a light squeeze. Every time she did, he would lose his train of thought and have to force himself to concentrate to get it back.

"How is your younger sister, Dud?" Mary chattered. "What a pretty girl she was. We all thought she was just an empty-headed little butterfly, always so flighty. But I'll never forget the day Nellie Casner's dress caught on fire, and it was your sister who had the presence of mind to knock Nellie down and scream, 'roll, Nellie, roll.'"

She looked at Boyd and Jesse flirtatiously. "Oh, there's just so much I could tell you boys about your uncle and his brothers," she said and giggled coyly.

From somewhere in the back of Dud's mind the thought came that what had been so attractive as a teenager did not have quite the same effect coming from a mature woman, and as Mary continued to flirt and wriggle, he could see a wall of politeness come into Boyd's and Jesse's eyes that hid a certain wariness and even dislike. Then Mary would squeeze his thigh again, and he would forget all about it.

When they finished eating, they complimented Mary and her mother on the meal, trying to speak loud enough so the old woman could hear.

"Oh, Mother cooked it all," Mary laughed. "She just insists on doing it. It makes her feel useful." She turned to her mother. "It was good, Mother."

The old lady beamed and stood up. The men stood up,

while Randall bolted from the room without a word. Mary paid him no heed.

"Come into the parlor," she instructed, and they dutifully followed her into the small front room while her mother began to clear the table. Mary motioned for Dud to sit on the sofa, and she took her place beside him while Boyd and Jesse sat in chairs opposite of them, looking uncomfortable. They talked about old times, people they had known years before, who married who, who had died. Dud received great pleasure in talking to someone who remembered the same people from his boyhood, especially his brothers. Boyd and Jesse joined in politely when they could. After a while, Mary announced, "Boys, I know Dud and I are boring you. Why don't you go back to the hotel and leave Dud here with me for a while?"

Although Boyd and Jesse tried to keep the looks of relief off their faces, they could not quite manage it, and they took their leave without a murmur of protest, thanking Mary again for the supper.

As soon as she heard the front door shut, Mary looked back to Dud. "I'm so glad you're here, Dud," she said, turning on the full power of her personality. "I've been so lonely."

He did not know how it happened, but she was suddenly in his arms, kissing and stroking him with the intense passion he had only experienced with women of a certain age.

Taken by surprise, he said, "Mary," and leaned backward, trying to catch his breath, but she would not let him. She was all over him, and his red-blooded male reactions began to give her the answer she wanted. He could not resist the silky smoothness of her flesh, nor did he want to. The thought that Mary, the most sought-after girl in his youth, desired him beat throughout his brain, puffing his ego to magnificent proportions.

"Let's go to my bedroom, Dud," she whispered, giving him a small tug.

He managed to catch his breath. "Honey," he whispered. "It's barely dark, and your mama and your son are in the house."

"Oh, Dud, don't worry," she said. "Mama can't hear thunder, and Randall is burrowed in his room at the back of the house reading a book."

Despite his misgivings, Dud allowed himself to be led to the front bedroom. The windows facing the front yard were open, causing light from the moon to stream into the room, allowing a gentle breeze to push the sheer curtains on each side of the window in and out.

Her bed felt as soft and enticing as her flesh. Even so, Dud refused to remove anything more than his boots. Keenly aware there were other people in the house, it would be bad enough to be caught with his pants down.

The prize that eluded him as a teenager now lay beneath him ripe for the taking. As he did, the passionate woman in her prime kept getting mixed up in his mind with the flirtatious teenager of his youth. Suddenly he was not middle-aged Dud Washburn anymore, but a lanky young man living in San Antonio, away from home for the first time, waiting to do battle in a war that made little sense, full of vigor and high hopes of glory.

He held her in his arms when he finished, remembering his brothers and wishing they were still alive. He would go to them and say, "You'll never believe what happened to me." After a time, Mary's even breathing

47

made him think she was asleep, and he gently withdrew his arm. Before he could get up, she clutched him.

"Dud," she said drowsily. "Stay here with me for a while. Sleep by me for a little while."

He kissed her cheek. "I'm not sleepy, honey," he said, removing her hand, and before she could protest, he got up.

"Are you coming tomorrow night for supper?" she asked.

"Of course," he said, pulling up his pants and fastening them. He sat on the edge of the bed and put on his boots. Getting up, he leaned over the bed and gave her another quick kiss. "I'll see you tomorrow," he promised.

He felt like a thief, sneaking out the front door. Old Tom lay on the gallery waiting for him, and Dud stopped to ruffle his fur. As they left Mary's front yard and the cool night air hit his face, Dud grinned and looked up at the moon. "Hot dang!" he cried, slapping his thigh. He walked back to the hotel as jaunty as Old Tom trotting off with the bone he had found in his sister's flowerbed.

He snuck into the hotel room, glad the others were asleep. The next day, the boys begged off going back to Mary's, giving the reason of wanting to meet girls. Dud paid them little heed; instead he left that morning, stopping by the general store to buy a small bag of candy. He took it by Mary's, not staying long, but wishing to be assured he would still be welcome for supper. She asked him to come at seven instead of six.

That night and every night thereafter for the rest of the week, the same passionate episode played out as soon as it grew dark and the other occupants were tucked elsewhere. Always, Mary asked him to sleep beside her for a while, but he refused, too wired to oblige her and conscious of other people in the house. At times, he felt guilty, as if he was stealing something, but he could not stop himself. While Mary and her mother did their own housecleaning, they had a black man who had worked for them for years doing odd jobs. When Dud tried to help him, the old man so begrudged the intrusion he had to stop. The only thing the old man liked about him was that Dud would sometimes fire his gun to scare away the coyotes that had taken to coming around Mary's house at night.

Randall seemed to resent him, too, and barely spoke to him; he even avoided looking at him. For someone who had always prided himself on his ability to get along with young people, Randall's snubs hurt.

It began to bother him, too, that Boyd and Jesse avoided Mary and her family. They never said anything, but had begun to ask him when they would be leaving for San Antonio.

"I'm tired of this town, Uncle Dud," Boyd said as they walked down the street to check on their horses. "There's not a girl around who isn't already spoken for."

"That's right, Uncle Dud," Jesse joined in. "And none of them are interesting enough to even try to steal away from a fiancé. Shouldn't we be moving on?"

Dud kept putting them off, even though he knew they were right. He stopped by the butcher's to get Mary's mother a special cut of beef she had mentioned—she liked him, anyway. As the butcher weighed the meat behind the counter, he asked who it was for since he knew Dud was staying at the hotel. When Dud told him it was for Mary Powell, a smirk crossed his face.

The anger in Dud burst up so hot and fierce, it shook him. He grabbed the butcher by the front of his shirt and pulled him across the counter.

"What was that supposed to mean?" he demanded.

"Nothing," the butcher replied. "Let go of me."

Dud, ashamed of his outburst, let him go. The butcher took his money without a word, but when Dud turned to leave, he spoke.

"Folks in this town like you and your nephews, Mr. Washburn," he said. He looked away and picking up a rag, began to clean the counter, indicating the conversation was over.

Dud did not understand what he meant. He would not mention it to Mary, partly because it might upset her, and mostly because he knew she would not talk about it. Any time he tried to talk about the present, Mary would somehow bring things back around to the past, reminding him again of the bond they shared together through people who were almost all dead and gone.

As he took the package of beef to Mary's house, he saw Boyd and Jesse lounging in front of the hotel, looking bored and lonely. He continued on without stopping, going to the backdoor and depositing the meat on the kitchen table. Deaf Mrs. Powell nodded and smiled her thanks, and Dud left.

As he made his way back to town, he saw Randall sitting on a footbridge that crossed the creek near the house, kicking his feet indolently while tossing pebbles in the water. Dud walked toward him, hoping to speak to the boy alone and make some kind of connection. As he approached, Randall twisted his head, and when he saw who it was, made a deep frown. He turned his face away and threw another rock.

"Randall," Dud said, reaching out his hand to touch the boy's shoulder. Randall gave him a quick glance, again turning his face away, and Dud let his hand drop. He tried once more. "Randall, sometimes things between grownups aren't always...." He stopped when Randall shot him a look of such malevolence, it startled him. The boy went back to throwing rocks in the water.

Dud stood looking down at him for several long seconds. Randall was right, Dud thought. He had been trying to give Randall an excuse, not a reason. He turned and walked away.

"We'll head out in the morning," he told Jesse and Boyd when he reached them. "I'll go to Mary's tonight and tell her we're leaving in the morning."

Although he knew she would be looking for him, Dud could not bring himself to sit through supper knowing he would have to tell her he was leaving. Instead, he went to the café with the others. Long cattle drives had taught them to fill up with as much good grub as they could the night before they left because it could possibly be the last decent meal they would have in a long time. Without consciously thinking about it, Dud, Boyd, and Jesse filled their stomachs with steak, potatoes, gravy, and biscuits. They ate two buttermilk pies between them for dessert. Finally, when he could put it off no longer, Dud went to Mary's.

As he approached the gallery, he could see her sitting by a lamp in the parlor. When he knocked, she got up swiftly and opened the door.

"Dud!" she said, opening the door for him.

"Mary," he said, taking off his hat. "We're leaving in the morning, and I just couldn't face you over supper to tell you."

She looked startled. "Come in," she said. "Sit in the parlor and I'll bring you some coffee. Please, I insist."

He did not want to, but he went into the parlor and sat down on the edge of the sofa. Mary returned with the coffee and placed a steaming cup in front of him.

"Have some coffee, Dud, and tell me what made you decide to leave so suddenly," she said.

He swallowed some of the coffee to oblige her. "We didn't intend to stay this long, Mary," he said. "The boys are getting restless."

"Oh, I see," Mary said, looking upset. "I'm so disappointed. Is the coffee bad, Dud?"

"Oh no," he answered, drinking more to show her he thought it was fine, although it tasted like hot bitter gall in his mouth. "It's just that," he began, but he had to stop. The room began to blur and move. "It's just that...," and he could not think of what he intended to say.

He looked at Mary and saw two of her. As his eyes tried to focus, she got up and leaned over him. "Mary, the room is spinning," he slurred.

She grasped his elbow. "Come along, Dud, you need to lie down for a while," she said, hoisting him up. She half carried him stumbling to her bedroom. He could not understand why his legs were wobbly, and the room kept growing larger and smaller. She set him on the bed, picking up his legs and placing them on the feather mattress. She bent over him, touching his brow with her hand. "Just sleep for a while, Dud, you're tired," she said.

He could feel Mary removing his boots, taking off his

vest and belt. He tried to struggle, but could not, and she took off his shirt and pants too, leaving him in his long johns. His eyes were so heavy, he had to shut them. He heard the howl of a coyote close to the house and Old Tom's barking. He had to get up. He forced his eyes open, and although his head felt like a lead ball, he turned it toward the window. Mary stood near a lantern on a table next to the opened window, going through his things. With an effort, he pushed himself up on his elbows. She found the map in his vest pocket and opened it.

Stumbling from the bed, he staggered across the room.

"Dud!" Mary cried when she saw him.

"What did you give me, Mary?" he asked in words so thick on his tongue he could scarcely pronounce them. "The coffee."

"It was just something to make you feel better, Dud. You're always complaining about your rheumatism. I thought it would make you feel better to rest."

She tried to lead him back to the bed, but he jerked away. Grabbing the map, he fell on one knee, but with a will that took everything he had, he got up again and clumsily gathered the rest of his things.

"Dud," Mary cried, her voice sounding desperate. "Please!"

He lurched to the opened window and threw out his clothes along with the map. Mary stood behind him, crying his name and tugging on his arm and underwear, but he crawled out the window nevertheless, falling to the soft ground, catching his long johns on the shrubbery by the house. While he swayed trying to free himself, Old Tom ran to him. Dud managed to get loose and pick up his belongings, and grasping them to his chest, he walked reeling up the street to the hotel.

When he got into the lobby, he flung himself on the registration desk, startling the clerk.

"My nephews," he mumbled. "Get my nephews. I've been drugged."

He slid to the floor, and the next thing he knew, Boyd and Jesse were picking him up.

"Bring us a pot of hot coffee," Jesse shouted at the clerk as he and Boyd grasped Dud under the arms, one on each side. "Try to walk, Uncle Dud," Jesse instructed. He turned his head to the retreating clerk. "And some castor oil if you've got it."

Once in the room, Boyd held him upright while Jesse shoved the china bowl under his chin. He instructed Dud to open his mouth, and with his other hand, he poked his finger in the back of Dud's throat. He stood back holding the bowl while Dud vomited into it. After he had heaved everything he had eaten at supper, Boyd and Jesse walked him up and down the room. When the knock on the door came, Boyd hollered, "Come in!"

The clerk entered carrying a large pot of coffee, his eyes wide with fear. "Do you want me to fetch the doctor?" he asked. "Is he going to die?"

"No, he'll be all right now," Jesse answered. "Did you find any castor oil?"

The clerk nodded and set it on the nightstand. He backed from the room, his eyes still on Dud. The boys thanked him, but all Dud could do was loll his head in his direction. Jesse stopped and picked up the bottle.

"No," Dud protested. "I threw up everything."

"Don't take any chances, Uncle Dud," Jesse said, and

holding Dud's nose so he could not breathe, he doused him with the castor oil as soon as his mouth opened. Dud swallowed it, choking.

Three hours later, every portal in his body emptied of its contents, so pumped with coffee he would not sleep worth a darn for a week, Dud lay on the bed and moaned.

"Lord, I don't know what that woman gave me."

Jesse and Boyd sat sprawled in chairs, exhausted from the night's work. "You're just lucky you ate all that food before you went over there, Uncle Dud," Jesse said. "She probably misjudged the dose."

"She saw the map," Dud said. "I'm sorry. I don't think she had time to give it a good look, and the light was poor, but she saw it."

"It's all right, Uncle Dud," Boyd said. "Don't punish yourself over it."

Nevertheless, Dud did beat himself because of it. "I was so stupid. Ev Reid set me up to go to Mary's. And I just fell hook, line, and sinker."

The boys were forgiving, and even though Dud realized Mary and Ev had probably used him, as a gentleman, he felt compelled to publicly give Mary the benefit of the doubt. On their out of town the next morning, he stopped by her house.

Without dismounting, he called, "Mary!"

She came to the door, and after searching his face, ran to him.

"Oh Dud," she said so sweetly he expected to see sorghum molasses dripping from her teeth. "I'm so sorry about last night."

"It's all right, Mary," Dud said. "I just wanted to say goodbye."

She grasped his leg, placing her bosom tightly against it. Looking up with widened eyes, she pleaded, "Take me with you, Dud. Take me with you."

He shook his head. "No, Mary. You've got your boy and your mother here."

"I can leave them for a while. I want to go with you, Dud."

He shook his head again and took up the reins.

"Well, will you promise to write me, Dud, when you get to Waco?" she begged. "Let me know when you're in Waco and how you're doing."

It was against his nature to tell that kind of a lie, and with men, his handshake and word were rock solid, but lying to women fell into a whole nether category. "Yes, Mary, I'll write. Tell your mother and boy goodbye for me."

She finally let go when the horse began to move.

SIX

THE NEXT MORNING, DUD ROSE FROM HIS BEDROLL, working the kinks out of his legs as usual. He saw Boyd and Jesse staring at him. "What?" he demanded.

Boyd and Jesse glanced at each other. "It's just that you didn't say anything about your arthritis, Uncle Dud," Jesse said.

Dud grunted. "I've learned my lesson, boys. From now on, I'm keeping my mouth shut about my ailments."

Boyd and Jesse burst into laughter, causing Old Tom to run between them, wagging his tail in excitement.

They could have made it to San Antonio easily in a day, but Boyd's horse threw a shoe, and Jesse had to go back to find it. Since Boyd weighed over a hundred and seventy-five pounds, and the ground contained one rock after another in a thin layer of soil, they decided it would be better to find a place to halt where they could put the shoe back on rather than risk going all the way to San Antonio without it.

They stopped at the first farm they came to. As they

rode toward the house, the quietness of his surroundings made Dud suspicious. In addition, it did not look like any farm or ranch he had ever seen, and for a minute or two, he could not think why. The fences, the barns, and the corrals were there, but aside from one old mule, there was nothing in them. Hog-pens sat empty, no chickens scratched in the yard. A big garden behind the house was partially visible, so someone had to live there.

Just when he wondered if he had passed through a gateway into an alternate world, three people came out of the house and stepped onto the gallery. A rotund older man with long hair and a heavy beard stood by a bony young woman with dark hair, while a small older woman with a face like a little bird hovered behind them.

"Hello the house," Dud called.

"Welcome strangers," the man said pleasantly. "Get thee down from thy horses."

"All-righty," Dud answered, trying to inject some sense of normalcy into a weird state of affairs. As he and the boys approached the gallery after dismounting, he swiftly assessed the people on it. The old man had a white face and lilywhite soft hands, a sure sign he was a lawyer or a professor. The old woman wore the abstracted, congenial look of someone who might be mentally incompetent. Aside from a dark mustache on her upper lip, frizzy hair, and a body that looked like it was made of angle iron, the girl was not too bad. Dud introduced himself, explaining about the shoe and giving the same spiel about being on a cattle and land buying trip that he gave everyone.

"We have no cattle here, friend," the old man said. "We bought this place last year, and there might be some tools in the barn left over from the previous owner; thee is welcome to look."

"Thank you, we'll do that," Dud said. The old man invited them to come back to the house afterward. "We welcome visitors," he explained. Dud nodded, and as he turned to go to the barn, he caught Jesse eying the girl in a speculative way. Jess suddenly gave her a charming smile, bowing slightly to her. She put her hand to her mouth and simpered.

Dud raised an eyebrow but said nothing. He liked women of all shapes and sizes and was a firm believer that all cats looked alike in the dark, but he could see nothing about the girl that warranted Jesse's extravagant attention. He shrugged it off and followed the boys to the barn.

The barn looked like a dusty museum, but after digging around, they found what they needed. Jesse left them to the job and disappeared. Dud did little more than watch Boyd nail the shoe back on.

Upon leaving the barn, they found Jesse sitting on the gallery in a swing with the daughter of the house. He faced her with one arm on the back of the swing, and as he and Boyd approached, Jesse raised his head and smiled.

"Uncle Dud, Miss Elzy and her parents have invited us to stay for supper and spend the night," he said.

Dud looked at Boyd, and Boyd shot him a puzzled look that replicated his own. "That's mighty nice of them," Dud said.

"Good," Jesse said, taking it for granted he meant yes. "Miss Elzy has been very kind to me," he said, lightly touching her hand and looking calf-eyes at her. She giggled again.

Boyd appeared just as mystified as he was by Jesse's

sudden infatuation. Again they shrugged it off and when invited, went into the house for supper. The old lady flitted around the table in the neat Victorian house, resplendent with expensive furniture and conspicuous bric-a-brac. Dud complimented the woman on her home, and she fluttered with pleasure.

The stout old man sat at the head of the table, with his daughter by his side. His wife sat on the other side of the daughter. They bowed their heads, and with a flourish, the old man took off on one of the longest and most boring blessings Dud had ever heard. He thought he would fall asleep before the old fellow ever reached the "amen."

He finally pronounced it and Dud opened his eyes, looking with anticipation at the food on the table. After seeing it, he had to try hard to keep his face from frowning. Everything on the table was green.

His host saw him, and his eyes gleamed defiantly. "We abstain from partaking of the flesh, friend Washburn. It is against our religion to do so."

Good manners kept Dud from saying it was against his religion not to do so. "It looks mighty fine," he said.

The lady of the house began passing dishes around the table. "Please help yourselves," she said. "It's so nice to have company in the house. No one comes anymore…."

Her husband shot her a hard look, and she grew more quivery and flustered. "I hope you like the food. It would taste better with a little bacon…," she trailed off again when her daughter gave her an angry stare.

"Mother!" the girl said sharply. "We've been through all this before." She turned a sugary smile to Dud and the boys. "Father believes all God's creatures are blessed, and it is a sin to kill any one of them. He's tried to preach that gospel to the heathens out here, but they hardened their hearts and refused to listen."

"Well, it's something to think about," Jesse said, giving the girl a deep, soulful look.

Dud and Boyd turned their heads simultaneously to stare at Jesse, a cattleman since birth, and both thought Jesse had lost his mind. Dud eyes moved to the over-and-under shotgun above the fireplace mantle.

His host saw the question in his eyes and chuckled. "That is fired merely to frighten away predators, friend Washburn, not to kill. Life, all life, is sacred."

"And God said," the old man suddenly bellowed. "Behold, I have given you every herb bearing seed, which is upon the face of all the earth, and every tree. To you it shall be for meat."

Boyd helped himself to a spoonful of spinach and plopped it on his plate. "And God despised the gift of fruit that Cain brought him," he said in a loud voice to no one in particular. "And he respected the killed fat that Abel offered."

The old woman's face lit up, and she turned to her husband. "That's right, Father. God didn't like Cain's offering of fruits and vegetables; he wanted Abel's meat."

"Be quiet, Mother," the girl ordered. "You are misquoting the Bible and don't know what you are talking about."

The mother looked down at her plate so defeated and crestfallen; Dud wanted to reach across the table, forget all about the sanctity of life, and slap the girl senseless.

The old man stuck out his lips in anger at his wife, and turning his gaze, cast a belligerent look at Boyd. Dud gave

Boyd a kick under the table before he started quoting chapter nine, verse three. "This food tastes delicious, ma'am," Dud said to the lady of the house. "Just the way it is," he added, giving Boyd a look of warning.

Diverted, the old man began to rail against his neighbors for their unbelief. As he ranted, Dud wondered how he stayed so big and fat on green beans, but as soon as he started stuffing his face with bread and jam, he understood. The old man devoured one whole loaf of bread by himself and a pot of jam. As they followed his lead, Dud guiltily realized they were probably wiping out a week's supply of bread.

As Dud sopped the spinach liquid with his bread, out of the corner of his eye, he saw his host give him a look of suspicion.

"Are thee baptized?" he thundered so loudly Dud almost choked on the bread.

"Washed in the blood," Dud said almost in a shout, clearing his throat of bread.

"Me and Jess, too," Boyd said. "Washed in the sacrificial *blood* of the *lamb* of God," he added loudly.

The old man pouted in disappointment at first, but then stared craftily at Dud. "But were thee immersed or sprinkled?" he demanded.

"Baptized in the Guadalupe River as a boy," Dud assured him. "Probably killed half the fish downstream," he added.

"Us too," Boyd said. "The Frio was running dry that year, and it took a while to find a place deep enough to dunk us, but they did."

Dud began to feel a little sorry for the old man, and

thought after all, they were eating his supply of bread, so he said, "We're just backsliding Methodists."

This pleased his host, who did not want any competition in the field of righteousness, and he began another torrent of abuse against the blackguards who lived around them for their refusal to be free-thinking and open-minded. As Dud scraped his fork against fine china, taking in the expensive furniture decorating the house, he wondered what the old man did for a living. When he began to fume about relatives back east who were equally unenlightened, a light went off in Dud's head—he was a remittance man, paid to stay far away from a wealthy family who did not want to hear any more about how sinful it was to masticate a good T-bone. In the meantime, Dud heard his suddenly deranged nephew offering to help skinny, smart-mouthed Miss Elzy with the dishes.

After rising, Dud and Boyd sat on the gallery and counted the minutes until they could escape to bed. The old man talked without pausing about his religion, a mixture of Christianity, Judaism, and some mystical Eastern religion that Dud suspected he bent to suit his fancy. When Boyd swatted a fly lighting on his leg, the old man interjected quickly. "Please friend, refrain thee from thy baser impulses. Remember that here we view all life as precious."

Dud could see his own precious life slipping away from him as he listened with half an ear to his fanatical host, meanwhile, puzzling over what had gotten into Jesse. They could hear sounds of laughter coming from the kitchen. Jesse and the girl joined them on the gallery later, sitting in the swing where Jess whispered in her ear. She responded with arch twitters and ignored everyone else. The crease of worry between Boyd's eyebrows grew deeper and deeper.

Their hosts had said they could bed down on a sleeping gallery at the back of the house, and as soon as the first rays of sun hit the western horizon, Dud excused himself. "I'm used to going to bed with the chickens," he exaggerated. Although Boyd was reluctant to leave his brother, he went with Dud to check on the horses before going to bed.

"What's wrong with him?" Boyd asked as he absent-mindedly patted Jesse's roan. "Has he taken leave of his senses?"

Dud went to his saddlebags and pulled out a handful of jerked beef strips, handing Boyd one. He kept one for himself and stuffed the rest in his vest pocket. After savagely ripping into the meat, he told Boyd, "Don't worry. I'm going to put a stop to this nonsense in the morning."

Boyd looked anxiously at the front gallery. "Will he be safe until then?"

They went around to the back of the house where three cots had been set up on the gallery. As they walked up the steps, their hostess came out the back door.

"I do hope you'll be comfortable here," she said in a vague way.

Dud assured her they would be. Her eyes fastened on his vest, and Dud realized she had spotted his two remaining strips of jerky. She did not say anything, but stared at them, running her tongue over her lips.

"Here ma'am," he said. "Have one. We sure appreciate your kindness."

"Oh, I couldn't," she said, but hesitated. "I really shouldn't," she whispered.

Dud placed one of the strips in her hand. She looked at it hungrily.

"Do you think God will forgive me?" she asked anxiously.

Dud nodded his head. "I imagine if you do your wifely duty joyfully tonight," Dud said, putting it as delicately as he could, "God will be happy to forgive you."

She looked a little puzzled, but then her face lit up as she saw the way out. "Yes, yes. I'll confess my sins, then I'll gladly do my penance, I mean my duty."

"Uh, wait," Dud said. "Don't confess tonight, confess tomorrow night. After we're gone."

She nodded conspiratorially. "Yes, that would be best. And I'll do my wifely duty tomorrow night, too, after I confess. That will make everything all right, won't it?"

"Yes," Dud nodded. "I imagine it will." He looked at the last piece of jerky, and taking it from his pocket, put it in her hand. "Well, if you're going to have to do your wifely duty twice, you might as well have two pieces."

"Thank you, thank you, Mr. Washburn," she said, closing her eyes and pressing the jerky against her bosom. She opened her eyes and smiled. "You are such a kind man, Mr. Washburn." Before he could say anything, she turned and hurried back into the house.

"That was the last of the jerky, wasn't it?" Boyd asked moodily.

Dud nodded. "Don't worry, tomorrow night, we'll be eating steak in San Antonio."

They could hear sporadic laughter coming from the front gallery far into the evening. Around midnight, Jesse came around to the back and fell into his cot without a word, falling asleep almost instantly. Dud stared at him in the darkness, while Old Tom went back to snoring.

The next morning, Jesse gave them chipper smiles but refused to answer their unspoken questions. Just as they were going into the house for breakfast, Jesse asked his hosts to excuse him for a few minutes.

"Please start without me," he said. "I'll be back in half a tick."

Their host smiled genially. "Of course," he said, and added significantly. "Son."

The girl gave Jesse a besotted and possessive smile as he went out the door. Dud and Boyd followed their hosts to the breakfast table—bread again and more jam. After another prolonged blessing, they began to eat, and Jesse slipped back into the house, taking his place at the table.

"Now young man," the old man said. "My daughter tells me thee has quite a little nest egg saved in the bank."

Jesse had the grace to blush, and he nodded.

"Well, well," the old man grinned, "that is fortuitous."

Dud thought the time had come to fire off the dynamite. He put his bread down, and looking at his host, he announced, "I am a divorced man."

When the girl and her father digested this information, they looked at one another in horror. The mother said, "Oh, I'm so sorry. That must have been painful."

The other two acted as if she had not spoken. "Divorced?" the old man said. "Well that changes everything. I don't know if I want my daughter marrying into a family that permits divorce."

Jesse leaned back and sat up straight. "Whoa, now," he

interjected, holding up his palms. "Who said anything about marriage?"

The words produced a catastrophic effect. The old man and the girl sat aghast and began to shriek at the same time. "What? What is this?" The girl cried, "But you kissed me! You took liberties with me!"

The old man looked at his daughter, his jaw jutted out, and he stood up. "You! You!" he sputtered, so angry he could not speak.

"Oh," the mother said with a flutter. "It was just a little kiss. What harm is just one little kiss?"

"Harm! Harm! You foul vermin," the old fellow roared.

Dud rose quickly. "Let's get out of here!" he told Boyd and Jesse. He stopped to bow his head to his hostess. "Thank you, ma'am, for your hospitality."

"You scoundrels! You sons of Satan," the old man yelled as Dud, Boyd, and Jesse pushed and fell against one another in their hurry to escape.

"Kill him, Father," the girl screamed. "Shoot him."

Dud, the last out the door, saw the old man going for the shotgun. "Run!" he hollered.

Once out the door, he and Boyd began for the barn, but Jesse yelled, "This way," and pointed to the horses tied to trees toward the main road.

With Old Tom in the lead, Dud pumped his legs as fast as he could to keep up with Boyd and Jesse. He could hear the old man's threats and the girl's screams. A shotgun boomed, and a tree branched fell to his left.

Jesse turned his head, grinning, and yelled, "What happened to the sanctity of life?"

"Knave!" the girl screamed while her father spat words that were not printed in the Bible.

"I'm going to kill you, Jesse," Dud threatened as he huffed and puffed, running as hard as he could to his horse. "You planned this, you rascal!" He looked back over his shoulder and saw the old woman struggling with the old man, trying to raise the shotgun while her daughter jerked at her arms.

"Run, Mr. Washburn, run!" the old woman screamed. She succeeded in pulling up on the shotgun, and the second shell fired high into the air.

"Thank you, ma'am," Dud hollered. In three more seconds he reached his horse, still cussing Jesse. As he jumped on his horse, he bawled, "What the hell was that all about?"

Jess reared his gelding and called with a grin over his shoulder as he gave it the spurs. "You and Boyd had your spells at being a fool over a woman; I thought I might as well have mine and get it over with."

As they raced away to the shrieks of "Sons of Beelzebub, you bastards!" in their ears, Dud and Boyd began to laugh. They laughed so hard they almost fell off their horses.

SEVEN

ONCE IN SAN ANTONIO, THE THREE ADVENTURERS LEFT their horses at a livery stable and checked into a hotel. Before they did anything else, they wanted to eat, and as they sat ingesting as much chow as they could hold, they forgot about the incidences on the trail. The quest for gold became uppermost in their minds again.

"I'll get cleaned up at the barbershop in the morning," Dud said. "Then buy a map."

Boyd and Jesse exchanged glances. "Uncle Dud," Boyd said. "I think you'd better splurge on some new clothes."

"What do you mean?" Dud asked indignantly. "There's nothing wrong with what I have on. This vest is only five or six years old, and your mama mended the holes in my shirt I had patched together with mesquite thorns."

"Well, that's just it, Uncle Dud," Boyd continued. "They are pretty much just one big patch. It's kind of embarrassing trying to impress women in a big city like San Antonio when our uncle looks like he sleeps in empty freight cars."

"Boys, women don't care what's on a man's back, just what's in his bank account," Dud said. "Show them a thick roll of cash, and they don't care how many rips a man has in his britches," but he agreed to buy new clothes.

The next morning, before they left their hotel room, Dud gave instructions to Boyd and Jesse. "Just to be on the safe side, go to the railroad station and buy three tickets for San Angelo. Make sure to get places for the horses on a livestock car."

"Are you sure you want us to spend the money?" Jesse asked. "We can just pretend to get the tickets."

"No, do the real thing. And don't get softhearted and give the tickets away to some down and out cowboy. I want it to look exactly like we are heading for San Angelo."

The boys nodded and Dud continued. "Let me leave the hotel first. I'll go to the barbershop. Come by and tell me you're headed for the train station. Mention getting tickets for West Texas."

The barbershop routine worked well; however, buying a map was not as easy as Dud expected.

"With nobody going on cattle drives anymore, Mr. Washburn," he heard over and over again, "we don't keep maps on hand like we used to. Everybody just hops a train nowadays."

Dud doggedly persisted, crossing street after street, going in one shop after another, asking clerk after clerk. He and the boys could pass through Austin, but it was not much of a town, and they would be much less likely to find a map there than San Antonio. If he could not find a map to buy, he would have to go to the courthouse or Fort Sam Houston and study their maps, inviting speculation.

At every store he visited, he met the same fellow either going in or coming out. Tall and big, with sandy hair and freckles, the middle-aged man dressed like a dude in a suit and vest with a white starched collar on his shirt. Dud could not believe he would be someone following them—he did not look the part. However, there was something about the way he carried himself that made Dud think he was not just a shopkeeper or a banker. He had the look of a man who had been in rough places and knew how to handle himself, despite his fashionable outfit.

"Oh, that's Woodrow Harrison, Mr. Washburn," a storekeeper explained as Dud leaned on the counter with one elbow and watched the retreating figure. "He's a railroad man. Used to live here in San Antonio; in fact, he was a neighbor of mine. Say, that's funny; he's looking for a map, too."

Dud looked back to the storekeeper. "Doesn't the railroad provide maps?"

"Sure," the little store owner said. "But his daughter came by his office one day to ask if she could have a kitten, and when he said she could, she got so excited she hugged his neck and accidentally knocked an ink well over on his map. Rather than have to explain what happened and wait for another map, he hoped he could just buy one. I guess he's not having any better luck than you are."

"I wish him the best," Dud said. "I hope he doesn't take it out on the little girl if he doesn't."

"Oh, he won't," the shopkeeper assured him. "He's crazy about his daughters—a real family man. It's a crying shame what happened when they lived in San Antonio."

Dud heard the word "daughters" and his ears pricked up. "What happened?" he asked.

"His little girls were walking home, and they walked by some boys who were deviling an old mule. You know how boys are. Suddenly the mule kicked, and it hit his youngest girl in the back of the head. She was unconscious for days. When she woke up, she wasn't quite right in the head. She's eighteen now and a beautiful young woman, but she has the mind of a ten-year-old."

"That's a pity," Dud said.

"Yes. You should see those girls, Mr. Washburn. Mr. Woody brought them to San Antonio last year, and two more beautiful girls you never saw in your life. The oldest one, she's about twenty, has dark red hair, pale skin, and huge green eyes. And that's not the only two things on her that are huge, too, if you get my drift, Mr. Washburn. Knocks the willies out of every man who looks at her. The other girl favors her mother, dark hair, big round dark eyes, good-looking little heifer, but as soon as she starts talking you know something ain't right." He stopped yakking long enough to shake his head. "Just a shame."

Dud ruminated on this information. Boyd and Jesse liked red hair just as well as any other color. "Whereabouts do these people live?" he asked.

"Somewhere out in the boonies where they're putting in a new railroad line. Mr. Woody has taken his family to some pretty tough places, but that wife of his and those two girls have always made him a decent home. It just seems a pity something like that should happen to a good family, when some of this trash hanging around San Antonio never has a bad cross to bear in their life."

"Yep," Dud agreed. "It's a shame."

It was a shame about the map, too. Dud left the gossipy shopkeeper and found a bench shaded by an oak tree. After sitting down, his eyes aimlessly looked at the bricked streets, pondering the situation. Old Tom rested, panting a little, beside him.

"We need a map," he muttered to the dog. "There ought to be at least one in this town." He got up to look again.

He found one in a junk shop. The shopkeeper, a small man with glasses and a humped back who Dud had dealt with many times before, specialized in buying things for resale from Fort Sam Houston army officers who had to strip down households after being reassigned.

"Dud!" he greeted him when Dud entered the cluttered store. "It's nice to see you again. I've found something for your sister. She's going to love this, Dud. Here let me find it. I put it back especially for you."

He dug around like a small mouse, coming up with an ornate china teapot. "See this, Dud? All the way from France. Perfect condition. She'll love it."

Dud scratched his chin and squinted. How many teapots had he bought her? Three? That left two empty spots in his nieces' hope chests. He and Ponder had already bought enough pots and pans for the girls to start ten households. He haggled a little over the price. "Okay," Dud said when they finally agreed. "But you have to store it for me. I'll be gone for several weeks, and I'll pick it up on the return trip."

"Of course, Dud. It's a pleasure doing business with you. Now, I have something else that might interest you. I know your brother-in-law likes Indian artifacts. Look at this blanket. Genuine Navajo. I got it from an Army officer who had been stationed in Arizona."

Dud looked at the filthy red and yellow blanket with skepticism. "It's kind of dirty."

"Dud!" he said, his small eyes growing wide with horror. "This is authentic! Do you think the Indians have a Chinese laundry around the corner? I'll knock off seventy-five cents."

Dud grinned. "All right, you talked me into it. But before you remember something else you think I just have to have, I'm looking for a Texas map, and a recent one, too. I don't want something with half the state missing."

The little man looked up at the ceiling, tapping his finger against a chubby cheek. "Of course," he said, pointing the finger upward. "Just the thing. Came in last week. A colonel died and his wife sold all his possessions. You know how it is, Dud. A woman dies; the man keeps everything and expects wife number two to like it. A man dies, everything gets tossed."

He scurried to the back of the shop and returned with a leather case. Opening the case, he pulled out a rolled map, and moving a few things off a Queen Anne buffet, he spread it out for Dud to see.

He had not exaggerated; it looked almost new. Dud made him an offer, but did not dicker long. "Hand me that blanket, I'll take it now," Dud said, and folded the blanket around the leather case containing the prized map so it could not be seen. A man taking a train trip to San Angelo did not need a map.

The others were waiting for him in the hotel lobby. As he walked toward them, he was hailed by a couple of friends, but with a wave of his hand, he made vague promises to see them later.

Boyd and Jesse jumped from the ornate sofa as he drew nearer. "Did you get it?" Boyd asked.

"You bet," Dud answered. "Took almost all day, but I found it. Come on, let's go upstairs and have a look. I'm getting gold fever."

Once in their room, they moved the table standing underneath a window into the middle of the room and rolled the map onto it. Thankful daylight still illuminated the room; the four of them searched the map while Old Tom dozed in the corner, courtesy of a few extra dollars put into the hotel manager's hand.

"Three rivers converging somewhere in Central Texas," Dud muttered, leaning over the map. "Here are the Lampasas, the Leon, and the Nolan, south of Waco," he said pointing. "They are the most obvious, but we don't know for sure—it might be three small creeks."

They made a methodical search of every inch of the map, deeming it better to be on the safe side and investigate further afield than just the middle area of Texas, but they came up with nothing other than the three rivers Dud first mentioned.

Finally, Dud straightened, regretfully concluding there could only be one answer. "It has to be where the Lampasas, the Leon, and the Nolan meet," he said. "But something doesn't feel right about it."

"That sounds like one of Uncle Ponder's old poker hunches," Jesse scoffed.

"All we can do is go there and find out," Boyd said.

Dud nodded. "I don't know. I do feel kind of like Uncle Ponder," he said, wishing for the first time that Ponder was with them. "I told Mary we were heading for Waco. Maybe that's why I feel wrong about it being there—I was hoping it wouldn't be."

He could not dispel his uneasy feeling, but just when he was about to suggest they put the map aside and go for supper, they heard a knock at the door.

He put his hand out. "Leave it," he whispered. "Just stand in front of the table."

The knock came again and a voice called out, "Mr. Washburn?"

"Keep your shirt on," Dud said, and opened the door.

His fellow map hunter stood in the hallway, hat in hand. "Mr. Washburn?" he asked. "My name is Woody Harrison. I think we've been after the same thing all day."

Dud studied him briefly and opened the door. "Come on in." He introduced the others while Old Tom sniffed at the man's pant legs and then nudged his hand to be petted. "What can we do for you, Mr. Harrison?"

While absentmindedly patting Old Tom's head, he answered, "I work for the railroad, and I'm in need of a recent map of the state. I believe you managed to purchase one this afternoon. If you'd be willing to sell it, I'm prepared to pay double for it."

Instead of answering, Dud led him to the table. Boyd and Jesse parted, allowing Harrison to examine the map.

"Yes, this is exactly what I've been looking for," he said. He put his finger on a spot some miles east of Austin. "Here's where we're putting in a new line, near where these three creeks join. A boomtown has sprung up, exploding almost overnight; that's why it's not on the map yet."

Dud felt a tingling at the back of his neck. He pointed

his finger at the same spot. "Those three creeks don't merge in one place. The third one joins further down."

"No," Harrison said. "The map is drawn incorrectly. Three streams converge near Tie Town: the Upper Yegua, the Lower Yegua, and Paint Creek. They in turn form the Middle Yegua. I went out with the surveyor myself."

Dud said slowly, "There wouldn't happen to be a few small hills north of these creeks, would there?"

"Oh yes," Harrison said, "the Yegua Knobs." He chuckled. "We call them the Yegua Knobs because of the creeks, but the Indians actually had another name for them."

"Oh really," Dud said. "And what was that name?"

"Let's see, Itana something. The Itanakaala, I think. It means the Walking Dead," he explained. "They believe the hills to be haunted by people unable to go to heaven. Evidently there is a natural phenomena around the creek that periodically causes a yellow mist to rise and float through the hills. I've never seen it, but they say it is rather spooky."

Dud hoped Woody Harrison could not sense their excitement. To try to hide it, he rubbed his fingers across his lips thoughtfully. "Tell me," he asked. "Why is it so important for you to have this map? I confess I asked a store clerk who you were, and he told me about your daughter spilling the coffee. But that doesn't explain why you want one so badly."

Harrison's already ruddy skin blushed. "Yes, I could request another map, but, I would have to fill out a form in triplicate, explaining exactly what happened, and it might take months to process and receive a new one." He paused before going on. "There is a lot of thievery that goes on in these kinds of jobs. If it goes on my record that

I requested a duplicate map, it might look suspiciously like I had sold the other one."

"I see," Dud said. In his mind, he also saw a beautiful young redhead for one of his nephews. "When were you planning on leaving town, Mr. Harrison?"

A hopeful look crossed the large man's face. "If I got the map, in the morning."

"I tell you what," Dud said. "You let us keep the map for a few hours, and then we'll give it to you. Are you staying in this hotel, too?"

"Yes, as a matter of fact I am." He reached into his pocket, but Dud stopped him.

"No, I insist. You take it. We'll bring it to your room in a couple of hours."

The man looked surprised, and again he protested. "I can't let you do that."

"Well, it's like this," Dud said. "We're on a hunt for land and cattle to buy as an investment, and a friend told us about a place where three streams meet with some small hills nearby, but he couldn't remember exactly where he'd seen them. So we'll mosey on up to this place you were talking about, Tie Town, is it? And we'll have a look at it."

"I can't believe it would be the right place," Harrison answered, still in wonder at his good luck. "The hills are heavily wooded, more suited for hiding outlaws than for running large amounts of cattle."

"Well, we'll check it out. I happened to hear that your wife is an excellent cook," Dud said, exaggerating slightly. "Once we're there, if you're still inclined to favor us, we would appreciate a home cooked meal in exchange for this map."

Dud watched as Harrison's eyes left him and went to

Boyd and Jesse. The man was no fool, and a light of understanding came over his face. He bowed slightly with a small smile. "I would consider it an honor." He was turning to leave when he caught sight of the Indian blanket thrown carelessly on a nearby chair.

"My word, is that an authentic Navajo?" He walked to it, reaching out to examine the nap. He turned back to Dud with a smile. "Would you consider selling this? I would insist on paying. You see, my daughter collects Indian artifacts. We've lived in so many out-of-the-way places, that many times she has so few friends; she accompanies me on fishing trips for entertainment. While I fish, she searches for arrowheads and pottery. She's accumulated quite a collection."

He smiled at Old Tom and added, "We used to have a little dog that guarded her every step of the way when she was smaller." He looked at Dud. "What do you say, Mr. Washburn? Can I persuade you to part with one more thing?"

Dud smiled. "I'm afraid that one is already spoken for. But we'll have that map to you directly."

Harrison walked back across the room to shake hands. "I'd invite you all as my guests for supper this evening, but I've already made plans to dine with a superior, and that's an appointment I can't break."

They assured him it did not matter, and they were looking forward to dining in his home at Tie Town.

As soon as he shut the door, Jesse whispered, "What was that all about?" and Boyd added, "Why did you give him the map?"

Dud grinned and rubbed his hands together. "Just trust your old Uncle Dud. You'll find out when we get to Tie

Town. Now one of you boys run downstairs and fetch a pencil and some paper."

Boyd started for the door, and Dud added, "And give that Indian blanket to the maid; tell her to wash it pronto and have it ready for us this evening. Grease her palm, Boyd, don't be stingy. We'll be leaving here around three or four in the morning."

"This is it, isn't it, Uncle Dud?" Jesse said.

"You betcha," Dud said. "What a lucky break."

After making a rough sketch of the roads and terrain between San Antonio and Tie Town, and the area surrounding the boomtown, Boyd and Jesse delivered the map and case to Woody Harrison. Dud waited in the lobby; afterward, they went out for supper.

As he stepped onto the smooth boards of the sidewalk after leaving the café, Dud felt full of good food and on top of the world. Everything felt right: the map business, Woodrow Harrison, even the blanket. As he stood making a casual survey of the people around him, he saw a familiar face. She was coming out of a store across the street, pulling on gloves. Dud would have betted they were expensive gloves, too. The sight of his ex-wife, now a matronly woman in her early forties, did not cause him pain or passion. As Ev Reid had put it, that ship had sailed.

Boyd and Jesse joined him and saw her. They knew who she was from previous times Dud had run across her in their presence. She did not like for him to acknowledge her, preferring to give friends and acquaintances the illusion her first husband was dead. Boyd and Jesse understood these things and made no comment. Just as he was about to turn to leave, Dud saw a man and teenage boy approach her.

Her husband meant nothing to Dud except to evoke vague feelings of pity. The boy, born long after he and she had parted the blanket, looked like his father. Dud watched as he joked with his father and spoke to his mother with a look of affection. All three smiled at some comment the boy made. Abruptly, Dud turned and headed for the nearest saloon.

He sat with a bottle at a table in the corner by himself. His sister's admonishments were working because it only took one bottle to make him slobbering drunk.

At the end of the evening, Boyd and Jesse placed his arms around their shoulders and guided him back to the hotel. As they helped maneuver his rubbery legs up the stairs, Jesse said, "Don't feel bad, Uncle Dud. You've got me and Boyd, anyway."

Dud thought he was going to cry, or maybe just puke—again.

EIGHT

DUD DID NOT KNOW HOW HE DID IT, BUT HE MANAGED TO wake up at three a.m. and get moving. No one made any comments about the high lonesome he went on the night before, and he preferred to forget it. They started north; again following the lesser known paths, this time to avoid detection in the off chance they were being followed.

They were almost sure they were not. Now that they were in a more thickly populated section, they stopped for dinner and supper at two different farms. Both were inhabited by hospitable Germans, and at one they spent the night in a rock barn so hygienic, his sister would have prepared meals in it without a qualm. The next noon, forced with the prospect of their own cooking, they forgo eating. Around two o'clock in the afternoon, after leaving the black-land farm country, they found a ranch house in a meadowland populated with large oaks.

Built of milled wood and painted white, the small house looked clean, and the gallery beckoned them invitingly. They passed a large, freshly tilled garden. From behind the house came the sounds of someone trying to chop wood—there was no rhythm to the whacks of the ax. Riding their horses around the side of the house, they saw a young woman attempting to wield an ax almost as big as she was. Old Tom ran to her, giving her a start, but she rested her ax and petted his ear.

"Where did you come from, big fellow?" she asked. Looking up, she saw them.

"Howdy, ma'am," Dud said, looking over the woman with a bachelor's eye for detail. She had dark circles under her eyes, and her blonde hair was parted down the middle and pulled tightly to the back of her neck in an unbecoming bun. Despite this, the petite woman, who could only be a few years older than Boyd, had a pretty face with full pink lips spread into a worried smile over even white teeth. Her big eyes were a shade of dark blue that reminded Dud of something, but he could not think of what.

"We're just passing through on our way to Waco, ma'am," Dud said. It was the story he told everyone. When they left this place, they intended to veer east and make their way to Tie Town. "My name's Dud Washburn. These are my nephews, Boyd and Jesse Callahan. The big pest's name is Old Tom. We'd like to water our horses and rest a spell, if that's all right."

"Yes, yes, of course," she said, and looked at the small pile of kindling with her lips pressed together in worry. With regret, she looked back at Dud. "Please, water your horses and sit on the gallery. I'll bring you something to drink." She put her hand up to her cheek. "Oh, please

83

forgive my manners, my name is Iris Talbot. My husband Lon and I lease this place."

When she said her name, Dud suddenly remembered what the color of her eyes reminded him of—the dark blue flag irises his mother grew beside their log home. He said, "Howdy do, Mrs. Talbot. We'd sure be obliged to you."

She put the ax down and hurried to the back door of the house. Dud backed his horse and with the others, returned to the front of the house where a water trough stood. After wiping their faces with wet bandanas, they walked to the house and stepped onto the gallery. Various ladder-back chairs and rockers lined it, and they sat down to await their attractive, but regrettably married, hostess.

She brought out cups and a platter filled with sliced buttered bread. "I usually have cookies on hand in case someone comes by, but I've been so busy," she said, again with an uneasy tone. "I put a pot of coffee on to boil."

"You're very kind, ma'am," Dud said. "We didn't mean to put you to any trouble."

She looked embarrassed. "Oh no, you didn't. It's just that...," she paused. "It's just that before my husband left for town, he gave me a list of things he wants done today, and I'm not very far along on the list."

Her soft gestures were like velvet. The bread had a light and fluffy texture; the butter tasted sweet. Dud believed she was wasting her charms chopping wood, and everybody knew wastefulness was a sin. "Ma'am," he said, "if we were to get those chores on your list done, do you think you could see your way to fixing us a good supper?"

Iris's eyes widened as she digested what he said. With a

face filling with hope, she leaned forward. "Really, Mr. Washburn? You'd do that for me?"

Dud glanced at Boyd and Jesse and saw they were agreeable. "Sure," he said. "You were chopping kindling just now. What else besides that is on your to-do list?"

Her cheeks flushed in excitement, and she answered shyly. "I'm supposed to clean out the barn and plant potatoes. I did some potatoes this morning, but I haven't even touched the barn."

"I'll clean out the barn," Jesse hurriedly said. Boyd said almost as quick, "I'll be more than happy to chop wood."

Dud shot Boyd the evil eye. "I bet you would," he said. If there was one thing all three of them hated, it was farming. However, diminutive Mrs. Talbot appeared so thrilled; Dud had to smile at her. "There you go, all the chores taken care of. But we've got a little time. Why don't you sit here and visit with us while we rest a spell before getting started?"

Iris's eyes danced in elation. "The coffee should be ready by now; I'll bring it out," she said, jumping up and racing back into the house.

She came out with a large pot and another cup. After pouring the coffee, she sat down and looked happily at Dud. "Did you come through San Antonio?" she asked.

Dud nodded, and she continued. "What were the women wearing?" she asked. "Are they still wearing bustles?"

Dud did his best to describe the clothes of the women in San Antonio. Boyd and Jesse added comments, too, and Iris looked back and forth between them avidly, but always directed her questions to Dud. She looked so young and sweet, Dud hated to see her hair pulled back so tightly it looked like it hurt her face. "The women there are wearing their hair piled up on the crown of their head in a loose bun," he added, hoping he could say it without hurting her feelings. "Not taut, kind of flowing like."

Iris nodded. "Yes?" she said, pleading with him to go on.

"And they wear bangs," Dud said, trying to figure out a way to describe the hairstyle he had liked best. "Full bangs," he said, "Almost down to the eyebrows," he added, touching his forehead with his finger. "Kind of long and wispy. Wouldn't you say that, Boyd, Jesse?"

Boyd and Jesse, looking amused, agreed. "That's right, Uncle Dud. Long and wispy."

Iris looked at them and smiled. "Oh you must forgive me. You must think I'm awful to pump you so hard about silly things like this."

They gave vigorous protests. Iris was a taken woman, but that did not stop three bachelors from thinking she was fun to talk to and pleasant to look at. She refilled their coffee cups, and Dud, looking at a swing hanging from a tree in the front yard, asked if she had children.

"No," she said, looking at the swing. "It was here when we moved in, and I begged my husband not to take it down. I thought maybe neighbors would visit and their children would enjoy playing on it, but we get so few people...."

She looked so sad, Dud regretted asking her. "Mrs. Talbot, they've got a new opera house in San Antonio, did I tell you that?"

"No," Iris said, her eyes wide with wonder. "Did you go to it?"

"No, we didn't have time this trip. To tell you the truth,

I don't much like listening to music unless I can dance to it," he said, somewhat abashed.

Boyd and Jesse snickered; they knew why he liked to dance. He gave them a sharp look, and their faces became angelic masks.

"I love to dance," Iris said. "Oh, I haven't been dancing since I don't know when. What kind of dances do you do where you live? We used to do so many reels back home. I grew up on a horse farm near Springfield, and someone was always having a dance."

Dud decided Iris Talbot could make monks forget all about vows of silence; she had them talking so much, starved for companionship as she was. After an enjoyable time conversing with her, Dud reluctantly said they had better start the chores.

Jesse walked to the nearby barn, while Boyd went around to the back of the house. Dud admitted he had not planted potatoes since he was ten years old, and Iris took him to the garden to show him how. As he looked down the long expanse of tilled soil, Iris refreshed his memory. "Just plant the eyes about two inches deep and a foot and a half apart." Dud tried to keep from scowling, and when she smiled and told him "thank you" again, he felt his disgust draining.

"Nothing to it," he assured her. "You just go do whatever you need to do."

She smiled again and paused, as if she wanted to say or do something else, but instead she said, "thank you, Mr. Washburn" again and left.

Dud heard the ax hit once, and in a minute, the whir of a grindstone. As he picked up a hoe, he looked at it distastefully. He hoped the barn was full of horse apples and Boyd would be chopping ironwood. He put the hoe down and picked up the burlap sack of potato pieces, chunking them in the rows while Old Tom sniffed.

"Get away from there," Dud scolded. That's all he needed was a dog stealing the bits he had already thrown down.

Boyd's chopping started, making a steady cadence, and in a minute, Dud heard chickens squawking. He hoped Iris Talbot planned on frying chicken. "I haven't had good fried chicken since you were a pup, old boy," he started to tell the dog, but Old Tom had deserted him to see what Iris was doing with the chickens.

When Dud had worked his way halfway through the garden, Iris ran out of the house. "Mr. Washburn," she said breathlessly when she reached him. "Which would you and your nephews prefer, pecan pie or buttermilk pie?" she asked.

Dud grinned. "Either one, Mrs. Talbot," he said. "Whatever you feel like baking."

She nodded her head and smiled. "Maybe I'll do both." She turned and ran back into the house.

Thoughts of pie kept Dud from cussing the ground too much as sweat poured from his brow. He finally removed his bandana and coiled it around his head, glad none of his enemies could see the depths a self-respecting cattleman like himself had sunk to. Boyd and Jesse must have been peeking around the corner of the house waiting, because they only showed their faces when he covered the last eye in the last row.

Dud tore off the bandana and called them a few choice names while they grinned. "Do you think this Talbot actually expected that poor woman to do all this in one afternoon?" Dud asked when he finished cussing them out.

Boyd shook his head and shrugged his shoulders. "Maybe he was joking, but she took him seriously. All I know is I was in agony the whole time I chopped wood, smelling those good whiffs coming out of the kitchen. I'm so hungry; I could bite a chunk out of my arm."

"I know the ax was dull," Dud said. "But how was the barn?"

"A healthy milk cow and a fine little Morgan don't have even a speck of dust on them," Jesse answered. "The rest have galls, saddle sores, and overgrown hooves. Looks like one person cares and another one either doesn't care or doesn't know beans about livestock."

They began to walk back to the house. "Uncle Dud," Boyd said. "You've got to tell me and Jess how you do it."

"How I do what?" Dud asked. "I know it's not how to plant potatoes, because you don't want to know that."

"It's women, Uncle Dud," Jesse teased. "They all love you. 'Run, Mr. Washburn, run!'" he mimicked.

Boyd laughed, adding in a falsetto voice, "'How about another piece of cornbread, sonny?' Now it's little Mrs. Talbot, plumb eating out of your hand."

Dud grinned. "Oh, that little filly knows she's a married woman and shouldn't really be carrying on with the two of you, but she thinks I'm so old I'm no threat."

"I don't know, Uncle Dud," Boyd kidded, shaking his head.

As they walked onto the gallery, Dud understood Boyd's talk of torment. Exquisite smells drifted from the kitchen. Iris Talbot must have heard their boots hitting the wooden boards, because she came out and asked Dud breathlessly, "What do you think? Did I get it right?"

She had rearranged her hair and cut a fringe of bangs across her forehead. That and her happy expression made an astounding difference—instead being a pretty woman, she looked beautiful. Dud gave her profuse compliments, and the boys joined in.

She blushed and smiled. "But what about the bangs?" she asked. "Are they wispy enough?"

Dud studied them. "I think they could be just a hair wispier. What do you think, Jesse?" he asked.

Boyd and Jesse moved closer. "I think you're right, Uncle Dud," Jesse answered, scrutinizing her forehead. "Maybe just a shade."

Iris turned and flew back into the house, coming out with a pair of scissors. "Here," she said, handing them to Dud. "Try to wisp them the way the ladies in San Antonio have them."

Iris stood still with her face held upward and her eyes closed. Dud fingered the scissors awkwardly and deliberated on how and where to cut. He passed the scissors to Jesse.

"I'd better let Jess do it. He curries horses better than anyone I know."

Iris nodded without opening her eyes. Dud looked around them. If her husband happened to walk up to his gallery and saw strange men crowding around his wife, there would be hell to pay. He did not see anybody and watched as Jesse took a few snips here and there.

"I think that's got it," Boyd said. "They look prettier than the eyelashes of a newborn colt."

Iris opened her eyes. She smiled, and taking the scissors, went back into the house.

"They look wonderful!" she called from inside the house. She came back outside. "Thank you so much," she said. "Come in the house and wash up. Lon and Benjamin, our hired hand, should be back any time."

They followed her inside. The kitchen, dining area, and parlor were in one large open area; to their right were two bedrooms. The floors were swept, the furniture waxed. She had one or two good pieces, others had seen wear. Lamps with little doilies underneath them, a few figurines, and some framed prints and portraits gave the house a homey feel. When Iris saw Dud peering to his right, she said, "I prepared the spare room for you and your nephews, Mr. Washburn. You might as well stay the night. It has a double bed and a cot by the window."

"Uncle Dud can take the cot," Boyd said with a laugh. "He and his dog snore so loud, Mrs. Talbot, you'd swear up and down they were sawing logs on both sides of the creek."

Iris smiled—a bundle of nervous energy. Dud wanted to tell her to calm down, that her husband would be suspicious if he came home and found his wife in such an excitable state with men in the house, but he did not know how to tell her. The bowls and platters filled with fried chicken, mashed potatoes, and various other vegetables along with baskets of biscuits distracted him.

He followed Iris to the kitchen sink to wash his hands. The long sleeves of her dress were pushed up almost to her elbows, and as she handed him the soap, he saw yellowing bruises on both arms. Although several days old, the bruises still showed distinct finger marks. Dud felt his blood run cold, and he handed Boyd, who was standing behind him, the soap without comment. Smiling, Iris's glance followed theirs to her arms. Her smile faded, and her face colored. She picked up a nearby spoon from the counter and placed it in a bowl of vegetables on the table. Turning away from them, she quickly rolled down her sleeves.

NINE

OLD TOM GAVE A COUPLE OF SHARP BARKS. FOLLOWING IRIS onto the gallery, they saw two men coming from the barn. Dud did not know what he had thought Lon Talbot would look like, but he had not expected him to be a dark-haired giant with smooth and regular features, the kind woman swooned over in romantic novels. Beside him trod a small, ugly man of mixed blood, Indian predominating. Both wore sour looks.

"We've got company, Lon," Iris sang out. "This is Mr. Washburn and his nephews, Boyd and Jesse."

A feeling of tenseness filled the air as Lon Talbot looked them over, a frown forming at the corners of his mouth. The Indian who Iris introduced as Benjamin said nothing and refused to look them in the eyes.

"We're just passing through on a land buying expedition, Talbot," Dud said, not wishing to spend an evening with Lon Talbot possibly trying to sell him cattle. "Your wife was kind enough to offer us supper and a place to stay for the night."

Talbot grunted. "Iris lets people take advantage of her," he said. He looked at his wife, and his face flushed in anger. "What have you done to your hair? You look like a French whore."

Iris opened her mouth, but no words came out, and he brushed past her to the door, ignoring Old Tom, who retreated with his head lowered. "Well, come on in since she's already shot her mouth off," he said over his shoulder.

Iris blushed in shame, and Dud exchanged glances with Boyd and Jesse. Feeling uneasy, they followed Talbot and the Indian inside in silence. Iris, standing behind her chair, smoothed her apron.

"What the hell, Iris!" Talbot said when he saw all the food on the table, making her jerk. "Did you think you were cooking for Buffalo Bill and his Wild West show?" He yanked his chair back and sat down. Benjamin, the Indian, who on closer inspection looked to be about sixty, sat down at the end of the table, silent and brooding. Dud, Boyd, and Jesse waited until Iris was seated before taking their places.

Dud sat directly across Iris, with her husband to his left at the head of the table. "Did you get all your work done?" her husband demanded.

She smiled and opened her mouth to answer when Dud caught her eye and gave the barest shake of his head. She stared at him for a second or two, before turning to her husband. "It's all done," she answered.

"'Bout time you got up and did something around here besides petting that old cow and babying your horse," her husband said. He reached with a fork to spear a piece of fried chicken, and Iris said, "Lon, we have guests."

He threw the fork down in anger and bowed his head. "Bless this food, amen," he muttered so fast, Dud did not have time to bow his head.

Iris looked around the table. "Please, help yourself," she said.

"It looks wonderful, Mrs. Talbot," Dud assured her, with Boyd and Jesse joining in.

"It ought to, by God," Talbot said. "This could have fed us for a week."

Dud commenced eating, putting morsel after morsel of scrumptious food in his mouth. He filled his stomach, and because of the look of gratification on Iris Talbot's face as she watched them eat with such pleasure, he refused to let his host's miserly comments slow him down.

While Iris brought out the pies, her husband began to ask questions about their mission. Dud dodged some of them and smoothed over others. He made sure Talbot understood they were supposedly on their way to Waco. Talbot in turn began to complain about the price of land, the price of cattle, and how hard it was to deal with Texans in general. Dud let him ramble, and even Boyd had no desire to interrupt. As bombastic and rude as Talbot was, it surprised Dud that he allowed Benjamin, who smelled rank, to sit at the family table. But Benjamin was an audience who did not answer back. After one particularly bitter and long tirade, Talbot must thought he had gone too far, and he began to try to be pleasant. Dud thought listening to that worse than his harangues, but he tried to be polite for Iris's sake. It was only too plain the man knew nothing about cattle and was floundering, sinking on a ranch he could not hold together.

Benjamin said nothing and stared at his plate. Iris held her tongue, and as it became more and more evident what a fool her husband was, Dud's estimation of her went up. She did not show shame, anger or false pride. She went from being a girl excited about having unexpected company to a young woman who accepted her husband just as he was with no apologies.

Evidently Dud and his nephews did not give Talbot the response he wanted to what he considered friendly overtures, and he began to be highhanded again.

"Look here, Washburn," he said. "You and kinfolks have had more than just a good feed at my table. I think for all the vittles you ate, you ought to be obliged to help me round up some cattle in the morning to sell."

Iris started to protest, but Dud, remembering the bruises on her arm, headed her off. "I reckon that's fair enough," he said. He gave the others a look warning them not to dispute him.

Talbot rose from the table. "Good," he said. "You can sleep in the barn tonight."

This time Iris refused to let Dud stop her from objecting, although she did it softly. "Lon," she said. "I've already made up the spare room for Mr. Washburn and his family."

Talbot glared at her in anger, and Dud said hurriedly, "That's all right, Mrs. Talbot. We don't mind sleeping in the barn." To put an end to any further argument, he began walking toward the door, but inside, he burned with fury. Boyd and Jesse followed, thanking Iris for the supper before they left.

Benjamin beat them to the door, and as they filed out, Dud looked over his shoulder into the house. Standing behind Lon Talbot, Iris's face drooped in loneliness and disappointment as she watched them leave. Talbot shut the door without so much as a goodnight, and before Dud and his nephews left the gallery, they heard the sound of a slap and a small cry.

Dud wheeled to go back into the house to beat the living hell out of Talbot, but Boyd and Jesse caught him by the arms and hustled him from the gallery.

"Uncle Dud," Boyd whispered, "You and Ma and Pa have pounded it into our heads all our lives not to interfere in other people's business."

"That's right, Uncle Dud," Jesse agreed as they dragged him to the barn. "What goes on in that house is between man and wife."

Dud jerked his arms, and they let go. He gave another outraged look toward the house, but stalked with his nephews to the barn. The Indian Benjamin had already preceded them and emerged from a small room carrying a bottle. He sat down on the dirt floor of the barn with his back against a pole. Uncorking the bottle, he muttered, "Bastard," and took a swig.

Dud could not sit or stand still. He paced the barn floor, stopping every once in a while to look out the opened doors to the house. The lanterns went out one by one, and it made him sick and irate to think of Lon Talbot crushing Iris beneath him. He was aware that Boyd, Jesse, and even Old Tom, watched him with troubled faces. Coyotes began to howl close to the barn, and Dud said, "I hope those bastards eat every baby calf he's got."

"You don't mean that, Uncle Dud," Jesse said.

"No," Dud said, stopping to take a deep breath and make his racing blood slow down. "I don't."

Benjamin, who had been drinking steadily, said in slurred words, "A man should beat his wife to make her happy, not to make her sad." He took another swig. "Bastard," he pronounced again.

Although they came from a culture with a different view of things, they understood what Benjamin meant. Dud felt his anger drain, and he sat down heavily by his nephews. If Iris Talbot wanted to stay with a man who would eventually knock those pretty teeth of hers down her throat, there was nothing he could do about it.

"Tomorrow is going to be a nightmare, boys," he said. "But we'll have to endure it for Mrs. Talbot's sake. We owe her that much."

Sausage and biscuits with milk gravy waited for them on the breakfast table. It was not the feast they had the night before, but it was hot and tasted good. Iris, quiet and thoughtful, had pulled her hair tightly back again, her bangs plastered against the sides of her forehead and held stiffly with pins.

They spoke little at the table, and Lon Talbot appeared anxious to get started. They just wanted to get it over with quickly and be gone. They thanked Iris for the breakfast without looking directly in her eyes. As Lon strode to the barn to get his horse, Dud stayed to the rear and slipped back into the house.

Iris, clearing dishes from the table, looked mildly surprised at his reappearance.

"Excuse me, Mrs. Talbot," Dud said. "But I don't want my dog to go with us. He might get in the way," he lied. "Would you mind keeping him in the house with you for a while?"

"Of course not," she said. "I understand, bring him in."

Dud opened the door. "Come here, boy," he said, and Old Tom trotted in. "Sit," he commanded and the dog put his backside on the floor. He instructed him to stay.

Looking back at Iris, Dud said, "Thank you, ma'am. You can let him out later. After we're gone a while, he'll understand and wait for us here."

Iris nodded and Dud, anxious that Lon Talbot should not catch him coming out the door, left the house before she had a chance to say anything else.

He caught up with the others just as Lon led his horse out of the barn.

"Did you leave Old Tom with Mrs. Talbot?" Jesse whispered.

"Hell yes," Dud hissed. "I didn't want that crazy bastard to get mad and shoot him if he took a notion to."

Dud had been riding horses when he could still count his age on the fingers of one hand. He and his nephews had worked countless numbers of cattle, but no roundup they had ever been on was as painful as the one Lon Talbot forced them to do. Carrying a bullwhip a yard longer than necessary, Lon led the three of them and Benjamin to a back pasture.

"I want to cut out about thirty head to sell," Lon told Dud. "We'll run them down into that arroyo," he said, pointing. "Benjamin can guard the rear to see they don't get out. Then we'll herd them back to the corral at the house."

They nodded, and Benjamin wheeled his pinto into the arroyo. For the rest of the time, no matter what happened, he wore the same inexpressive face as when he started.

It became apparent from the first "hi-yi" that Talbot

had no idea what he was doing. Instead of merely popping the whip to use the sound to guide the cattle, he beat them with it. Dud thought at one point, Jesse was going to grab the whip and wrap it around his neck. They tried not to look at Lon while they cut out culls and left the best of the cattle to use as stock to build up his herd because every time they did, they had to resist the urge to kick him off his horse and thrash him. Talbot had no idea the difference between good or bad, and while screaming, yelling, pushing his horse through bunches of scared cattle and pounding them with the whip, he herded in cows and bulls in their prime into the arroyo and kept back ones with legs so hocked a whiskey barrel could have fitted through them and others that had tits dragging the ground.

They dared not say anything to him; if they infuriated him in any way, he would take it out on Iris. Every time Dud looked at Boyd and Jesse, he saw grim compressed lips that mirrored his own. Cattle ran everywhere in fright, and what should have taken less than an hour took all morning. By the time they finally managed to get thirty head into the arroyo, Dud's teeth and jaws ached from being clamped shut.

Herding the cattle back to the home corral would have been easy any other time or place. As Benjamin and his pinto steadily kept the cattle near him in line, Dud wondered how he could stand working with Lon. Talbot kept the animals so riled; it took everything they had to keep the cattle from stampeding, but like the rest of them, Benjamin said nothing.

One bull who was perfect in every way except temperament gave them trouble the entire time. He swung his vicious rack of horns constantly, stomping the ground and bellowing every step of the way. Dud came close to suggesting they leave the bull behind, but the belligerent thrust of Lon's jaw when he approached him to make the proposal made him change his mind. Instead, he fell back and tried to stay out of the way.

They somehow managed to get them penned in the corral, but the rogue bull snorted and bawled, twisting and turning his horns in fury. As frightened cattle moved out of his way, he charged the boards of the corral.

"Hey now! Get back!" Lon shouted, popping his whip, infuriating the bull even more.

He finally realized he was causing more harm than good as the bull continued to crash against the boards. Talbot turned to them. "We've got to get him out of there. He's going to tear up my corral." He looked at Boyd and Jesse. "Get in there and get him out," he ordered.

Boyd and Jesse just stared at him. With lips held tight and jaws locked firm, they shook their heads. Trying to keep Iris from getting slapped around was one thing, suicide was another. Lon turned to Dud, but one look at his face told him not to even try to order him. Lon's face contorted with fury as the bull's horn busted through one of the boards.

"All right, you yellow cowards," he yelled. "I'll go in there myself. Open the gate, Benjamin, and keep the other cattle from getting out."

As Talbot took the whip and reined his horse, Dud wished him dead. If it had been any other man, he would not say a word and only think "good riddance." However, because he hated Lon Talbot so much, his conscience made him say, "Talbot, you best not go in there. See if he'll calm down on his own, or prod him with a pitchfork to get him away from the fence if you have to, but don't go in there."

Lon stared at Dud for several seconds, and then whirled his horse, forcing it into the corral. He cracked his whip at the bull, trying to get him to go toward the opened gate while the rest of the cattle milled in the back of pen in a terrified circle.

Just as Dud expected, hell broke loose. The frightened horse reared, bucking Talbot off. The bull charged, goring him in the stomach and throwing him in the air. The rest of the cattle stampeded, and Benjamin got out of the way fast. Dud, Jesse, and Boyd, waving their hats and yelling, managed to turn them toward the pasture they had come from, the rogue bull leading the way.

Going back to Lon Talbot's inert body, they got down from their horses and examined it. His neck had broken in the fall, mercifully, so he had died before being trampled. "I don't want Miss Iris to see this," Dud said. "But she's got to know. Can we cover the worst of it with a blanket?"

"I'll get something out of the barn," Jesse answered. "You better be the one to tell her, Uncle Dud."

He nodded and stood up. Looking down at the bloody remains, all the hatred he felt for him withered. Lon Talbot had been an ignorant young man with a fine physique and a flawed character, and Dud hoped Iris would not take it too hard.

TEN

"MISS IRIS," DUD SAID, GIVING A SLIGHT KNOCK ON THE front door. He opened it and was greeted by Old Tom wagging his tail. Dud stroked the dog's ears. "I bet you've been begging scraps from Miss Iris all morning," he whispered. Looking up, he saw the door to the Talbots' bedroom was shut. "Miss Iris," he called again, walking toward the door.

She opened it as he reached it. "Yes?" she asked. Behind her, Dud saw saddlebags and rolled up clothes on the bed. He tore his eyes away.

Fingering his hat in his hands, he said, "Miss Iris, I'm sorry to tell you this, but there's been an accident. A bull gored your husband."

Iris's eyes grew round. She swung back into the room and began pushing things off the bed. "Bring him in here," she said. When Dud did not move, she paused while still leaning over the bed. "What is it?" she asked.

Dud shook his head. "It's too late for that, Miss Iris." He put his back against the open door and waited for her

103

to pass. She stared at him, walking by him to the front door. Once outside, as he followed, she began to run, stopping abruptly when she came to the body. Falling to the ground beside her dead husband, she stared for several seconds before putting his head gently in her lap. Caressing his hair, she muttered, "Oh Lon, poor Lon."

Dud waited a few minutes, then kneeled beside her. "Miss Iris, do you have some friends or neighbors you want us to fetch?"

Without looking at him, she shook her head. "No. They tried to be friendly when we first moved here, but Lon chased them away."

"And family?" Dud persisted. "You don't have any folks nearby?"

Iris shook her head. "They're all back east." Suddenly remembering something, she turned and blurted, "I had two brothers who came to Texas and disappeared. I usually ask every person who comes by if they have seen or heard about them. I forgot to ask you at first, and later Lon didn't give me a chance." She began to cry, and Dud did not know if she was weeping for her husband or her brothers.

He let a few tears fall, and then asked, "Miss Iris, is there a town near here?"

She wiped her eyes and gave a nod. "Just a few miles up the road."

Dud paused, trying to think of the right way to say things. "Miss Iris, we need to take the body into town for other folks to see. We could bury him out here, but that might give rise to gossip."

Iris gave him a bewildered look. "Gossip?" she asked.

"I don't want any whispers to start about you, me, or

Boyd and Jesse having something to do with his death," Dud said, deciding to be blunt. "He wasn't the most pleasant of men, Miss Iris."

She flushed and nodded. "I understand."

"Good. I saw a wagon in the barn. You get ready while we hitch it."

Iris gently removed Lon's head from her lap. Standing, she said, "Dinner is on the table. I don't feel like eating—but there is no reason why you shouldn't eat something before we leave."

Dud nodded. "Thank you, ma'am. We may have to spend the night in town. We may not get him buried until morning."

A frantic look came in her eyes. "But my milk cow? I can't leave Bessie; she'll need to be milked."

Dud looked around for Benjamin, but he had disappeared as soon as he had seen that Lon was really dead. Dud put his hand on Iris's arm and began to lead her to the house. "We'll tie Bessie to the back of the wagon. Don't worry."

While they ate, Iris changed her dress. When she came out of the bedroom, her eyes were red, but her bangs were down and her hair put up in the prettier style. After they had eaten, she cleared the table while they went outside. Benjamin appeared carrying a saddle as they were hitching the wagon and loading Lon's body into it. Benjamin threw the saddle into the back of the wagon and got in, sitting stiffly in the back. He stayed that way, without speaking, while they drove into town. Once there, he disappeared, and Dud did not expect to ever see him again.

People were morbidly curious, as Dud expected, but

they were also kind. Lacking a hotel, one family took Iris in for the night, while Dud and the boys slept in the stables. The next morning, they scrounged for breakfast among the few supplies the general store carried. The store owner dropped a comment about Talbot's bill in such a way Dud was sure to understand his meaning. Dud nodded and went outside with Boyd and Jesse. While they sat on the steps, munching crackers, a man wearing a dark suit and tie came out of the bank.

"You gentlemen are friends of Mrs. Talbot's?" he asked.

After Dud agreed, he continued. "I don't want to say anything to the widow, so I'll tell you. Her husband had mortgaged the cattle, and I'll have to repossess them."

Dud nodded again, thankful Talbot had died before he involved them in a scheme to sell cattle the bank owned. "I'll tell her," Dud said. "Did he leave her any money in the bank?"

"No, I'll be honest with you gentleman," the banker said. "He came here with a lot of cash and favorably impressed us all at first. It didn't take long before his true colors began to show. He went through that money and borrowed heavily. We won't mourn his death, but we do like and feel sorry for his widow. She's a lovely young woman in every sense of the word. I hate to distress her; that's why I'm putting the responsibility on you."

Dud nodded and said he understood. Later, as soon as the funeral ended, the same story was repeated by Talbot's landlord.

"I don't want to bother Mrs. Talbot," the older man said. "But her husband was three months behind on the rent, and I have people who are willing to give me cash money if they can move in now. I'm not a hard man," he said, pleading with Dud for understanding. "It pains me to evict a widow, especially one as kind and gentle as Mrs. Talbot. I'll forgive the three months rent if you can convince her to vacate right away."

"I'll see what I can do," Dud promised. The people Iris stayed with the night before had prepared a luncheon, and more people in town were bringing food. Dud let Boyd and Jesse go on ahead, while he stood back, rubbing his chin and pondering Iris's situation.

A beautiful young widow, alone in the world, who would soon need the comfort of a good husband, and him with two bachelor nephews—what more could he ask for? Iris was slightly older than they were, but age did not matter.

"I just don't know if I can convince her to go with us," Dud muttered.

In the back of his mind, a voice that sounded a lot like Ponder's said, "You dang sure better give it your best shot."

On their way back, while Dud drove the wagon and Iris sat beside him, he wondered how to get started. Iris, however, said it for him.

"Mr. Dud," she asked. "Will you let me ride along to Waco with you? I won't be able to stay here—I don't know anything about cattle, and I wouldn't even know where to begin. So I'll have to try to find a job in Waco."

Dud expelled a breath. That had been easy, except that they were not going to Waco. "Miss Iris, we're not going there. We tell people that because, er," he had to think of a lie really quick. "Er, we've had some shady characters following us, and we were trying to shake them."

"Are you wanted by the law?" Iris asked, as if she believed such a thing impossible.

"Oh no," Dud said, glad she had such a good impression of them. "They just know we're carrying a little money because we want to buy some property."

"Oh, okay," Iris said. "Where are you going?"

"We're going to a boomtown, a railroad town northeast of here—Tie Town."

Iris nodded. "I expect I can find some kind of work there, too. Would you mind terribly having me ride along, Mr. Dud?"

"Of course not," Dud assured her. "But we'll have to travel light, Miss Iris. There is not much of a road, and most of what we'll be on will just be cattle trails."

"I understand," she said.

He explained in the kindest possible terms what he had been told about her financial situation in town. While he talked, Iris flushed, looked down and nodded her head.

Dud squirmed a little in the seat. "Uh, Miss Iris, now if you're feeling poorly or if you think you might feel poorly in the next week or so, we can postpone this trip until you are better."

Iris turned a puzzled look upon him. As she realized what he meant, her face blushed. "I wasn't feeling very well last week," she said carefully. "In fact, I told my husband last night I still didn't feel very good. But I'm fine today. Just fine." She turned her head and pretended to be interested in the scenery.

She had been smacked around the night before, but had managed to ward off her husband's advances, and this unexpectedly elated Dud. Things were going easier than he had hoped.

Iris wanted to leave a clean house. As she dusted, she picked up a teapot and looked at it with trembling lips. Shutting her eyes briefly, she put it down and vigorously began polishing the table it sat upon. After supper, Boyd and Jesse washed dishes, and Dud cleared her husband's desk while she packed. He found an empty wallet and two dollars hidden in a chubby hole.

When she came out of the bedroom, she walked to a china closet, easily the best piece of furniture in the house, and stood in front of it. "Do you think the storekeeper would accept this in trade for the bill I owe him?" she asked.

"I don't see why not," Dud said. "It's a mighty fine piece of furniture."

"It was my mother's," Iris said, stroking the polished wood with her hand. Tears came into her eyes again. "I let Lon waste my inheritance, and now I'm losing this, too," she whispered.

"Why don't you let me pay the bill, Miss Iris?" Dud said, feeling sorry for her. "You can pay me back some other time. Maybe he'll store it for you until you get a place of your own."

Iris wiped her tears and tried to smile at him. "No, I can't let you do that. But thank you." She looked back at the china closet. "My mother would under-stand. If she was alive, she would rather see me pay my debts than to try to hold on to belongings that aren't really that important." She looked back to Dud. "The rest of my things aren't worth that much, but maybe the landlord can hold an estate sale to get back some of the rent money he so kindly forgave me."

Dud understood. She looked around the house. "I'm tired. I think I'll go to bed."

"You do that," Dud said. "We'll see you in the morning."

She had insisted they sleep in the spare room, and they were thankful for one good night's rest before starting on a journey to Tie Town that would be uncomfortable much of the time. Dud took the cot under the front window before Boyd or Jesse could squawk about his snoring. He fell instantly asleep, but awoke a little after midnight. He lay still as the faint sounds of repetitive creaking filtered into the room. Sitting bolt upright, he glared at the bed on the other side of the room, but Boyd and Jesse lay in two large lumps, their breathing heavy and steady. As Dud remained motionless, he realized the creaks were not coming from Iris's room, but from outside. Leaning over, he moved the curtains aside a few inches and looked into the front yard.

The moonlight shone on someone in the swing under the big oak tree, swinging to and fro as high as it would go. Dud pushed back his covers, and reaching for his pants, pulled them on over his long johns. Padding lightly through the room, he quietly opened the bedroom door. Leaving it partially open, he moved stealthily to the front door. Turning the knob, he pulled it without making a sound and peered outside.

Iris wore her nightgown, her long hair flowing behind her back. Back and forth she worked the swing, raising her head up as she went forward, the wind pushing against her gown, showing an outline of two exquisite breasts. Every time the swing went upward, the wind blew her gown around her knees, exposing small bare feet, narrow ankles, and two shapely legs to go with them.

Boyd joined Dud at the door. He stood behind him silently watching. In a moment, Dud turned, expecting to see him salivating as he had over the rat-eating girl. However, Boyd surprised him. He looked appreciative, as any man would, but the light from the moon also revealed a face filled with compassion. Dud gave him a slight nudge, and they retreated back into the house, shutting the door quietly.

"Is she trying to draw back to a time before she married that fool?" Boyd whispered.

Dud nodded. "I reckon she's swinging away from what happened here and reaching for the future," Dud said. "Let's leave her alone while she wrestles with it."

As soon as Boyd had gone back to bed, and Dud could hear the heavy breathing that signaled sleep, he got up on one elbow. Holding the curtain aside, he watched for another few minutes before lying down again. It took him a long time to go back to sleep.

The next morning, as Dud walked toward the barn, he saw Boyd and Jesse deep in conversation as they stood next to the wagon. As he approached, they spied him and fell silent, moving around the wagon, rocking it to see if it was steady and looking at the brake. Dud felt his face redden. Boyd and Jesse had never before kept secrets from him, and he had to shake off hurt feelings.

"Is Miss Iris ready?" Boyd asked.

"Yes," Dud nodded. "You better get the cow." Iris realized age prevented her pet from going on another long journey and had agreed to give her to one of the neighbors.

The amount Lon Talbot had allowed to accumulate on his bill at the general store made Dud's eyebrows raise, but the owner, after getting his wife's approval, said the china closet and the wagon would cover it. From there they found the landlord, who wishing Iris the best of luck, said he was sure he could recoup his losses by a sale of the household items she was leaving behind.

"Don't fret, Miss Iris," he said. "My wife always was partial to that little rocker you had by the window."

"And another thing," Dud added to keep Iris from choking up again. "In a few months, you'll have enough potatoes on that place to feed every Irishman in Harris County."

Iris rode her little black Morgan, and they told every person who asked they were heading for Waco. After getting a late start, they traveled for miles on the main road before veering northeast, stopping to camp for the night in a clump of post oak trees.

It had been a difficult day. They silently ate a few hard rolls leftover from the funeral dinner. Iris looked exhausted, so Dud prepared her bedroll, and she quietly sank down, pulling the Navajo blanket over her. Boyd, balancing on his haunches, took a stick and poked the campfire while Jesse leaned on one elbow with his legs extended. Dud sat crouched, watching the flames. Over the flickering light, they looked at Iris and then at one another. With muted movements, they bedded down for the night.

The next day, Iris spoke little, but seemed determined to pull her weight and not cause any trouble. She took care of her horse and kept whatever pace they set without complaint. That whole day they saw neither man nor dwelling, to Dud's mild surprise. He watched Boyd and Jesse closely to see which one would get the edge in with

Iris. To his puzzlement, neither one tried to move in on her. They were polite to her, and he could tell with every look they glanced her way that they liked her and appreciated her beauty. Nevertheless, she might have been their sister for all the respectful attention they gave her. And she did not eye them when she thought no one was looking, either. Dud could not understand it, except to chalk it up to the fact that she was so recently widowed.

ELEVEN

THE NEXT EVENING, IRIS HELPED TO GATHER FIREWOOD AS Old Tom roamed, sniffing the ground and bushes. Boyd shot a wild turkey; Iris dressed it, and Jesse built a campfire to roast the bird. Holding the turkey while watching Jesse get the spit ready, Dud wished he could say or do something that would break Iris's silence. She had chattered with so much fun on the front gallery of her home with them, and Dud liked to listen to women talk.

He was just about to put the turkey on the spit when Old Tom commenced a loud barking. It was not his danger bark; nevertheless, Dud turned his head in the dog's direction. They could hear something crashing through the brush, and before Dud could blink twice, a huge buck with a rack that spanned four feet came hurtling through the camp with Old Tom barking at his heels. As the deer came dangerously close to Dud, he leapt back, so hungry all he could think about was protecting the turkey. The deer bounded over the fire in one graceful

114

leap and disappeared into the night, but Dud lost his footing, fell and landed in a cactus patch.

With thorns jabbing his behind, Dud let out a yelp and jumped forward, still determinedly clutching the turkey while Old Tom sauntered back to camp wearing a satisfied smirk. "Son of a...," he said, curses streaming from his mouth. Dud cussed the deer and Old Tom with every epitaph he could think of while he danced in pain.

He caught sight of Iris and fell silent, managing to say between spasms of pain, "Beg pardon, ma'am." However, she did not appear shocked or mad. On the contrary, she appeared to be trying not to laugh. Her hand went up to her mouth, and she bent over trying not to giggle. Boyd and Jesse smothered chuckles.

"Are you okay, Uncle Dud?" Jesse said, swallowing hard. "Let me see if you've got any thorns in your backside."

Boyd took the turkey. Dud glared at all of them while Jesse walked behind him. "Yes, I think I see some. You'd better lie over your saddle, Uncle Dud, and let me pull them out."

Dud stalked to his saddle, giving it a vicious kick to get it closer to the fire so Jesse could see in the fading light. Iris stifled another laugh, and Dud stuck his lower lip out at her in a grimace. Lying down in the most undignified position he could imagine, with his butt in the air over the saddle, Dud clamped his teeth as tight as he could while Jesse, using his knife and thumb, began to pull out thorns.

"Uncle Dud," Jesse said, choking down another snigger, "I believe you're going to have to drop your drawers so I can make sure there's nothing left."

Dud glowered at Iris again. "Turn your head, woman."

She nodded with knuckles pressed hard against her lips. As she turned her back, it began to shake with repressed giggles.

Dud stood up, pulled down his pants and unbuttoned the back flap of his long johns, He lay back down and barked, "Hurry up back there."

He made a stony face while Jesse probed, and rose quickly when he announced he could not find anything else. Boyd put the rescued turkey over the fire and grinned at him.

"Well, I guess you're all happy I provided you with a little entertainment tonight," Dud said in a huff.

They smiled at him. "Here, Mr. Dud," Iris said. "Let me get you some coffee." She went to the pot and poured some in a cup. As she handed it to him, she smiled sympathetically. "Does it hurt bad?"

Dud thanked her, his anger melting. "No, I'll just be a little raw tomorrow."Thereafter, she gradually opened up and became the Iris they had first met. As the turkey dripped juice, the fire hissing and flickering while slowly turning the bird a golden brown, Iris told them about her horse, raising it from a colt on her parents' horse farm in Missouri. She asked about their ranches, and Dud made light mention of his. Boyd and Jesse talked about their sisters. After supper, Iris again brought up her brothers.

"They left Missouri for Texas several years ago," she explained. "And we never heard from them except for one or two early letters. I feel something must have happened to them, or they would have written."

As Dud stared at her, a slow dawning of realization came over him. Even before Iris said her maiden name,

Dud knew it. Why had he thought the child in the tintype would still be a little girl?

Dud had told Boyd and Jesse's mother about the incident, but had not stated Missouri, and he doubted they even remembered him mentioning it. With clear faces they told Iris they had not heard of or seen her brothers. When she looked at Dud, he shook his head. Two days after her husband's burial was not the time to tell her that her brothers had been murdered.

"Lon would get so mad at me because I asked every person I met about them," she said. "But I just have to know if they are all right."

Dud would tell her later when her spirit had a chance to heal. At the mention of her husband, Boyd, ever direct, asked, "Miss Iris, would you mind telling us how it was you came to marry Mr. Talbot?"

In the soft light, Dud saw her blush. She picked up a nearby stick and began to draw circles in the ground with it. "My parents had died," she said, dropping the stick and wrapping her arms over her knees. "Two of my brothers had disappeared. My oldest brother was trying to provide for a wife and children, along with me, my older sister and her blind husband, and another brother who is feebleminded. I had a lot of beaus, but when Lon came around, he …," she paused. "He drove up in a carriage with a livery driver. He put on a good show. Later, I realized the reason he had a driver was because he hadn't wanted us to see his ignorance, not because he was a big shot. My brother was hesitant about him, but my sister-in-law was all for him; she was tired of having to put up with all her in-laws living with them, even though it was a family farm. I was frantic to get to Texas to find out what had happened to my other brothers. When Lon said he wanted to start a ranch in Texas, I let my sister-in-law push me in his direction."

She looked up, turning to each of them. "I shouldn't blame her. I agreed to go because I thought it was the only way I could find my brothers. I didn't have enough gumption to strike out on my own. Lon talked my older brother into giving him a cash settlement on my interest in the farm." Iris dropped her head in shame. "Poor Lon, he should have married someone who really cared about him instead of someone who just used him as a ticket to Texas."

It explained a lot of things, but Dud still thought all Lon Talbot had needed was a good hanging. As he rubbed the ears of the sleeping dog beside him, he said, "You shouldn't think about it anymore, Miss Iris. That was yesterday, and yesterday's gone."

Boyd and Jesse murmured much the same thing. Dud, following Boyd's opening, grew bold. "Miss Iris, when I came to tell you about your husband, you had your saddlebags and clothes on the bed. Why?"

Iris stared at him and flushed again. "I was going to give you a day's head start, and then try to catch up with you to ask if I could ride along to Waco. I figured you wouldn't want to interfere with a married couple, but I knew once out on the road you wouldn't have much choice but to help me. A circus had come to town a couple of weeks ago, heading south, and all Lon could talk about was how sorry the circus people were. I'm afraid it was a very poor excuse for a circus, and most of the people working it were picking pockets and trying to get money out of simpleminded people with shell games. I thought if

I left him a note telling him I had run off to join the circus, he would be so disgusted he wouldn't come looking for me."

She looked at Dud with pleading eyes. "You understand why, don't you?"

Dud said yes, and they all nodded.

"I'm going to get a job and earn my own money," she said. "And use it to find my brothers instead of trying to use other people."

"We better go to sleep, Miss Iris," Dud said. "We'll be worn out tomorrow if we don't get some rest."

The next day, they stopped at a farmhouse, Dud taking an instant dislike to the couple who owned it. The woman, although handsome, bullyragged her husband incessantly and gave Iris extended glances that Dud could only describe as peculiar. When Iris jumped after the husband pinched her behind, they left. At the next town, they stayed in adjoining rooms in a hotel, but Dud had to get up three times during the night to chase away amorous drunk cowboys banging on Iris's door.

As they grew closer to Tie Town, the sky darkened and storm clouds began to build. Dud looked repeatedly at the black horizon, his worries over Iris being caught in inclement weather increasing. Thunder rumbled and the wind began to rage, almost blowing off their hats. Just when Dud thought the clouds were about to explode in a calamitous squall, they overtook a covered wagon.

Dud rode to the front. A large man with two boys riding beside him drove the wagon. Swarthy with dark hair, they wore ragged clothes and caps. Even before they opened their mouths, Dud knew by their raw looks they were immigrants.

"My name's Dud Washburn," he hollered above the wind. "I've got a young woman riding with us. Would you let her ride this storm out in the back of your wagon?"

"Sure, sure," the man shouted and motioned his hand for them to come on. Dud rode around the back as the man brought the wagon to a halt. After helping Iris down, Dud assisted her into the back of the wagon. The man turned, showing a big grin with a wide gap between his front teeth. "Ugor Darst," he said loudly, pointing to himself. He pointed to the boys beside him on the wagon seat. "My sons, Franz and Miklos. The woman," he said, pointing in the wagon. "My wife, Zizi, and my boy Kristof. Gaspar—the baby."

Iris, climbing in the back of the wagon, smiled at the woman sitting on a cot. She returned Iris's smile with a shy one of her own and moved to make room.

"We're much obliged," Dud yelled, the wind carrying away his words so he was not sure Ugor Darst even heard him.

Lightning struck and water began to pour on them. Hunkered down in slickers, Dud, Boyd, and Jesse rode beside the wagon, rain lashing at their faces, making them miserably wet even though they had lived through the same thing innumerable times. When the rain finally let up to a gloomy drizzle, Dud rode to the back of the wagon and peered inside.

Iris and Zizi Darst sat cross-legged on the cot, combing one another's hair amidst smiles and giggles. Dud grinned in pleasure at the sight of thick hair tumbling down their backs, one blonde and the other raven. Men could get along by themselves on the trail for months at a time and be just fine, but women pined for the company of other women.

That night, they camped with the Darst family. The older boys were like thin dark weeds, ranging in ages from about fifteen to eight. Their shy faces lit up in excitement and pleasure at meeting new people, while the little one buried his face in his mother's ample chest, only to peek out again at Dud. Zizi Darst, although younger than her husband, had lost the first blush of youth. Nevertheless, her large dark eyes and expression of timid sweetness made her appealing.

"We are from Budapest," Ugor said, and when he saw the look of incomprehension on their faces, he added, "Hungary."

Dud nodded, and after introducing himself and the others again, uncharacteristically told them where they were from and where they were headed.

"Sure, sure," Ugor said, nodding his head vigorously. "We, too. We go to Tie Town. I am blacksmith, and heard of someone looking to, what you say, hire a blacksmith."

Zizi could not speak more than five words of English, and Iris did not know squat about Hungarian, but that did not stop them from getting along together. The two of them flitted around the campfire, cooking the most savory smelling stew Dud had ever had the pleasure to whiff. The boys, shy at first, knew more English than either of their parents. At first they played with Old Tom, and as Dud talked with old man Darst, he kept half an eye on them to make sure they did not tease or bedevil the dog. They were kind and gentle with him, however, and Dud put Old Tom through his tricks to please them. As the hour wore on, their glances at Boyd and Jesse grew in frequency to the point they began to openly admire them, enthralled at being so near real cowboys. By the end of the evening, they were imitating the unconscious swagger and confident manner of Boyd and Jesse. When Dud accidentally called Franz "Frank," the other boys asked him to give them American names, too. "Gaspar, too, please, Mr. Dud." Miklos became Mike. Kristof, built much smaller than his older brothers, became Kris, and because little Gaspar could be so quiet and then suddenly burst into a torrent of speech, he became Gabby.

Over an early supper, Ugor Darst explained he was the seventh son of a seventh son and would receive no inheritance. Trained like his brothers in metalwork, their small mountain village could not support another blacksmith, and Ugor had taken his family to the city where they lived in a slum, working and saving until they had enough money to immigrate to Galveston. He dreamed of having his own home and of giving his sons opportunities. Zizi watched her husband and nodded solemnly, seeming to know just by the look on his face what he was saying.

"I know Constitution; I know Bill of Rights," Ugor proclaimed, slapping one fist on an opened palm.

Dud smiled. "In Texas, you might get further knowing about the Alamo and Santa Anna," he said.

Ugor's broad face crinkled in puzzlement. "What is this Alamo and Santa Anna?"

Dud explained about the revolution and the Republic of Texas. "When they hollered 'Remember the Alamo!' it wasn't just a cry for revenge," Dud said, "but a reminder that to give in would mean certain death.

"Say," Dud added with a grin, remembering something

else. "There was a Darst who died at the Alamo. Maybe he's some of your kin."

Ugor laughed. "Maybe so, an uncle, eh?" He looked at his sons and they beamed. "Hear that, my sons? We have relative die at this Alamo."

Before night fell, while Dud sat petting Old Tom, Boyd and Jesse had target practice with their pistols, teaching the boys firearm safety and how to fire a gun. Frank and Mike, somewhat bashfully, brought out knives and showed off their skills. Their thin ragged arms could throw a knife through the air so fast, it became almost invisible. Mike, especially, was a whiz at hitting whatever target he aimed at with one deadly flick of his wrist.

After supper, Ugor brought out a fiddle and began to play happy, toe tapping music. Kris took over; his knife throwing skills may not have matched his brothers, but he could make a fiddle *beszélni* in perfect time. Ugor and his wife began to dance. Dud stood up, bowed to Iris, and taking her hand, joined in. Hungarian dancing involved more foot stomping than what they were used to, but they soon got the hang of it. The women took turns dancing with the men and boys, Iris's face glowing in a continuous happy smile.

As Dud watched Iris twirl and step, he realized all she would have to do would be to point her finger at one of his nephews and say "you're it," and he would fall at her feet in humble adoration. To Dud's irritation, she did not do so, neither did they give her any indication they wanted her to. He could not understand it.

The Darsts invited their group to ride with them. Seeing how much Iris and Zizi Darst craved companionship, despite the language barrier, made it easy for them to agree. Along the way, Dud looked into the wagon and found them sewing. Iris would pick up something and say its name in English. Zizi would say it in Hungarian, and then pronounce it in English. Iris would repeat the Hungarian word, and Dud thought by the time they got to Tie Town, Iris would be speaking Hungarian like someone who just got off the boat. He had his doubts, however, about Zizi Darst and the English language.

TWELVE

APPROACHING TIE TOWN, THEY SAW A MUDDY, BUSTLING, sprawling raw village that looked as if it had newly sprung from a hammer, which it had. They parted company with the Darsts, who wanted to camp at the edge of town. After farewells, Dud began the search for a decent boardinghouse while Boyd, Jesse, and Iris rubbernecked behind him. He managed to get Iris's attention long enough to give her a small lecture.

"Miss Iris, I'm going to talk to you like you were my little sister," he began, trying to sound firm. "There are a lot of men out here who hear the word 'widow' and think it's an invitation to take up immediately where the husband left off. Now you can do what you want; it's none of my business. But if you don't want every man treating you like your bedroom has an open door, don't be telling every so and so you meet that you're a widow woman."

Iris flushed a deep red. "Should pretend I've never been married?" she asked anxiously.

"No, don't fib," Dud advised. "It will catch up with you. Just don't be hollering it out."

Iris nodded, and Dud let out a deep breath of relief. Iris was as sweet as mother's milk and almost as unworldly as the newborn who suckled it. As far as Dud was concerned, Iris needed a husband and needed one bad. He threw a dark look at Boyd and Jesse just thinking about it.

Dud would not have let Old Tom sleep in one of the boardinghouses they came across, and the others were full. They finally found one that could squeeze Iris in if she did not mind sleeping with the landlady's deaf and sometimes incontinent mother. Iris did not object; however, she did not appear too thrilled about it either, but Dud did not want her in a hotel after the previous experience they had. After speaking with the landlady, who was built like a two-seater outhouse, Dud found the other boarders seated around a dining table eating chicken and watery dumplings. He introduced himself and Iris, and removing his .45 from his gun belt, placed it on the table.

"If I get word that someone is harassing Miss Iris, or that some man is knocking on her door in the middle of the night, this gun of Mr. Colt's is going to shoot some-body's ass dead. Do I make myself clear?"

The men, mostly old drummers, looked shocked and nodded. A few old women looked thrilled to the bone. Dud replaced his gun, and Iris followed him to the door.

"You're not just going to leave me here, are you?" she asked.

Dud patted her cheek. He had no intention of dumping Iris in town and leaving her to fend for herself.

"Eat some supper, go to bed, and get some rest, gal," he instructed her. "I'll come by tomorrow and get you."

Iris nodded. "Okay, Mr. Dud. I'll be waiting for you." She looked back at the group around the table and made an expressive face of apprehension and doubt. "I guess the old man on the end with the false teeth won't bite me."

Dud grinned. "Behave yourself, gal. I'll see you tomorrow."

He and his nephews walked into the hotel just as someone checked out; otherwise, they never would have gotten a room. Leaving the hotel, they rode to one of the two stables in town and made arrangements for their horses and the mule. The stable owner, a puny man with an oversized handlebar mustache, found he knew some of the same people Dud knew, so they become somebody in his book instead of just three drifters joining the rest of the crowd.

Most of the town's sidewalks were boarded with raw wood. Walking along, they found a barbershop. Since it was the middle of the week, they did not have to wait long for baths, haircuts, and shaves. Dud hoped Iris was not having any trouble convincing her landlady to let her take a bath. Maybe, he thought, when he was making his Mr. Colt speech, he should have turned and said Iris could take a bath whenever she wanted.

The barbers disgorged the cascade of knowledge Dud had hoped for. Tie Town sat in the center of a new line of track being built by the railroad; it was named after the railroad ties cut nearby and stored in massive piles on the outskirts of town. On Friday and Saturday night, the town became so packed with railroad workers; the risk of being hit by a stray bullet became so great, it was not safe to hang around the streets. Sunday mornings were generally quiet, but the town did not entirely empty of drunken cowboys from nearby ranches, disgruntled outlaws left over from the Civil War, and railroad men until Monday. There were five saloons in town, the best being the Gilded Lily, run by an old tart named Lottie. At the mention of the name, Dud wondered if it was the same Lottie he knew. According to the barbers, the Gilded Lily Saloon had one special attraction that put it far ahead of the others—a beautiful and mysterious young French singer by the name of Suzette who wooed crowds on Thursday, Friday, and Saturday nights and ignored them the rest of the week.

Dud put out feelers about property and gradually came around to the land with three adjoining creeks.

His barber turned to a coworker and grinned. "Who owns that land this week, Bub?"

The other barber stopped cutting hair and scratched his cheek with his scissors. "Don't rightly know. I think Seth Thompson may have it."

With a smile, Dud's barber enlightened him. "There's a high stakes poker game once a month at the Gilded Lily. The property you're talking about changes hands might near every game. I think Luke Wallace lost it to Seth Thompson this last Saturday night."

"You don't say," Dud ruminated. What could be lost could be bought.

Dud parted with Boyd and Jesse upon leaving the shop. What he did not know they did, he would be unable to confess to his sister should she try to worm it out of him later. He wandered somewhat aimlessly around town, getting his bearings. A small residential section had been built to the south and away from the gaudy saloon district. Trees, mostly oaks, a few pecans, and cedars lined the dirt streets. Dud stopped in front of a half-built home on a large lot that stood away from the others. From the weather-beaten poles of the frame, he guessed whoever started it had stopped some time ago. It had rafters, but lacked a roof, outside walls, and a floor, but it looked sturdy enough. In the back, a long shed covered a few pieces of leftover lumber. The back wall had been boarded and one end was cornered off, but otherwise it stood open.

"It goes up on the auction block for back taxes this Saturday at the county seat," a voice with a tinge of an Irish accent said behind him.

Dud turned and saw a small older man wearing a dark suit, brocade vest, and high top hat. "Howdy," Dud said. "I'm not too interested. Just looking."

Holding a gold-tipped cane in one hand, the little man put out his other. "Felix O'Brien, the unofficial mayor and justice of the peace of Tie Town. Call me Mayor, Your Honor, or Felix, if you please. O'Brien was my pappy's name."

"Dud Washburn, Felix," Dud said, shaking his hand.

"I heard you were asking about the Yegua Creek place. It's haunted you know."

Dud nodded. "I heard rumors."

"You won't be able to buy it either," Felix said. "The men get too much enjoyment trading it back and forth in poker games, and they wouldn't consider it selling it to an outsider. You'll have to win it if you want it."

Dud put his hands on his hips and stared at him. "My

brother-in-law's name is Callahan. Is there any reason why I should believe the word of an Irishman?"

Felix put his head back and laughed. "Right you are. But you've a bit of the Irish in you too, Washburn, don't deny it."

"I wouldn't dream of it," Dud said with a grin.

"Tell you what, cousin," Felix said. "You rent a buggy or a wagon, and I'll take you out tomorrow morning and show it to you."

Dud raised an eyebrow. "It has a good road enough for that?"

"Oh, yes," Felix assured him. "They cut a road through there to get timber. The railroad used to lease it for timber, but it got so spooky for the men, they refused to work out there after a time."

"All right," Dud said. "Seven-thirty suit you?"

"Oh man!" Felix said. "I don't get up until at least nine. Make it ten."

Dud agreed. Felix added, "Are you going to bring the pretty lassie you left at the boardinghouse?"

"I was planning on it," Dud said.

Felix's eyes lit up, and his face made a wicked grin. "Good. I promise Mr. Colt won't have to have a little talk with me, however."

Dud watched as Felix bobbed away to find out the latest scoop on some other newcomer. Poker! He stood in front of the half-built house and stared with unseeing eyes. He could only play a fair hand of poker at best, and Boyd and Jesse had even less skill than he did. He thought and thought, the word poker going round and round in his brain. He knew of only one man who could beat anybody at cards. He procrastinated back and forth.

Finally he realized there was only one thing to be done, and he did it.

"What!" Boyd and Jesse cried in unison when he told them. "I know you told us Uncle Ponder was the prince of poker players, Uncle Dud," Boyd said. "But that was before he got married and quit. He hasn't played for more than toothpicks in fifteen years! And didn't you say he's getting so forgetful he almost caught the house on fire?"

"Well, what am I supposed to do?" Dud countered. "I can't beat high stakes players, and you can't even win in a penny ante game. Uncle Ponder ought to get here in a couple of weeks. I sent a telegram to San Antonio for someone to fetch him and put him and one of the other hands on a train as far as they can go. They'll have to catch a ride on the mule train the rest of the way. Once he's here, we'll get him back in practice."

"I swear, Uncle Dud!" Jesse exclaimed. "We're going to be up a creek, not buying one."

"Unless you can come up with a better idea," Dud thundered, "just forget about it for the time being. You've got one month to concentrate on something else, women, for instance!"

They flushed and hushed, but Dud did not stop worrying. How could he keep them out of trouble for a month? And Iris was not going to be happy hanging around that boardinghouse with nothing to do. She kept talking about a job, but she lacked the knowledge to teach school, and jobs for decent women were few and far between.

When he approached the boardinghouse the next morning, he saw Iris waiting on the gallery for him, but she was not alone. Three men sat with her. As he drew near, their talk died.

Iris, however, smiled. "Howdy, Mr. Dud!" she said, jumping up. "I've been waiting for you."

"That's good," Dud said, giving the men on the gallery the once over. "How would you like to go for a buggy ride in the country? The mayor is going to show us a piece of property."

"Sounds great," she said cheerfully. She turned to the men on the gallery. "I'll see you gentlemen some other time."

They called "Goodbye, Miss Iris," with too much intimacy as far as Dud was concerned. As he led Iris away, he commented, "That one young fellow looks like he has shifty eyes, Miss Iris. I'd watch out for him if I were you."

"Do you mean the one with the high buttoned collar?" Iris asked. "That's the minister, Mr. Dud. He just came by to invite me to church on Sunday."

"Humph," Dud grunted, steering Iris by the elbow around a mud hole. "Just because a man is a preacher doesn't mean he wouldn't like to give comfort to a pretty widow woman."

"Well his wife might not like it," Iris said.

"Having a wife hasn't stopped many another man," Dud said darkly, "including preachers."

Iris laughed. He scowled at her, but did not mean it and found himself grinning back. She had a clean, fresh look, and smelled faintly of soap and violets. Before Dud could compliment her, Frank Darst and his brother Mike ran up to them.

"Mr. Dud, Mr. Dud," Frank said, out of breath. "The man at the stables does not want to hire my papa. My mama asked me to fetch you, but she asked not to tell my papa because he might get mad. Oh, excuse me, Miss Iris."

The two boys gave Iris a short bow.

"Can you do something, Mr. Dud?" Mike asked. "Can you help my papa?"

Dud patted the boys on the back. "Calm down. I'll see what I can do."

They followed him to the stables and agreed to stay outside, out of sight with Iris, and wait for him. He paused at the door, looked to his right and saw the boys, with Iris right behind them, scampering around the side of the building where they could put their eyes to any knotholes they could find.

Old man Darst and the stable owner were going round and round when Dud entered.

"How you doing, Darst?" Dud asked casually.

"Do you know this fellow, Washburn?" the owner said.

"Well, he's by way of being a friend of mine," Dud said, tugging at his earlobe. "Why? What's the problem?"

"He does not want to hire me, that's problem!" Ugor said. "He think I'm not American enough."

"It's not just that, Darst," the owner protested. "I don't know you from Adam."

Ugor's face flushed, his dark eyes snapping. "I American. I know Constitution. I know Alamo," he boasted. "I know Davy Crockett. I know Jim Bowie. I know…."

Before he could start in on William Travis, Dud interrupted. "Say, Darst, you had kinfolks die at the Alamo, didn't you?" he said. He turned to the stable owner. "Don't you remember? There was a Darst who died at the Alamo."

He flushed. "Well, no, I didn't remember that," he said. "Say, is that true?" he said, questioning Ugor. "That some of your kin died at the Alamo?"

"Same name, we kin," Ugor said, holding his breath and giving a small roll of his eyes.

"Well," the stable owner vacillated. "I'd hate to turn down somebody whose kinfolks fought at the Alamo." He turned to Dud. "You say you know him, Washburn?"

"That's right," Dud said. "Why don't you check the condition of his horse and wagon and look at the knives he made his boys if you want to see some of his work. I'll vouch for his character."

Frank and Mike appeared almost in an instant, holding out their knives. Iris brought in the horse Ugor had tied outside. The stable owner looked at the knives and examined the shoes on the horse.

"All right, Darst," he said. "I'll put you on trial for one month. You and your family can stay here and live in the back room until you can afford something better."

"Thank you," Ugor said with dignity.

THIRTEEN

AFTER UGOR LEFT TO FETCH HIS WIFE AND POSSESSIONS, Dud talked to the livery owner about renting a buggy. He had a fairly new Kimball with a jump seat, to Dud's surprise, and he was only too happy to rent it.

"The cowboys only want my little one-seater so they can tear around the countryside showing off to a gal squeezed next to them, sitting practically in their lap," he groused. Evidently, he was the father of daughters.

Dud commiserated with him and made a mental note to tell Boyd and Jesse about the smaller buggy, perfect for courting. While the stable owner hitched a team to the larger buggy, Felix walked in, sweeping his hat off in a courtly gesture to Iris.

"And a top of the morning to you, Miss Iris," he said, intensifying his Irish brogue.

Iris smiled and Dud grouchily asked, "How many generations has it been since your family has seen Ireland?"

He might have been invisible. Felix flowed on as if he

had not spoken. "You're looking as lovely as your name-sake, Shiver me timbers! If you aren't the loveliest lass this town has ever seen."

"I'm going to shiver your timbers if you don't get in the buggy, Felix," Dud said.

Felix held out an arm to Iris. "Allow me, Miss Iris," he said.

Dud intercepted them. "You sit in the back," he said. "Miss Iris is going to sit on the jump seat with me, away from your shivering timbers."

"All right, Washburn, just give an old man a chance to get in."

Finally, they got situated. Dud asked, "Which way?"

"Well, if you stop by the Iron Horse Saloon, I can get my bartender friend to fix us up some sandwiches to take along, with a couple of pints of beer and a bottle of sarsaparilla for the lady."

Dud looked at Iris. She nodded hopefully. "All right," Dud said. "While you're getting the sandwiches, I'll stop at the hotel for a blanket."

Of course, Felix had to have money for the beer and sandwiches, since he had left his wallet at home. Dud handed it over without a quarrel and left to fetch the Navajo blanket.

At the hotel, he stomped up the stairs to their room, got the blanket and tromped back down again, spurs jingling. He met Boyd and Jesse as he walked through the lobby.

"Where're you going, Uncle Dud?" Boyd asked.

"Felix, the mayor of this mud hole, is taking Iris and me to look at a piece of property I'm interested in. I told you last night."

"Oh, that's right."

"Do you want to go along?" Dud asked.

Boyd opened his mouth to say yes, but shut it again, glancing at Jesse. "No, that's okay, Uncle Dud. You go on ahead. Jess and I have things to do around here."

"All right," Dud said, heading for the door. "Stay out of trouble."

He walked outside, and as he chunked the blanket onto the back seat of the buggy, he was hailed by Woody Harrison.

"Hello, Washburn," the portly man said. "I heard you were in town."

Dud shook hands. "Nice to see you again, Harrison." He turned to Iris. "Miss Iris, this is Woodrow Harrison. He's the railroad man we met in San Antonio. Harrison, this is a friend of ours, Iris Talbot."

"Miss Talbot," Harrison said, doffing his hat.

Iris smiled in return, and Harrison continued. "If you'd still like to have supper with us, Washburn, why don't you come by tonight around six? Bring your nephews and Miss Talbot, too," he said, with a nod to Iris. "We live on Pecan Street in the white Victorian-style house on the corner."

"Is that the opposite end of the house that's unfinished?" Dud asked.

"Yes, that's it. Pity about that house. Things run rather loose and fast in these boomtowns. Here today, gone tomorrow type people. Shall we see you at six?"

"Yes," Dud answered. "We're looking forward to it."

Harrison bid them good day and went on his way. Dud got into the buggy, and said, "Is that all right with you, Miss Iris? They seem like nice people."

"Of course, Mr. Dud," Iris said, leaning forward to face the day, smiling. "Anything you say is fine with me."

Dud supposed after the lonely miserable hell she had been living through, the people and excitement of Tie Town were a giant improvement. Oddly enough, she seemed to read his thoughts.

"You know, this is so much fun for me," she said. "But last night at the boardinghouse, I kept wishing we were back in the country with the animals and a clear night full of stars."

"I reckon I feel the same way," Dud admitted. It meant he was going to have to find some nice young rancher for Iris to marry, since his nephews insisted on acting like morons and ignoring their chance. "I might as well open up an office and put up a sign that says matchmaker," Dud grumbled under his breath.

"What did you say, Mr. Dud?" Iris asked.

"I said there's Felix," Dud said.

As Old Tom trotted behind them, Felix chattered and gossiped on the way to the three creeks at the Yegua Knobs. Because of the rain, the deep sand they normally would have had to traverse had packed down. As Harrison had first said, it was heavily wooded and showed numerous tree stumps where railroad workers had gathered lumber before they refused to go back. There were spots of flat meadows with rocky ground where the sand had washed away. The rocks were not like the ones in South Texas—these were reddish brown, some sort of iron ore, Dud thought.

"Anybody ever use these rocks for building homes?" Dud asked, interrupting Felix's flow of words.

"Some do. Very few," Felix said. "It's too much work to gather the rocks when lumber is so abundant and cheap."

Dud nodded and Felix continued a discourse that Dud only half listened to.

The three creeks were at the foot of the Knobs, water spreading over the countryside, flooded because of the recent rains upstream. Dud scanned the landscape, but the thick brush and trees made it hard to see anything that could be a landmark that might indicate a bull or sign of a bull.

"What do you think, Washburn?" Felix asked. "Kind of rough, isn't it?"

Dud nodded, for any other reason, he would have little use for it. The story he had told about it being so dry in South Texas and wishing to find land with more water had sounded good, but even with the flooded creeks, he did not much care for the Knobs. That was something he would have to hide from Felix's prying eyes, however—or maybe not. It would not do to appear too interested.

"Rough as a corncob next to a hemorrhoid," Dud said. "Pardon me, Miss Iris. I didn't mean to be crude." Iris gave him a smile and did not pay any attention to his lapse of manners.

They went to high ground and found an open area to spread the blanket. As they sat eating, Dud let his eyes roam. Where would they begin to dig without the last key to guide them? There was no bull—no sign of a bull. Maybe there had been some bones lying around when it was first hidden, and whoever buried it thought they would return in a short time for it. He knew he was borrowing trouble—until the land was officially his, he could not or would not dig on it. Rocks, however, were a different matter.

"Mr. Dud," Iris said. "You're a million miles away."

Dud turned to Iris and feeling kind, smiled. "Just studying on something. Felix," he said, turning to the old man. "Do you reckon the man who owns this property now would mind if my nephews and I came out here and gathered some rocks? I might bid on that property in town, and if I get it, I want to rock the walls."

Felix looked surprised. "I'll ask him when I see him, if you want, Washburn. Do you know how to do masonry?"

"I've dabbled in it," Dud admitted. "Keep it under your hat about me wanting to bid on that property, and I'll buy you a steak dinner with all the trimmings."

"For a steak dinner and a ride to the courthouse to watch you bid on it," Felix grinned, "you've got a deal."

"All right," Dud agreed. "But you've got to let my dog ride in the back of the buggy with you. He's tired."

Once back in town, after getting rid of the loquacious Felix, Dud walked Iris back to the boardinghouse.

"Do you really want to build a house here in Tie Town, Mr. Dud?" Iris asked.

Dud was silent for a moment, looking around the town. "Not particularly," he answered. "But it will give Boyd and Jesse something to do to keep them out of trouble until I can conclude my business here. And it will give you some place to hang out instead of that blasted boardinghouse."

"Mr. Dud, I really need a job," Iris began again. They stopped in the middle of the street. Old Tom sat down and nudged Iris's hand with his head. She absentmindedly petted him. "I want to find my brothers, and, well...," she said. "You've been awfully good to me, Mr. Dud, but I don't want to be a kept woman."

Dud let out a long breath of air, refusing to look at Iris. Is that what she thought he was trying to do? He could not bring himself to tell her about her brothers just yet. "I didn't intend to insult you, Miss Iris," he said, facing her again. "But let me look for you something, will you? Will you let me do that for you?"

"I'm not insulted, Mr. Dud," she said, her eyes wide and full of some emotion he could not read, except he knew she still liked him. "Thank you so much for everything."

"I'll be back later to take you to the Harrisons," he said. He did not want to look for Iris a job, but knew if he did not get on with it, she might decide to do it herself, and he feared what she might come up with on her own.

School teaching was out. The town already had a teacher, and Iris had confided to him that her schooling had been sketchy. The boardinghouses were family owned and managed with the help of relatives. Instead, Dud went to the dressmaker, to the milliner, but no, they did not need help. He stopped by Woody Harrison's office, but he did not know of anything. He found Felix, but even Felix drew a blank. He talked to the Baptist minister who promised to ask some of the members of his congregation if they needed help in their homes. However, the longer Dud thought about it, the less he liked the idea of Iris working in a private home where she might be subjected to someone's lecherous husband.

In disgust, he sat on a bench in front of the general store. He had been there first and knew their answer, so he did not bother to go inside again. As he sat looking out over the street, pondering his situation, a young woman came out of the store. She looked about seventeen or eighteen, but she did not wear her hair up as a girl that age would normally do, and her dress was decked in ribbons and bows befitting someone much younger. Her long dark hair hung down her back, held together with a wide bow, an innocent contrast with the large dark eyes and full mouth that would make any man sit up and take notice. She stared at him and began swinging herself around the gallery post as a child would do.

"Howdy," she said.

"Howdy, ma'am," Dud answered.

"My papa knows you," she said, swinging first with one hand, then with both.

"He does? Who is your papa?" he asked.

She stopped and stood nearer. "Mr. Woodrow Harrison," she pronounced. "My name is Annabelle. What's yours?"

"My name is Dudford Washburn," he said. "You can call me Mr. Dud if you want to. It's nice to make your acquaintance."

"Call me Annabelle," she said.

"Maybe I'd better call you Miss Annabelle," Dud said.

"Okay. Do you like dogs? I like your dog. May I pet him?"

"Sure," Dud said. "He's a gentle old fellow."

As she bent down to stroke Old Tom, the storekeeper came out with a broom. As he pushed the broom, he fussed at the girl.

"Miss Annabelle, you run along home. You know your papa doesn't like you hanging around town."

She looked up from Old Tom and protested. "I have to

wait for my sister. She's across the street at the hat lady place."

"All right, but don't you be pestering anybody," he said, shooting Dud a look and going back into the store. Dud realized the storekeeper had no concern for him, but was giving a stranger in town a backhanded warning not to bother the girl.

Across the street, the door opened and a gorgeous young woman with a figure as curvy as an Indian trail came out carrying several boxes. Her hair, piled high on her head, was a vivid shade of natural red, a striking contrast with her pale skin. "Annabelle," she cried, spying the girl.

"Sissy, come here!" Annabelle rose and called. "I want you to meet Mr. Dud, Papa's new friend."

Looking both ways, the young woman started across the street. Dud rose, and meeting her, offered to carry her packages. As he took the boxes, he looked down at the biggest bosom he had ever seen on a woman that age and size. Tearing his eyes away, he followed her across the street.

Taking the boxes from him, she put them in Annabelle's hands. "Don't shout across the street, Annabelle," she remonstrated. She turned to Dud and smiled, showing glowing white teeth and lots of pink lip. Dud understood what the clerk in San Antonio had been trying to tell him.

"I'm Elizabeth Harrison," she said. "You must be Mr. Washburn. Papa told us all about you. I believe you're going to have supper with us this evening."

Dud removed his hat. "Yes ma'am, nice to meet you."

"Wonderful! We'll see you later then, Mr. Washburn," Elizabeth said. "Come along, Annabelle."

"You can call him Mr. Dud," Annabelle said, trying to juggle the hat boxes. "He said for me to call him, Mr. Dud. Didn't you, Mr. Dud?"

Dud smiled. "That's right, Miss Annabelle."

"See, Sister?"

Elizabeth gave Dud a small smile and roll of her eyes. "Come along, Annabelle." She turned and led the way down the sidewalk. As Annabelle followed with the boxes, she twisted and called to Dud. "Bring your dog, Mr. Dud, Mama and I will save him a bone."

"I will, Miss Annabelle," Dud called back, grinning as Elizabeth took Annabelle by the elbow to hurry her along. Dud amused himself by wondering which one would fall the hardest, Boyd or Jesse.

FOURTEEN

Dud walked back toward the hotel, taking his time. On the other side of the hotel stood a brick surveyor's office, beside it, a small café. Iris's boardinghouse was just down the street. He did not want Iris working as a waitress—too many loose women who used it as an easy pickup for johns gave the profession a questionable name, but there did not seem to be anything else. On the plus side, he thought it would be an ideal place for Iris to meet a nice man to marry. There were three restaurants in town; one was a tent that served soups and stews from open kettles to men who found seats on benches next to crude tables; another was in the hotel, a much fancier one with white tablecloths and private booths, perfect for conducting business. The third was the small café with a row of windows across the front. He did not want Iris working in a mess tent, nor did he want her in a hotel where the close proximity of beds would be uppermost on the mind of every man who looked at her. He walked into the small café on the other side of the surveyor's office, thinking the windows would allow him to check on Iris without ever having to enter.

At that time of day the café had few customers. The place looked clean enough, but the gray-haired woman behind the counter had a slightly slatternly air about her. She had fat cheeks and round, shrewd eyes. A bent older man who resembled a skeleton smoked a cigarette near the stove.

"What will you have, stranger?" the woman asked.

"A little of your time," Dud answered.

"Time we got plenty of, buddy," she said.

Dud introduced himself and learned her name. "I've got a friend in need of a job, Miss Ruby. She's young; she's pretty, and she'll double your business in a week if your hire her as a waitress." Taking a hint from the mysterious French singer he had yet to see, Dud added, "She can only work Thursday, Friday, and Saturday nights."

Ruby stared without speaking at first. Slowly, she said, "Friday, Saturday, and Sunday nights are our rush times."

"Okay," Dud agreed. "There's one thing that has to be clear. She's not to be pinched and used as a quick feel by anybody, and that includes cookie over there," Dud said, pointing at the old man. "How much would you pay her?"

Without committing herself to anything, Ruby haggled with him over wages. Dud insisted Iris get to keep all her tip money. Finally, Dud gave in on the salary when Ruby relented on the tips. She said, "I'll hire her, Washburn, on one condition."

"What's that?" Dud asked.

Ruby threw a glance at the cook. "You and Mr. Colt explain the facts of life to Joe over there." She lowered her voice and leaned closer. "He ain't much, mister, but he's all I got."

After a little talk with Joe the cook, Dud found Boyd and Jesse in the hotel lobby. They listened with interest to the recounting of his day.

"If I bid on that house and get it, I don't have any intention of going after it hammer and tongs," Dud said. "A female leery about approaching a man in a hotel lobby probably wouldn't mind stopping by a house being built to talk and visit. You and Jess can work on the outside, while I piddle on the inside. And it will give Iris somewhere to go when she gets bored. She's used to working in her own home."

"And if we can haul rocks from this Itanakaala, or Yegua Knobs, it will give us a chance to study the lay of the land before we dig," Boyd said, his eyes eager with excitement. "It's perfect, Uncle Dud. I don't know how you think up these things."

"It's a lot of ifs, though," Dud warned. "If we get the winning bid on the unfinished house, if we get permission to haul rocks from the present owner, if we can get Uncle Ponder here in time to prime him for a big stakes poker game, and if he can win."

Boyd and Jesse exchanged looks. "Oh well," Jesse said with a shrug. "At least we got an invite for a home-cooked meal tonight."

"It's more than vittles," Dud said with a grin, but he refused to elaborate. Later, however, once the word got around the hotel lobby, several men explained to Boyd and Jesse about the treat they were in for. If they had left well enough alone, it would have been all right, but after extolling Elizabeth's attributes to an overblown proportion, they had Jesse and Boyd so edgy, that when the time came, both were so nervous, they wanted to back out.

"Oh no, you don't," Dud said, pushing them out the hotel door. "Remember, God hates a coward."

"But he's not too partial to blundering idiots, either," Boyd muttered, as he unwilling followed Jesse down the sidewalk.

After fetching Iris at the boardinghouse, the four of them walked by the café while Dud explained the job. Iris clutched his arm and stared at the windows with wide eyes. "Do you think I can do it, Mr. Dud?" she asked, suddenly frightened.

"Oh course you can," Dud said. "Just don't let them talk you into working more than those three days. That's when you'll make your biggest tips, and there is no reason for you to wear yourself out working six days a week when you're going to be making most of your money on those days anyway."

Iris agreed with his idea, and Dud asked her if she wanted to ride with Felix and him the next morning to the county seat. He explained they would have to spend the night, get up early to bid on the house, and afterwards come back to Tie Town, getting in late on Saturday night. Boyd and Jesse had already informed him they did not want to go; they were much more interested in the French singer everyone was talking about.

"Oh dear," Iris said. "I promised the landlady I would help her with the baking tomorrow." She bit her lip and said determinedly. "I want to go with you, so I'll just have to play the man card."

"What's the man card?" Dud asked, glancing at Boyd and Jesse, who looked as clueless as he was.

"Well, that's what my father called it," Iris explained. "My mother liked to do things for people, but sometimes it got to be too much, so she would tell them my father said 'no' or had something else he wanted her to do. And my father would laugh and say she was playing the man card. I'm not sure what he meant by card, but between women, it was understood that what the man wanted came first."

"It was the trump card then," Boyd said.

Iris looked puzzled. "Trump?"

Dud explained. "The bigger card wins or "trumps" over the smaller card. Nobody ever used me for a man card, I can guarantee you that."

"Oh no, Mr. Dud. You were used a lot of times and just didn't realize it," Iris assured him. "Say you asked a girl to go for a buggy ride, but she had already promised her friends she would stop by and visit with them. Well, all she had to do was explain that you had asked her, and they automatically understood and released her from her obligation. And you never knew it. Now if she wasn't that interested in you, she could use her previous engagement as a means of not going with you. Or, she might use it if she thought you were taking her for granted, and she wanted to play a little hard to get."

"Stop, you're making my head spin," Dud moaned. "Satan, thy name is woman!"

"Oh, Mr. Dud," Iris said, laughing. "You're so funny."

Dud sighed. Saying things like that had infuriated his ex-wife, but Iris just thought it amusing. It must be a sign he was getting old. Old people could say anything they wanted and get away with it. Young folks just laughed at them.

"Well, men use it, too, in a way," Boyd said. "I've heard plenty of men say, 'I can't do that because my wife won't let me,' when all along it was them who didn't want to do it. And I know if some girl asked me to do something, I'd blow off any plans I had with a man in a heartbeat."

"You really must learn to play harder to get, Boyd," Jesse kidded in a falsetto voice.

Boyd grinned sheepishly.

They found the Harrison home to be a new, two-story, white Victorian house with lots of gingerbread trim. A velvet carpet of grass covered the front yard; green shrubs and flowering rose bushes skirted the house's foundation. Annabelle opened the front door and ran onto the airy gallery to greet them.

"Did you bring your dog, Mr. Dud?" she called.

"Yes ma'am, Miss Annabelle," Dud said with a smile. "He's right here."

She stooped to pet Old Tom. Her father came to the door, smiling a welcome. "Annabelle, don't leave our visitors standing on the gallery. Come in, come in."

With hats in hand, they walked into the wide hall of the house. Dud told Old Tom to stay outside and gave Annabelle permission to feed him scrapes after supper. Mrs. Harrison bustled forward, a full figured woman with dark, gray-streaked hair. As her husband made the introductions, her eyes widened, and she stared at Dud.

"Dud Washburn?" she asked. "Not Dudford Washburn?"

Dud nodded his head, said, "yes ma'am," and wracked his brain trying to remember where he knew her from.

She pressed her fingers to her opened mouth. "Law! Dudford Washburn! I'm Nellie Casner; your sister saved my life when I was a little girl. Oh my, and are these her sons? Oh my, oh my. Girls!" she called, looking around her. "Come meet the boys whose mama saved me when my dress caught on fire."

She looked at Dud as if she was seeing a dead person come back to life. Behind her, her husband said, "Daughter, would you and sister finish supper and put it on the table so Mother can visit with Mr. Washburn?" They both answered, "Yes, Papa." Dud became aware of a myriad of details—Woody Harrison had addressed the younger daughter; Boyd and Jesse's eyes were wide with nervous apprehension at the sight of the luscious Elizabeth; Iris looked scared, as if she felt out of place.

"Come into the parlor, Mr. Washburn," Mrs. Harrison said, "while we wait for supper. My, it is so good to see you again after all these years."

Iris did not seem to know what to do. She looked toward the kitchen as if to follow the girls and ask if they needed help. Dud took her by the arm and led her into a parlor filled with good quality furniture. A pipe stand stood next to an easy chair. A piano sat near windows covered in clean, flouncy net curtains. Dud steered Iris to a horsehair sofa, and after she and Mrs. Harrison had sat down, he took a seat next to her.

Nellie Harrison explained the incident to Iris. Dud said, "I didn't hear about it until just recently. My grandmother died after her skirt caught fire, and it terrified my father that the same thing might happen to my mother and sisters, so he impressed upon them repeatedly what they were to do. It was so ingrained in my sister; I don't imagine she gave it much thought."

"Well, I did. At the time, all I could think of was to run,

the very worst thing," Nellie said. "My father was head surgeon at the San Antonio hospital, and he knew all too well how fatal it could have been. He asked your father if there was anything he could do for your younger sister to show our gratitude, but he said no, that she was the type of person who could find happiness in any situation life put her in, but he was deeply worried about your older sister. She had literally been left at the altar and had become very embittered by it. She had expressed an interest in nursing, and your father asked if my father might take her on and train her as a nurse."

"Yes, I remember that," Dud said.

"My father always said that despite her brusque personality she made the best nurse he ever had. She fell in love again, you know, a young soldier who had been terribly wounded in the war. When he died, she just seemed to give up, and when she contracted yellow fever, she was gone within a few days."

"I didn't realize she had fallen in love again," Dud said politely. He wondered who the poor slob was, but was glad his sister had found happiness before she died.

"Oh yes," Nellie said, her eyes looking away, remembering days past. "My father respected people's privacy, but he would often tell my mother and us girls harmless little gossip as a way of sharing his work. We followed your sister's love affair avidly, thinking it so romantic. And now, I just can't believe these young men are your baby sister's boys." She gave them a benevolent smile, and Dud sent up a silent prayer of thanks for an unfortunate incident that happened thirty years previously.

"Supper's ready, Papa," Annabelle said, coming in to the room.

Dud had feared he would have little in common with Woody Harrison, but the family had lived all over the state, were used to entertaining and knew how to converse. Boyd and Jesse had trouble keeping from staring at Elizabeth, who knew it and thoroughly enjoyed it, but they managed to hold their own during the parley at the table. When Woody started talking about fishing, it astonished Dud to learn how much Boyd and Jesse liked fishing, too, especially since they seemed to have developed a predilection for it that very evening.

While they devoured some of the best home cooking Dud had ever eaten, Nellie talked about his sister and growing up in San Antonio. With a gentle and wily determination, she extracted information from Iris. Dud, after exchanging glances with the others, confessed that Iris was recently widowed.

"We all thought it would be better if she did not advertise it in a rough and tumble boomtown like this," Dud explained.

Nellie's face shone with compassion. "I think that's very wise of you, my dear."

Having satisfied Nellie's inquisitiveness about Iris, at least temporarily, Dud began to fret about Old Tom. Annabelle noticed the quick looks he gave the direction of the front of the house, and she asked, "Are you worried about your dog, Mr. Dud?"

"Sort of," he said, smiling kindly at the girl. "Old Tom is bad about digging, and it sure worries me that he might be digging in your mama's pretty flower beds."

Annabelle nodded and looked at her mother. "May I give Old Tom the ham bone now, Mama, just to make sure he won't dig?"

"Yes, dear," her mother answered. "But come right back to the table."

They watched as Annabelle trotted to the kitchen. Dud had already explained Annabelle's affliction to his three companions, and they looked at her with mild, but not insensitive, curiosity. Annabelle came back in and sat down at the table with a smile. "He's fine. No digging."

Dud let out a sigh of relief. He did not want Old Tom screwing up Boyd or Jesse's chances with the Harrison girl. Nellie Harrison looked slightly relieved, too.

When they finished eating, their hostess rose, suggesting the men retire to the front gallery while she and the girls cleared the table. "Would you like to help, Mrs. Talbot?" she asked.

Iris nodded her head. "Oh, yes." She looked at Dud and the boys. "If I may be excused?"

"Of course, Miss Iris," Dud said, while Boyd and Jesse agreed.

Woody fetched his pipe and led the way to the gallery, giving them permission to smoke or chew if they were so inclined.

"That's okay, Mr. Harrison," Jesse said. "Uncle Dud's only vice is his dog."

Woody laughed and they settled down to discuss politics in a desultory way. Jesse talked in a natural, if somewhat reserved, manner, but Boyd added little to the conversation, and Dud read mild puzzlement and confusion on his face. Woody brought the subject around to Iris and apologized for his wife's curiosity.

"That's all right," Dud said. "It's only natural for women to be inquisitive." He thought for several seconds and added, "You know, Iris's husband dealt with her in a heavy-handed way." Wishing to be on honest terms with the Harrisons, he explained the circumstances of their acquaintance with Iris.

Woody puffed on his pipe and nodded his head. "It's hard to stand back and watch something like that happening," he said. He added with a wry smile, "Are you sure you didn't encourage him just a little to go after that bull, Washburn?"

"No, as a matter of fact, I told him not to do it," Dud said. "Unfortunately, with a man like that, I might as well have poured coal oil on a flame."

Elizabeth came out of the house and approached Boyd and Jesse. They jumped to their feet. "Would you gentlemen like me to show you our garden in the back of the house?" she asked. "There's enough light left, I believe."

Of course they agreed. After they left, Woody said, "Nice boys you have there, Washburn."

"Thank you," Dud said. "My sister and brother-in-law did a fine job with them."

In a short time, the other three women came out of the house and sat with them. Nellie Harrison gave an unconscious pat to her husband's leg. Iris sat near Dud, and Annabelle sat on the gallery playing with Old Tom. As they talked, Dud sensed a kind of empathy between the two older women, and guessed that Nellie extracted Iris's life history in the kitchen. Iris, transparent and guileless, had responded with a desire for friendship.

"My, this night has brought back so many memories," Nellie said. She gave a small chuckle. "You know, when I was young, when you boys first visited San Antonio, we girls would play a game—we would pick and choose which Washburn boy we would most like to marry."

Dud laughed. "I bet Rayford won every time."

Nellie gave a tinkle of laughter. "He was by far the favorite. What a dashing boy! We heard he got engaged to a girl in Virginia before he died. Oh the consternation of the girls back home!"

"Rayford never lacked for female admirers," Dud agreed.

"Now don't be modest, Mr. Washburn," she scolded. "There were quite a few girls who secretly admired a skinny young man named Dudford."

Iris gave Dud a surreptitious poke and repressed a giggle. "Well, it's nice to hear that," Dud said. "I sure didn't know about it at the time."

"And your brother Milford! Such a clown. My father so wanted my younger sister to marry Milford. He said there would never be a dull moment with Milford around. She confided to me that she wanted to marry Milford, too, but she could never pin him down."

"That was Milford, all right," Dud said.

"He and Bradford died at Shiloh, didn't they?" Nellie asked. "So, so sad."

"Were you all named Ford?" Iris asked.

"Yes," Dud said. "My pappy's name was Ford, and my dear old mama was so attached to the old man, she named every one of her sons after him."

Elizabeth and the boys came back to the gallery, but sat at the opposite end, Jesse on one side of her, Boyd on the other. The sound of Elizabeth's vivacious voice carried across the gallery, but they were unable to hear what was being said. Dud looked down at Annabelle and saw her staring at the group. In a minute, she got up and quietly went over, unobtrusively sitting behind Boyd. Dud looked at Iris and wondered if he should suggest she join them. Her status as a widow put her in a different position. Before he could decide what to do, a tall young stranger came up the walk. Woody introduced the tow-haired man as the town's surveyor, owner of the building between the hotel and the cafe. After perfunctory greetings, he joined the other group. Almost immediately afterward, another young man appeared whose name Dud promptly forgot.

"How did you meet Mr. Harrison?" Iris asked.

"You know, it's a funny thing. A young man my father didn't approve of came courting," she said. "And suddenly I got a letter from my older sister in Houston asking if I would come help with her new baby. I never thought a thing about it at the time, even when after I arrived it was plain my sister was perfectly capable of handling the infant on her own. I met Woodrow and fell in love. It was only years later, after Elizabeth came of age, that I realized my father had planned the whole thing to get me away from that undesirable young man.

"I haven't thought of him in years. I wonder what became of him. What was his name? Something odd. Ev. Ev something. Ev Reid, I think. It ended well for me, anyway."

"I think he was a friend of Milford's," Dud said slowly. "But the friendship cooled before Milford left."

"That's right, I do seem to remember that," Nellie said. "I don't know what it was about him; I just know my father did not approve of him."

As Dud contemplated this, she looked at Boyd and

Jesse. "At the time, we all wondered why your younger sister married your brother-in-law. He was gruff and not particularly handsome, and she had her choice of beaus. Later I came to realize how wise she had been, how just right he was for her."

Dud agreed with her. She looked at him through eyes that had grown serious. "You have two fine nephews, Mr. Washburn. I hope you all get whatever it is that you came to Tie Town to find."

FIFTEEN

THEY WERE IN! DUD REJOICED. EVEN IF THINGS DID NOT work out with the sought after Elizabeth, Boyd and Jesse had entered into the good graces of respectable society in Tie Town. He hoped that Iris, too, would benefit from her association with the Harrisons, offsetting any negativity her job might bring.

She was not to start until the following weekend and looked forward to the trip to the county seat. Nellie Harrison had asked if they might pick up a bolt of muslin; the general store in Tie Town had been out for weeks. Woody had forgotten to get his favorite brand of pipe tobacco in San Antonio and asked Dud if he would mind looking for it. He insisted on paying Dud in advance.

After leaving the Harrison home, Dud and Iris walked to the boardinghouse while Boyd and Jesse veered toward the Gilded Lily saloon. "You're not going to see the naughty French singer?" Iris asked.

"Oh, I'll get curious some other time," Dud said, holding Iris by the elbow as they walked through the darkened town. "We're leaving early in the morning, and I'll need my beauty sleep tonight."

Iris's laughter rang pleasantly through the still night air. Almost immediately, two shots boomed from down the street and the sound of men cursing could be heard. Iris grabbed Dud's hand, and he urged her forward. "Let's hurry," he said.

Once they were safely away, Iris asked, "Is your life always this exciting, Mr. Dud?"

"Lord no," Dud said. "Most of the time I'm sitting on a ranch out in the middle of nowhere staring at the rear end of a cow."

He could feel Iris's smile rather than see it. They walked up the steps of the boardinghouse. Dud opened the door for her and said goodnight. "I'll fetch you at first light, Miss Iris."

"Thank you, Mr. Dud," she said, squeezing his hand and slipping into the house.

The next morning, there were several men already at the livery stable. Ugor Darst had the fire going and his anvil set up, busily hammering on a horseshoe. The owner pitched hay into a stall in the corner. A heavy-set man with big jowls and a large nose stood next to Felix. He removed his hat when he saw Iris and spit out a chaw of tobacco.

"Pleasure to met you, ma'am," he said when introduced.

"Thompson here wants you to pick up a roll of barb-wire, Washburn," Felix explained. "Until the train can come through, it takes a coon's age before we can get freight hauled in. Darst said we could use his wagon."

"I don't see any problem with that," Dud said, studying

Seth Thompson, the owner of the property he wanted. It might fare him well to do Thompson a favor.

"How's your wife, Thompson?" Felix asked.

"Poorly," he answered. "That woman took poor the day after we married, and she's been poorly ever since."

Unlike Woody Harrison, Thompson did not offer to send money to pay for the wire. Ugor refused to take payment from Dud for the use of his wagon. Before they left, two other men in town who had heard of the trip came in and asked Felix and Dud to bring them back items from the county seat. This time, however, Felix took their money.

An all day trip at best, Felix managed to make it longer by stopping to chew the fat with every stranger they met. He did wrangle an invitation to dine at noon at a farmhouse, and twice they got offered something the locals called "bust-head whiskey," a mixture of wine made from wild mustang grapes and molasses. After the first sip, Dud politely declined any further offers, much to Iris's visible relief. Felix drank almost two quarts with no effect other than to burst into singing "Beautiful Dreamer" and later falling asleep in the back of the wagon with Old Tom. Iris asked Dud to sing some of the songs he used to quiet cattle on the trail, and he did, desperately trying to remember the words to the less raunchy ones. He taught Iris a few of them, and they sang together the rest of the way.

On the outskirts of town stood a large two-story house profusely lit, with tall white columns across the front—almost a mansion. Horses, buggies, and wagons circled the place, and sounds of laughter could be heard rippling through the evening. Felix roused himself from the back of the wagon, and straightening his top hat, said, "Stop here."

The three of them got down, and a small boy came running. "I'll take your mules, mister," he said. After glancing at Felix, who acted as if this was only to be expected, Dud tossed the boy a nickel and said his thanks. As they walked up the wide steps, the front door flew open, and a lady bedecked in her finest jewelry and lace greeted them. Felix bowed elaborately and kissed her hand.

"Madam, I can only say that no wanderer in the desert of life was ever greeted by a more beautiful sight."

She blushed and happily bid them to come inside. Once in, Felix began to circulate, speaking heartily to almost every man he saw and stopping to bow and kiss the hands of all the women. Someone pushed a glass of punch into Dud's hand, and a young woman approached Iris and took her by the arm.

"Here, come upstairs with me, and you can freshen up from your journey."

Iris looked questioningly at Dud as she was being led away, but Dud shrugged his shoulders and nodded his head. The girl who had Iris by the arm began a stream of conversation, and Iris smiled in return. Dud ambled from one group to another, being grateful Felix had come along and thinking it odd he had not told them they were going to a party. He soon found a cluster of cattlemen and forgot all about Felix.

Later a band began to play. They did square dances, waltzes, reels, and every other kind of dance anyone could think of. Iris's blue eyes were shining, her face radiant. She danced with him repeatedly, with Felix many times, and with two dozen other men who by the looks on their faces thought she was prettier than a paid off mortgage.

At four o'clock in the morning, the partygoers began to thin out. The young woman who had taken Iris upstairs offered to let her stay the night. Dud searched for Felix and told him he was going to bed.

"I'll go with you to the hotel," Felix said, setting his spiked punch cup down. Dud had never seen a small man like Felix who could hold so much liquor.

"Hotel, my foot!" Dud exclaimed. "I'm not paying for a couple of hours of sleep. You can find me at the far corner of the stable, sleeping in the hay."

Dud went through the kitchen, telling any woman who might be his hostess what a pleasure it had been, that he had never been to such a successful and fun party with so much good food. The last part was not entirely true, but he made it sound that way, and he was rewarded with charming smiles and giggles. He sweet-talked a few scraps from the cook and went outside, whistling for Old Tom.

After giving Tom the scraps, he made his way to the barn and found an empty stall toward the back. Kicking aside some dried horse manure, he fetched armfuls of clean hay from a pile, throwing them down. After making himself comfortable, he fell asleep, only vaguely aware sometime later that Felix had joined him.

If Old Tom had not licked his face, Dud might have overslept. He sat up, took a deep breath and tried to remember where he was. Giving Felix a soft kick, he said, "Wake up, old man. We've got a date on the courthouse steps."

Felix groaned, sat up and held his head. "Go without

me," he said thickly.

"No, you wanted in on this trip. Come on, get up," Dud said. He stood up and shook the stiffness from his joints. "Why didn't you tell me we were going to a party?" he asked. "Iris and I wouldn't have stayed out so late the night before if we'd known."

Felix looked at Dud through bleary eyes. "I didn't know we were going to a party."

"What do you mean you didn't know? Aren't these people friends of yours?" Dud asked.

"I thought they were friends of yours," Felix said, rising and dusting off his pants. "You were the one right in the big middle of that group of cattle barons, fabricating lies with the rest of them."

Dud's breath came faster, and he could feel his nostrils flaring. "Do you mean to tell me we let Iris sleep in a strange house, and we don't even know who lives there? Of all the...," and he began to spew curse words at Felix.

"Please," Felix said, looking at him distastefully. "She's perfectly all right. You know, the longer I know you, Dud, the more you remind me of an old mother hen."

"Come on," Dud said roughly, giving him a slight push. "I'm fetching Iris and getting to that courthouse."

The maid who opened the door looked as if she just got out of bed, too. "The ladies are still asleep," she informed them and began to shut the door.

Dud stuck his foot on the threshold. "Please get Miss Iris up immediately," he said. "Tell her Mr. Felix and Mr. Dud are waiting."

They stared at one another like two poker players over a game of Mexican Sweat, but she finally said, "Yes sir," and went up the stairs.

Dud turned to Felix. "This could have been a cathouse for all you knew."

"I think you would have picked up on that, Dud," Felix said. "You've probably been in enough of them."

Iris came down the stairs, her face puffy with sleep and her hands busy pushing pins in her hair. "I'm sorry I overslept," she said breathlessly when she reached them.

"That's okay," Dud said. "We just got up. Let's head for the courthouse and see what the action is there."

As they approached the small assembly, Dud feared they had missed the bidding on the house altogether. Standing on the steps and half listening as two mules were being auctioned; he quietly asked around and found the house had not yet gone on the block. Dud relaxed and let his eyes wander, noting the elaborate and ornate newness of the marble and granite courthouse. In the crowd of men that also contained a smattering of women, he saw the Nordic surveyor he had met at the Harrison home.

"And now we have for auction a lot in Tie Town with half a house on it," the auctioneer said. He stopped, wiped his brow and took a swig out of a bottle he had in his jacket. He looked like one of the revelers of the previous evening. He also looked like he had a headache. "What do you give me?"

Dud did not open the bid. One or two others started with ridiculously low amounts—they were not serious about the lot, just looking to pick up a bargain. When the bids began to climb, the young surveyor joined in. As others fell away, Dud began to bid, and soon it came down to him and the surveyor. When the bids became dangerously close to the cutoff figure Dud had previously decided upon, the surveyor shrugged his shoulders, gave a wry grin and shook his head.

"Sold! To the gentleman with the pretty young lady," the auctioneer called, relieved to be finished. "Cash on the barrel, sir, right here."

After paying, Dud found the surveyor. "No hard feelings, I hope," Dud said.

"No," he said with a shake of his blond head. "I'm always running across something. I just thought I might pick it up cheap." He turned a deep red. "I'm trying to save my money. The Harrisons expect Elizabeth to marry well. When Mr. Harrison dies, Elizabeth will be responsible for her mother and Annabelle."

"Yes," Dud said. "I can see that. But Harrison's got a good job; he ought to have a little pile stashed away."

The surveyor nodded. "Ja," he said, reverting to his Swedish roots. "But he spent a lot of his savings on doctors for Annabelle, and he doesn't like to deny them the things they want now. I just thought if I had a house close to theirs, it might make them look more favorably on me. They will try to keep Elizabeth close."

The big Swede's words made sense and gave Dud a feeling of foreboding. He came from an old-fashioned family where the husband pointed his finger at the wife and said this is where we are living and expected her to deal with it. It would be difficult to convince Elizabeth and the Harrisons that she belonged with Boyd on an isolated ranch. Had that not been a problem in his marriage? It was not the one that broke it, but it had not helped.

"Will you join us for breakfast?" Dud asked. Looking up in the sky, he added, "or maybe dinner."

"No, I have a job to do, thank you," he replied. "I imagine I will meet you again at Elizabeth's. I see lots of men there."

Dud gave him a pat on the back. "Don't give up heart," he said. "In a situation like this, it's fair to pray that the best man wins and all the others feel lucky they got away."

The surveyor laughed. Iris and Felix had joined them, and he bid them goodbye. When he left, Dud turned and said, "All right, let's eat."

They hunted up a café in town where Dud and Iris watched in amazement as Felix shoveled in the groceries. For dessert, the waitress brought him a piece of pie. He said, "No darling, I want the whole pie."

Dud paid for everything and ordered food to take with them. Tired, they had to search for the items people had requested, but finally found everything and headed home. In the late afternoon, Iris crawled into the back of the wagon and fell asleep. Old Tom wanted in, too, so he joined her. In a while, Dud's head began to nod, and he handed the reins to Felix. "You slept yesterday, brother," he explained. "Today it's our turn." Iris did not say anything when he got in the wagon bed with her. She sleepily moved over and did not complain about a smelly dog lying next to her and a tired old man with a sawed-off shotgun on the other side of it.

Dud slept lightly, vaguely aware it had grown dark and that the mules had slowed to a steady deliberate clop. Old Tom snored, snorted once or twice, and twitched his leg. Iris turned over and grew still.

Some time later, Dud suddenly sat up. The wagon had stopped moving. He looked toward Felix and shook his head. Peering out the back, he saw they were in Tie Town in front of the livery stable. He eased out the rear of the wagon. "Come on, Old Tom," he said in quiet tones. "Out, boy, we're home, such as it is."

Old Tom jumped out, and Dud reached in, grabbing Iris by the foot and shaking her leg. "Wake up, Miss Iris. We're back."

She sat up, rubbed her eyes and with heaving breaths crawled out the back with Dud's assistance. "Why didn't you drop me off at the boardinghouse?" she pouted. "Now I'll have to walk back."

Dud took her by the arm. "Come here," he said, guiding her to the front of the wagon. "Look at our driver."

Felix lay sprawled on the wagon seat, his chest rising and falling with profound snores, the reins tied around the brake handle. Dud prodded his shoulder. "Get up, Felix, we're back."

Felix sputtered, gave a start and sat up. "What? What did you say?" He looked around through squinted eyes. "Where's my pie?"

Dud did not answer. Instead, he told Iris, "I'll saddle the horses, and we can ride back to the boardinghouse."

"I can ride bareback," Iris said. "Just put a bridle on my little Morgan. He'll let us ride double."

"Let's get the wagon in first," Dud said. "These mules have had a hard day."

Inside, the Darsts had lanterns lit, and they helped with the mules and unloading. For the loan of the wagon, Dud brought Ugor some pipe tobacco, Zizi a few yards of calico for curtains to put over the one window in the cubbyhole they lived in, and the Darst boys some candy.

They gave copious thanks, and Ugor asked, "Did you get the lot?"

Dud nodded. "Yes, despite almost being led astray by that durn Felix. I'm going to put a bridle on Miss Iris's mare and take her back to her boardinghouse."

"Franz!" Ugor called. "You and Miklos put a bridle on Miss Iris's horse for Mr. Dud."

"Yes sir, Papa!" they answered. "But Papa, our names are now Frank and Mike."

"Aw, get out of here," Ugor said, waving his hand. "This late at night I'm supposed to remember new names?"

The boys brought the horse around, and Dud got on, swinging Iris up behind him. They said their goodbyes and waved; once outside, Iris leaned forward, whispering in his ear. "Thank you, Mr. Dud, for taking me along, for giving me a roof over my head and taking care of my horse. I don't know how I can ever repay you for all you've done for me."

"You can keep me and Boyd and Jesse company while we work on that house," Dud said, "if you've a mind to."

"Sure," she answered sleepily. "If you'll get me some pots and pans, maybe you can help me learn how to cook over a campfire."

"Well, gosh darn it, Miss Iris!" Dud fussed. "Why didn't you tell me that this morning? We could have found all kinds of pots and pans in town."

"Because I didn't think about it until just now," Iris said.

She felt so good pressing against his back; he would have forgiven her anything. All he could think of was how stupid his nephews were, especially when she squeezed his hand again as she said goodbye before running into the house. He returned to the stables and got the pipe tobacco and muslin for the Harrisons. The hotel looked like a morgue—the noise coming from the Gilded Lily Saloon roared through the streets like a bear in heat. Dud, still tired, went to bed, but stayed awake until Boyd and Jesse came in.

"Did you get it, Uncle Dud?" Boyd asked.

"Yep," Dud answered. "I'll search out Thompson tomorrow and ask if we can collect rocks."

"What about the poker game?" Jesse asked. "Are you going to feel him out about that, too?"

"I hope he brings it up," Dud said. "We don't want to appear too eager. How was the French tart?"

Even with the dim light of the lantern, he could see something going on as Boyd shot a glance at his brother. "She's beautiful and can sing like a nightingale," Boyd said. "You'll have to find out for yourself, Uncle Dud."

"It will have to be next weekend," Dud said. "Iris wants to go to some special church service tomorrow night, and she doesn't want to go alone or with her landlady, so I said I'd go with her. I guess lightning won't strike the chapel if I walk in."

Boyd glanced at his brother before speaking. "I think I'll go, too, Uncle Dud," he said. "There will probably be a lot of pretty girls there."

Jesse sat down and removed his boots, getting ready for bed. "What about you, Jess?" Dud asked.

"No, that's okay," he answered. "You two go along. I'll find something else to do."

Boyd looked at Dud, but said nothing, and then he, too, got ready for bed.

SIXTEEN

"Is he planning another practical joke?" Dud hissed to Boyd as Jesse walked ahead of them to the café for breakfast.

"No," Boyd muttered, his eyes on Jesse's back. "I almost wish it was that."

"What do you mean?" Dud asked.

"I may be mistaken," Boyd whispered. "Just go to the Gilded Lily and hear Suzette sing—but wait until next Saturday night. If you don't see anything, I'll know I was wrong."

Because Boyd was not often wrong about Jesse, it worried Dud. He had to put it aside for the moment, however. He had other plans to make.

Later, at the livery stable, a hard-eyed cowboy with a clipped dark mustache introduced himself to Dud as one of Seth Thompson's cowhands.

"Mr. Thompson sent me after the barbwire," he explained in a laconic drawl. "He said he'd pay you for it the next time he saw you."

"I've been wanting to speak with him," Dud said. "If you don't mind, I'll ride out there with you."

The cowhand stared at him in wariness. "It's an all day ride out there and back."

"I got all day," Dud said mildly.

After looking at him intently for a few more seconds, the cowhand said, "Mrs. Thompson sure has been down. It might do her good if you could bring Miss Talbot along with you."

Iris had not even been in town a week, and all the men knew about her. Dud preferred to have Boyd and Jesse with him, but had no desire to appear threatening or crowd Thompson in any way. Although he realized the cowboy was the one who probably hoped Iris would do him good, not Mrs. Thompson, Dud decided it might be better if Iris went along. "She had a pretty rough trip yesterday," he said. "But if you can wait, I'll see if she wants to ride along."

He said he would wait. Dud saddled his horse and Iris's in the hope she would agree. When he reached the boardinghouse, he went up the steps and knocked on the door. The landlady opened it, standing with fingers as big as corncobs wrapped around a broom handle. Dud explained he needed to see Iris.

"She's worn out from yesterday," she said. "What do you want her for anyway?"

"None of your business, woman," Dud said, but not too unfriendly. "Just get her for me, please."

"All right," she snarled. Leaving Dud standing at the door, she hollered up the stairs. "Iris! That overbearing, domineering, cow man who thinks you ought to be at his constant beck and call is here again!"

"Mr. Dud?" Iris's muffled voice floated down the stairs. "I'll be right down!"

The landlady glared at Dud and went into another part of the house. Iris came down the stairs, dressed, but barefoot, her hair brushed, but not pinned. "What is it, Mr. Dud?"

He explained and she said, "Sure, but I haven't had breakfast yet."

"This isn't a restaurant!" a loud grating voice called from the other room. "You slept through breakfast, missy, and don't even think about going into my kitchen and digging around!"

Iris rolled her eyes and shut them. Dud yelled back, "I'll get her something at the café. Don't get your drawers in a wad!"

"I'll be ready in a few minutes, Mr. Dud," Iris said over the muttering in the background. "If you wouldn't mind waiting for me on the gallery."

Dud said that would be fine. Iris must have rushed, because it was not long before she came out, pinning on a wide-brimmed hat. "Are we going to miss the church social tonight?" she fretted. "I guess it doesn't matter anyway. I was going to ask the landlady if I could bake something to take, but that's out. I can't go without bringing something."

Dud told her he thought they would be back in plenty of time. "I'll ask them at the café to make a couple of pies and some rolls or something we can pick up later."

"Oh, that would be nice," Iris agreed. "But it's just embarrassing not to be able to bring something home cooked. The landlady already thinks I'm worthless because I slept in; now everyone will think I can't even cook."

"She's just mad because you played the man card on her," Dud laughed.

At the stables, while Iris spoke to Zizi Darst in a mixture of English and Hungarian, Boyd and Jesse came in. Dud took them aside to explain the situation. "We can't keep borrowing Darst's wagon," he added. "See if you can find one for sale cheap, but don't buy it until I get the final okay from Thompson. Darst may even want to sell his. Also, be on the lookout for some used pots and dishes. Iris is willing to cook over a campfire at the house."

"Hells bells," Boyd said. "I'll buy her new ones if she'll cook."

"Yeah, me too," Jesse said. "I'm already sick of café food."

The Thompson cowhand offered to let Iris ride in the wagon with him, but she thanked him and said her horse needed the exercise. He held the reins in almost total silence, answering Dud's innocuous questions with terse answers—not out of anger, but apparently because it was his nature. The ride to the Thompson ranch house did not take as much time as he had insinuated it would, and not nearly as long as it would have if Iris had agreed to ride in the wagon with him, Dud thought.

Seth Thompson strode out of the house as they pulled into the front yard. His shrewd eyes swept over the three of them, and stayed briefly on Iris. "What's the matter, Washburn?" he asked, looking back at Dud. "Afraid you wouldn't get your money for the wire?" He spit tobacco juice onto the ground and laughed at his own joke.

"Nope," Dud said, getting down from his horse and assisting Iris off hers. "Came to make a trade."

Thompson's eyes squinted in suspicion. "What'd you mean?"

Dud drew closer to Thompson, but stood relaxed. "I bought the unfinished house on Pecan Street as an investment, and I want to rock it. If you'll let me collect some of those iron ore rocks on your place on the Yegua, and let me cut down a few cedars for shingles and such as that, I'll give you the wire."

"You ain't much of a trader, Washburn," Thompson said, laughing and spitting again. "I'd let you do that for nothing, but I'll sure take the wire now." He turned to Iris. "Miss Talbot, it's a pleasure to see you again."

Before she could reply, his cowhand said, "Miss Talbot heard Mrs. Thompson was feeling poorly and thought she might like some company."

"Well, it won't be much of a pleasure for you, Miss Talbot," Thompson replied. "But you can go on in and say howdy."

A middle-aged woman came to the door. Her thin lips made a dour frown when she saw them. Thompson introduced her as his sister.

"I didn't plan on company for dinner," she said sourly.

Iris blushed, and said, "I ate a late breakfast, and I really don't care for anything, anyway, thank you."

"Well," the woman said, moving aside an inch. "Come on in, then. She's in bed, leaving others to do her work as usual."

Iris glanced at Dud, but followed the woman. Thompson's eyes stayed on Iris until she disappeared within the house.

"Come on, Washburn," he said. "We can rustle up some grub in the bunkhouse."

Dud's time with Seth Thompson was neither pleasant nor unpleasant. The food they ate in the bunkhouse tasted decent enough, the conversation they had about horses and cattle adequate. Thompson did not mention what Dud was hoping he would until walking back to the house to fetch Iris so they could leave.

"Say, you play poker, Washburn?" Thompson asked. He added craftily, "If you like that piece of land on the Yegua, there might be a chance of winning it in a friendly game. Title to that property floats around like a whore on payday."

"Nooo," Dud said. "I'm not much of a hand at poker. And no need to buy the land when I can get the rocks and timber off of it for nothing."

Thompson looked crestfallen, and Dud added, "But I've got an uncle heading this way who is a poker playing fool."

"Oh really?" Thompson said, perking up.

"Yeah," Dud said. "He loves the game and has the money to play. Trouble is he's getting on in years."

"Is that right?" Thompson said innocently. "Maybe he would like to join our little game. We play the first Saturday of the month at the Gilded Lily, and quite a few of our players have lost their three-times-in-one-night vigor." He gave a little chuckle.

Dud looked down at the ground and tried to appear as if he were weighing the idea in his mind. "Well, it's like this," he said. "Now don't get me wrong—I'm sure you wouldn't dream of doing anything. It's just that his mind isn't as sharp as it once was, and I'd sure hate for someone to take advantage of him."

"Oh, we play an honest game, Washburn," Thompson assured him angelically. "We're willing for anybody to play with us as long as they can put up the stake."

"I'll talk to him when he gets here and see if he wants to," Dud said. "How much of a stake are you talking about?"

Dud had prepared himself for the answer and did not blanch. "It's not a closed game, is it?" he asked. "I mean, you don't mind spectators, do you?"

"It's in a room upstairs, but we let a few extra people in," Thompson said. "You and your nephews can watch— if you've a mind to."

"Well, thank you, we just might do that." Dud breathed a silent sigh of relief. Far better to play up to Ponder's age than try to hide it.

Iris came out to meet him as he walked to the house. From the look on her face he realized something was wrong, and he quickened his steps so he would reach her before Thompson did.

"Mr. Dud," she said in low tones. "That woman needs a doctor. She's in a bad way."

Dud turned to Thompson when he reached them. "Miss Iris thinks your wife needs a doctor, Thompson."

He scowled. "There ain't a thing wrong with her that hasn't been going on for years. Besides, there ain't no doctor in Tie Town."

"My nephew Jesse is a fair hand at doctoring animals and sometimes humans. Would you mind if he came out here at daylight and looked at her? It would ease Miss Iris."

"He can do what he wants," Thompson said. "Won't do a bit of good, though."

"Thank you, Mr. Thompson," Iris said. "It would make me feel better."

On the way home, Iris described the situation to Dud. "Lying on the bed like that, in so much misery, poor thing," she said. "And that wretched sister of his!

"And all that spitting, spitting, spitting. Blah!"

Dud repressed a grin; glad Iris had not been taken with the Thompson family. "That cowhand of his is a nice enough fellow," he added. "But he sure would be a hard man to live with. Probably wouldn't talk to his wife, and she'd never know where she stood with him."

Iris gave Dud a strange look. "Yes?"

Dud tried to look innocent. "I was just making a comment, that's all."

Iris gave a sigh. "Do you think Mr. Jesse can do anything for her?" she asked.

Dud shook his head. "I doubt it, but he can try. Maybe he can talk old man Thompson into carrying her to a doctor."

Once in town, Dud dropped Iris off at the boarding-house. "Now, Miss Iris," he said. "You get some rest. You're tired and upset about Mrs. Thompson, and you need to lie down and relax. Don't let that old battleaxe make you feel bad or try to talk you into helping her with her work. I'm paying good money for you to stay there, so you're not obliged to her for nothing. If she says anything, you tell I said you had to get some rest. I'll pick you up for church later."

Iris nodded. "I know you're right, Mr. Dud. I'm sorry I was crabby."

"That's all right, now you run along."

Dud found Boyd and Jesse waiting for him in the hotel lobby. "We cleaned underneath the shed," Boyd said, "and made some shelves for the pots and pans we bought. Mr. Darst will sell us his wagon, but he wants to keep the canvas."

"Fine," Dud said. "We can get started tomorrow. I'm going upstairs for fifteen minutes of shut-eye. Jess, I hope you don't mind me volunteering your services. Are you sure you won't go to church with us?"

"No, that's all right, Uncle Dud," Jesse replied. "I don't mind going out there. And I believe I'll just hang around town for now."

Dud exchanged glances with Boyd, but said nothing.

After resting and getting himself cleaned up enough to be presentable for church, Dud left the hotel and walked outside. Many people were already heading in the direction of the church. He waved to Woody Harrison and his family as they walked by. Boyd trailed behind them, reminding Dud of a large dog.

"That boy would follow a pair of big t...," Dud stopped when he became aware that Kris Darst was standing next to him and watching his face with round eyes. "Howdy, Kris," he said hastily. "What are you up to?"

"Nothing much, Mr. Dud," Kris answered. He made no effort to speak again or move; he just stood silently watching Dud.

Dud shrugged. "You want to go to church with me and Miss Iris?" he asked.

Kris nodded his head. "Yes, sir, sure."

"All right, then, let's go fetch Miss Iris," Dud said. "First we have to make a stop at the café."

Iris was waiting for them on the boardinghouse gallery, smiling with the buoyancy of youth. Once at the church, Dud led them to a seat in the back; the Harrisons and Boyd sat a few rows ahead. From his place in the sanctuary, Dud could see part of Boyd's face when he turned to speak to Elizabeth and Annabelle. Dud felt sorry for him; he looked baffled, like a man out of his depth. Services started and Kris began to squirm.

"Settle down, boy," Dud said, and Kris became still.

During the services, Dud let his eyes wander over the congregation. Iris was by far the prettiest woman there, even better looking than the Harrison girls to Dud's mind. Evidently, other minds also thought so, because he caught a lot of male eyes light in her direction and stay there.

After the service, they filed out of the church, following the rest of the congregation to a wooden barrack some yards behind it.

"Did you like the service, Mr. Dud?" Iris asked.

"Too wishy-washy," Dud replied. "I've had buttermilk and cornbread that had more bite to it. Give me some hellfire and brimstone. I want my money's worth."

Iris grinned and they took their places in line for food, eventually finding a spot to sit across from the Harrisons. The surveyor arrived, and Boyd had to share Elizabeth's attention with him. Boyd did not say much, however, and let the Swede monopolize Elizabeth.

Kris, when he thought no one was looking, was stuffing rolls, biscuits, and anything else he could, inside his shirt. He asked if he could get seconds, and Dud told him yes. After eating more than Dud would have thought he could possibly hold, he asked to be excused so he could go outside and play with the other boys. Dud nodded, and Kris, looking oddly bumpy, hurriedly left the barrack.

When Dud and Iris finished eating, they talked for a while with the Harrisons before getting up to mingle with the rest of the crowd. Dud went to a back window and looked out. Sitting on the steps were the four Darst boys, devouring the food Kris had smuggled out and handing bits and pieces to Old Tom. Dud walked away from the window without comment and was stopped by Felix.

"How's it going, Dud?" he asked. "I heard you went to Thompson's place to ask him about gathering rocks for your house."

"That's right," Dud said.

"Heard his wife is bad off, too," Felix said.

Dud nodded. "Jesse's going out there at daybreak to see if he can do something for her, but the way Iris described her, I think it's too late for any kind of help."

"'Tis so," Felix said. "That Thompson is a hard nose. Did he talk to you about the poker game?"

Dud nodded. "I'm not much of a hand at poker," he said and saw Felix's face fall. "But I've got an uncle coming who likes a game now and then. He might want to play."

Felix's eyes glistened. "Is he any good?"

"He was," Dud answered. "Thompson already has his eye on Iris for his next wife. I've got to find that girl a good husband before she gets mixed up with somebody like that s.o.b."

Felix looked across the room where Iris stood, laughing and talking with several men. "I'm partial to her myself," he said.

Dud looked at him sharply. "I said a good husband, not an old fart like you."

Felix shrugged. "That man on her left is no good."

Dud looked. "What's wrong with him?"

Felix looked around, lowered his voice and said out of the corner of his mouth, "He drinks." He shook his head.

"We don't want him, then," Dud agreed. "What about the other fellow, the one with the brown hair?"

"No, mercy no," Felix said. "He lives off his widowed mother. Hasn't hit a lick of work since Old Tom sucked a teat."

As first one, then another approached Iris, Felix found fault with all of them. "I don't know the new fellow, though," he said about the latest arrival.

"I don't like him," Dud said. "He's got mean eyes. Let's get Iris and get out of here. We can go by the livery and see if we can talk old man Darst into playing his fiddle for us."

On his way to fetch Iris, Dud accidentally bumped into her landlady. Instead of giving him an evil stare as he expected when he said "excuse me, ma'am," she smiled and with a voice full of sugar said, "Well, hello, Mr. Washburn. It's so nice to see you."

Dud leaned forward and said softly, "You're going to die and go to hell for being such a hypocrite, old woman."

"Aw, go stuff your face in an ant bed," she growled. "And take that mangy cur with you."

"I'll have you know Old Tom hasn't got a speck of the mange on him," Dud said.

She waved her hand in front of her face. "Not him! Felix!"

SEVENTEEN

D<small>UD</small> <small>SPENT THE FOLLOWING WEEK CHOPPING TREES,</small> hauling rocks, searching for signs that might indicate a bull, and teaching Iris how to make change. Iris had not been joking when she said her schooling had been haphazard, and Dud had a hard time understanding how someone who could pick up the Hungarian language so quickly could have so much trouble counting out nickels and dimes. Nevertheless, he sat with her under the shed at a makeshift table, patiently handing her bills and admonishing her not to let the café owners cheat her out of her tips.

Iris scorched her first pot of beans and burned the cornbread, but she stuck with it, and soon she was mastering the art of campfire cooking. Despite her success, Dud worried about her skirts being so near an open flame and that she had to bend over constantly. Remembering the outdoor kitchens he had seen in Mexico, he drove the wagon seven miles to a brickyard an

Irishman from County Cork had started and bought a load of firebricks. He used some of these, and the first stones they hauled in, along with a wagon bed of sand and one of cement, to build a waist high rock oven under the shed with a grill to the side. Ugor Darst saw what he was doing and fashioned a metal door to cover the oven. Felix supervised.

"You can be clear across town, Felix," Dud said, "and hear cornbread batter being poured into the pan."

Iris talked often of her brothers, making Dud fidget in guilt. When Iris said she intended to ask everyone who came in the café if they had seen her brothers, Dud finally broke down and told her. She began to weep.

"Where are they buried?" she asked.

"On my ranch in South Texas," he said miserably.

Sniffing, Iris asked, "Will you take me to their graves when you leave here?"

"Of course," Dud said, feeling helpless. "I truly am sorry, Miss Iris."

She cried more, and he begged her to stop. "Would you prefer to go back to the boardinghouse?" he asked.

"No," she said emphatically. She looked at the ground, trying to stifle her sobs. "I want to visit the Darsts."

"Sure," Dud said, anything to stop her tears.

When they arrived at the stables, Iris ran into Zizi Darst's arms and began sobbing. Dud explained to the Darst boys what had happened, and they in turn told their mother. She held Iris, caressing her hair, crooning something that sounded similar to "poor baby" over and over again. Every man inside vacated the premises.

On Saturday morning, Dud went to the Iron Horse

Saloon to watch Felix's court. Smaller than the Gilded Lily, the Iron Horse sported an abundance of bullet holes in the walls and ceiling. Felix had a table set up in the back. People milled around, waiting for court to begin.

Felix walked in from a door in the back of the saloon wearing his inevitable brocade vest and top hat. He placed a Bible, a ledger, and a gavel on the table. Looking at the crowd, he picked up the gavel and banged on the table.

"Court is now in session," he announced and sat down.

Dud listened as Felix heard each case, surprised at his rudimentary knowledge of the law, despite his somewhat unorthodox approach to it. There was a squabble over a fence line being built too far into another's property and a saloon owner requesting compensation from railroad workers who demolished his establishment. He had hog-tied them the night before and brought them to court at gunpoint. They shamefacedly admitted their guilt and agreed to pay for damages and court costs, Felix adding that he would have their jobs if they did not. A tart with bleached hair and cheap perfume brought charges against a cowboy for forgetting his manners and dipping his finger into the icing on the cake for a lick.

Felix scratched his chin and thought for a minute before throwing the case out of court. "Madame, you are in a business. The haberdasher cannot bring charges against a customer who tries to feel the cloth before purchasing it. Case dismissed."

"Wait a minute, Judge," she screeched. "A fellow has no right to take a bite out of a biscuit he's thinking about buying."

A twitter of laughter ran through the saloon. Felix hit

the gavel on the table to restore order. "Madam," he said. "On the contrary, I often have. Now leave the courtroom before I fine you for contempt."

Dud suppressed a grin as the soiled dove, or as he thought in her case, a rather dirty hen, threw her grimy feathered boa across her shoulder, scowled at Felix and gave a hateful glare at the cowboy before exiting the saloon in a wave of exalted injury and entirely false innocence. Felix turned to the cowboy and said with all the severity of his position, "Keep your hands to yourself, bub, or I'll sic that painted cat on you next time."

After the civil cases came several couples who wished to be married. Felix rose majestically, and as each couple took turns standing in front of him, he performed the ceremony with a flowery language that far surpassed any Dud had ever heard. Once they said their "I do's," Felix would painstakingly write out a certificate of marriage in a convoluted hand on an equally elaborate certificate.

A man standing next to Dud nudged him, pointing his chin toward Felix. "Felix always has a crowd of people on Saturdays to be married," he said. "People come from all over to get them fancy certificates so they can hang them on their wall. Lots of people done been married for years get hitched again just to get one."

One couple asked Felix if he would predate their wedding. They already had three children. "What with one thing or another," the husband drawled, "we just never made it in to town to get it done."

"I think it's fairly obvious what the one thing or another was," Felix agreed dryly, looking at their offspring. "How old is the oldest child?"

"Six."

"All right then, I'll mark it back seven years," Felix said, and proceeded to dip his pen in the inkwell. They happily paid the fee, and Felix pocketed the money. Dud wondered just how legal these marriages were, but Felix carefully wrote down the names in his record book, and Dud had to admire his entrepreneurship.

Dud did not see Iris until that evening. As they walked to the café where she would begin her job, Iris said, "I'm going to save my money to buy a tombstone for my brothers after I pay you back for what I owe you."

"Miss Iris, you don't owe me a darned thing," Dud said. "You're just like family. If you want to save your money for a headstone, that's fine. I think you ought to buy yourself a little finery first, though, and then you can start worrying about other things."

In front of the café, Iris put her hand in his. "I'm scared, Mr. Dud."

"You don't have to do this," Dud reminded her.

She gave an understanding nod of her head, but her jaw firmed. She straightened her back and giving his hand a squeeze, went inside. Dud left her there, and then came back later with Boyd and Jesse to eat supper. Nervous, high-strung, yet eager to please, Iris soon had the place packed with men raring to be near her. When Dud stopped by at closing time to escort her to the boardinghouse, she was so exhausted she was in tears and could barely put one foot in front of the other. Dud thought he was going to have to carry her up the stairs and put her to bed.

The next morning, Dud and Boyd looked at another

section of property, one they had no interest in and only wanted to use as a blind. Jessie came back from the Thompson's in the late afternoon. By the time he arrived, he said, Mrs. Thompson was too far gone to save, and the best he could do was to browbeat a bottle of whiskey out of old man Thompson to ease her pain. He stayed with her until she died. Thompson said to pass the word around in town, but he planned on burying her that evening in a grave his cowhands had already dug.

Dud again escorted Iris to her job and went for the first time into the Gilded Lily Saloon. He pushed opened the batwing doors and entered, thinking for a new boom-town, it was not bad. The bar had varnish and behind it a large mirror with elaborate lamps. The tables and chairs for the most part were whole. A stage with velvet curtains stood at the far end of the room, next to it, an upright piano. On his left was an ornate staircase leading upstairs, and at a round table beside the stairs sat a middle-aged woman with plump arms and full breasts that overflowed from an opulent gown; her large eyes protruded above a broad nose and thick lips. She stared at him with interest.

He walked to her and said, "Lottie."

Her mouth curved into a wry smile. "Dud, have a seat," she said.

He sat down on the side allowing him to view the stage. Across the room, he spied Jesse sitting alone at a table, nursing a beer. He turned to Lottie. "You haven't changed a bit," he said, but noticed that her hair, once a natural auburn, now had a brassy hennaed look to it. "Gorgeous as ever."

"And you are as big a liar as ever," she said with a

laugh. "I heard you were in town and wondered when you would finally show your face."

"Aw, I've been busy, Lottie," he said.

Lottie motioned for one of the girls to bring Dud a beer. "So I've heard," she said. She looked at Dud with amused eyes. "So tell me, Dud, did you come to see me for old times' sake?"

Dud felt his face flush slightly. "I'm trying to walk the straight and narrow, Lottie. That boy sitting alone over there," Dud said, giving a nod in Jesse's direction and feeling thankful he had an excuse. "He's my nephew, and I promised my sister I wouldn't lead her boys into any mischief."

Lottie laughed at him. "That's all right, Dud. See that man over there in the black suit with the string tie? That's my Johnny."

Dud twisted and glanced at the man she referred to. Wearing a white ruffled shirt and a flashy ring, he looked like a tinhorn gambler. He also appeared about twenty years younger than Lottie. Dud turned back in his seat. "Nice looking kid. Looks a little green."

"Unripe fruit is always so firm, though. Are you sure it's your sister holding you back, or that young filly at the café?" Lottie asked.

"Noooo," Dud protested. "She's just a friend. I had hoped I could get one of my nephews interested in her," Dud said peevishly. "I don't know what's the matter with those boys."

Lottie looked in Jesse's direction and smirked. "He's got it bad for someone else."

That was what Dud was afraid of. "Tell me about this Suzette girl," he asked.

Lottie took a sip from her glass. "Nothing much to tell. She came in here about a month or so ago and said she would dance for tips and room and board. She insists on earning her money standing up and not on her back, but she knows the score, Dud. I've been in the business too long not to know. Somewhere, at sometime, she turned tricks. She's knows everything that goes on, but she walks around here like some kind of ice maiden, refusing to hardly speak."

"You don't know where she came from?" Dud asked, rubbing the center of his lips lightly with his forefinger.

"Nope. Like I said, she doesn't say more than three words to anyone. The only person she has anything to do with is the old black hag I hired to clean the place. Rashtah hates my guts, but for some reason, she's taken up with Suzette. She collects Suzette's tips for her, and when she goes to town, Rashtah is right there with her, ready to scream her head off if any man so much as speaks to Suzette."

Lottie looked at the stage with a frown of dissatisfaction. "I should have made her give me a cut of her tips."

"What do you care?" Dud asked. "You're packing them in." The tables had filled to capacity; Jesse now shared his with strangers. The back of the saloon bulged with men milling impatiently.

"Not if they're all like your nephew," Lottie snorted. "It's a rip-roaring night for him to have two beers."

A man with a derby perched crookedly on his head sat down at the piano and began to play. The talk around the room rose above it. In a little while, the men began to shout. The noise continued, rising to a crescendo, with feet stomping, voices hollering, hands clapping. The piano player valiantly played louder. Finally, when Dud thought the men in the room would storm the stage at any minute, the pianist began something that sounded like a drum roll. The audience immediately grew quiet, and all that could be heard in the room was the piano slipping into a soft melody and the sounds of the heavy breathing of women-hungry men.

The curtains opened. On the stage were a few props; an easy chair, a small table, a fake fireplace and mantle. A young woman wearing a velvet dress and plumed hat came onstage without looking at the audience, carrying a parasol, humming a tune as if she were a young wife just in from an afternoon of shopping. She took off her hat, and began to sing in a soft pleasant voice, hanging the hat on a rack near the chair. A petite girl, the coal black hair piled high on her head glistened and shone. She sang softly and walked across the room, removing her gloves and setting them on the table.

The piano player slipped into another tune, a slightly livelier one, and the young woman picked up the tempo, raising her voice a little. This time she removed her cape, walking back across the stage as she sang, placing the cape on the rack. Her slow, deliberate movements had every man in the saloon almost breathless. Dud looked across to Jesse and immediately saw the same thing Boyd had seen.

Jesse watched her, his face almost expressionless. To Dud and Boyd, however, who knew him so well, that blandness covered deep emotion. Dud felt sick—sick and sorry for Jesse. The piano player began yet a faster tune, and Dud turned his eyes back to the stage.

Suzette stood in the middle, singing sassier, pulling the long sleeves off her dress, leaving little puff sleeves at the top and showing bare white arms. Next off was a dickey that she twirled to the shouts of the crowd and threw onto the chair. She leaned forward and shook her bosom, the top half showing high and firm, the other half barely covered by green velvet and ruffles.

As each song hit a faster beat, Suzette's singing became increasingly interspersed with boisterous French words, and more of her clothes came off. Dud shifted in his chair, feeling slightly scandalized. He had never seen anything like it. When she detached the lower part of her skirt and showed her knees, he swallowed so hard, he almost choked. He would have enjoyed it, but he could not erase the picture of Jesse's face, even though he tried not to look at him. Suzette removed two large pins from her hair, and it cascaded down her shoulders. She flung it loose and rowdy yells stormed the building.

"Suzette, Suzette," the men roared. Some hollered words of love; one old man stood on his table and shouted, "Come to me, darling! You've awakened something that's been dead for years!" His companions pulled him down amidst riotous laughter.

Kicking her legs high, Suzette hopped and twirled while she sang a song in French that sounded raucous. The crowd around him went wild with cheers and whistles. Just when Dud thought she could not possibly do another thing, she turned around, flipped her skirt up and shook her black satin covered behind at the spectators. Dud thought he was going to have a heart attack.

She left the stage smiling and blowing kisses to the audience, yet Dud thought she did not really see them. Men flung cash at her, and the stage floor became littered with dollars and coins. A toothless old woman in a faded dress with a rag tied round her head went around with a basket, collecting tips. Dud put in a few coins, and saw Jesse throw in some too. Dud hoped they were not silver eagles. He looked away from the old woman and from his vantage point, was shocked to see Suzette hiding behind the curtains, her large dark, expressionless eyes searching the faces of the men in the saloon. She left almost immediately.

He turned to Lottie. "How in the world have you managed to keep her from getting run out of town and having this place closed down?"

Lottie laughed and rubbed her fingers against an opened palm. "You'd be surprised what a nice donation to the school or church will let me get by with. But in Suzette's case, it's because she's just selling the peep, not the whole chicken. She won't even speak to any man, woman, or child she meets on the street unless it's absolutely necessary. Rashtah follows her like a dog, and even she doesn't get much conversation out of that frigid French stick."

With Suzette gone, a stampede of men and women began up the stairs. Dud looked up in amazement. Lottie saw his expression and grinned. "The other girls are jealous of Suzette," she said. "But the end result makes them so much money they can't bitch too much."

Dud turned and saw Jesse get up and quietly leave the saloon. Lottie put her hand on his. "You know, Dud, a woman like me likes a little change in her diet every once in a while," she said, her white fingers running lightly across his rough, brown skin. "We once meant a lot to each other. You did me a tremendous favor once." When he did not immediately respond, she added, "Besides, I can always use the cash. The overhead on this place is killing me."

Dud rose from the table and leaned over to kiss her on the cheek, giving her a soft caress. "Not this trip, honey." Somebody else could pay for Johnny's upkeep.

Dud left the saloon, thinking about Iris. As he walked down the sidewalk toward the café, he did not find Jesse, but Felix appeared beside him.

"Did you see her?" he asked.

Dud nodded his head. "I thought I'd seen everything," he commented.

"It's the truth you're telling," Felix said.

Felix followed him to the café. Dud peered through the windows; the place was empty. He and Felix entered and sat down.

"Hi Mr. Dud, Mr. Felix," Iris said, looking tired but pleased to see them. "Can I get you something?"

"Bring us some pie and coffee," Dud said. "Not the whole pie, just a couple of pieces. Get yourself a piece, too, if you want one."

Iris brought them the coffee and then cut two slices of pie and brought it to the table. "Sit down, Miss Iris," Dud said.

Iris looked at the Ruby and Joe. "I'm not sure," she said.

"Miss Iris, there is not a soul in here," Dud said. "If someone comes in, you can get up." He rose and pulled out a chair for her, turning his head at the same time to shoot a hard look at Ruby that told her not to even think about saying a word. Ruby huffed and turned away, reaching for a snuff can under the counter.

Dud put his plate between them and shared with Iris. A few men trickled in, and then the dam broke and Iris was too busy to even speak to them. He haggled with Felix over who would pay. "We ought to at least go Dutch, as much money as you racked in this morning."

"Rent money, Dud, just rent money." But he paid his half and they left, going to the hotel lobby to sit and talk while Dud waited for Iris to get off work.

"Has your poker playing ringer come in yet?" Felix asked.

Dud glanced around the lobby to make sure Felix had not been overheard. "Hush, Felix," he hissed. "What do you care for anyway?"

Felix did not answer. Instead, he pushed his legs out in front of him and interlaced his fingers over his stomach. "I hope Iris doesn't get mixed-up with the last man who came in the café. He has too hot of a temper."

"Which one was he?" Dud asked.

"The one with the flat nose," Felix said. "He's missing a couple of teeth."

"I didn't have a very high opinion of him either," Dud said. "I think I'll mention to Iris the reason why he's missing a few teeth."

"No, they just rotted," Felix said.

"So what? She won't know the difference. Not unless your big mouth tells her."

"You have so little faith in me, friend," Felix countered.

Jesse entered the hotel lobby, saw them and began his way past the ornate Victorian furniture and potted plants. Just as he reached them and said hello, a bedraggled woman entered the hotel, keeping her head down as if in shame, but her eyes darted back and forth. She had a hungry look, and clutched her worn shawl around her bony shoulders as if keeping a snarling dog at bay. Spying

Jesse, she set her jaw in determination and approached them.

"Mr. Callahan?" she asked.

"Yes, ma'am," Jesse acknowledged.

She swallowed hard. "Forgive me for coming up to you like this, but I'm desperate. My man is down sick. He's got malaria, and he can't hold down any quinine; he keeps vomiting it up." She began to cry. "I don't know what to do. One of the Darst boys plays with my boy, and he told him that you were a good hand at doctoring." She lifted her eyes. "Please help us, mister. Please come look at him. There ain't a doctor here, and we ain't got money for one anyway. Please, mister. Please. We need my man. I don't know what will become of me and my children."

"Shh," Jesse said to soothe her. "You've got quinine, and it's helped before, but he just can't hold it down this time, is that it?"

She nodded through her tears.

"You got any lard in the house?" Jesse asked.

She nodded. "I've got a little bacon grease."

Jesse gave Dud a brief glance before continuing. "Go to the café and tell Miss Iris to give you about a quart of grease. Tell her me or my uncle will settle with her later. Take the grease, mix the quinine you have with it, and rub it all over your husband's body. The quinine will soak in through his skin."

Her eyes lifted in hope. "It will?"

"Yes," Jesse assured her. "You run to it, and if doesn't help, you can come back here and fetch me."

She covered her mouth and tried to hold back tears. "Thank you," she murmured. "Thank you."

"That's all right, now go on," Jesse said.

They watched her leave, and Dud turned to Jesse. "Where did you pick up that piece of knowledge?"

Jesse shrugged. "I don't know—somewhere." He thought for a moment. "You know, Uncle Dud, I've just realized, every time someone mentions horses or cattle, your ears and Boyd's prick up. But mine prick up when someone talks about remedies and doctoring."

EIGHTEEN

THEY HAD SUNDAY DINNER WITH THE HARRISONS. IRIS barely got out of bed and dressed in time to join them. Dud assured her she would soon get used to the work and urged her to sleep late on Monday morning. He found himself sleeping later, too, because he was keeping the same hours in order to see her home. Boyd and Jesse did not complain when he no longer got out of bed at three-thirty in the morning.

When Felix pressed her for an answer, Iris admitted she had garnered fifteen proposals those first few days. Yet she was at the lot on Pecan Street Monday afternoon, laughing, talking, and firing up her new outdoor oven. Dud sat near her, cutting shingles with a small ax while Boyd and Jesse began rocking the north wall of the house. The Darst boys came by and took turns cutting shingles and helping mix cement. They possessed an inherent knack with tools and horses, but refused payment for their work. Instead, Dud and Iris fed them, and after several days of this, he questioned Gabby when his brothers were out of earshot.

"You got enough to eat at home, boy?" he asked.

Gabby nodded. "Frank say we eat away from home as much as we can. My mama lost two babies already," he said, holding up two chubby fingers. "And Papa work hard and need lots of food. So this way, we help."

Other men came by, looking hungrily at the pot, making inane conversation. Dud looked over every one as a potential prospect for Iris, but none seemed good enough for her, so he managed to run most of them off without being too offensive. Felix was even better at getting rid of them than he was.

"Miss Iris," Dud said as he sat working on the shingles. "I can't let you keep doing all this cooking for us without doing something for you in return. At least let me keep paying your rent."

"No, Mr. Dud," she said, shaking her head. "My land-lady is always hinting things as it is, and it embarrasses me. I enjoy doing this, please don't worry about it."

"That old biddy," Dud groused. He said firmly, "I will pay for stabling your horse, no ifs, ands, or buts, about it. And when I eat at the café, I'm going to leave you as big a tip as I want, and don't you dare let Ruby and Joe get their hands on it."

Iris smiled. "Okay." She leaned down and kissed him on the cheek. "Thank you, Mr. Dud."

Dud blushed. There was nothing an old man liked better than to have a pretty girl give him a kiss. Well, there was that one other thing. He wondered if there was something wrong with his nephews. Here Iris was, so delectable every man who saw her wanted to eat her up, and Jesse was mooning over a French hussy and Boyd had fallen for an outrageous flirt who loved toying with men like a little girl playing at hopscotch. Dud decided it must be the Callahan in them.

He had to admit, however, that Boyd did not act the ardent suitor. After supper, the Harrisons often sat on their gallery until dark, where young men from around town and neighboring ranches joined them. If the air started to chill during the Indian summer evenings they were experiencing, everyone retired to the parlor, and Elizabeth would talk or play the piano. At ten o'clock promptly, Woody arose and started blowing out the lamps, signaling everyone to go home. Dud strolled by the house on one of those evenings, and as he approached, he saw Boyd in the group of men on the gallery, but he sat with his hat in his hands, leaning forward, arms resting on his legs, silent and patient, not really even looking at Elizabeth. Annabelle saw Dud and called to him. Although Woody and Nellie were in the house, Dud, feeling curious, joined them for a while.

Elizabeth reigned as the natural center of attention, and Dud spoke a few words to her, but did not try to enter the conversation. He was used to hearing Boyd say exactly what he thought when he thought it, if it pleased him to do so, and it puzzled Dud to see Boyd sitting wordless and not even glancing with appreciation at Elizabeth's overflowing bust and tiny waist. Yet Boyd sat there night after night. Dud caught Elizabeth peeking at Boyd several times in perplexity, and later aggravation. Whatever he was doing was driving Elizabeth to distraction, and Dud could only guess that Boyd was taking Jesse's jesting advice and playing hard to get.

"How does he do it?" Felix asked after witnessing it once himself.

Dud shook his head. "I don't know. I've never seen a man exhibit more patience and self-control. Makes me wonder if we're even kin."

Jesse kept his post in the saloon every evening Suzette sang, and otherwise stayed away from it when he realized Suzette never darkened the downstairs when she was not performing. He was more apt to see her walking in town during the day, head up, eyes straight ahead, but he did not dare presume to speak to her. In the meantime, despite his failure with Mrs. Thompson, he had multiple people approach him to cut out bullets or doctor sick animals.

Their lives were not completely taken up with lovesickness, much to Dud's relief. There seemed to be a marked increase in the number of parasols strolling up and down Pecan Street when Boyd and Jesse worked on their masonry. Indeed, as soon as a female was detected heading their way, their chests puffed out, and they managed to pick up the biggest rock or lift the heaviest board just as she walked by. Sometimes the girls stopped, and although he could not hear what was being said as he worked in the back of the lot, Dud could hear lots of giggles.

Poor Annabelle Harrison came several times a day, petting the dog, talking to Dud, helping Iris, but she most liked sitting on a large stone and watching Boyd and Jesse work, especially Boyd. Probably, Dud thought, because Boyd treated her as a young lady, not a child. Once Dud even heard Boyd chide Annabelle after she lisped baby-talk.

"Miss Annabelle, you're not an infant, don't be talking like one."

It relieved Dud to hear Boyd being his usual outspoken self with at least one Harrison. Nevertheless, Boyd only did it when none of the other family was around.

Sometimes Elizabeth would stroll by, pausing to chastise Annabelle for bothering them, although they told her repeatedly that Annabelle was welcome. Dud supposed it just gave her an excuse to stop.

"Do you really think she's right for Boyd?" Felix asked.

"No," Dud answered shortly. "But she's a decent woman who comes from an excellent family, so there is not much I can object to."

"That she's selfish and lazy?"

"Felix!" Dud said. "Don't you have something else to do?"

"Nope," Felix answered. "Not a thing. When is that ringer of yours coming in?"

"Any day now," Dud fumed. He wondered when Ponder would show up and hoped nothing had happened to him along the way. In the meantime, he and the boys went out in the mornings for lumber and stones, watching with careful eyes. While two gathered the materials they needed, the other would hunt through trees and shrubs, looking at large rocks and older trees for signs of arrows, bulls—any kind of markings whatsoever. Their eyes swept the hills and searched the ground for other signs, too. If anyone else was around, they could not find evidence of it. The flood waters had receded, but the debris it left made finding anything almost impossible.

Iris asked Dud if they might invite the Harrisons for

Sunday dinner since they had dined with them several times. The Darsts had already shown up frequently in the evenings to dance, talk, and sing. Dud smiled at her. "Anything you want, Miss Iris, honey," he said.

The weather remained mild after the torrential rains that happened before they arrived, and the repast with the Harrisons became like a picnic. Annabelle, proud knew her way around, set the table while her mother helped Iris with the finishing touches. Elizabeth sat and looked beautiful. Afterwards, Woody mentioned he had not been fishing in a while. Boyd immediately asked him if he would like to go that afternoon to the Yegua.

"Papa, may I go too?" Annabelle asked. "Please, Papa?"

Woody gave his daughter an indulgent smile. He turned to Boyd. "Do you mind if Annabelle goes too? She loves to hunt for arrowheads and things like that while I fish."

"No, not at all," Boyd said, smiling. He immediately grew serious and turned to Elizabeth. "Miss Elizabeth, would you care to go, too?"

"Oh, good heavens no," Elizabeth said. "Thank you kindly for the invitation, though. I'll just let you menfolks run along."

"Elizabeth has to watch her complexion," Annabelle said seriously. "Or else she freckles dreadfully."

"Annabelle!" Elizabeth said. She wiped the cross look from her face and smiled again at the men. "A girl does have to be careful."

Iris looked down at her tan hands and hid them behind her back. Dud felt like slapping his forehead. Why had he thought it would be the older daughter who liked collecting Indian artifacts? He should have taken one look at Elizabeth and realized she would never have an interest in anything remotely like that. It was a relief, though, because he no longer wanted to part with the Navajo blanket. Iris would need it on the trip back to see her brothers' graves.

"Woody, I don't know about her going," Nellie said, a worried look creasing her brows.

"Take Old Tom along," Dud offered. "Let him roam with Miss Annabelle so he can scare any critters away."

"I was just about to suggest that," Boyd said.

"See, dear," Woody said. "She'll be fine."

"All right," his wife reluctantly agreed.

"Miss Annabelle," Dud said, "If you felt like giving Old Tom a bath in the creek, I sure wouldn't object."

"May I, Mama? May I?" Annabelle begged. "It's warm enough still."

Nellie smiled and gave her permission. "Just don't go in higher than your knees," she warned.

Although Dud would have liked to do a little fishing, he and Jesse begged off going, and they sat talking with Elizabeth while Iris and Nellie washed dishes. The surveyor stopped by and offered to see Elizabeth and her mother home.

"Nice dinner," Dud told Iris after they left. "You cook better than my mama."

Iris grinned and blushed in happiness. "Mr. Dud, you're full of more blarney than Mr. Felix, but I sure appreciate the compliment," she said.

"No, Miss Iris," Jesse said. "I've never heard him say that to anybody, including my mama."

Dud laughed. "Come on, let's stroll downtown before

Iris has to go to work and see if we see any sign of Uncle Ponder."

They did not find Ponder, but they did meet Suzette walking on the opposite side of the street, holding herself regally aloof. Her cool eyes passed over Dud and paused briefly on Iris and Jesse before moving away.

"That girl scares the dickens out of me," Dud said, exaggerating in hopes of making Jesse give some kind of response. "I think she'd kill somebody in a heartbeat."

"No, Mr. Dud," Iris protested. "I don't agree with you. I think she's lonely and scared."

"What do you think, Jesse?" Dud questioned.

Jesse did not answer immediately and continued walking with his eyes ahead. Finally, he said in resignation, "I think it doesn't matter what I think."

Dud exchanged glances with Iris, but did not reply. He was not exactly happy, but it relieved him to see Jesse facing reality.

That night, Dud had an argument with Boyd over the Navajo blanket.

"You ought to give it to the poor kid," Boyd said. "She washed your stinking dog for you."

"Hell, you washed half of him," Dud said, knowing Boyd had bored of fishing and stopped to help Annabelle with the dog. "I want to keep the blanket. Iris will need it. I'll find something for Annabelle that will impress Elizabeth, I promise."

"Well, you should give Iris something," Boyd agreed. "You've got her practically sitting on your lap spooning food in your face, just like a dirty old man."

Dud drew in a deep breath and protested. "You don't have

any call to say things like that to me, boy. What about you? Every time I go looking for you, I bump into that poor little dimwit, Annabelle. The girl almost stoops to the ground to kiss your footprints, and her sister uses any excuse to come over and see how many muscles you're flexing that day!"

They stared at one another until Boyd burst into laughter. "All right, Uncle Dud."

Although Dud had told the boys labor on the house would be desultory, they were used to hard work, and in almost no time the walls were up and half the roof shingled. Late one afternoon, he and Jesse sat on stumps inside the house, discussing how to do the fireplace. Soon they would board the inside walls and put in a floor. Iris was at work; Boyd had left to get cleaned up for his vigil at the Harrisons; Felix was God only knew where, because most of the time he could be found with them, giving instructions, gossiping and eating Iris's cooking. All that remained besides Dud and Jesse was Old Tom, who lay next to Dud's feet.

A shadow crossed the room and Old Tom lifted his head, but did not bark. Dud looked at the doorway, shocked to see Suzette standing in it, dressed in a new purple satin gown with elaborate white silk ruffles at her neck and cuffs, a small purple hat containing a white plume perched rakishly on her head. She looked down at them imperiously while holding a small kitten in her hands. Jesse sat frozen and only rose when Dud did.

"Come in, Miss Suzette," Dud said, as if it was the most natural thing in the world to have her arrive at their unfinished house dressed like the queen of France. "Have a seat, and tell us what we can do for you."

She entered, looking around without a trace of self-consciousness. Rashtah followed her in. When Suzette reached Jesse, she stopped and held out the kitten.

"It is my kitten," she said. "There is something wrong with her ears. She scratches all the time and shakes her head."

Jesse gulped and took the kitten into his hands. Dud noticed they shook slightly, but stopped when he began to examine the feline. "It's a he, not a she," he said automatically. "He has ear mites—tiny little insects in his ears."

"You can fix, yes?" she asked.

Jesse nodded, unable to look her in the face. "We'll need some sweet oil from the drugstore."

She turned. "Rashtah?"

Rashtah immediately left the house. Suzette turned back to Jesse. "Rashtah will fetch it."

"Sit down," Dud said, offering her his stump. While she positioned her skirts and sat down delicately, Jesse shot Dud a silent plea not to leave. Dud leaned against the closest wall to watch and let Jesse have the other stump, which he did not take. They stood silent for several seconds. Finally, with a wave of her lace handkerchief, Suzette told them to please continue what they were doing.

Dud walked to the other wall. "I think we ought to put it here," he told Jesse. Jesse gave him a blank stare.

"It will warm the living room, and maybe some of the heat will go into the bedroom."

"Oh, yes," Jesse said, relief crossing his face as Dud's meaning finally sunk in.

"What do you think, Miss Suzette?" Dud said. "Do you think this is a good spot for a fireplace?" He had yet to meet a woman who did not have an opinion about the inside of a house, but for an instant, he thought Suzette would refuse to answer. Finally, taking a slight breath, she looked behind Dud. "That is the bedroom, yes?" Dud nodded.

"I think," she said slowly, as if not used to conversing. "I think you should put in a double fireplace—one for the living area and one behind it in the bedroom." She turned her head away as if she had spoken all she was going to say, her hands continuing to caress the kitten.

Dud turned to Jesse. "What do you think? It sounds like a good idea, but could we use the same flue? A chimney that won't draw is worthless."

"I've seen it, but don't know how they did the flue either," Jesse admitted. "Do you think that Irishman you bought the bricks from would know?"

Dud rubbed his chin, looking at the imaginary wall between the living area and bedroom. "I hate to have to drive all that way out there, and then he might not know or be the rear end of a horse and not tell me."

Rashtah returned with a small bottle of sweet oil. Suzette spoke a few rapid sentences to her in French. Rashtah responded with a few melodious words, Creole, Dud thought, and Suzette turned to them. "The man who used your quinine cure was formerly a brick mason. When he is better, he will come instruct you. He cannot lift rocks, however."

"Uh, thank you, ma'am," Dud said. He looked at Jesse, but Jesse still would not meet Suzette's eyes. He managed to walk forward and take the kitten from her hands.

"I need a towel, Uncle Dud," he said, stroking the pet to calm it.

Dud nodded and found one that was not too encrusted

with dried cement. Jesse took it and expertly wrapped the cat, leaving nothing but the head exposed. Rashtah opened the bottle of sweet oil, and he poured a small amount in each of the unwilling animal's ears, rubbing it in with his fingers.

"He'll need it done again in a few days," he said, "as more mites are hatched."

Suzette nodded. "I will return." She reached into her pocket and brought out a small beaded purse while Jesse disentangled the kitten. "I will pay you, yes?" she said.

Jesse raised his head, this time looking her in the face, and replied with a firm, "No."

She gazed at him. "You disapprove of me? My money is no good because you think I am bad?"

"I think you are the most beautiful creature I have ever seen," Jesse said matter-of-factly, continuing to stare at her.

She dropped her eyes. "I cannot thank you publicly," she said. "Someone might shoot you in the back in jealousy. When you see me touch my cheek like this," she said, lightly putting her index finger to her cheek, "you will know that is my signal to you." She removed the kitten from his hands, placing it against her cheek briefly. "I think my kitten does not have *les* ear mites. I think he has *une* bad *maladie* that will require my return and much treatment. Rashtah will remove the label from the bottle of sweet oil."

"Uh, yes, ma'am," Jesse said, and he and Dud followed the two women to the door. As they stepped outside, they saw a familiar figure coming their way. Suzette stopped and turned to them.

"It is the man you have sent for, yes? The man who will win for you the land in the haunted hills?"

Dud did not bother to hide his shock. "Is that what everyone is saying? Is that what people think?"

"No," she replied. "Just me. Rashtah overheard Lottie and Johnny as they spoke of it. They know you sent for someone when you heard about the game of poker. They think Felix put it up to you."

"Felix?" Dud said, puzzled. "What's he got to do with it?"

"You must ask him," Suzette said, and lifting her head, sashayed away with Rashtah following. When they passed Ponder, Suzette acted as if she intended to sail right past him, but Ponder tipped his hat and smiled. Suzette surprised Dud by slowing down, as if almost against her will, and she returned his smile. Rashtah eyed Ponder curiously before giving a toothless grin. Nodding to the ladies, Ponder put his hat back on. Just before he reached Dud, he spit a stream of tobacco juice.

"I have just three things to say," Ponder announced. "I want a horse; walking is for old ladies and little children. Why have you summoned me to this Godforsaken town, and who was that beautiful bag of goods and what was she doing here?"

"You said a lot more than three things," Dud said. "I don't know exactly who she is or where she came from, but she sure doesn't act like a frigid iceberg in my book." More like a smoldering volcano. He shook his head. Just when he thought Jesse might be getting over her, the dark-haired little vixen had to come over and light a match to his wick.

"Come on in, Uncle Ponder," Dud said. "I'll explain. And where is the other cowhand? I sent for two of you."

"I'm not senile yet, Dud," Ponder grouched. "I don't need an escort."

Dud brushed it aside. The important thing was that Ponder had made it. Dud did not waste too much time explaining about Suzette; poker was what he was interested in.

"You made me come all the way up here to this shithole for what?!" Ponder roared in response. "Have you lost your mind?"

Dud took a deep breath and counted to ten. "I think the treasure is buried on that sorry piece of land," he said, spelling it out, "and the only way I can get it out of there in good conscience is for you to win that property for me in a poker game."

"Hell, no, dunderhead!" Ponder said. "You're crazy. Don't even think about it. Find somebody else."

"There is nobody else!" Dud yelled. "You have to try."

"Dud, I have not played a serious card game in almost twenty years."

"Don't worry about it. It's just like riding a horse," Dud said. "It will come back to you." He hoped.

NINETEEN

DUD TOOK PONDER TO THE CAFÉ FOR SUPPER. IRIS SMILED, but got called away by a hungry patron demanding more gravy. Ponder turned to Dud and gave him a suspicious stare.

"I knew you were always partial to blondes, Dud," he said, "but I never knew you to chase after the freshly weaned ones before."

"I'm not chasing her!" Dud said. Taking a deep breath, he continued. "She's just a sweet young woman who latched onto us because she doesn't know anybody else. What would you have me do? Throw her to the wolves? Besides, I explained all that to you or has it already slipped your mind?"

Instead of retorting, Ponder ruminated on what he said. Dud expected him to launch into a long diatribe, but Ponder surprised him by asking, "Can she cook?"

"A lot better than you can," he replied shortly.

"Hmm. Where are Boyd and Jesse?" Ponder asked. "I want to talk to them."

"Boyd's sitting like a mute over at the Harrisons', and Jesse is mooning around, hoping Suzette will come by and drop him a crumb," Dud replied. He took his attention away from Ponder and watched the other customers. A good-looking young buck with a full head of dark hair kept calling Iris over to his table. She gave him the same cordial treatment she gave everyone. Dud watched him, however, weighing whether the young man would be good marriage material for Iris. He decided definitely not, and tried to quiet a niggling little voice in his head that said his main dislike was that head of luxuriant thick hair. Either way, Dud kept one hand free and close to his gun belt just in case, but the man kept his hands, if not his comments, to himself.

"If she's just a friend, Dud," Ponder said, innocent as a baby, "let her have a chance with that boy. He ain't no different than you were at that age."

"Why the hell do you think I'm so worried about her?" Dud said, but he rose anyway. "All right, come on, I'll take you back to the hotel."

"I ain't sleeping in no hotel when you've got a perfectly fine home for me to bed down in," Ponder protested. "I just want a horse."

"Okay!" Dud said, throwing money on the table and not caring if Ponder pitched a fit over the amount. "I ain't gonna argue with you over where you sleep."

Once outside, a group of young cowpunchers were hanging around the front of the surveyor's office. A tall, toothy boy poked a round-faced young man sitting on the bench Dud usually sat at while waiting for Iris.

"Get up, you manner-less shifty outfit," he said with a wide grin. "That's old man Washburn's waiting bench."

They broke out in loud guffaws. As he walked through the crowd, Dud said, "All right, all right. Let an old man pass." He tensed, ready for a fight if need be, but they laughed uproariously again, and he and Ponder continued without incident.

Dud led Ponder to the livery and got a horse for him. He would try to find an old army cot so Ponder would not have to sleep on the dirt floor. Amid protests that there was no need for a guide, he shepherded Ponder back to the house and left him there for the night. He gave a casual look through town for Felix, but did not feel like going through all the bars so he gave up the search. Instead, he went to the stables and talked to the Darsts. A young cowboy with a bright new bandana came in and began to question him about cattle.

"I heard you was a real good cattleman, Mr. Washburn," he said. "I thought maybe you could give me some pointers."

At first Dud hesitated, but the tender-faced boy seemed so serious, Dud soon found himself talking about cattle and ranching. He tried to keep track of the time, but whenever he made to look at his pocket watch, he was asked another question, and it blew his ego up a little to be able to instruct such a willing listener.

"Gol durn, them coyotes are getting close," Ugor groused as the yaps and howls grew louder.

Dud stopped talking, suddenly realizing something was wrong. Before he could make a move, however, Kris came running into the stables.

"Mr. Dud! The café closed early. Some man is bothering Miss Iris."

Dud galvanized into action. Realizing it would be

faster to run to the café than to bridle a horse, Dud left the building with Kris at his heels.

"Hell fire, I was set up," Dud murmured as he raced to the café.

In the dim light of the street lanterns, Dud saw Iris trying to pull away from a man. As he neared, Dud recognized the dark-haired buck who had been in the café earlier.

"I don't want to go walking with you," Iris cried, struggling as the man tugged on her arm.

Dud walked behind him and popped him in the head with the butt of his pistol. The cowboy let go of Iris and sank to his knees, holding the back of his neck and looking befuddled.

"I knew you were trouble the minute I laid eyes on you," Dud said to the kneeling man. "The next time you bother this girl, it will be a bullet hitting the side of your head." Dud turned and took Iris by the arm. "Come on, Miss Iris, I'll take you home. I'm sorry I'm late—I let one of this hombre's buddies detain me," he said, ashamed he had let someone play on his ego and trick him. Or maybe the comment about old man Washburn's waiting bench had stung him more than he realized.

"That's okay, Mr. Dud," Iris said smiling through teary eyes and taking deep breaths. "You're here now."

At the boardinghouse, Iris's landlady met them at the door. "About time you brought her home," she snapped. "What are you trying to do, ruin her reputation?"

"Shut up, you old biddy," Dud said. Iris took his hand, squeezed it and smiled before running into the house and up the stairs.

"Well, what are you standing there for?" the landlady

said. "Go home! Or back to whatever hole you crawled out of." And she slammed the door in his face.

"Aw, get on your broom and fly away," Dud muttered as he turned and walked down the steps, forgetting that Kris Darst was dogging his steps.

"Yeah, get on your broom and fly away," Kris mimicked at the closed door and laughed.

Dud placed his fingers on Kris's bare head and rubbed his hair. "I can see right now I'm going to have to watch my language."

As they drew near the hotel, Dud said, "Kris, go straight home."

"Yes, sir, Mr. Dud," Kris agreed. "See you tomorrow."

Dud bid him farewell and watched as the small boy raced up the street, dodging in and out of the shadows. Before Dud reached the hotel entrance, he met Felix on his way to the small room he rented above the surveyor's office. He smelled of whiskey and cigars, walking with unsteady steps.

"Where have you been?" Dud asked. "I want to talk to you."

Felix stopped, raised himself up and stood swaying. "I've been getting drunk. I saw the man you brought in to play Thompson, and the situation looks utterly, completely, and absolutely hopeless. I thought there was nothing left to do but drown my sorrows in the fruit of the vine." He nodded his head, and Dud caught him to keep him from falling on his face.

"Get over here," Dud said, pulling him into the alley between the hotel and surveyor's office. He leaned Felix against the wall to keep him from toppling. "Now listen to me, you old drunk. The minute I came to town, you latched on to me like hair on a hide. You tell me why this poker game is so important to you and what Lottie and Johnny have to do with it."

Felix's head hung down, nodding like a puppet. "Dud, Dud, Dud," he muttered. "I believed from the first time I laid eyes on you that if anyone could bring it off, you could. Then you said you didn't play poker, then you brought in a dribbling old coot who can't even hold his own urine, much less a hand of cards. Oh merciful Jesus, I thought you could do it."

"Do what?" Dud demanded, shaking him.

Felix finally raised his head and looked him in the eyes. "Win the Gilded Lily back for me."

Dud looked around them, peering into the street. He brought his eyes back to Felix. "What are you talking about?"

"I lost it," Felix said, weeping the tears of a drunk.

Dud took him by the elbow. "Come on, I'm going to pour some coffee into you. You got any in your room upstairs?"

Felix nodded and allowed Dud to haul him up the stairs. Dud shoved the door open and plopped Felix down on a small bed by a window overlooking the street. It took several minutes to get a fire roaring in the small potbellied stove and a few more to find the coffee. A pail stood nearby; Dud picked it up, sniffed it and hoped it was drinking water.

While Felix fell asleep and snored, Dud sat in a chair and waited for the coffee to boil. When the coffee was ready, having no mercy, Dud forced him awake and shoved a cup in his hand. After sputtering and spitting, Felix finally grew sober enough to talk straight.

The story was not unusual. A hot poker game and everything Felix had saved for years went down to the three aces held in Seth Thompson's hand.

"It was that bust-head whiskey," Felix moaned. "I had no idea it could be so potent, and they just kept pouring it in me."

"Felix," Dud said. "Start over from the beginning."

Felix took another gulp of the scalding coffee. Taking a deep breath, he began. "I was a policeman on a beat back East. I used to make my rounds and go inside some of the taverns, checking things out. My old woman left me, taking the boy with her." He gave Dud a pitiful look of misery. "She turned the boy against me. Do you know what's it's like to have your own flesh and blood sneer at you?"

"No," Dud said. "But if my first wife and I had had a child together, I have a feeling I would have found out."

Felix nodded in commiseration. "Aye. After that, I would get so lonely, and look at the people in the taverns, and I'd think, that's what I'd like. I'd like to go out West and have a little place of me own.

"I saved and scrimped until I finally had enough. I came out here and built the Gilded Lily. It was a nice little place then, Dud. You would have liked it. But I made the mistake of playing cards. Lottie was new to town, working at the Iron Horse, but she already had Seth Thompson twisted around her finger. She kept pouring that bootleg liquor down my gullet. He won it from me in my befuddled state and sold it to her at a ridiculously low price, thinking she would favor him and become his mistress. She added the upstairs, brought in all the whores and Johnny with them. She tries to convince Thompson that Johnny is just a fixture to keep the gossip down about the two of them. She doesn't want to lose Thompson's patronage entirely. I think he realizes deep down he has been made a fool of. He just doesn't want to admit it."

"So you've been saving again to try to get it back?" Dud asked.

"I know it's stupid, Dud," Felix admitted. "I'm ten times happier being a minor little official than I ever was a saloon owner. It's the best thing that could have happened to me, and yet, it galls me to be taken like that."

"And you thought I could win it back and sell it to you, is that it?"

Felix nodded, hanging his head miserably.

"Felix, Lottie is no fool. She's not going to let Johnny put the Gilded Lily up in another game. Johnny doesn't mean that much to her."

"Oh, but yes he does," Felix said, looking up. "And you don't know how bad his gambling compulsion is. He's already been after Lottie to bring opium in and addict the girls to it as a means of raising more cash for his games. But Lottie's resisting. She knows I'll raise a hell of a stink if she does, and she can't grease her way out of that throwing money around."

Dud did not answer, but sat staring through the isinglass of the stove at the fire flickering inside. He only half listened as Felix moaned again about Ponder. "And here I was believing there might be a chance," he concluded.

"Don't knock Ponder yet, Felix," Dud said. "Fifteen years ago, he was the best." He rose to leave. "Sleep it off, Felix, and then come by the house tomorrow. We've got to get Ponder in shape, and we'll need your help."

"All right," Felix agreed. As Dud reached the door,

219

Felix added, "I'm not really blaming Seth Thompson. He was and is an unhappy, lonely man. He just went after the wrong woman."

"Yeah," Dud agreed as he opened the door. "We've all done that."

The next day, Dud argued with Ugor Darst over the boys. He wanted their help every day after school. He had little more than two weeks to get Ponder in poker playing condition, which meant that almost every waking moment Ponder had to be playing cards with somebody. The work on the house could come to a standstill, but that would cause gossip and keep them from finishing the roof, something Dud wanted done. Ponder already insisted on sleeping in the unfinished house, and Boyd had declared he thought he should stay with Ponder. Jesse had not offered to join them, and Dud knew he wanted to stay at the hotel because it was closer to Suzette. He did not want to stay at the rock house either; the hotel was near the boardinghouse.

Ugor had agreed the boys could help with the house as long as he did not need them at the stables, and after discussing it with Zizi, said they could also help Ponder with his card playing. However, he refused cash or to allow Dud to buy them new clothes. Dud rebelled.

"If I can't pay them, then I don't want them there at all. I don't want to be accused of taking advantage of my friends," he said. "Especially little kids."

"No, no," Ugor said. "They with you, they stay out of trouble."

Dud put his hands on his hips. "Darst, you won't let me pay them cash money, you old Hungarian hardhead, but you've got to let me do something for them. They need new outfits, especially shoes."

Zizi clutched her husband's sleeve and whispered something to him. Ugor stared at Dud. "What you do with that house when you leave here?"

"Sell it, I don't know. Why?" Dud asked.

"My wife, she like that house," Ugor said. "Let boys work on house, when you leave, you sell to me and carry note. I send money every month for house."

"That's a deal as long as you let me buy them new clothes," Dud said.

Ugor laughed. "Ha, ha, very funny. Maybe Hungarians not only hardheads, eh?" He looked at his wife and shrugged his shoulders. "All right, Washburn, you buy clothes, you sell house to us, and boys work hard for you. Also, you allow me to make new knives for you and your nephews. Yours is no good. Agreed?"

Dud opened his mouth to protest that there was not a darn thing wrong with his knife except that the blade had a few nicks and was wearing a little thin, but he stopped himself and grinned. "Agreed," he said.

Nevertheless, Dud fretted about money going out the door while none was coming in. He told himself repeatedly that he had already earned plenty and what he was doing was an investment in the future. He could not count on buried treasure being there, but the women of Tie Town were real.

"But merciful Jesus," he muttered under his breath, "I think I'm speculating on a French whore and a beautiful, but next to worthless, redhead."

He met Elizabeth and Annabelle on his search for something that would keep Ponder off the ground at night. He stopped on the sidewalk, removed his hat, and smiled at the girls.

"Howdy, Mr. Dud," Annabelle said cheerfully. "We've been shopping."

"That's nice, Miss Annabelle," Dud said.

Elizabeth gave her brilliant smile, the one that showed her perfect teeth. She looked at Annabelle. "You take the packages and run along home, Annabelle. I'll be behind you in a minute."

"Yes, Sister," Annabelle said, and obediently started toward home.

After Annabelle had walked away from them, Elizabeth lowered her voice and leaned closer to Dud. "Whomever I marry must understand that Annabelle is my responsibility, Mr. Washburn. God has given me an obligation toward my sister, and I shall not shirk my duty."

She spoke so sanctimoniously, Dud felt the sudden urge to shake her, and yet, at the same time, he realized Elizabeth was completely sincere. No matter what happened, she would take care of Annabelle. "Yes, ma'am, Miss Elizabeth," Dud said. "I think we all realize that, and we admire you for it."

She fluttered her eyelashes and smiled at him. "Thank you, Mr. Washburn. I just thought it was something that needed to be said."

He assured her he understood and after she left, he stood for a moment watching as she walked away. He suddenly felt sorry for her—doomed by circumstances to forget about her own desires and make the best possible match for the sake of her family. Unable to enjoy sunshine for fear of freckling and ruining her creamy complexion, discouraged by her mother from work because it might roughen her tender skin, strapped into a corset with strings pulled so tight she could hardly breath, all so she could be attractive enough to snare a prize catch. But Boyd had responsibilities, too, and Dud wondered if he had explained them to Elizabeth.

TWENTY

"WASHBURN!"

Dud turned. He had just enough time to recognize the young man who had been sitting on the surveyor's bench the previous evening before he had to block a punch. The young man jabbed him in the stomach, knocking half the air out of him. Mad, Dud came back swinging, and soon they were rolling in the streets, fighting. Old Tom came as close as he dared, barking and baring his fangs, just waiting and hoping for the signal from Dud to join in.

Tiring, Dud managed to rise to his feet. Kicking his assailant, he backed away a few steps. He pulled his pistol and as the young man got on his feet, Dud let off a few shots, making him dance.

"What the hell are you doing?" he cried to Dud. "Stop before you shoot my foot off!"

"Well, what the hell are you doing clouting me out the blue?" Dud demanded, holding his gun, but no longer aiming it. "What'd I do to you?"

The cowboy picked up his hat and dusted it against his

pants sheepishly. "I'm in love with Miss Iris," he confessed, looking down at the ground in boyish bashfulness.

"Well, tell her," Dud said. "Don't tell me. She's a free woman."

"Aw shucks, mister," the young man said. "I'd rather fight you than do that."

"Fighting me ain't gonna do no good," Dud said. "It will just make her mad."

"Yeah," the young cowboy agreed. "Can I buy you a drink to make it up to you?"

"I'll have to catch you later," Dud said. "I've got an errand to run."

He left the young cowboy and found a man with half-a-dozen army cots for sale. Dud did not want that many, but the fellow was on his way out of town to escape an irate husband who objected to his wife being bounced up and down on them. Dud took the cots to the house on Pecan Street, dumping them in a corner. He looked up and called to Boyd and Jesse as they hammered on the roof.

"Where's Uncle Ponder?"

Boyd pointed his hammer toward the shed.

Going back outside, Dud found Mike and Kris forming a line by the ladder, passing shingles up to Boyd and Jesse as they were needed. Nearby, Frank separated stones, piling them by size as Gabby tried to help.

"You boys be careful of snakes," Dud warned.

"Yes sir, Mr. Dud," they said in chorus.

Ponder sat conversing with Iris under the shed. Zizi had brought food over, as she often did, to cook with Iris. While Ponder sat in a nearby chair talking, Iris and Zizi stirred food in pots and checked on more in the oven. Iris turned, saw Dud and smiled. "Hello, Mr. Dud," she said cheerily. When he reached her, she took a second look. "Why is your lip bleeding?" she asked. "And there's a big bruise coming up on your cheek."

"Oh, I accidentally ran into someone's hand," he said. "What are you cooking?"

Iris made a face. She wet a towel and dabbing his lip said, "Beans and salt pork. I charged them at the store like you said I could. We're making cornbread, too."

"That's mighty sweet of you, honey, but you ought not be putting yourself out—you've got to work tonight," Dud said.

"That's okay. This is where all the fun is anyway," she answered. "Zizi is excited because you agreed to sell them the house."

Zizi gave him a shy smile. She glanced at Ponder. She lowered her head and stirred the beans again; as if afraid she might be intruding.

"I'm glad you are happy about it, ma'am," Dud said, unsure if she could even understand him. He called to Boyd and Jesse. "Boys! Get down off the roof! It's time to get Uncle Ponder back into the poker playing frame of mind."

Ponder sighed, looked away and shook his head. "Come on, Uncle Ponder," Dud said, ignoring the frown. "Let's move over in the corner."

They went to an old round table Dud had bought from the Iron Horse and repaired. His patch job would not pass inspection in any woman's parlor, but it was good enough for them. The partial wall hid them from view of anyone passing by, but allowed them to be seen by Iris and Zizi. Dud instructed the Darst boys to stay back for the time being while he, Boyd, and Jesse sat down with Ponder. After getting situated, he handed Ponder a new deck of cards. "All right, Uncle Ponder, let's get started."

Ponder took the deck in his long slender fingers. Looking down on the brown skin of Ponder's hands, Dud suddenly noticed just how wrinkled they had become. He looked up, startled to see uncertainty on Ponder's face. Ponder attempted to shuffle the cards, but his fingers did not want to cooperate. He tried again, but the unyielding deck stayed stuck in clumps.

Dud froze. He moved his eyes upward and saw the same rigid look of shock reflected on Boyd's and Jesse's faces. They knew Ponder would be rusty, but had no idea how much. At the same time, Dud became aware that Iris and Zizi had crept closer.

Ponder did not take his eyes from the cards, but the atmosphere grew so thick, Dud knew he felt it. Ponder's hands shook, but he tried again, even harder this time, and the cards shot all over the table. His shoulders slumped slightly; otherwise, he went as stiff as the rest of them.

Iris came over to Ponder, placing her hand on his shoulder. She leaned close to his ear and spoke almost in a whisper. "Uncle Ponder," she said softly. "Would you teach me and Zizi how to play cards instead? We would really like to learn."

Ponder looked up at Iris; he stared at her and moved his eyes to Zizi. Her eyes went round; her mouth drooped open, and she pointed her finger at her chest, saying something in Hungarian.

"Sure, Zizi," Iris said. "Uncle Ponder will teach us. It will help you learn English."

Dud, Boyd, and Jesse shot out of their chairs in relief and held them out to the women. Iris sat down on Ponder's left, but Zizi stuck to Iris's right.

Walking away, Dud made a motion to Boyd and Jesse, and they disappeared. The Darst boys knew something was wrong, but did not know exactly what. Dud looked back. Ponder sat slowly shuffling the deck, talking. Iris was nodding and hanging on to every word. Zizi, with lips parted, stared at Ponder in awe. Even though he was old with fumbling fingers, Dud guessed Ponder still cut a dashing cowboy figure to someone like Zizi.

Dud turned to the Darst boys. "Come on, let's rig us a table. You might as well start learning, too." He added under his breath, "Although a fat lot of good it might do."

They put up another makeshift table close to Iris's stove, sitting down on upturned kegs and crates. Picking up a deck of cards, Dud looked around the table. Frank, Mike, and Kris sat facing him, while Gabby stood next to Frank. Four pairs of wide dark eyes stared at him trustingly, causing Dud to falter momentarily. He rolled his eyes heavenward, sending up a silent prayer to be saved from the fires of hell, or at least the wrath of his sister if she found out he was teaching little boys how to play poker.

Dud looked down at the small heap of matches on the table. "We're going to need more
matches."

"Gabby can go," Frank spoke up. "Gabby is good at running errands."

Gabby nodded enthusiastically, and Dud realized Frank wanted Gabby to have new clothes, too.

"All right, boy," Dud said. "Go to the general store and

get five big boxes of matches. Tell them to put it on my bill."

Dud spent the next several hours patiently playing and explaining the rules of poker to the boys. He cast surreptitious glances at Ponder, noting in relief that Ponder's fingers had limbered somewhat. Every so often, either Iris or Zizi would jump up and go to the stove to check on their food.

"We're still not out of the woods yet," Dud murmured in worry. "Not by a long shot."

"What did you say, Mr. Dud?" Kris asked.

"I said there is not much that can beat the smell of beans and onions simmering on the stove. I'm sorry, Mike, but four of a kind beats a full house."

"What beats the smell of beans and onions cooking then, Mr. Dud?" Frank asked.

Dud shuffled the cards and said, "Oh, women do, I reckon."

The boys burst into laughter, and Iris said, "Hey, what's so funny over there?"

"Mr. Dud is being fa-ce-tious," Mike said, pronouncing the word carefully. "Mr. Felix says Mr. Dud is always being facetious."

Dud looked up from the table and saw Felix coming toward them. "Speak of the devil," he said. "Dinner must be ready."

Ponder looked up, surprised. "Are those beans already done?" he asked.

Iris nodded. "I soaked them in salt water last night."

"I'm surprised that spavined-faced mare at the boardinghouse let you have the water to soak them in," Dud said.

"Miss Iris cooks better than Mr. Dud's mama," Kris said. "He said so."

Boyd and Jesse strolled back with Elizabeth and Annabelle between them. Annabelle set about to help find enough mismatched plates, saucers, and cups to serve food in, while Elizabeth flirted with the boys. Zizi prepared a pie plate heaping with food to take to Ugor, but the boys stayed behind.

When they finished eating, Dud told Iris if she wanted to take a short nap on one of the cots in the house, he would awaken her in time for work. Annabelle offered to wash dishes, and Boyd, used to a houseful of sisters and probably homesick, helped her. After a short time, Dud woke Iris, and he and the Darst boys walked with her. Leaving Iris at the café where she would probably receive five marriage proposals and numerous other kinds slyly spoken in innuendo, Dud took the boys to the dry goods store.

"What about Gabby?" Frank asked. "Can Gabby have new clothes too?"

"Sure," Dud said. "He's doing his part, too."

The boys picked their own outfits—as close to replicas of Boyd's and Jesse's as they could get. Frank and Mike protested when Dud also told Kris to choose a Stetson.

"He's too little," Frank said. "Yes, Mr. Dud," Mike agreed. "None of the other boys his age wears a hat; they all have caps."

"No," Dud said firmly. "Kris deserves a hat."

The man who took the quinine cure came early in the week and with his help, the fireplaces went up with remarkable speed, despite being one man short because someone had to be playing cards with Ponder every waking moment. Relentless in their efforts, every so often they would nevertheless have to help Ponder up and force him to hike the streets to keep limber. He complained about it bitterly.

"I'm sick in tarnation of all this walking."

"Hush up, old man," Dud scolded. "If we didn't make you stagger around a little bit, you'd get so stove up; we'd never get the kinks out of your back."

It took hours of play before the rust left Ponder's game. After starting with Iris and Zizi, he played with the Darst boys. As children, the boys had little talent or understanding of the game, but Ponder acted as if they were just as worthy adversaries as any other poker playing cowboys he had ever met, which they adored. The language barrier hindered Zizi, but Ponder somehow managed to communicate with her through the cards.

Although Thompson and his crowd preferred draw poker instead of the usual faro, in addition to those two games, Ponder taught Iris three card monte and stud poker. Dud felt more guilt over watching Iris handling cards than he did the Darst boys, but she enjoyed playing. Felix came every day. At first skeptical of Ponder's abilities, Felix grudgingly began to admit Ponder was not too bad.

To Dud's surprise, Iris became Ponder's star pupil. He listened one day as Ponder patiently explained to her that with experts; she should play conservatively, staying in only if she believed she had the best hand or that the odds were in her favor.

"In draw poker with nothing wild," he said, "holding jacks or better is a good hand, but with deuces wild, for example, it ups it to three aces."

Later, after Iris left, he questioned Ponder. "Why are you so willing to tell Iris all your secrets? You never helped me."

Ponder looked up, cards flying from nimble fingers as he dealt from the deck without watching. "Cause you ain't near as cute and sweet as that little honey." He added dryly, "She's not the usual whorehouse trash you like to associate with."

"I don't know why I put up with you," Dud muttered and rose to get another cup of coffee. He spied Seth Thompson riding his horse to the house, a big sorrel with four distinctive white socks. Dud would not have the horse where he came from, but since Thompson's land was almost entirely deep sand, it did not matter. Thompson left the horse out front and sauntered to the back where they sat playing. Dud offered Seth his place.

"We're just passing the time," Dud explained, "playing for matches and who has to get up to make coffee."

Thompson grinned knowingly, spit a stream of tobacco juice and sat down on Dud's cowhide stool, his heavy thighs spread wide and his beefy hands eagerly taking up the cards. "Let's see what the competition has to offer," he sneered and spit again.

Dud gave a silent snort and went to Iris's stove for more coffee. After pouring a cup, he looked up and saw Suzette with her kitten and Rashtah approaching the house where Jesse worked inside putting the finishing touches on the fireplace mantles. Glancing back at Thompson, who could see nothing in the protected corner where he sat, Dud whistled softly and strolled back to the table.

"Believe I'll sit in again," he said. Almost as soon as he

sat down, he caught another movement outside. Looking up, he saw Iris peeking around the corner and beckoning to him. He stood up. "Believe I'd better hold off a few minutes. Nature is starting to knock at the back door."

Ponder grunted and dealt two cards to Thompson, eyeing him under emotionless lids. Thompson grinned, taking the cards, and Dud was able to walk outside unnoticed. Iris caught him as he rounded the corner.

"Is that Seth Thompson in there?" she whispered. "I thought I recognized his horse."

Dud nodded, and Iris grimaced. "I've got some stew meat," she said, talking low and holding up a brown package. "I'll take it over to Zizi's and cook it. You can come over there later and eat if you want to, or fetch me after old blubber-butt leaves."

"Miss Iris," Dud admonished, suppressing a grin.

Iris grinned back at him, but grew serious. "I'm charging an awful lot of food at the store, Mr. Dud. The bill is running up."

"Do you hear me complaining, Miss Iris, honey? You don't know the sh…, I mean stuff, we'd be eating if not for you. I'll go by in the next day or two and pay the bill if it worries you."

"Okay," she whispered and smiled. "Is the French singer in the house?"

Dud nodded.

"They say when she wants to, she can cook marvelous delicacies," Iris continued. "She'll go down to the kitchen and cook up a storm every once in a while and leave it for the others to finish off."

"How do you know?"

Iris drew her brows together. "Men talk when they eat, and I'm not deaf, Mr. Dud."

Dud looked at the house—maybe there was more to the French whore than he realized. He turned back to Iris. "You watch yourself down there at that café. You're a sweet, kind woman. I want you to stay that way—don't turn into a hardened old harridan like Lottie or Ruby—but you've got to be careful."

"Don't worry so much, Mr. Dud," Iris said with a smile

As she turned to leave, Dud stopped her. "Don't let Zizi put sour cream in that stew," he hissed.

"I can't help it, Mr. Dud; that's the way those people eat," Iris hissed back.

"I don't care; I don't like all that sour cream in everything. Play the man card on her if you have to. Tell her I've got a hankering for a good old American stew or Irish stew or whatever you call it."

"Okay," Iris whispered. "Give us a couple of hours."

Dud watched Iris as she walked back to town. He shook his head. A man could not help but worry over a woman like Iris.

TWENTY-ONE

Dud and Ponder, along with Boyd, kept Seth Thompson playing for almost three hours, with Thompson never knowing that Suzette lingered in the house with Jesse almost the entire time. Given the feelings Jesse had for Suzette, going to the Gilded Lily to see her dance seemed so much like incest, Dud could not make himself go back, and Boyd must have felt the same way because he did not either. Nevertheless, they found out through gossip that Suzette had on all three nights touched her finger to her cheek at the close of her act. The first night it was noticed; the second night it was commented on; the third night, every man in the saloon was sure it was a signal to someone, and the whole town was wondering who that person could be.

When a few days later Thompson came back to the shed, Dud made sure to put him in the blind corner again. While he sat down, Dud rose and on the pretext of getting coffee, watched the street. He saw Rashtah approaching, and when she noticed him, he inclined his head to the inside of the shed. She nodded, turned and left. In a minute, Suzette and her kitten hurried along and disappeared into the house. This time, Rashtah stayed outside, sitting partially hidden behind a cedar tree.

Dud turned to the players. "Jesse," he said, and by his tone, Jesse knew to get up. When he reached him, Dud said so low Thompson could not hear, "You've got a visitor."

Jesse looked back at the table. "Take over my hand, would you, Uncle Dud?" he said loudly. "I'm going to get a shave before the barber's towels get too bloody."

Despite admiring Suzette's cunning in keeping Jesse from being shot in the dark—no one else in town would question his death as they would Thompson's—Dud wondered if he was doing the right thing encouraging them to meet.

Rashtah kept a watch for Thompson's horse, and when he dropped in on Dud, Suzette would slip into the house unnoticed by him. It humiliated Jesse to be so secretive, but Suzette insisted on it, and Dud was inclined to agree with her. He felt fairly sure Thompson did not realize she was there, or if he did, he was using it to his advantage. Iris said Thompson had a big enough ego to believe Suzette was in the house solely to gaze lovingly on him from afar. The other men who participated in the monthly poker games called on Ponder and played, but Thompson never came with them. He always arrived alone, swaggering, grinning, and spitting tobacco. Iris, who never said a word about Ponder's habit, frowned when she saw Thompson's dried brown spittle next to her stove.

"He's here hoping to rub up next to Iris and for no

other reason," Ponder scoffed at Dud. "You're just too big of a jug-head to realize it."

"She doesn't pay him a bit of mind," Dud said so quick he surprised himself, feeling thankful, too, that Iris always disappeared when Thompson showed up. "She's got some sense, anyway," he added.

"More than some people I know," Ponder said, throwing Dud a dark look. He tapped his cards. "Hit me again."

Dud dealt him another card. "I'd like to hit you," he muttered. "Why my poor old pappy had to die in the war and I be left with you, I'll never understand."

Ponder looked at his cards. "Married four times and nary a child out any one of those women. Instead, I had to get stuck with you. Three aces," he said, throwing down his hand.

Ponder's concentration had come back, and now when Felix came, it took everything he had to keep from getting trounced. "Saints preserve us, Washburn! Have some pity, man," he said one afternoon.

Iris, who had been playing, too, smiled and got up to fetch the coffee pot. Felix continued, "Where are Boyd and Jesse?" he asked.

Ponder scooped up his matches. "Boyd's over at that good-for-nothing worthless redhead's, and Jesse is off chasing the French tart," he said.

"Well, Uncle Ponder, why don't you just tell us how you really feel about it?" Dud said, but dropped the sarcasm when Iris came back with the pot. After replenishing the cups, she got back in the game.

As Dud looked at the cards in his hand, he began worrying about the truth in Ponder's words, so much so, he did not at first realize they were watching him. After running a bluff with a pair of deuces, Dud heard Iris squeal, "You were right, Uncle Ponder. He does!"

Dud looked up. "Does what?" he asked.

Iris laughed. "Uncle Ponder told me you always scratch your nose when you bluff, Mr. Dud, and you do! You've done it three times since we started playing!"

"I do not," Dud protested.

"Yes, you do," Iris said with a grin.

Dud took a deep breath to make another objection when he remembered he had scratched his nose when he decided to bluff. He felt foolish. "Well, horse-feathers."

"Most people don't realize it," Ponder said. "You see, Miss Iris, a man can use that to his advantage, though. A really good player will consciously rub his ear or his chin, something like that, when he's running a bluff on small stakes. Another good player will notice it. Then when it comes time for the big show down, he'll do it to convince the other fellow he's really just bluffing again."

"Ponder," Felix said. "You're a devious fellow, and I wished I'd met you ten years ago."

"I'll never scratch my nose playing cards again," Dud grumbled. "Miss Iris, we've played long enough. How about me and you heading over to the Darsts? Maybe we can talk old man Darst into playing his fiddle, and we can dance." He wanted to do something that would take his mind off the coming card game and his nephews' tangled love lives.

"Believe I'll join you," Ponder said, closing up the deck. "I love a good dance."

"Fine, fine," Dud said, thinking if the treasure hunt

accomplished nothing at all, it had at least brought the old Ponder back. "Let's all go."

The Darst boys met them halfway, running and out of breath. "Mr. Dud, Mr. Dud," they all said at once, and Frank shushed them so he could speak. "My papa sent for you. There is a strange man and woman at the stables. They are asking about you."

Dud patted Frank on the back and began to walk quickly to the stables. Who could it be? Ev and Mary?

But he was too late. "They've already gone," Ugor said, "a big heavy man with dark hair and a beard, a woman with a veil. They ask why you go to the land at the Yegua. They demand many answers I cannot give them."

The others gathered around them, and Dud could see the questions in their eyes, too. Iris and Felix knew only that he wanted the land, but not why. "Which way did they go?" Dud asked.

Ugor shook his head. "No, Dud. Do not try to follow them. It grows dark. They will waylay you. I think they no good."

"He's right, Dudford. Leave it for now," Ponder said.

"We came to have a dance," Felix said. "Send the boys to the store for lemons and sugar. We can have lemonade and a dance."

"Yes, yes," Ugor said, "a party with music. Kristof— Kris, fetch the fiddle."

Dud nodded, reluctant to let Ev and Mary slip away, if that's who it was. He looked down at the loose dirt in the stables. Iris had a small, but slightly wide, foot. Zizi Darst had tiny feet, too, but she could not afford the pointy-toed shoes that were fashionable and had to make do with a pair of boots someone had given her. The footprints in the dirt of the stable showed a long, narrow woman's shoe. He looked up and stared at the stable door. He wanted to wring Mary's neck and beat Ev Reid to a pulp, but the woods around Tie Town were made for hiding out. It would be a waste of time to search for them.

He had only himself to blame. He had put up with a crook and thief in his backyard because he had once been friends with his brother. He had allowed himself to be seduced by Mary because it vaunted his ego. He looked at the faces who were looking up to him, the Darst boys, Iris. He forced himself to smile.

"Would you boys mind going to the store for sugar and lemons? Charge it to me. Your papa is going to give us a party, and I'm providing the refreshments. Bring us some cheese and crackers, too."

Their faces split into grins. "Yes sir, Mr. Dud!"

He looked once again at the door and with a shake of his head, turned and faced the others. It dawned on him that he had not been so happy in years. He bowed to Iris as Ugor drew the bow across the strings. "May I have this dance, madam?"

Iris smiled and curtsied. "Of course, kind sir."

The next day, Dud again forced Ponder to walk around the block. When they came back to Pecan Street in view of the house, Dud looked at it with fresh eyes. The boys had done a good job rocking the walls with the reddish brown stones, and the shingles on the roof were straight and even. He and Ponder walked beside the house on their way to the shed. As they approached an open window, they heard the sound of soft tears.

"Suzette, Suzette," Jesse murmured softly.

"You have healed my kitten," Suzette cried. "But can you heal my broken heart?"

Ponder pushed Dud to one side of the window, and he took the other. With backs against the wall, they froze in place, invisible to the occupants of the house. They heard Jesse's gentle murmuring in return. Dud debated whether to remain or force Ponder away and leave them alone. Rashtah dozed on the other side of the house. The promise he made to his sister took precedence over etiquette, Dud decided in an instant, especially when he heard the beginnings of Suzette's story.

Old Tom ambled over, and as they listened, Dud rubbed the dog's ears. It was not totally unlike many other stories he had heard pour from the lips of girls sucked into a life of misery and sin. A sin he, unfortunately, had always been all too eager to join them in. He had learned early on that prostitutes, while some of the laziest of women, could be the most proficient of liars. He tried to take the sorrow out of Suzette's tale and weigh what was left with a cool mind devoid of emotion.

He and Ponder eavesdropped without a qualm of guilt and only moved after hearing Felix greet Rashtah. Dud wanted to talk to Jesse, but after Suzette left, there was always someone around.

The next day, Ponder went with him to the general store. Cowboys circled throughout the crowded store, hanging around the counter and gossiping. The fat, squatty grocer gabbed as he tallied Dud's bill.

"She's got a man; I'm telling you," he told the crowd.

"It's got to be a man with money," an unshaven young cowboy added.

"Hell yes, and here he comes now," another said, and

all eyes turned to the plate glass windows in front of the store.

Seth Thompson walked in. "Afternoon, boys," he said, grinning widely.

"Here's your bill, Mr. Washburn," the grocer said, placing it in front of Dud. "Howdy, Mr. Thompson."

After giving Thompson a brief glance, Dud looked the bill over and began peeling greenbacks off a roll.

"We've just been talking about you and Suzette, Mr. Thompson," another cowboy said.

"That's right," the grocer interjected. "Last week, Suzette heads down Pecan Street. Seth Thompson heads down Pecan Street. Suzette comes back smiling. She's been smiling ever since."

"Come on, Mr. Thompson, give," the unshaven cowboy said.

Dud, pushing his money across the counter, watched him. Thompson smirked and hoisted his pants. With a sly, lewd grin he said, "You boys ever had frog meat?"

The grocer and the cowboys laughed. Thompson looked around their faces, moving the chaw around in his mouth with his tongue and smiling. He turned to Dud and the smile froze. For a second, his eyes changed, the laughter in them turning into something quite different. Derision quickly replaced whatever it had been, and he said, "What about you Washburns? Ya'll ever had any?"

"Had it?" Ponder said with a snort. "My second wife was a black-haired Cajun from New Orleans. I had it so much, every time someone said 'Ooh,' my la-la stood up."

Laughter again filled the store. Thompson looked around. "Cajun!" he said, mocking Ponder. "That's just that bastardized version from Lousy-anna."

Ponder lunged for Thompson, but Dud grabbed him. He shoved Ponder toward the front door, holding on with an iron grip while jerking the door open and pushing him outside, slamming the door behind them.

"He's just trying to get to us," Dud said once they were on the sidewalk. "You know that."

Ponder shook free and nodded. "I know it, darn it," he replied. "Come on, I've got to talk to you."

Dud followed him into the Iron Horse Saloon. Ponder walked past a line of cowboys drinking at the bar and took a table in the back. Dud sat down. "All right," he said. "What is it?"

"Dud, I don't think I can do this by myself," Ponder confessed. "Sometimes these games go on all night. I may not be able to last."

Dud nodded. Ponder only spoke what he had feared. "You think I'm good enough?" he asked.

"Maybe," Ponder said. "I think you could take him; you've practiced enough and matured as a player. But I'm going to tell you something, Dud. He'll find a way to kill you if you win. You saw the way he looked at you in that store. I can beat him without retribution because Felix has been spouting off about me all over town. Thompson can convince everyone that no one could have whipped me. You're an outsider; you're not one of the boys that will be around long enough for him to beat later on in another game. Besides that, he's jealous as hell of you because of Iris."

"What do you mean, because of Iris?"

Ponder rolled his eyes and shook his head. "Do I have to spell out everything to you? I've told you this before. I declare, Dud, if I didn't know your mama loved my

243

brother almost more than God, I'd swear you didn't have a flea's worth of Washburn blood flowing in your veins. Thompson is crazy about Iris, but she prefers hanging around your sorry ass. God only knows why, but there it is."

"Oh, she's just lonely," Dud said hastily. "She's like Felix; she likes to be in the big middle of things."

Ponder turned his eyes heavenward again, but said, "I may not make it, Dud."

"So you're saying you can't do it by yourself. Who do you want with you then if not me?"

Ponder took a deep breath. "Iris."

Dud stared at him. "You're joking. She can't even make correct change. The café owners routinely beat her out of tip money."

"Dud, she's got the knack. Her only fault is that she can be bluffed out. She can't always tell when someone is bluffing."

Dud shook his head and looked around the bar in disbelief. "No, Uncle Ponder."

A commotion started in the front of the saloon. Two cowboys began an argument that turned into a fist fight. Dud only glanced at the men, and Ponder did not bother to look.

"Dud," Ponder said. "I know what I'm talking about. Iris can do it. She'll be nervous as hell, but if you tell her you're sending her in the game to bolster my confidence, she'll do it. Once she's in, and she starts playing, she can take over if I have to drop out, and she can win."

Dud refused to answer and turned his face away. One of the cowboys pulled a gun and shot the other one. Dud watched the dead cowboy's friends carry him out the door with it barely registering in his brain what they were doing. Ponder continued to talk. "Dud, the only way you can be sure of getting that property on the Yegua is to send Iris in to play."

"No! Whatever is on that property is not worth the risk. I've already put her and the rest of my friends in enough jeopardy as it is," Dud said, his voice getting louder with every word. "I'm not taking her into a whorehouse, Ponder! I'm not!"

He became aware that the chatter in the saloon had come to an abrupt halt. He looked at the row of men at the bar who were now staring at him. "What are you looking at?" he hollered at them. They shook their heads and went back to their beers.

"Dud," Ponder said. "We will be right there with her. You won't be risking her to danger. What if she wins? Put yourself in Thompson's shoes. He will tell everyone he let her win because he wants to marry her or sleep with her or whatever. Every man can understand that. He can save face if Iris wins, and she'll be in no danger. If you play and you win, you're a dead man."

"Let me think about it," Dud said. "Let me think about it and talk it over with Boyd and Jesse." He looked at Ponder. "Are you sure, Uncle Ponder?"

Ponder nodded. "Sure as shooting, Dud. She's got the gift."

At that moment, Dud wished Iris had the gift of playing the piano like Elizabeth Harrison instead of poker, but he could not change things.

TWENTY-TWO

POURING COFFEE FROM THE POT ON IRIS'S OUTDOOR stove, Dud explained Ponder's proposal to Boyd and Jesse.

"Are you going to let her, Uncle Dud?" Boyd asked.

"I don't know," Dud said. "What do you think?"

At that moment, Annabelle Harrison stepped out of the shadows. Fearing she would not get the hang of what they were doing or that her parents would disapprove, she had not been allowed to play poker. Sometimes the Darst boys or Boyd would feel sorry for her and play Old Maids or Hearts with her. Old Tom approached her, and she reached down to pet him. "Maybe you should ask her, Mr. Dud," she said.

"I think Miss Annabelle's right, Uncle Dud," Boyd said and Jesse agreed.

"I'll put up the money for her if she wants to," Dud said, giving in. "We'll split Ponder's stake like we agreed, but I'm backing Iris."

Iris's initial reaction was much as Dud expected.

"Oh, Mr. Dud, I don't think I could do that. What if I lost all your money?"

"It's like this," Dud explained. "Ponder is afraid he won't be able to last the whole game. He asked if you could play, too. You can't play as a team, but just being in the game with him would help him and bolster his confidence. It would be just like the two of you playing here under the shed. I'm not worried about the money, Miss Iris."

"Uncle Ponder wants me to?" Iris questioned, and Dud nodded.

"What about you? What do you want, Mr. Dud?"

"I want you to do whatever you feel comfortable doing, Miss Iris."

Iris pushed her lips together and let her eyes gaze to her right. "I think," she said. "I think I want to help—if you're sure about the money, Mr. Dud," she said, looking back at him.

"I'm sure, sugar. I just don't want to put you in any danger or hurt your reputation. But don't worry about the money. It's a gamble, I know, but it's the only way I can get my hands on that land legally. Everyone else in the game hopefully believes I'm after the Gilded Lily."

"How much is the stake?" she asked, and Dud told her.

"I have my tip money saved, Mr. Dud. May I pay for half my stake?"

Dud shook his head. "No, I won't let you do that, Miss Iris."

"Then I won't play," Iris said stubbornly. "And I want to. If I win, you could have the land and let me split the cash winnings."

"Miss Iris," Dud explained. "That is not good arithmetic. You could put up a third of the stake, and then if you won the land, I'd take it and split the pot with you, as long as it evened out."

"Okay, we'll do that," Iris said, and turned to walk away.

Dud gasped. "I didn't agree to that. And where are you going?"

"To buy a new dress!" Iris said over her shoulder, as if she could not believe Dud even had to ask.

Dud gave in, but as luck would have it, Iris could not find a suitable dress to buy and there was no time to make one. Annabelle offered to loan Iris one of their gowns, explaining artlessly that she had her mother's permission after her father insisted. A full afternoon was spent at the Harrisons' trying on dresses. Iris finally found a dress Elizabeth had outgrown that would fit, with a few nips and tucks. According to Annabelle, who told Boyd everything, the dress was too low-cut to wear to a poker game, but her mother had found a pretty linen and lace fichu for Iris that would make it more modest and fitting to wear.

Dud later went with Iris when she told Ruby and Joe she would need Saturday and Sunday off. She wanted to work as usual on Friday night because she felt it would keep her from thinking and worrying too much about the coming game. Even she realized, however, that if the game lasted all of Saturday night and into Sunday, she would be unable to drag herself to work.

"What'd you want off for?" Ruby growled.

"That's her business," Dud said.

Ruby swelled like an unrelieved bladder and said, "Iris, if you don't show up here on Saturday, just don't come back."

"Okay," Iris promptly said. "Do you still want me tonight?"

It shocked Dud that Iris was willing to give the job up so easily after she had been so insistent on getting it. It must have shocked Ruby, too, because she started to crawfish. "Well, uh, well," she mumbled at first. "You have to work next Saturday night by yourself then! There's a big barn dance planned. Me and Joe will go, and you'll have to man the café alone."

"Wait a minute," Dud said. "You're not going to have any business anyway! Let Iris go to that dance."

Iris put her hand on Dud's arm. "I'll be happy to cook and wait tables by myself next Saturday night, since you're giving me this Saturday and Sunday off."

"Well, okay," Ruby said, agreeing ungraciously, taking her rag and giving it violent shoves around the counter while shooting Dud fiery looks.

Iris walked him to the door. "Don't worry, Mr. Dud. I don't care about that dance anyway. I'll see you later."

"All right, Miss Iris, honey," Dud said. "Don't let that she-devil cheat you out tip money tonight, because I can just about guarantee she's so mad she'll try."

"Okay, Mr. Dud, okay," Iris said soothingly. "I'll try to get out of here tonight as soon as I can."

When he left the café, Jesse caught up with him at the hotel. "Uncle Dud, I've wanted to speak to you all day, but I can't ever catch you alone."

Dud nodded. "Come on up to the hotel room. We won't be interrupted there."

Jesse and Old Tom followed him up the stairs. Once in the room, Dud shut the door. Old Tom went to his place in the corner and after circling three times, lay down. Dud and Jesse pulled two chairs close to the window. As Jesse talked, haltingly at first, Dud remained silent, letting him it tell his way. Looking at Jesse's fine head, his young body made rock hard by eating the dust of countless beeves, Dud remembered him when he was a boy. The incident that stuck his mind and refused to leave was when Jesse insisted on picking for his own the runt in a litter of puppies. Dud had told him the dog would never amount to much, but Jesse had insisted. He had been right; the dog, timid and shy, was killed by coyotes before it was a year old because it lacked enough gumption and cunning to escape. He had never said "I told you so," and Jesse had never complained. Dud wondered what he should say to Jesse about Suzette.

As the boy poured his heart out, and Dud listened to the story for the second time, he began to realize Suzette was not like that puppy.

"I believe her, Uncle Dud," Jesse said. "I know you get mad sometimes and tell me and Boyd that half of what women say is a lie and the other half is undependable, but I believe her. I think she's being honest with me."

Dud put his hand on Jesse's shoulder and squeezed it. "I do, too, boy. I don't know why, I just do. Probably because I heard she can cook."

Jesse burst into laughter, releasing and dispelling the heavy passions he had been carrying. "Uncle Dud, the only man worse than you are is Uncle Ponder," he said with a grin.

"I know it, boy. Do you think she'll have you?"

Jesse grew serious again. "I don't know. She's scared. Hell, I'm scared."

Dud rose and gave him a reassuring pat. "I've got to

get to the saloon and have a word with Lottie before it gets crowded. Have you talked to Boyd?"

Jesse nodded. "He understands."

Dud nodded in return. Boyd would.

Later that afternoon, Dud pushed the doors of the saloon open and looked around the room. As he expected, it was almost entirely free of customers, caught in the lull between busy times. Lottie stood at the end of the bar playing solitaire while her bald bartender polished glasses. Dud gave another swift look around as he walked toward Lottie, but Johnny was not casting a shadow downstairs.

Dud stopped at the corner next to her and rested his arms on the bar. Lottie called to the bartender for a beer, but Dud waved the offer aside. "This is business, not social, Lottie."

"Oh really?" she said, placing a jack on a queen while watching Dud's face. "What is so important that you have to come see me in the middle of the afternoon?"

"Oh," Dud said casually, looking at the rows of bottles on the wall. "I just wanted to talk about Johnny and a few other little things."

Lottie bristled immediately. "What about Johnny?"

"Oh, it's just that I've met a lot of men like him, Lottie. They're always on the run from something," he said, turning his head to look at her. "They're never quite straight. They have to chisel somebody out of something and leave town in a hurry, that kind of thing. Maybe not anything more than petty theft, but they're always wanted for something."

"And your point being?" Lottie said sharply, nostrils flaring.

Dud shifted his body to face her, still leaning one elbow on the bar. "I'm going to have two people in that game tomorrow night, Lottie," he said. "And if they get anything stronger to drink than coffee, I will dig and dig until I find every piece of dirt on Johnny I can, and I'll see to it that he gets covered in it."

Lottie's eyes blazed so furiously, the bartender took a step in their direction. Lottie waved him back curtly without taking her eyes from Dud. "You'd do it, too, you bastard," she said. "Are you putting Felix in that game?" she demanded. "Because if you are, I can tell you right now you're wasting your time; he'll never get the Gilded Lily away from me. Never!"

"Did I say Felix?" Dud countered.

She stood like a motionless fury, ready to explode. Taking deep breaths, she forced herself to be calm, making an effort to hide her anger. "We were once close, Dud," she said, trying to make her voice seductive. "You once helped me out of an awful jam. I can't believe you'd be like this to me."

"Lottie," Dud said, "I've thought about that incident a lot over the years, and I've come to a few conclusions. At the time, I was an inexperienced young man, ready to believe a story an attractive girl told me about self-defense—ready to go to the marshal and back up her story for her. But as I've grown older, I realize I only saw what that pretty girl wanted me to see, not what really happened." He looked Lottie in the eyes straight and hard. "I figured out how you did it, Lottie. I know what really happened."

She put the cards down, her nostrils still flaring, but this time in fear.

"You don't know what you're talking about," she said.

"Oh yes I do," he said. "If I don't get your promise that my people don't get anything stronger than coffee put in their drinks, that their food is not doctored in any way, I will go to that dead boy's brother and sister, and I will confess to them how I was hoodwinked as a young man, and I will lay down my belief of what really happened. And since they now own half of Fort Worth, I don't think they would mind hiring a battery of lawyers to run you to the ground and string a rope around your neck."

"You son of a bitch!" she cried through clinched teeth.

"Promise!"

"All right," she hissed. "I promise!"

Dud took a few steps to leave.

"Stop!" she said.

He stopped and waited.

She squared her jaw and raised it. "Seth Thompson gives me fifty dollars a sucker." She did not have to explain what for.

Dud reached in his pocket and peeled off two one hundred dollar bills, throwing them on the counter in front of her.

"He'll beat me and rape me for this; you know that, don't you?"

"If you open those pretty legs of yours to him willingly like you've done so many times before, then it won't be rape, will it?" Dud said. "And I imagine with a few of those crocodile tears you're so good at, you can escape a beating."

With fists balled, her face suffused in impotent anger. Dud, however, continued. "Just remember, woman, there is no statues of limitations on murder. And if you're thinking about having me shot in the back, you ought to know that *my* attorney," he said, pointing to his chest, "has a copy of what really happened in that killing twenty years ago right next to where he keeps my will."

"Get out!" she screamed. "Get out!"

As he headed for the door, she yelled, "And tell Felix I said he doesn't have a snowball's chance in hell!"

TWENTY-THREE

DUD WALKED IN THE HOUSE ON PECAN STREET EXPECTING to find Felix, but Ponder said Felix wanted to be alone. "He said he'd see you tomorrow before the game," Ponder added. "I'm going to bed."

"Uncle Ponder, it's barely dusk," Dud said.

"I don't care. I'm going to sleep, only get up to pee, and then go back to sleep," Ponder said. "If you take my advice, you'll do the same. You may not be in the game, Dud, but somebody's got to be watching our backs. Iris get any rest?"

"She said she slept all day until it was time to go to work," Dud said. "Uncle Ponder, are you sure...."

"There ain't no sure thing," Ponder interrupted. "Get out of here and leave me alone. Don't come back until thirty minutes before the game begins."

Dud reluctantly left. He started to walk to the Harrisons, but he did not want to see Boyd sitting like a patient lump; it was driving him crazy, too. He could stop at the livery and visit with the Darsts, but they would be hustling with Friday night business. Jesse would be at the Gilded Lily, his inscrutable face staring at the woman he loved and wishing he alone possessed her.

When Dud looked up from his ambling steps, he found himself in front of the café. Giving a sigh, he decided he might as well eat something before taking Ponder's advice. Iris, busy as usual, gave him a smile when he entered. The tables were full, but Dud found a place next to the cowhand who had ridden with them to Seth Thompson's place.

"Sorry to hear about Mrs. Thompson," Dud said, trying to be sociable even if he did not feel like it.

The cowhand did not even try. He nodded his head with no pause from chewing. "She was a good woman," he said.

Dud, watching him eat, grew irritated. "Why do you work for that bastard anyway?"

"He's my stepfather," he said, still looking at his plate. He paused and added, "He buried my mother, too."

There was not much Dud could say to that, so he grew silent. The young cowhand mopped the last of his gravy with a biscuit, eating it in three bites. As he rose from the table and reached for his hat, without looking directly at Dud and seeming to address the wall across the room, he said, "Make him state what they consider winning hands before you start to play. Sometimes he'll beat someone with a blaze or a skip and suddenly announce it's legal. He'll misdeal in hopes of fouling someone out of a hand to try and break a winning streak. They all sandbag a little, but he's the worst."

As he walked away, Dud murmured, "Much obliged," to his back.

Iris brought Dud a glass of water and whispered, "Is the special okay?"

Dud nodded, still looking at the retreating cowhand as he left the café. "Sure, honey."

He ate what Iris put in front of him without tasting it. They did not speak again, but exchanged numerous solemn glances with one another. Dud put Iris's tip on the table and gave Ruby the money for his food, which she accepted with ill grace. He paid as little attention to her as he had the food and went back to his hotel room to doze until it was near time for Iris to leave work.

Jesse came into the darkened room as Dud rested on the bed. He did not light the lantern, but stumbled until he found a chair.

"Uncle Dud, are you asleep?" he asked. When Dud answered no, he said, "What if we don't win that land tomorrow? What then?"

"Then we'll figure something else out," Dud said. "I'm not going to take something off someone else's property without their permission."

Jesse sighed. "I know. Uncle Dud, do you think Suzette really likes me?"

Dud rolled his eyes in the dark. "She's not sneaking around trying to see any other man in town as far as I know." He sat up on the edge of the bed. "You want to go down and wait for Iris with me?"

"No, you go ahead," Jesse said. "I think I'll go to sleep."

Dud pulled his boots on and called to Old Tom. "Come on, boy. I've got to keep Iris out of trouble. Or maybe Iris is keeping me out of trouble."

"Yes, thank God," Jesse murmured.

Dud started to grin and make a smart remark, until he realized Jesse had not been joking.

Iris came out earlier than Dud expected. "She must have really took you for a lot of tip money if she was willing to let you go early," Dud said.

"I imagine," Iris said. "But I was so ready to leave, I didn't care. Can we sit and talk for a few minutes before I have to go back to the boardinghouse? I'm more nervous than a snake in a hog-pen."

"Sure, honey," Dud said. The surveyor slept in the back of his building, but Felix's bed was next to the window on the second floor. What the hell, Dud thought, and led Iris back to the darkened bench.

"I spent the first part of the night listening to what a promiscuous rascal you were. Ruby is sure you and Lottie knew each other previously," Iris said. "Then someone came in and said you had gone to the saloon and laid the law down to Lottie about something, and after that, you became a mean tyrant who abuses women every chance you get."

Dud gave a snort. "I didn't know I was such a bastard."

Iris grinned. "Is everything going to be okay about tomorrow?"

"I think so. I told Lottie not to give you and Ponder anything stronger to drink than coffee. That's one of their tricks for hoodwinking people out of money—getting them intoxicated on that piss-foul bust-head whiskey."

"Oh, and I did so want to get plastered," Iris teased.

Dud leaned forward, placing his elbows on his thighs, looking out over the darkened street. "Suzette offered to let you use her room for the breaks." Felix had already told Dud that the men would have two or three thirty minute breaks a night to eat or do other things that Dud did not want to have to explain to Iris. She and Ponder would use them to snack and rest.

"That was nice of her," Iris said. "Do you think she'll marry Mr. Jesse?"

"I don't know," Dud answered truthfully. He looked back at Iris. Would Jesse and Suzette want Iris to know what had happened to her? He did not know if they wanted it or not, but he did.

"Suzette's parents were immigrants from France," Dud began, trying to talk low so Felix would have to really strain to hear. "When she was about thirteen, they died, and she was sent to live with some distant relatives. They were lice-picking poor, and life with them was pretty bleak. Her parents hadn't been well off, but Suzette told Jessie they had been a happy, lighthearted couple. A neighborhood boy began coming over to see Suzette, and out of boredom, they began to do what comes naturally in those dreary circumstances. Her guardians caught them in a compromising position—they hadn't actually done anything, but they were pretty darn close. Close enough that it gave the guardians an excuse to sell Suzette."

"Sell Suzette?" Iris asked, puzzled. "What do you mean?"

"In Oklahoma, there is a certain unsavory saloon with a cathouse upstairs. The upstairs has a long hall, and on one side of the hall is the 'broke' girls, and on the other side is the 'unbroke' girls, chained to their beds. I'd heard rumors of it, but had never been there and never wanted to."

Iris sat up. "What? Do you mean they sold Suzette to

a…, a house of ill repute that chained her to a bed? I don't believe anyone could be so evil."

"Well, you'd be surprised," Dud said. "She fought like a little devil, but that didn't stop it. There are a lot of men who enjoy that kind of roughhousing. She got beaten regularly, and she told Jesse there were times she fought hard, just hoping someone would kill her. One of the girls who brought her food and emptied her slop jar finally whispered to her that if she got 'broke,' they'd put her across the hall and give her much more freedom, and she could probably talk some man into taking her away. So she submitted the best she could, and ran off with the first man willing to help her escape."

"Poor girl," Iris murmured.

"He was a gambler," Dud said. "He started working the riverboats, and while he gambled, she would sing. Nothing like she does now, just regular singing. She knew he was no account, but she got pregnant and stuck with him because of the baby. Then she got sick, lost the baby, and wasn't able to sing for a while. Money got tight, and when he wanted her to sleep with a wealthy steel magnate who was willing to pay top dollar for her, she took what clothes and money she could and ran."

"Oh Mr. Dud," Iris said, shaking her head in pity. "What an awful thing. How did she end up here?"

"Heard it was a boomtown and figured there was money to be made for a while, anyway," he answered. "She wasn't making hardly enough to eat with regular singing, and she remembered a dance her mother used to do for her father when she was a little girl. Her mother had an aunt who worked in some place called Pig Ally in Paris; she was some kind of 'courtesan.' That's the way of the

French; the lower something is in the dirt, the fancier the name they tack on to it. Anyway, when her parents became engaged, her father told her mother he would not allow this aunt in his home. He was very strict about such things. To get even, the aunt taught her mother this dance, secretly thinking he would see it and be horrified because he was so straight-laced. Instead, he loved it, but threatened to kill her if she did it for anyone but him. You know how men are, Miss Iris."

"No," Iris said slowly, "but I'm beginning to understand how you are."

Dud gave a grunt of good humor. "Anyway, Suzette started doing this dance to make enough money to keep out of prostitution. She told Jesse that while she does it, she pretends she is her mother dancing for her father. She said when she saw him; she started pretending he was her pa because he favors him."

"Well, she does care about him then," Iris said.

"Yes, but Miss Iris, the girl has been so abused, I don't know if she'll ever recover from it. She blames herself for getting mixed up with the neighborhood boy in the first place, something she knew her parents would have disapproved of. She has all kinds of guilt she's carrying around with her."

"Why shouldn't she get over it?" Iris demanded, her voice becoming louder with every syllable. "Just because she made a stupid mistake? Was it her fault she got beaten and had to sleep with men she didn't want to sleep with?"

Tears sprang into Iris's eyes; she began to tremble, and her words were almost screamed at him. Dud looked upward, wondering if Felix was listening.

"Why shouldn't she get over it and be happy?" Iris

demanded. "Why should she have to pay for it the rest of her life?" She raised her fists to her eyes and began to sob.

"Honey, sugar," Dud said, grasping her shoulders. "I didn't mean to upset you."

Iris buried her face in his chest and wept. Dud stroked her hair. "You're always so happy," he whispered. "I thought you had forgotten all about that son of a bitch you were married to."

Iris straightened and wiped her tears. She nodded through wet eyes. "I almost had. I think I'm just strung up about tomorrow. Please forgive me for going to pieces."

"Of course," Dud said. "But I think you'd better go to bed and get some rest."

She nodded, and they rose to leave. They walked across the street in silence, and when they reached the boardinghouse gallery, Iris turned to him and said, "Mr. Dud, I know you probably don't realize it, but letting me go off the handle tonight will help me keep it under control tomorrow. Thank you, Mr. Dud. Thank you for everything." She stood on tiptoes and kissed his cheek before turning and hastening into the house.

Dud shut the door before the landlady had a chance to yell at him. He stood with his hand on the knob, wondering why his first wife could not have been more like Iris.

TWENTY-FOUR

PONDER SNORTED AND MUMBLED A FEW CURSE WORDS under his breath when Dud passed the information from Thompson's cowhand to him. Iris, looking like a gorgeous young debutante about to meet a roomful of beaus, questioned him. "I don't know what a skip or a blaze is, Uncle Ponder," she said.

The blue dress Iris wore made her eyes flash an even darker blue. The gown had short puff sleeves, as if proclaiming her honesty to the world, while the white fichu covered her bosom prettily as Annabelle had said. After her husband had made his wishes clear, Nellie Harrison had joined in the excitement and graciously loaned Iris an expensive lace shawl. Ponder had nodded in approval when Iris walked into the house on Pecan Street with Dud, and now he assured her not to worry.

"Blaze and skip are just a couple of winning hands people in different pockets of the country throw in sometimes. Hardly anyone uses them, and if we question the men about it, they will deny they ever play that way. And if they say they do, I'll explain. Just be sure to count your cards as they are being dealt. If they are wrong, point it out to the dealer before picking them up. You remember what sandbagging is; just remember if you are bidding after Thompson, not to take too much notice of what his opening bid is."

Iris closed her eyes and trembled. "Okay, okay," she said. Dud squeezed her forearms lightly. "You don't have to do this, you know, and you can back out at any time."

She nodded her head. "I know, but I want to. I'll be all right."

"Okay," Dud said. He turned to Felix and tried to persuade him not to go near the Gilded Lily, much less join the onlookers. "Lottie will never let Johnny put up the saloon if you are standing there watching."

"I know. I know you're right. But I can't stay away," Felix said, pleading for understanding. "I've got to be there."

Dud looked over his group. Ponder and Iris cleaned and poised, Boyd and Jesse wary and ready for whatever the evening might bring, and Felix shaky, teary-eyed and hopeful despite the grim outlook of the Gilded Lily ever being on the table again. Even Annabelle had come to wish them luck.

"Do you want me to look after Old Tom for you, Mr. Dud?" she asked.

"No, thank you, Miss Annabelle," Dud said kindly. "If there's trouble, I'll need the dog." He turned back to his people. "Are you ready, troops?" he asked.

They nodded and filed out the front door. Annabelle shut it behind her, waving goodbye.

The saloon, swelled with people in every corner and

nook, grew silent when they entered. Lottie stood near the bar, her face grim. "No dogs allowed," she said.

"Piss off," Dud said. "And what I told you earlier goes for the dog, too."

She clamped her jaw and with an ugly flounce, bounded up the stairs ahead of them. They followed, and Dud held Iris's arm, keeping her close to him. At the end of the hall, Lottie opened a door to the right and jerked her head toward the room.

Ponder, who knew every swindle there could be with mirrors and reflections, swept his eyes over the walls, floor, and ceiling. A large round table stood in the center with chairs around it. Above it hung a fancy chandelier with heavy, thick candles that Ponder paid particular attention to. On another table close to the window was another lamp. Chairs for spectators were lined against a wall, far from the round table where Thompson, Johnny, and two other wealthy men Dud rather liked waited for them. When they saw Iris, they rose to their feet.

"Why we are honored," Thompson said, his coarse cheeks grinning. "We never expected to have such a beautiful visitor, Miss Talbot."

Iris, who appeared pleasant, but reserved, did not answer. Thompson looked at Felix. "Well, Felix, we heard you might be joining us. Welcome back."

The minute he had left the house on Pecan Street, Felix had put on a cheery front, and he kept it. "No, you heard wrong," he laughed. "You've got two much better poker players than me joining you tonight."

Johnny and Lottie exchanged looks. Thompson eyed Dud and said, "Washburn?"

Dud walked forward with Iris in one hand and Ponder

on his other side. "I think you gentleman all know my Uncle Ponder and Miss Talbot. They'd like to join your game tonight."

Four blank faces stared at him. Iris kept her composure, and just as Felix had put on his persona, Ponder suddenly became an enigma. It took Dud several seconds to remember the last time he had seen Ponder look that way—it was while listening to a general's orders, right before Ponder went out and shot up a Yankee battery.

"May we sit in?" Ponder asked politely.

Johnny grinned, but Thompson shook himself slightly. "Miss Talbot, we appreciate your presence, but we would never dream of taking advantage of you in a game of chance."

"I don't think that will be the case," Dud said. "Why don't you let her play? After all, you told me at your ranch the game was open to anyone who had the money."

"That's right, Thompson," Felix interjected. "Surely you're not afraid to face a little bitty thing like Miss Talbot across the table, are you?"

"Oh, let her play," Johnny said.

Thompson, cornered, said, "Why no, no, have a seat, by all means."

Iris murmured her thanks and sat down in the chair Ponder pulled out for her. He moved around the table, got another chair, and sat across from her. Dud crossed the room to a man with a strongbox and bought chips for them. As he set the chips on the table, he watched Thompson. Thompson sat staring at Iris, and suddenly, he grew jovial.

"Well, well, this is nice," he boomed, looking as if he had convinced himself Iris had a personal interest in him, not the game. The other two men glanced at one another and Thompson, but giving a shrug of their shoulders, did not object.

Dud walked across the room to join the other spectators. Ponder held up his hand a few inches. "Before we begin, what are the house rules?"

Thompson looked around the table and back at Ponder. He gave a short grunt. "House rules? What do you mean? We play straight draw poker here. Guts opens, you can draw three cards. Bet whatever the hell you want, but you've got to back it up. I thought you knew that."

"What constitutes a winning hand," Ponder began. Before he could say, "for example," Johnny interrupted. In a bored, monotonous tone that said all too clearly he thought Ponder had dementia, he began, "Ace high, pair, two pair," and went through straights and flushes, ending with a straight flush.

Ponder did not look at him, but waited until he finished and then asked bluntly, "Do you consider blazes, little dogs, big dogs, skips, or round the corner winning hands?"

Thompson again exchanged glances with the other men. "Of course not," he said with a blustery lie and shot a hard glance at Felix. He picked up a new deck of cards, rapped them on the table and with large fingers, opened the package and began shuffling the cards. Spreading them on the table, he said, "High card wins first deal."

Dud hoped Iris would not win the first deal, and she did not. The cards were dealt, and after that began the most gut jerking night of Dud's life. After the first few difficult minutes, for the next seven hours of play, if Iris and Ponder had nerves, Dud never saw them. Although they did not exchange words as they played, he knew they were feeding off one another emotionally. With Ponder as calm as a dead bolt on a Tuesday night, Iris bid, raised, and called in a rhythm free of doubt and anxiety. As Dud watched her play, making the game look easy, he knew Ponder had been right. Iris had a natural flair for it. She knew every bid around the table, every call, every raise, and how many cards each man drew. When the other players got cocky and started playing around with high-low games, she never lost the thread. The "after the first Queen, one-eyed Jacks, and low hole wild," nonsense ended when Thompson insisted they stop after he forgot what was wild and lost a hand he otherwise might have won.

Both Iris and Ponder played a conservative game, folding many times when a brash player would have stayed in. During the evening, at different times, both Iris's and Ponder's chips grew so low, once Dud whispered out of the side of his mouth to Felix, "I'm going to have to sell the ranch to keep them in." He did not think they even noticed. Slowly their piles came back around, and it became apparent as the night wore on they were formidable adversaries.

The other players did not make it easy for Iris when they saw how well she could play. Once she told Thompson, "I'm sorry, Mr. Thompson, but you've dealt me six cards."

Thompson looked at her pile in mock consternation. "Well so I have, little lady. Do you want me to just take one away or call for a re-deal?"

"That won't be necessary," Iris said, charming as usual. "Just take the last card you dealt me and discard it, please."

When Johnny tried it several hours later, giving her four cards instead of five, which she caught immediately, he said, "Oh, sorry about that, Miss Talbot. Another card?"

This time Iris asked for a re-deal, just as good-natured as before, but Dud wondered if she, too, had seen Johnny peeking at the top card. In any case, he gathered up the cards from the table in a snit of anger and re-dealt in a pout.

When drinks were first called for, Iris asked for a glass of water. Lottie had a pitcher on the table at Thompson's back, and Dud poured a glass, taking a sip before giving it to Iris, looking at Lottie as he did. Lottie clamped her lips and let her eyes shoot fire in his direction. Thereafter, when Iris or Ponder wanted something to drink, Dud would get it for them, not always tasting it first, but doing so at odd intervals to get the message across to Lottie. As the game went on, Thompson repeatedly began urging them to drink something with a little more "kick" to it. Each time they refused, and unable to hide his mounting anger, he threw a sharp glance at Lottie. She saw his look and returned it with an angry jerk of her head in Dud's direction.

At the first break, Thompson stalked from the room, dragging Lottie by the elbow with him. He slammed the door shut, and in a few seconds they heard the sound of a slap and a sharp cry. The men in the room turned to Johnny, but he smoothed his coat sleeves down unconcernedly. "See you gentlemen and lady," he added mockingly, bowing to Iris, "later."

Suzette appeared and led Iris and Dud toward her room down the hall. Loud noises filtered through closed doors— ribald laughter, filthy cursing, and the sound of

269

bed springs squeaking. Dud covered Iris's ears with his hands as they walked. She cocked her head at him, smiled and gave a giggle, but kept walking. It was only after Suzette closed the door that Dud took his hands away. "How am I doing, Mr. Dud?" Iris said with a smile and a large gasp of air.

"Wonderful, honey; you're doing fine. Here, sit at the table and eat a little something. Suzette made sandwiches." Suzette had made not only a pile of sandwiches, but pots of tea and coffee along with a plate of cookies.

Iris sat down at the table, but could not eat immediately. "He's an awful player," Iris said.

"Johnny?" Dud asked.

"Yes, he's terrible. The only thing going for him is that he is totally unpredictable." She stopped chattering and looked around the room. "What a lovely bedroom," she exclaimed. "Is this Suzette's room?"

Dud nodded and looked around. Instead of the usual whorehouse flash and stench, Suzette's room smelled fresh and bore a quiet country charm. Iris picked up a sandwich. "Eat something, Mr. Dud. There's plenty for both of us. Eat something and tell me what you think of the other players."

Dud picked up one of the sandwiches, and taking a bite of the thinly sliced, but piled high, flavored meat, he exclaimed, "Dang! These are good."

Iris nodded vigorously. "This is awfully nice of her to treat us this way."

A knock sounded at the door, and Ponder entered. He pulled a chair to the small table where Dud and Iris sat. "You're doing great, Iris. You've got them on the run," he said. "Have you noticed that? They are beginning to bet wild." Picking up one of the sandwiches, Ponder chomped on it and stopped talking long enough to gaze at it in surprise.

"Good, aren't they?" Dud said.

"Better than snuff and not near as dusty," Ponder said, taking another huge bite.

Iris laughed. "I hope Suzette says 'yes' to Mr. Jesse. Maybe she'll teach me some of her cooking secrets and how to dance."

Dud choked and spit, spewing bread all over his shirt. He shot Iris a stern look and said pointedly, "Getting back to poker."

They talked poker while they ate. When they finished, Ponder rose, admonishing Iris to lie down and rest. Rashtah had a cot for him in her room. He left and Dud followed soon afterward, promising Iris he would fetch her at the right time. He met Boyd and Jesse in the hall.

"They're doing great, aren't they?" Boyd said, talking low so not to disturb Iris, something that seemed incongruous amidst the other noises of the night.

Dud agreed. "Jesse, tell Suzette we appreciate all the trouble she's gone to."

Jesse colored faintly and nodded his head. Dud turned back to Boyd. "Boyd, would you mind standing here by the door while I go outside and get a breath of air? I don't trust anybody in this rat hole except Suzette and Rashtah."

Going down the stairs, he, Jesse, and Old Tom met a drunken barmaid coming up. With her dress askew, one breast exposed, she stopped Dud. "I like you," she lisped.

He removed her hand gently from his arm and squeezed it. "I like you too, sugar, but I've got to take a leak before I wet my pants," he said.

She nodded. "Don't go out the back," she slurred, weaving back and forth. "They're waiting for you."

"Who's waiting for me?" Dud asked.

She giggled. "Johnny has some men waiting for you in the alley."

Dud nodded. "Thank you, honey. Maybe me and the dog will just go piss in a corner."

She laughed and nodded, letting them pass. Dud glanced at Jesse as they continued downward. "See?"

"What are you going to do?" Jesse asked.

"Find a spittoon or an open window," Dud said. "I'm sure as hell not going outside just yet."

When the game resumed, Lottie had a black eye and a split lip. There were traces of powder and blood marks on Johnny's cuff, not Thompson's, but he looked smooth and unruffled. Thompson looked put-out, but trying not to let it show; the other men looked chary. Plainly, Thompson wanted to end the game, but Felix's presence stopped him. Felix would not harass anyone who lost, but he would spout obnoxious comments all over town about anyone who tried to stop the game just because Iris was good.

Nevertheless, the chips in front of Iris and Ponder dwindled again to a dangerously low level, but this time Dud refused to get too edgy, and in a while, the piles went up even higher than before. So high, in fact, two players had to drop. They took another break. This time Iris could neither eat nor talk, only flop on the bed in exhaustion. As Dud waited outside her door in the hall, Felix came up to him and asked in a low voice, "How much longer do you think Ponder can last?"

Dud shook his head. "Not much longer."

Felix gazed at him. "Johnny's about out."

"Don't get your hopes up, Felix. Lottie hates me even more than she hates you," Dud said. "But what about the land, when's he going to bet the land?" Dud demanded. "I thought that title floated around throughout these games."

"No," Felix said, shaking his head. "I thought I explained that to you. It's always used at the end, at a showdown."

"No, you didn't explain that to me," Dud said. "All you could think about was the Gilded Lily."

"Well, I'm telling you now."

Dud could only shake his head and wish the game would soon end.

Iris had dark circles under her eyes when she came back to the table; otherwise, she was all right. Johnny's luck had left for the night. In a frantic effort to win one last pot, he threw a dark beseeching look at Lottie, but she shook her head and hissed, "No!" giving Dud a triumphant look of hatred. Her refusal to back Johnny any further threw him out of the game, and he left the room, trying to act the cool, sophisticated gambler and failing. Lottie did not go after him.

When that hand ended, Ponder rose on unsteady legs, resting his trembling hands on the table. "You'll have to excuse me," he said, taking deep breaths. "But I have to cash out. Miss Iris, you have played a fine game." He turned. "Jesse, if you wouldn't mind, cash in my chips for me, please sir."

Jesse leaped forward to do as Ponder asked. As he did, Ponder turned and stumbled. Dud gave a start, but checked himself in time. Ponder righted himself, and with head held high, he walked slowly across the room. He had pushed himself almost beyond endurance, playing with a skill that earned him the respect of every person in the room. Every eye watched him as Boyd jumped up to give him his chair. Ponder sank down, utterly done in.

"I'd be much obliged for that drink now, Boyd," he said.

"Yes sir, Uncle Ponder," Boyd said, his voice resonating with veneration.

Dud gave Ponder a nod of thanks. From the look of his pile, Ponder had more than tripled his stake. Across the room, Lottie smirked in satisfaction. Johnny may have cost her a packet, but she had deprived Dud and Felix of the Gilded Lily. Felix stared at her with cool eyes from under pinched brows, but said nothing. Lottie turned away with an arrogant expression that did not completely cover the disquieting thoughts assailing her.

"Well, Miss Talbot," Thompson said as he began to rise from the table. "I guess you'll want to quit now, too."

Iris looked at Dud and swallowed. She looked back to Thompson. "Why no, Mr. Thompson, I wouldn't mind playing a few more hands."

While Lottie's mouth fell open, Thompson sat down slowly in his seat, a dawning of pleasure spreading across his face. "Why, it would be just you and me, wouldn't it, Miss Talbot?" he asked, making it sound like a salacious tryst.

Iris nodded.

"Lottie," Thompson called, not taking his eyes from Iris. "Get us a new pack." When she did not move, he turned and snarled, "I said a new pack, woman!"

Thereafter, Thompson smiled, he purred, he cooed, and played with the abandonment of a charlatan in a crowd full of rubes. For the next two hours they played, head to head. Thompson nervously put chaw after chaw of tobacco in his mouth, spitting on the floor carelessly while he stared at Iris with unabashed lust in his eyes. Iris continued to play well, but without Ponder, she lost some of her confidence. She blinked every time Thompson spit. Dud could see she was beginning to struggle, although her pile of chips had grown even bigger than Thompson's despite his sideshow antics.

As Iris looked down at her cards, Thompson's gaze became so openly lustful; Boyd had to squeeze Dud's shoulder to keep him from bounding across the room. Thompson wiped the sweat from his forehead and giving his cards a mere glance, looked at Iris and said, "You sure are pretty little woman, Miss Talbot."

Boyd's hold on Dud's shoulder tightened. Without looking up, Iris responded absentmindedly. "That's what my husband used to say until after the wedding."

As soon as the words left her mouth, she realized she had made a mistake. She tightened her eyelids shut, while Thompson's widened in surprise. Opening her eyes, Iris said, "Two cards, please, Mr. Thompson."

Thompson grinned, handing her two cards and taking three for himself. "I didn't realize you were a widow-woman, Miss Talbot," he said. "Or should I say, Mizz Talbot?"

Iris handled it well. "Yes, but I don't like to talk about it. I bet three hundred," she said, pushing her chips in the pot. Thompson automatically did the same.

"You know what they say poker is like, Mizz Talbot?" he asked. "They say it's like making love to a widow-woman. A man never knows when he is supposed to stop."

Boyd again had to forcibly hold Dud back. Iris put her cards on the table. "Three aces," she said. Thompson placed his face down. He took a handkerchief out of his back pocket and started to blow his nose. He looked across the table at Iris and stopped. He put the handkerchief down, and leaned to one side of the table. With one eye on Iris, he blew snot out of his nose onto the floor and pinched it off with his fingers. Iris gave an involuntary shudder.

Unable to endure it any longer, Dud broke free from Boyd and interrupted the game.

"I think Miss Iris should take a break," he said. "It's been over three hours since the last one."

Iris closed her eyes and let out a soft sigh. "Please," she said. "If you don't mind, Mr. Thompson."

"Well, of course, little lady," he said, trying to pretend his clothes were not wringing wet with perspiration. "I'll meet you back here in thirty minutes."

Iris nodded, and Dud helped her from her chair, leading her into the hall. As soon as the door shut behind them, she crumpled, burying her face in his shirt. She looked up, her eyes full of tears.

"Daddy, I don't think I can do it," she whispered and began to weep.

Dud held her in his arms. "You don't have to, sugar baby" he said, reaching up to stroke her hair.

"But I want to," she cried with a jerk of her head and a snap of her foot. "I want to."

Dud stood silent for a moment. "Come to Suzette's room with me," he said, taking her by the shoulders. As they walked down the hall, he whispered in her ear. "He's spitting on the floor constantly because he knows it bothers you. He's doing everything he can to irritate you from picking his nose to farting as loud as he can."

"Why that!" she cried impotently. "I wish I could do something to shake him,"

Dud opened the door to Suzette's room. "Maybe you can," he said.

TWENTY-FIVE

"WHAT DO YOU MEAN?" IRIS ASKED AS THE DOOR SHUT behind them.

Dud led her to Suzette's dressing table, noticing Suzette had again left coffee, tea, and various small tidbits that looked like women froufrou food, but would probably be all Iris could stomach, anyway. Steering her to the stool in front of the table, he put his hand on her shoulders as she sat down, and he looked at her in the mirror.

"Iris, honey, I hate that bastard right now, and I hate the way he's looking at you, but if you insist on staying in this game, we've got to do something to turn the tables on him." With clumsy hands that were more suited to throwing a lasso, Dud began removing pins from her hair. When he got them out, he brushed her hair down her back. Searching the knickknacks on Suzette's table, he found a hairclip. Taking the sides of Iris's hair, he pinned it back with the clip. He took some of the long hair down her back and brought it forward. Finally, with callused fingers, he ruffled her bangs. "There, that helps."

Iris slanted her eyes in his direction and said, "You think so?" Dud paid no attention to her questioning look. Instead, he held his hands over her shoulders, hesitantly at first, finally placing them on the fichu and taking it off. With the fichu removed, Iris's firm white breasts peeked enticingly from the gown.

"There," he said again. "I dare any man to sit there and play poker and keep his mind on the game."

"Do you really think this will help, Mr. Dud?" she asked.

"It won't hurt unless you feel a draft and catch cold. Now go lie down and shut your eyes for a while."

She nodded and made her way to Suzette's bed. "Mr. Dud," she pleaded. "Please don't leave me. Sit here and hold my hand, please."

"Okay, honey, you just lie down," he said, pulling a chair to the bed. He squeezed her hand, and she shut her eyes.

"Will you sing to me? Will you sing one of the songs you sing to the cattle to quiet them?" she asked.

"Sure, honey," Dud said. He looked at a small porcelain clock on the table near the bed. In a soft voice, he began a song he had sung a hundred times on open starry nights, feeling alone in the world with nothing but the backs of cattle as company. How many times had he dreamed of women while singing that song? Every time?

Iris's breathing began to deepen, her chest rising and falling in rhythm. He dared not let her sleep longer than fifteen minutes. Any longer and she would be so groggy she would never be able to concentrate on a single hand. He sang lightly, barely making a hum, and watched the clock. In fourteen minutes, he shook her shoulders. "Wake up, little baby. It's almost time."

She opened her eyes and looked at him. "Okay," she said, and got up from the bed.

As they went out, Suzette met them at the door. She gave Iris a startled glance, but said nothing. Iris stopped and told her how much she appreciated everything Suzette had done. Suzette listened with her face turned away. Dud tugged on Iris, but before they took two steps, Suzette called, "Wait!"

She ran back into the room and came out with a bottle of perfume, spraying some of it between Iris's breasts. She handed Dud the bottle and wrapped Iris's shawl around her shoulders, covering her bosom. "Do not open it until you sit at the table," Suzette instructed. "You want the grand effect."

Iris nodded like an acolyte, and Suzette, taking the bottle back, continued. "If you win, and I think you will, for your own safety, let him pretend he is throwing the game to you."

"Yes, I understand," Iris said, looking at Dud, and he agreed.

Suzette kissed her cheek and wished her *bonne chance* before bolting back into her room. Iris looked at Dud again, took a deep breath and nodded her head.

The room had become packed with people—barmaids, cowboys, ranchers, and anyone of importance in town either up that late, or up that early, because sunrays were seeping through the windows. The crowd parted for Iris as Dud led her to her chair and pulled it out. Men who looked at her for over an hour every Friday, Saturday, and

Sunday night now gaped as if they had never seen her before. Iris's blue eyes were wide with fright.

Thompson stared as she sat down. Despite her nervousness, Iris let go of the shawl around her shoulders in a casual drop. Thompson's mouth hung open, and he began bellowing for everyone to get out. "Just the ones who were here earlier," he said. "The rest of you beat it!"

The room slowing emptied amid a low drone of protests. Ponder gave Iris a smile and a nod, and she acknowledged it with a return nod and small smile. Thompson called again for a new deck, and the play began, but this time, Iris had the advantage. Her confidence slowly grew and it showed in the cool way she dealt the cards and made her bets. One shoulder of her dress would drop, and she would give it what Dud at first thought was an unconscious tug. When he noticed that the shoulder crept down every time Thompson tried to decide what to discard, Dud began to feel almost sorry for him and wondered how Iris managed it.

It must have been getting to Thompson worse than Dud imagined, because in less than thirty minutes after they resumed play, he looked at the cards in his hand and pushed half the chips he had in front of him. He grinned while Iris looked at her cards. She matched him with hardly a bat of an eyelash, but did not raise his bet. She took one card; he took two.

With a smirk, Thompson pushed the rest of his pile into the pot. He opened his jacket, and brought out a folded piece of paper, throwing it casually on top of the chips.

"That's the title to that land out at the Yegua," he said.

"It and my chips ought to equal what you've got in front of you."

Iris never missed a beat. "What land?" she asked.

"It's the land where three creeks meet at the foot of the Yegua Knobs. Washburn," he said, throwing a nod in Dud's direction, "he's been out there picking up rocks and lumber. He knows what I'm talking about."

Iris stared at Dud with round eyes and then back to her hand. As she sat there concentrating on the cards, Dud glued his eyes on Thompson and tried to decipher what he could be holding—a straight, a flush? Thompson began grinning—the same self-satisfied leer he wore when people asked him if he and Suzette were lovers.

He was bluffing! Dud knew it as surely as he knew he had two balls hanging in his pants. He looked back at Iris, and for the first time that night, indecision showed on her face. Dud exchanged glances with Ponder, and also for the first time that night, Dud was able to read Ponder's expression—he knew Thompson was bluffing too. Ponder lowered his eyelids and put his head down as if telling him to do something. But what?

Ponder again jerked his head as if to say, "Do something, Dud, darn it!" And then Dud remembered. When Iris swallowed and looked up at him with questioning eyes, he scratched his nose.

She looked at Thompson and back at Dud, but he dared not repeat it. It was not necessary anyway, he knew from the look on her face she had caught it.

She swallowed again and said, "That land isn't worth much to me, Mr. Thompson. I'm just a poor working girl."

Thompson smiled and leaned back in his chair,

thinking he had her buffaloed. Ponder and Dud looked at one another; both wondered what Iris could be doing.

"However," Iris said, "I think I will see your bet if you allow me to match it with this amount." She moved chips forward on the table. "Since the land's value is in doubt, perhaps this will cover it and your chips, leaving me with something in the event I should lose."

The smile paled on Seth Thompson's face. He stared at Iris's remaining chips. They equaled two-thirds of the original stake. Dud bit his lip in emotion; Iris believed in her hand, but she was determined not to lose his money.

Thompson's shoulders slumped, just a little, but he knew he was beat. Iris could bet every chip she had and still win. His only possible decision was how to handle losing. He made up his mind and leaned forward. "Mizz Talbot, would you allow me the pleasure of taking your hand?"

Iris slowly put her hand across the table, unsure of what he planned to do. Dud felt himself move forward as everyone in the room crowded closer to the table and held their breaths. Thompson took Iris's hand and stroked it with his big, stubby fingers. "Mizz Talbot," he said, "you are one of the most beautiful young ladies I have ever met in my life, and it has been a pleasure sitting across the table from you all these hours."

Iris, speechless, nodded her head. For seconds, all Dud could hear was a clock ticking on the wall and Felix's labored breathing. Thompson, still holding her hand, said, "Mizz Talbot, would you show us your cards?"

It was not according to Hoyle, but Iris did not demand he flip his instead. She pulled her hand gently away and turned over her cards. The crowd leaned forward in one collective body and gasped—a full house, a pair of deuces and three tens.

"A helluva hand for just two players," Felix whispered in admiration.

Thompson pretended not to notice the stares around him. He gazed into Iris's face and pushing the pile of chips with the deed toward her, he said in a tone that held a contrived combination of hopefulness and generosity, "Mizz Talbot, I want you to have this. Maybe then you'll think about poor old lonely Seth sometimes. Just take it, honey, it's yours." He drew his hands back and in one swift, smooth move, shoved his cards in the remaining deck.

Iris let out a sigh of relief. She smiled and said, "Why, thank you, Mr. Thompson."

Everyone spoke at once, smiling, laughing. Thompson had robbed Iris of the satisfaction of winning on her ability, but she did not care. She smiled at everyone, her face returning to Dud's repeatedly. Felix, Ponder, Boyd, Jesse, himself, all wore huge grins of relief. Dud cashed in Iris's chips and handed her the money. They swept toward the door along with the rest of the people, with Boyd and Jesse next to them. Dud stopped by Lottie as Iris got carried away with the crowd.

"You kept your end of the bargain, and I'll keep mine," he told Lottie in the now empty room. "Just remember, I'm a lot better off to you alive than I am dead."

She remained mute, staring at him with hard eyes and a pursed mouth. He had fooled her in the beginning, but he could see by her expression that her intelligent mind now questioned his reason for wanting to win the game so badly. He expected her to turn without a word and storm from the room. Instead, she asked with narrowed eyes and tightened lips, "You ever fish for carp, Dud? Because if you have, you ought to feel like his kin. Your little 'sugar baby' has hooked you and is playing with you like the bottom-feeding, walleyed, oily bastard you are. You can watch your back, Dud, but don't be looking in my direction while you're doing it."

This time, she did turn and storm from the room.

Above the roar in the hall, he heard Iris call his name. She popped back into the room and ran to him, her face brilliant with happiness.

"Mr. Dud, Mr. Dud, I won, I won," she cried holding up the wad of cash. "I won my inheritance back, Mr. Dud. All that money my parents worked so hard for, and I allowed Lon to waste, I won it back." Tears sprang into her eyes, and she wrapped her arms around his waist and hugged him, rocking back and forth in happiness.

He put his arms around her and squeezed in return, smiling and kissing the top of her head. He looked up and saw that Thompson had reentered the room. He stared at them, turned on his heels and pushing past Ponder, stomped away.

Dud kissed Iris's hair again; hugging her made him feel like he was keeping the snakes away. But had one of those snakes been telling the truth? Iris leaned back, still holding on to him. "Thank you, Mr. Dud. Thank you, thank you, thank you."

"Iris," Dud said, looking down in her upturned face. "I believe I should be thanking you."

Boyd and Jesse burst back in. "Come on," they shouted. "Let's get out of here and celebrate!"

Dud followed Iris to the door, but Ponder caught him by the arm.

"You didn't have to rub it in his damn face," Ponder hissed, his face dark with anger.

"She hugged me first!" Dud said. "What was I supposed to do? Stand there like a cigar store Indian?"

Ponder looked at the door. "This means you are really going to have to keep an eye on her, Dud."

"You're the one who said she would be all right!" Dud said, furious at Ponder.

"That was before you decided to plow with the little heifer right before Thompson's eyes, you dimwit!" Ponder paused. "I swear to God, Dud, if you hurt that woman, I'll kill you."

"I'm not going to hurt her!" Dud said, aghast.

"I know how you are, Dud!"

They left the room, glaring at one another.

The Darst family was waiting for them outside the saloon. Annabelle peeked around them, and when Iris finished hugging Zizi, she hugged Annabelle. Dud drew closer and leaned next to Annabelle.

"Miss Annabelle," he whispered, his voice a little shaky from his encounter with Ponder. "Would you mind running home and asking your papa if he would open his office for us and keep this money in his safe tonight until the bank opens in the morning?"

She nodded, and Boyd, who was close enough to hear, said, "I'll go with her." Boyd probably realized Annabelle had snuck out of the house to await the news. He would go to the front door and send her around to the back to creep in without being noticed.

Dud's anger with Ponder did not last long. Besides

splitting the pot with Iris, he insisted, with Boyd and Jesse agreeing, that Ponder keep at least half of his winnings, even though he protested he did not want anything.

"All right, all right," Ponder finally said. "Good God in tarnation."

"I guess you'll be wanting to go home now, Uncle Ponder," Dud said.

Ponder looked at him as if he were crazy. "I guess you think wrong. I believe I'll stick around here for a while yet."

In the end, they decided to put the money in the bank on Monday and go to the county seat on Tuesday to register the paperwork at the courthouse that would make everything legal. Ponder cautioned Dud not to take Iris along.

"Don't push him, Dud," he warned.

Dud thought about the look on Thompson's face when he saw Iris with her arms around him; even so, he did not want Iris out of his sight for that long. He had nightmares of Thompson kidnapping Iris and molesting her.

Sunday night was so hot and still, they slept naked and would have rolled miserably in sweat if they had not been so tired. Dud predicted a norther. On Monday morning, Ponder vanished; leaving word with Felix he would be back late that night. The norther hit that afternoon. As Dud stood in the stables, the wind rocked the building, whipping the flame in Ugor's fire pit as they stood hovering around it. Ugor disappeared into the rear of the stables and came back holding a knife.

"Here, this yours," he said, handing it to Dud.

Dud turned the polished horn handle in his hand—a good stout knife with a strong, sharp blade, just the right size for his scabbard. Someone had etched in the shining blade "DW." Dud thanked him and praised the knife.

"Mike, he did it," Ugor said, trying to look modest. "Well, most of it."

"Mike did this?" Dud asked, admiring the craftsmanship.

"Sure," Ugor said. "Mike, he got the feel to work with metal. It's born in him. In the old country, he would follow my footsteps. Frank, Kris, they good, but don't have the *ösztönt*, what you say, instinct, for it. In old country, they would be shepherds. Here," he shrugged, "maybe be cowboys."

"And Gabby?" Dud asked with a gentle smile. "What about him?"

Ugor shook his head. "I don't know. His mama, she spoil him. I say, 'don't spoil that boy,' but she no listen. I told the older boys, 'promise me you keep him out of prison.'"

Dud smiled again. "Oh, life has a way of knocking the spoiled out of us. He'll be all right with the older boys watching out for him."

Ugor shook his head again. "I worry about those boys. They good boys, but you know how it is."

Dud did not know how it was, but he pushed aside that old familiar stab of pain. "Only secondhand," he answered. "But you don't have to worry, Darst; they're good boys."

The next morning, Ponder handed Iris a box. With Dud looking over her shoulder, Iris opened it and found an ornate silver comb and brush set. She looked up, her eyes brimming with sentiment. "Oh, Uncle Ponder.

They're beautiful." She hugged his neck and kissed his cheek. "Thank you so much."

As Iris left to show her gift to Annabelle and Zizi, Dud looked at Ponder, shocked to see a blaze of emotion in his watery eyes.

"You're a fool, Dud," he said, and turned and walked away.

Unable to understand Ponder, Dud suddenly felt homesick. He made up his mind to start the treasure hunt in earnest as soon as he got back from the county seat, even if he had to dig up both sides of the creek and dodge bullets from Ev Reid or some unknown stranger while he did it.

TWENTY-SIX

IGNORING PONDER'S WARNING, DUD TOOK IRIS WITH HIM to the county seat. Annabelle yearned to go, too, and had Elizabeth convinced to join them, but Elizabeth became indisposed that week and her parents refused permission. Iris said Annabelle cried and pouted to her parents, but not in front of Boyd. In any case, Boyd and Jesse again decided to stay in Tie Town and let Felix ride shotgun as chaperone while Iris sat in the middle of the wagon seat.

"May I take my horse, Mr. Dud?" Iris pleaded. "We can tie him to the back of the wagon. I'd like to be able to ride him for part of the trip or in town."

Dud did not really want to fool with all those animals, not counting the dog, but he could not turn down a request from Iris. While Dud saddled Iris's horse, without thinking why, he asked Ugor to fetch his grulla. With his horse and Iris's saddled and tied to the back of the wagon, the three of them set out in the cold blustery wind.

Dud held the reins loosely in his hands. Iris huddled next to him, smiling and talking despite the biting wind.

She wanted to find something special for Elizabeth because she had given her the dress she wore to the poker game. Nellie had a fondness for chocolate, and Iris hoped to buy, if nothing else, at least a box of cocoa for her. She wanted to get Annabelle something too, but did not know quite what. Felix sat on the other side of her and made suggestions, most of them useless.

"I promised Boyd I'd buy something for Annabelle because she keeps Old Tom so clean and combed out," Dud said.

Iris nodded. "Boyd will always be good to Annabelle," she said.

"He's made sure Elizabeth knows that," Dud agreed dryly.

They left the flat country and began to drive the horses into a small dell with heavily wooded rises on either side. Before Dud could voice his fears about Elizabeth and Boyd, he noticed Old Tom sniffing the air. The dog then put his nose to the ground, picking up a scent. At the same time, the horses shied nervously.

"Felix," Dud began, but the crack of a rifle shot stopped him.

"Hi ya," Dud shouted, popping the reins as hard as he could. The horses bolted; Iris fell against him, grabbing her hat and the edge of the seat. Felix did the same while Dud repeatedly whipped the horses forward and Old Tom ran behind them.

"What was that?" Iris screamed. "What's wrong? Oh my God, your ear!"

Dud paid little heed to the stinging sensation on his right earlobe as he urged the horses forward. Felix slipped and struggled to climb back in the seat. Old Tom kept pace beside the racing wagon. Finally, when Dud thought they were out of rifle range, he brought the horses to a halt, throwing the reins to Felix.

"Take Iris into town—shoot anybody that tries to stop you," he shouted as he jumped from the wagon. As he ran to his horse, he could hear Iris calling frantically.

"But you're bleeding, Mr. Dud!"

Dud untied the horse and jumped in the saddle. He rode to the side of the wagon, reared his horse and popped the team as hard as he could. "Get moving!" he yelled at Felix.

He did not have to tell Felix twice. He watched the wagon take off before he turned back. The shot had come from the wooded ridges now on his left. He looked around and picked the highest spot and rode to it. When he reached it, he looked down at the road, but could not see anyone making tracks back to Tie Town or following the wagon. Scanning the horizon, he saw nothing but trees and brush.

Cursing under his breath, he rode his horse slowly back to the spot where they had heard the rifle shot. He rode on a little further, and then pushed his horse into the undergrowth, mentally cursing the pine trees around him. "Indians, Tom," he warned the dog. He soon saw the signs, and began patiently following them, thankful whoever it was had a well-fed horse. Old Tom quickly picked up the scent Dud was after and together they zigzagged their way through the forest. The trees that could hide their enemy could also hide them.

In a while, Dud thought he heard noises, and he put his hand up, stopping the dog with a soft command while he listened. He rode slowly forward.

"Washburn, Washburn," a voice came through the trees. "I'm hurt; I'm down."

Dud moved with even greater care, searching the trees for signs of an accomplice as he headed toward the voice. He saw no one until he came into a small clearing. Seth Thompson's horse stood while Thompson lay sprawled on the ground nearby. He saw Dud and called again.

"Washburn, come here. I fell off my horse and broke my leg." He groaned and touched his thigh. "Come here and help me. I didn't mean to hit you. I just meant to scare you. My horse reared and made me fire wild. Look, there's my rifle."

Dud glanced at it. The rifle lay far enough away it could not be snatched in a hurry. He cautiously made his way closer, his pistol pulled. Thompson clutched his leg with one hand while the other arm lay near a fallen log. He moaned and cursed. "Come on, Washburn. I'm hurting here."

If Thompson's horse had reared, he would have fired up, not down, and Thompson's right hand had not moved from beside the log, although he writhed as in agony. Dud realized his only decision would be if he should shoot it out with Thompson, kill him and get it over with, or go straight to the log with his gun trained on Thompson and kick the pistol he knew was there away, taking him into town for attempted murder.

While the seconds ticked by, Thompson watched him. Dud did not believe a jury would convict him—it would be Dud's belief of what happened against Thompson's protests that it had all been a mistake.

"You know something, Thompson," Dud said. "Even though you're a bastard, I always halfway liked you and felt sorry for you. But you shot my right ear and not my left, and that scares the hell out of me." He pretended to lower his defenses and made to put his gun away. Thompson made a grab for the pistol under the log, but before he could raise it, Dud shot him.

The firing of his .45 sounded like thunder in the woods, the familiar smell of gun smoke rising and dispersing through the chilly air. Dud looked at the body, picked up Thompson's pistol and put it in his belt. He went to Thompson's rifle and found a bullet jammed in the chamber as he expected. No longer able to be a sniper, instead of high-tailing it out of there, Thompson had resorted to a ruse. Struggling with the heavy man, Dud threw him over his horse and tied him. He went to his horse, about to get in the saddle and leave, but his arm began to tremble. The trembling went down in his legs, and he found himself sinking to the ground.

Old Tom nosed him, and Dud threw his arms around the dog and hugged him tight, trying to stop the erratic breathing in his chest and the tremors shooting through his muscles. He'd killed many men, shot men and had their brains splatter on him during the war. When it was over, he went to his deserted childhood home, and he'd been so jumpy for a long time he'd start at any sound. His brother-in-law had wanted to move, and he did, too. Then it was Indian trouble, and he'd lived through that. This was different; this was unlike anything he'd ever felt before.

Dud took his hands away from the dog and covered his face with them. "Oh God," he cried rocking back and forth, "That bastard shot to my right side."

Only a sliver of sun shone on the horizon when he

found Felix waiting for him in front of the hotel. Dud got off his horse slowly, throwing the reins over the rail and stepping onto the sidewalk. "Where's Iris?" he asked, in control of himself once again.

"I sent her upstairs," Felix said. "She refused to move from the bench all afternoon, looking like her best friend had died, but I finally convinced her to rest by telling her you might need her." He walked to the sorrel and pulled Thompson's head up by the hair, letting it drop almost immediately.

"Sheriff's office next to the courthouse?" Dud asked.

Felix nodded his head. "I'll go with you. Let me tell the desk clerk where we're at in case Iris comes down."

Dud nodded, and when Felix came back, they found the sheriff. Felix backed his story, and nobody could deny the blood all over Dud's neck and shirt.

"I don't think they'll be any trouble," the sheriff said, "unless the family wants to squawk over it."

"The only squawking they'll do will be over the will," Felix said dryly.

As they approached the hotel, Iris saw them and ran toward them. "Mr. Dud!" she sobbed, trying unsuccessfully to hold back tears. "You're hurt. There's blood all over you." She came closer and when she saw his ear, she put both fists against her mouth. "He shot your earlobe off!"

Dud reached up and found she was right; instead of just a nick as he had thought, his right earlobe was gone.

"Come upstairs and let me clean the wound for you," she said, taking him by the hand. Her fingers trembled in his.

In the hotel room, Iris wanted to call a doctor to stitch the lobe closed. "It's bleeding again," she cried.

"Oh, it will be all right. A man always looks like a stuck hog when he gets a cut to his ear or his head," Dud said.

"It's more than just a cut," Iris persisted.

"It just means I'll never be able to wear earbobs, that's all," Dud said.

Iris laughed through her tears. "Oh, Mr. Dud!" She finished dressing the wound and went into her bedroom to wash before they went to supper.

As soon as she walked through the connecting door to her room, Felix asked, "Do you think she realizes he was aiming at her?"

"Don't say anything. Oh God, Felix, Ponder warned me not to take her along."

Felix shook his head. "It's water under the bridge now, Dud."

Iris came back in, and they went to supper, but Dud's ear throbbed, and Felix and Iris were as exhausted as he was. Uninterested in anything else, they went back to the hotel room, and Dud flopped on the bed.

"Iris, honey, my ear feels like a Chinaman is beating on it with a hot iron," Dud said. "Could I talk you into taking my boots off and rubbing my feet for a while to take my mind off that pigtailed little devil?"

"Of course, Mr. Dud," Iris said. She removed his boots, and sitting on the edge of the bed, she began to massage his feet.

Felix looked at him in repugnance. "Washburn, you are revolting."

"Oh, Mr. Felix," Iris said. "He's hurting, can't you see that?"

"That's right, Felix," Dud said, reveling in having his feet manipulated by Iris's tender hands. "I'm hurting."

Felix said a word he should not have and took a chair near Iris. As Dud's eyes grew heavy, he heard Iris telling Felix she hoped she did not have to look at another deck of cards for a long time. Relieved he had not led her into a life of sin, Dud let Iris's gentle ministrations lull him to sleep.

Dud did not know anything until the next morning when he opened his eyes and saw Old Tom staring at him patiently. He got up, taking the dog down the stairs and out back, leaving him to take care of business while he took care of his own. Returning upstairs, he roused a protesting Felix out of bed. He knocked on Iris's door and hollered for her to get up—he was hungry.

After eating and tending to the deed business, Felix walked to the print shop to pick up his order of marriage certificates while Dud took Iris shopping. She found Elizabeth a brooch and the chocolate for Nellie. Jesse had said that Suzette needed a new pair of shoes, and Dud paid for those while Iris bought her a shawl similar to the one Nellie had loaned her.

"I wish I had a narrow foot like Suzette instead of these short stubby things I've got," Iris moaned. "It's so much more refined looking."

"Just be glad you have two feet, girl," Dud said. "And don't worry about how refined they look."

Buying something for Annabelle proved challenging. The Harrisons kept Annabelle in little girl finery, something Iris disliked.

"It really bothers Annabelle that Elizabeth has a hope chest and she doesn't," Iris mourned with a shake of her head."And we can't buy her anything like that—it would give Annabelle false ideas and upset the Harrisons."

As they gazed through the storefront windows, Dud spied a curious-looking tea set. "Take a gander at this, Iris. Don't most girls like to have tea parties, no matter what age they are?"

"Well, I had a cousin who insisted on wrestling hogs instead, but most of the rest of us do," Iris said as she peered through the glass. In place of the usual painted flowers and whatnots, it had outdoor wildlife scenes—water fowl and deer—on the set. "That is uncommon," Iris agreed. "And Annabelle loves nature. Do you think the Harrisons would mind if I got it for her?"

Dud studied the teapot. "I don't think so; she could always use it playing with her dolls. It might make her feel like she has something similar to Elizabeth's things. Why don't you let me get the pot, the creamer, and the sugar bowl, and you buy the matching cups?"

Iris agreed. After making their purchases, they split up, deciding to meet back at the hotel. Later, Dud found Felix in one of the saloons, giving a hand by hand account of the poker game to a small crowd of men. Dud stood at the edge and noticed that Felix was not intoxicated, remembering also that he had not touched a drop during the night of the game either. Dud glanced to his left and saw the county employee who had auctioned the house on Pecan Street. As he quietly drank his beer, Dud introduced himself and asked, "Are those marriages Felix does legal?"

He nodded his head. "Oh yes, they're legal. That settlement is lucky to have Felix. Anybody else but that talkative old man would have been killed a long time ago in that shoot-'em-up hellhole."

After supper, the three decided not to stay another night. Instead, they limped back to Tie Town by the light of a rising moon. Dud's ear pulsated in pain, and Iris and Felix looked as exhausted as he felt. Once home, Dud dropped Felix off at his apartment above the surveyor's office and took Iris to the boardinghouse. Reaching in back of the wagon, he lit a lantern and handed her a velvet-covered box.

"I don't want to hear any of that stuff about how a decent woman can't take expensive gifts from a man," Dud told her. "This isn't that kind of gift. You did me a tremendous favor, Iris, and I won't ever forget it."

She stared at him, and then opened it with fingers that trembled slightly. She touched the earrings of sapphires dangling from small balls of gold, saying in a soft, quiet voice, "Thank you, Mr. Dud."

Her lack of enthusiasm rattled him, but he thought perhaps she was worried about accepting so expensive a gift, despite his words. He got out of the wagon and walked around to help her down. "Don't wear them to that dratted café. If you drop one, Ruby will try to steal it from you."

Iris nodded. "Will you come in the morning and take me to the Harrisons with you so I can give them their presents?"

"Sure," Dud said. Iris walked away carrying her box, but before she made it to the gallery, she turned and ran back to him, giving him a quick hug. "They're beautiful!" she cried, and ran into the boardinghouse.

TWENTY-SEVEN

AFTER EXPLAINING TO EVERY PERSON WHO SAW HIM WHY HIS earlobe was no longer there, and having to face Ponder's glares of "I told you so," Dud, feeling grouchy, went with Iris to give the Harrisons their gifts. Nellie and Elizabeth made a big to-do over their presents, but Annabelle stared at her tea set and clutching it to her breast, took it into her bedroom without a word.

"Annabelle!" Nellie remonstrated as she walked away, but Annabelle shut the door quietly behind her.

"I'm so sorry," Nellie apologized. "Annabelle usually exhibits lovely manners."

"I think we understand," Dud said and stopped Nellie from going after the girl.

They left Suzette's gifts with Jesse. Even though Dud felt like an old stallion ridden a hundred miles too hard, he and his nephews went to the land where the creeks met on the Yegua. They studied the map again to see if there was anything they missed. Searching through brush the rest of the day, they came up with nothing, dragging back into town at dusk.

"The only bull is this map," Boyd muttered dejectedly.

"And how are we going to find anything anyway in all that debris left over from the flooding?" Jesse complained.

They went again the following day, taking Ponder with them, hoping he would see something they missed. They fought their way around thick stands of trees and yaupons, hunting through clearings and crossing the creek to explore just in case the map had the heart on the wrong side. All the while, they looked for signs that someone else might be searching, too, but found no indications. Because of the Yegua's reputation, they could never be certain if their vague feelings of being watched were real or imagined. Dud began to wonder if it had been Mary and Ev who approached Ugor Darst. It could have been curious locals with nothing better to do than stick their noses into a stranger's business. Regardless, even with Ponder's help, their hunt proved futile. They rode back to town in silence, not bothering to hide the gloom they felt.

Felix dropped by the house on Pecan Street, drawn by the smells of Iris's cooking and full of news.

"They claimed the body. The sister thought about raising hell over what happened, but when the sheriff told her they'd have to hold up the estate settlement if she insisted on an investigation, she shut her trap fast."

"What about the stepson?" Dud asked as he spooned something delicious Iris called burgoo, made with squirrels he and the boys had brought in along with chicken and sausage and whatever else Iris could find to put in it.

"Nobody ever knows what that closed-mouthed biscuit-eater is thinking," Felix said, licking escaped burgoo off his chin. "I'm reading the will in court Saturday—that's probably all they're worried about, is who gets what."

The next afternoon, Dud's horse lost a shoe, and since part of the ground around the Yegua was rocky, they came back into town early to have Ugor put on a new one. Jesse and Boyd left Dud at the stables. Because their teacher either had food poisoning or a terrific hangover, the Darst boys were out of school for a couple of days.

The weather had warmed slightly, and the wind had died. While he waited for the shoe, Dud strolled outside, leaned on a wagon and began talking with Mike Darst about his new knife. Two girls walked by, their budding breasts just beginning to show the signs of womanhood to come. They looked at Mike and giggled. Dud might as well have been invisible. "Hi, Mike," the older one said. "Where's Frank?"

Mike turned a deep shade of red. "He's asking our uncle a question about mules," Mike stuttered. "Well, he's not really our uncle, but we think of him...," he trailed off as the girls sashayed on their way.

Dud grinned, but before they could return to their conversation, Annabelle approached, carrying a new doll. Another group of smaller girls walked past, laughing and talking, and Annabelle attempted to show them the doll.

"Leave us alone, Annabelle," one pig-tailed girl said.

"That's right, you're too old to play with us," another added disdainfully.

Annabelle stood still, staring at them while the doll

hung limp in her hand. The girls circled her, and going around in a ring, began to chant.

"Annabelle, Annabelle, kicked by a mule," they sang. "Annabelle, Annabelle, too dumb to go to school. Annabelle, Annabelle, dumb as a mule."

Tears sprang into Annabelle's eyes, and the circle of girls broke up in a gaggle of laugher as they ran away. Dud and Mike said nothing, and Annabelle turned. She walked toward them like a sleepwalker, but when she reached the wagon, she took the doll and began beating its head against the wagon's wheel as she burst into tears. The doll's china face cracked and broke, and Annabelle flung it down.

"Stop bellering, Annabelle," Dud said quietly.

She sniffed, and while tears still filled her eyes, she stopped her wild crying. She stared at the shattered doll, her face drawing up in horror. "Oh no, what am I going to tell Papa?" she cried. "He just gave it to me."

Mike stepped forward, chin up. He lifted his foot and stomped his boot on the doll's head. "I will apologize to your father for stepping on your doll, Miss Annabelle," he said, his high, cracking voice sounding tragically noble. "I will offer to pay for it."

Annabelle stared at him, while Dud watched with interest.

"No," Annabelle said slowly. "That would be wrong. Thank you, but I will confess to Papa." She put her head down, tears streaming down her cheeks. "Papa won't let me go to the dance Saturday night," she said in a small voice. "Elizabeth gets to go, but I don't."

Dud felt sorry for the girl, and Mike was not the only

one who could be noble. "Mike," he said. "Do you think your papa and brother would come over tonight and play for a dance? Maybe Miss Annabelle's parents would let her come to a small party at my house."

Annabelle looked at Dud in awe, then hopefully at Mike. Mike grinned and said, "I shall ask them." He turned on his heel and called out, "Papát, Papát! Can you and Kris play tonight at a party for Mr. Dud?"

"Sure," Ugor's big voice boomed from inside the building. Zizi came to the door. "Party?" she asked.

"Right," Dud answered. "Come over to my house tonight for a party."

When Mike translated, her face filled with pleasure, then drained. She cried something in Hungarian and turned, rushing back into the building.

"Hmm, I guess I better warn Iris," Dud said.

Iris's had a similar reaction to Zizi's, and she cried out in English, "The food! What shall I cook?"

Although Dud assured her it would be a small party, after receiving a look from Iris as if he were insane, he felt prompted to add, "Just make that burgoo stuff again." In the end, Iris had him fetch her landlady's cast iron wash pot, and then sent him off to kill and dress something to put in it. When he returned, he was asked to go back to the landlady's for her big stone crock and extra cups and plates, but he managed to foist that job on Jesse.

Annabelle came by to say they were coming, and her mother was frying chicken. "I don't know why we couldn't just have cheese and crackers again," Dud muttered. The intricacies of women's social rules and obligations were too much for him to figure out.

Iris worked all afternoon, trotting outside to cook, dragging in tables and chairs, collecting enough utensils. She had just put the Navajo blanket on a table to use as a tablecloth when she suddenly clapped her hands to her cheeks. "Oh, Mr. Dud," she cried, looking at him. "I'm so sorry. I've been running around like this is my house and my party. I'm afraid you've spoiled me. You'll probably get married, and I'll be just like Seth Thompson's old maid sister, mad because I have to take second place."

Jesse and Boyd overheard and broke into hearty laughter. "I believe it's going to be the other way around," Boyd said. "One day you'll get married, and Uncle Dud will be crying buckets of tears because he won't have you to run and fetch for him."

Iris grinned and Dud tried to smile, but it came out looking like a sick slit. Iris, almost skipping in gaiety, went back to the boardinghouse to change clothes.

Felix brought an extra fiddler to spell Ugor and Kris. Kris especially wanted to hang around the other boys at least part of the time. After Felix, the Darsts arrived, Zizi carrying a large pan. "Strudel," she informed Dud.

Dud, with glands beginning to slobber, took the pan, shut the door behind the Darsts and carried it across the room to the table Iris had set up. The Darst boys went immediately to Ponder to talk about an unusual horse someone had brought into the livery stable. Hearing a knock that sounded like someone had used a foot to hit the door; Dud went back and opened it. Iris stood juggling boxes of napkins, cookies, and more cheese and crackers. Her head hung down sheepishly, and she gave him a "please don't be mad" look because behind her towered her landlady. "Well, Washburn," she boomed over Iris's head, "are you going to let us in or not?"

Dud moved aside to let Iris in, and when he saw the landlady had a pie in each hand, he let her pass, too. She shoved the pies in his hands as the musicians tuned their instruments and began to play. "Where's that mangy Felix?" she asked peering into the room. Seeing him, she hollered, "Felix, you son of a stray cur, you're dancing with me." Dud shut the door behind her with his elbow while she made a grab for Felix, his head jerking back and forth looking in vain for an escape.

The Harrisons arrived soon afterward with the surveyor at their heels. The big Swede looked around the house, nodding in approval. "Ja, the house looks fine," he said. Annabelle clutched her tea set to her chest. "She insisted on bringing it," Nellie said apologetically. "I warned her it might get broken." Dud smiled and told Annabelle they would be careful. Iris greeted them and asked Annabelle where she would like to put the set.

Annabelle carried it to the table and set in smack in the middle. "Here," she said happily. Iris smiled and wrapping one arm around Annabelle's waist, hugged her. Iris wore her poker dress, but instead of the old-fashioned fichu, she had tucked a gauzy scarf around the neckline to keep from being too exposed. Her new earrings dangled on her ears, and Dud thought she looked utterly beautiful. As the music played, Dud looked around the room; he had never seen one with so many good-looking women in it. Even Iris's landlady cleaned up well.

A little later, an unexpected knock came at the door, surprising Dud because most of his friends walked in without knocking. The only reason Iris had knocked was because she could not get the door open. Dud went to the door, and opening it, got a shock. There stood the man who had given him the offhanded advice at the café, Seth Thompson's stepson.

The cowboy leaned against the doorframe casually, and although Dud tightened, ready for a confrontation, the young man took off his Stetson, handed it to Dud, and removing his gun belt, placed it in Dud's hands.

"I heard there was a dance tonight," he said, looking into the room instead of Dud's face.

"Come on in," Dud said. "I'm sorry I had a trouble with your step-pa."

The cowboy sauntered in, pausing and speaking from the corner of his mouth as he looked elsewhere. "I bet he pulled the 'I'm hurt, help me,' stunt on you."

Dud nodded. The young man continued. "I did you a favor by tipping my hat about the poker game. You did one for me when you put a bullet hole through that bastard, something I've dreamed of for years. I'd like to dance with Miss Talbot if I may."

Dud's hands paused in midair. Without looking at the cowboy, he said, "You'll have to ask her," and finished hanging the hat and gun belt on a nail in the window frame close to the door. While the cowboy went after Iris, Felix walked over to Dud. "What do you think?" he asked, eyeing Thompson's stepson.

Dud gave a shake of his head. "He's a peculiar bird, Felix. But he was good to his stepmother, and he didn't like Thompson." He added, "I still don't think he's right for Iris, though."

Felix looked at him askew, and to Dud's relief, he said, "There's no question of that. Good heavens, man."

All the men, including Ponder and the Darst boys, took turns teaching Annabelle to dance. The Harrisons looked pleased, and taking Dud aside, Nellie said, "You do realize why we have to be so careful with her, don't you?" Dud nodded, and Woody added his thanks. "It made her ecstatic to get to come. She's talked of nothing else for hours."

Jesse slipped out a little before nine. A short time later, he opened the door with Suzette by his side. It so shocked the fiddlers, they stopped playing. Suzette raised her head a notch and looked even more arrogant than usual. Placing his arm around her back, Jesse guided her in.

Iris smiled and went to her. "Hello, Suzette," she said, squeezing her arm. Iris turned and faced the quiet room. "This is my friend, Suzette. Suzette, this is Ugor and Zizi Darst, and their sons, Frank, Mike, Kris, and Gabby." Iris continued on until she had introduced everyone in the room. Suzette said nothing while she looked at each person in turn, her face white and her nostrils flaring. "Come in and get something to eat," Iris said. "Mrs. Harrison made some wonderful fried chicken, and Zizi Darst brought a fabulous dessert."

Jesse guided Suzette into the room. Before she walked more than a few feet, the haughty façade crumbled. Clutching Jesse's chest and hiding her face, she began to weep. He continued to walk with her, holding her up as he took her to a corner of the room and sat down on a bench beside her. Suzette kept her face hidden and cried almost mute, bone-wracking, tears. Iris stared imploring at Dud, but he did not know what to do either. He looked at the Harrisons, so protective of their daughters, and was sure they would leave. Nellie gazed into her husband's face, and reading something there Dud could not see, she said, "Woodrow, would you mind if I danced one dance with that slender young man from my youth, Dudford Washburn?"

He patted her hand and smiled. "Just one, dear."

Dud looked at the fiddlers, and nodding their heads, they began to play again. Dud bowed to Nellie and swept her into his arms. "You are a lovely person, Nellie," he said.

She blushed. "Better keep it Mrs. Harrison, Dudford," she said with a smile. "My husband is just a teeny bit jealous of you."

Dud grinned. "Your husband is a good man, and you have two of the finest girls I've ever had the pleasure to know."

"I think so, too," Nellie said with a smile.

Jesse and Suzette did not dance, but remained in the corner. Rashtah slipped in and sat near them. Iris took them plates loaded with food, but while Rashtah fell on hers hungrily, and Jesse ate his thoughtfully, Suzette did not touch hers. They sat together holding hands for a long time before quietly leaving.

Later, the fiddlers stopped playing and while the men congregated on one side of the room, the women sat on the other near the table of food and the fireplace, gossiping with one another. No longer able to dance with Iris and being almost incapable of holding prolonged conversation, Thompson's stepson left.

"Sure, you can relax now, Washburn," Ugor teased. "He gone now."

Dud quickly changed the subject, and without giving away secrets, made a comment about the dense brush on the property at the Yegua Knobs. Woody, thinking he was complaining because of the lack of grass for cattle, said that in other areas, the Indians had often burned land to make it easier to hunt on.

"It will kill the undergrowth, but not hurt the big trees in most instances," he said. "Then you can get some really good pasture growing."

Ugor made a few remarks about cattle in Hungary. He rarely talked about his homeland, just as Dud hardly ever mentioned Goliad. Once, when two old Germans were in the blacksmith shop extolling the virtues of the fatherland, Dud had witnessed Ugor grow angry.

"I tell you something," he thundered, pointing to the ground. "This your land now. This new life, new start. You forget about that old one, or else you might as well go back."

Tonight, Dud listened as Ugor switched over to talking about his wife. "That woman, she driving me crazy this week. It is that time, you know."

The other men commiserated with him, and he asked Dud, "You go to your land tomorrow?"

When Dud said yes, he asked if he could ride along. "I want to get away for few hours. Boys can run stable."

Dud laughed and agreed, although he did not know how they would handle looking for symbols of buried treasure with Ugor along.

It turned out much simpler than Dud thought. After a late start, Ugor talked and joked expansively on the way out, but once there, he asked to roam alone, explaining he had little time by himself. Dud readily agreed, and using the excuse that they were going to check fence lines, he and Boyd and Jesse left him for a few hours while they continued their search.

"What do you think about Mr. Harrison's idea of burning off some of this brush, Uncle Dud?" Boyd asked.

Dud paused, moving a yaupon branch to keep from getting popped in the face. "Better not," he grumbled. "We might burn down the only sign there is."

TWENTY-EIGHT

ON THE WAY BACK INTO TOWN, UGOR DARST TOLD JOKES about the Hungarian farmer's daughter. As they laughed, he took a deep breath, taking in the countryside and expanding his chest. "I'm happy," he said, "'tis good." Once back at the stables, he kissed his wife resoundingly on the lips and hollered good-naturedly at his sons. Dud turned away, and finding Jesse and Boyd watching him, felt a light flush of blood suffuse his face.

Friday night passed uneventfully. Everyone had, by that time, heard about his run-in with Thompson, but no one tried to kill him over it. On Saturday morning, Dud stood near Felix while he read the will in court. Thompson's stepson sat like a tombstone, while Thompson's sister fidgeted with her lips drawn together in a tight, puckered line. After reading a lot of legal mumbo-jumbo, Felix looked up and said, "In other words, Thompson left his everything to his stepson."

"What?!!" the sister cried, jumping to her feet. Amid the murmurs that broke out in the room, she began screaming protests. "I'll sue! I'll tie it up in court forever!"

"Silence!" Felix yelled, banging on the table with his gavel. He pointed to the stepson, "You! Approach the bench."

The cowboy rose slowly to his feet and walked forward, hat in hand and never changing expression. Dud turned his ear, the one that did not ache, toward Felix to better catch what was said.

Felix leaned closer, eying the cowboy. "Listen here, young fellow," he said. "You can't kick his sister off that place. It wouldn't be Christian. So unless you like the idea of having her hanging on your neck like a singletree, take my advice. Get her a place to live in town, with a small monthly income. Let it be known you'll make a generous settlement to the first man who'll marry her." Felix slanted his body and looked at the pinched-faced angry woman. "Better make it a big settlement."

The cowboy nodded in agreement, and Felix sent him back to his seat. He pounded on his gavel. "The beneficiary has agreed to supply Seth Thompson's sister with an abode in town along with a small monthly income until such time she can find a man to marry. On that happy occasion, the groom will receive a fair and generous settlement to take her off his hands."

The people in the courtroom nodded and murmured in approval. "That Felix," a toothless old woman said, "he's a wise one." Thompson's sister, however, had other ideas and stood up to shriek more threats, but Felix again banged on his gavel and pointing it at her, said, "Madam, if you choose to fight my ruling, you will lose your house in town, your monthly stipend, and your dowry. I advise you to consider matters carefully, because I also have a witness who is willing to swear in court that you and your brother willfully and with malice withheld medical treatment from the recently deceased Mrs. Thompson. Now madam, what shall it be?"

She sat down with a thud and looking at the unfriendly faces around her, said, "I accept."

"Court is now over," Felix pronounced. "Belly up to the bar."

Watching the cowboy leave the saloon, Dud asked Felix, "Wasn't that kind of unusual, Thompson leaving everything to a stepson who hated him instead of some of his own kinfolks?"

Felix grunted. "He knew where the dead bodies were. He forced Thompson in here six months ago and watched while I wrote out the will."

"That's a hard way to earn money," Dud said, shaking his head.

He left the bar soon afterward and later walked with Iris to the café. Ruby and Joe were there, still determined to go to the dance and leave Iris in charge. Dud tried to feel sorry that Iris could not go, too, but for a reason he did not really want to face, he could not quite make it. He told Iris he would see her later and left.

Felix caught up with him on the sidewalk. "Aren't you going to the dance tonight, Dud?" he asked.

"No," Dud said. "Ponder's going, but I'd feel guilty knowing that Iris was sitting there at the café all alone. I'll go by there later and check on her."

Felix gave him a sharp look. "Maybe you just know she won't be there all alone for long," he said. When Dud refused to answer, Felix changed the subject, saying he had to circulate it around to all the old bachelors that Thompson's sister would inherit a nice dowry.

"Why don't you take her, Felix?" Dud ribbed. "You might talk him into giving you a big enough dowry to buy back the Gilded Lily."

Felix looked thoughtful, but shook his head. "No, it wouldn't be worth it. Had one just like her once and don't want another."

Dud grew serious and nodded his head. "I messed up my life, too, when I was a young man, Felix."

"Good God man!" Felix said crossly. "Quit looking so pathetic. That bullet shot your earlobe off, not your balls."

Dud laughed. "All right, have fun at the dance; I'll see you later."

Boyd, Dud knew, would probably be at the Harrisons', sitting patiently while Annabelle insisted on serving tea from her new set before the dance began. Jesse would go to the Gilded Lily later that night to see Suzette. With news of Thompson's death, the men in the saloon had waited with anxious breath to see if Suzette would rub her cheek with her forefinger, and when she did, every man turned and looked at his neighbor suspiciously. They remembered all the trips to Pecan Street, and with Thompson no longer around, they cast eyes at Dud. He could see what they were thinking. Had he killed Thompson just to get at Suzette? But after giving him a look or two, they shook their heads and turned to Boyd and Jesse. Since Boyd practically lived in Elizabeth's lap, Jesse became the target, and Dud hoped no trouble would erupt. One mutilated person in the family was enough. Jesse would not appreciate him trying to be his keeper, but Dud nevertheless let it be known around town that if someone shot Jesse, they better shoot Boyd and him at the same time if they wanted to live.

He killed some time at the stables. Ugor had been busy Friday night and earlier in the day, but almost everyone who intended on coming to town was already there, so by late Saturday afternoon, things had quieted down considerably for him. Although still early, Dud decided to mosey to the café to sit with Iris.

As soon as he saw the front of the café, he realized his prediction of a slow night could not have been more wrong. Horses lined up next to the hitching posts and more cowboys were walking toward the café, spurs jingling and hats pushed cockily to one side, all of them wearing their best clothes. Walking in behind them, he found the tables full. Iris, looking flustered, talked to one group of men, and then ran back to the kitchen, her hands busily trying to flip steaks, shove biscuits in the oven, and make gravy all at the same time.

Dud pushed his way across the crowded café, and above the din of men boasting and telling jokes, he went behind the bar to the grill and spoke to Iris. Iris turned and almost swooned in tears. "Oh thank God, Mr. Dud. Can you please help me? Please?"

Dud reached over and taking Joe's apron from a nail in the wall, replaced it with his hat. "You got plenty of beef and potatoes?" he asked.

Iris nodded. "Yes."

"Good," Dud said, wrapping the apron ties around his waist. "Whatever anybody orders, tell them all they can have is steak and potatoes tonight."

Iris took a breath and looked at him dubiously. "But

Mr. Dud," she said anxiously. "Don't you think I should cook, and you should wait on tables?"

Dud took her by the shoulders and turned her to face the crowd. Railroad workers with swollen knuckles and callused hands mingled with slit-eyed, leathery cowboys. Old men with beards, young men barely old enough to shave, all made up the jumble of sweaty muscled flesh in front of them. "Look at those men, Iris. Every one of them is here because he is in love with you. There is plenty of food at that dance. They came in here because they want to see you. If I go out there instead, we'll have a riot on our hands."

Iris looked at the men, her eyes round. She nodded her head.

Dud gave her a gentle shove. "Now get out and tell them steak and potatoes is what they're having tonight." Dud gave another look at the crowd, turned and threw more steaks on the grill without bothering to count them. Thereafter, he worked like he always did, steady and calm, flipping steaks, cutting potatoes and throwing them in grease to fry. Iris ran back and forth, taking full plates out, returning with empty ones she pitched into hot soapy water and washed when she could. She made coffee, filled cups, dipped water into glasses and when she had a free minute, threw flour, milk, and lard together for the biscuits the men demanded. Thirty minutes after Dud took over the grill, the Darst boys entered the café, slipping through the crowd.

"Our papa thought you might want some help," Frank said.

Dud nodded. "Frank, you help Iris clear tables. Mike,

get over there and wash dishes. Kris, I need you to peel potatoes."

Pudgy little Gabby came forward. "What about me, Mr. Dud?"

"Run to the store and buy me a couple of cigars," Dud said. "Get each one of you boys and Miss Iris a piece of candy, if you want. Tell them I said it was okay." Iris had never charged so much as a hair ribbon for herself on his account, and he found the Darst boys equally trustworthy.

Gabby nodded and darted out the front door while the other boys took to their posts and began working. Kris took one slice with Joe's knife, put it back, and removed his from its scabbard. Mike put on a kettle of water to heat, while Frank found another of Joe's aprons to wear. When Iris realized he could make change faster than she could, she let Frank take the money as well. Gabby came back carrying licorice and a peppermint for Iris. Dud stuck one of the cigars in his mouth to chew and placed the other in his pocket. Kris put Gabby in a corner behind the counter with a bag of potatoes and ordered him to start peeling. After watching how to long to leave the potatoes bubbling in grease, Kris took over that, too.

As Frank brought dirty plates to the kitchen, he surreptitiously began putting the remaining scraps in his mouth. Mike saw and said a few sharp words in Hungarian. After that, as Frank brought the dishes to the pan of soapy water, he would pop part of his leftovers into Mike's mouth while Iris and Dud pretended not to notice. Kris, also nobody's fool, made a few caustic Hungarian remarks, and when Dud's back would be turned, he'd get his share and so would Gabby. The men in the café soon noticed, and many of the kinder-hearted ones began leaving large chunks of meat and potatoes on their plates for the hungry boys. Frank saved all the bones, and when he had a small pile, took them outside to Old Tom.

Iris smiled and laughed with the men, and Dud thought he had never seen her be as kind as she was that night or as beautiful, even with sweat plastering her hair against her forehead and the loose strands curling around the nape of her neck. When Kris caught Dud holding a fork in midair, gazing at Iris over his shoulder, he began to tease him. "Mr. Dud, my papa says you are really in love with Miss Iris; you just don't want to admit it."

Dud turned to stare at the boy. He looked back to Iris. "A man like me doesn't have any business being in love with a woman like that," he said. He turned the fork back to his steaks and forced his mind to concentrate on them again. Out of the corner of his eye, Dud could see Kris watching him, but he went back to his potatoes without comment.

Iris rushed to the grill with another five orders. Grabbing ready plates, she said, "Mr. Dud, one of them said shave its hair, wipe its butt, and throw it on the plate."

"Hells bells, Iris, that makes me ill," Dud, who liked everything well done, said. However, he cooked it just the way she asked for it and wondered if Iris, who never cursed, realized she had said "butt" in a public place.

It lasted for hours, the Darst boys staying with them until suddenly it was over, and the café emptied of customers, a wreck of dirty tables, chairs scattered every which way, and a floor littered with crumbs, tobacco ashes, and spit. As the boys helped Iris clean, Dud threw six more steaks on the griddle. Iris looked up from wiping the counter.

"They're for the boys to take home," Dud explained. "They earned them. You want anything?"

Iris shook her head. "No thanks. You go right ahead."

Like the Darst boys, he had already snitched bites here and there, and he did not need anything else. He finished with the steaks, found brown paper and wrapped them with a pile of fried potatoes to take home. Iris insisted they split the tip money six ways, but Dud, spitting out the second cigar he had chewed to a nub, told her to split it five ways. "The boss says so," he added.

Iris and the boys grinned. "Yes sir, boss," they said. The boys went on their way, laughing and talking with packages under their arms, their pockets full of money. Dud opened the door for Iris and shut it after her, which she stopped to lock carefully.

"Are you ready to go home? Or would you like to look in on the last of the revelers?" Dud asked, the music from the barn dance drifting in their direction.

She shook her head. "Can we just sit here on the steps for a little while and listen?" she asked.

They sat down on the wooden steps leading to the café, the cool night air crisp and pungent with the odor of horse manure and dried leaves that had collected in a heap against the sidewalk. Iris heaved a sigh of contentment. "I don't think I've ever worked so hard and enjoyed it so much," she said.

"You're not sorry about missing the dance?" Dud asked.

"Oh no," she said. "I have just as much fun when we get to dance to Ugor Darst's fiddle anyway. Maybe more so."

She grew quiet and turned her ear to the music, listening, head in hand, arms resting on her knees. Dud breathed heavily beside her. He felt beat, but exhilarated.

"When Lon and I first married," Iris said in a soft voice, "we would go to dances or suppers, and the other women would stare at Lon and look at me so enviously. I wanted to tell them...I wanted to tell them...," she broke off and could not finish.

Like a man in a dream who has no control over his actions, Dud found his arm wrapping around Iris's shoulder. She turned her face toward him, lifting her lips and lowering her lashes. His fingers touched her chin as his lips bent down on their own accord, but before they could meet hers, a cry rent through the night air.

"Mr. Dud! Mr. Dud" one of the Darst boys screamed. "Someone shot my papa!"

Dud and Iris both jerked their heads. Kris raced toward them, tears streaming from his eyes. Dud jumped up, taking Iris with him.

"Someone killed him; someone killed him," Kris continued to cry.

"Come on, Iris," Dud said, pulling on her hand, and together they ran to the stables, following Kris.

The other Darst boys were in a weeping huddle around the fallen body of their father. Zizi screamed and cried, rocking back and forth as she hugged her husband's body. Dud touched the boys with a light hand, moving them out of his way as gently as he could. He pulled Zizi from Ugor, noting the deep gash on her forehead as he handed her over to Iris. "Move them back to the door, Iris," he said, probing the body of his friend, hoping to find a spark of life.

Ugor had been shot in the stomach and looked as if he

had not lived long afterward. A belligerent expression still showed on his face.

Frank Darst stood with clinched fists. "I will kill whoever did this to my father," he said.

"Not yet, Frank," Dud said. "Don't go off halfcocked; you may get the wrong person. You boys go fetch Uncle Ponder, Boyd, and Jesse for me. I need them."

Frank nodded, and he turned, disappearing into the darkness with Mike and Kris at his heels. Iris, eyes wide with shock, stood holding Zizi as she cried piteously. Dud looked at the ground around Ugor, but it had not been swept and was a labyrinth of footprints. Nevertheless, he thought he could make out the markings of a quick, but deadly, skirmish. He went to Zizi and asked Iris to question her about what happened. Iris spoke a few words of Hungarian, and Zizi spilled a slew of hysterical sentences. When she finally wound down, Iris turned to Dud and gave a shaky translation.

"She said a masked man dressed in black, and a woman with a heavy veil, also dressed in black, came in here and demanded to know why you wanted the property at the Yegua Knobs so badly. The man hit Ugor repeatedly, and when Zizi tried to stop him, he hit her with the butt of the pistol, knocking her out. As she came to, she heard a shot and saw the couple running away."

Dud nodded. Frank and Mike arrived with Boyd and Jesse. Kris came in leading Ponder by the hand. Dud warned the younger boys to stay back to let the older ones read the signs. Ponder stood next to Iris and Zizi while Boyd and Jesse carefully went over the ground, their eyes making sweeping movements as they slowly walked toward him. At one point, Boyd stopped and got down, balancing on his haunches. Jesse joined him, and together they searched.

"A woman stood back here," Boyd said, pointing. "I don't think she walked forward." He got up, eyes down, and came to where Dud stood. "The man came closer. It looks like they struggled."

Boyd paused and Jesse pointed to the bruised bumps on Ugor's forehead. "He was pistol-whipped before being shot."

"See the powder burns?" Boyd said. "He must have jammed the gun into old man Darst's guts." Boyd grimaced. "Is that the way you read it, Uncle Dud?"

Dud nodded. "That's pretty much what Zizi said. I didn't see the woman's footprints. Are they long and narrow like before?"

"I can't tell," Boyd admitted, and Jesse agreed; they might or might not be the same. They drew nearer and Boyd whispered. "Do you think it was Mary Powell and Ev Reid, Uncle Dud? Everybody in town knows old man Darst went out to the property with us yesterday."

Dud shook his head. "I can't believe Mary would stoop to murder," he whispered. "Thievery, chicanery, yes, but surely not murder." He didn't want to believe it. "Somebody better get Felix."

However, a crowd had already formed at the door, and someone had gone for Felix. He pushed his way through, growling, "Get back. Get back."

When Felix reached the body, he stared down and shook his head, his lips in a tight line. "Dud?" he asked, and Dud told him about Kris's cry for help and what Iris had gotten out of Zizi, omitting his suspicions of Mary and the hunt for treasure on the Yegua.

Felix nodded and turned to the Darst boys. "Boys, come here," he said.

"Felix," Dud began, but Felix stopped him.

"I know it's hard on them, Dud, but it's better to get it over with now and in the presence of witnesses so they won't be bombarded with questions later."

Dud nodded while the Darst boys came forward. Felix looked at each one in turn, and then said, "Tell me exactly what happened tonight, from the very beginning, lads. Start at the last time you saw your father alive."

Frank looked at his brothers. He turned back to Felix and began. "Someone told my papa that Mr. Dud and Miss Iris were working alone in the café with a lot of customers, so he sent us there to help. We stayed at the café working until it closed. When we came back, we found our father like this." He swallowed to keep the tears down.

"Do you boys know of anyone who would want to hurt your pa?"

Frank shook his head miserably.

"You boys go on and stand back now with your mother," Felix said. He looked at the circle of people crowding at the door and raised his voice. "You hear that folks, a man and a woman, both of them dressed in black and masked, slipped in here around nine o'clock tonight and manhandled old man Darst. His wife tried to stop them, and they knocked her out. They shot Darst and ran. If anybody knows anything, say it now or tell me later, but don't keep it to yourself.

"Dud, we'll get some men, take Ugor, and lay him out at your place. We'll bury him in the morning," Felix said. He added in a lower tone, shaking his head, "Whoever did it picked the perfect time for it. Everyone at the dance, and you tied up at the café."

Dud agreed with Felix, and there was nothing else he could add. "Uncle Ponder," he said. "Would you take Zizi, Iris, and the boys back to the house and stay with them?" Ponder nodded, putting his arms around Zizi's shoulders. He hugged her and gave the top of her head a gentle kiss. Dud spied Suzette peeking in from behind the door. "Suzette! Go with Iris and help her, if you would."

Suzette looked surprised. She glanced around the crowd. "Me?" she asked.

"Yeah, you!" Dud barked because he was upset. "It's about time you realized you're not the only woman who's had bad things happen to her."

"Uncle Dud," Jesse remonstrated mildly.

A quiet murmur went through the crowd. Jesse walked over to Suzette. He looked into her eyes and then at the crowd. "Just so you all know, I'm in love with Miss Suzette and have asked her to marry me. While she is in my house, I'll treat her with the honor and respect she deserves."

Suzette gave a teary smile. While in the back of his mind Dud applauded Jesse's good sense—it was a lot easier to justify shooting a man who was trying to have sex with a woman you loved than one who said he would not—he nevertheless had other things to think about. "Go on with Iris, Suzette. I don't want you girls going anywhere alone."

Iris, trying hard to keep from bawling, said, "Mr. Dud, Zizi wants Ugor to be laid out in his best clothes."

"All right, go get them," Dud said, as his stomach

roiled. "Boys, get whatever things you want to keep, because from now on, you'll be staying with me."

While they went into the Darsts' living quarters, Boyd and Jesse leaned closer. "Uncle Dud, what are we going to do?"

Dud looked down at the bodies of his friends. Finding Mary and Ev would be almost impossible, and proving them guilty of murder even more so, but he had to do something to prevent more carnage.

"We're going to burn that land to the ground," he said. "This has got to stop."

TWENTY-NINE

BOYD AND JESSE, ALONG WITH A FEW OTHER MEN FELIX appointed, brought Ugor Darst to the house and placed him on a table in the front room. Although gentle and kind to Zizi and the Darst boys, Dud knew by the narrowing of his eyes and firm set of his jaw that inside, Ponder was white-hot with fury over what happened.

Zizi clothed Ugor in a red scarf and purple vest from their native land. People came and went, the women crying and bringing food, the men looking stern and trying not to show the worry and curiosity that consumed them. Iris and Suzette snatched sleep when they could in the bedroom, taking turns staying near Zizi. Dud and the rest of the boys lay on pallets wherever they found an empty spot, dozing off and on during the night.

The house filled with people again in the morning. The funeral lasted into the afternoon, and Dud wondered if he had ever experienced a day so long. Iris had dark circles under her eyes, red rimmed from the tears she tried to cry in private to keep from upsetting the Darst boys. Frank could handle his grief only by being angry and telling anyone willing to listen that he would extract retribution from the man who killed his father. Mike held everything inside, staying near Ponder and hugging Old Tom, burying his face in the dog's fur. Kris followed Dud like a scared shadow. Gabby clung to his mother and Iris, unable to fathom what happened.

Late in the night, after the house finally emptied of people, Jesse and Boyd stood with Dud by the fireplace. Frank sat in front, staring moodily at the blaze. Kris crouched on the floor close to Dud, while Mike leaned against Ponder.

"Uncle Dud," Boyd said. "The wind is still blowing from the south. If we're going to do it, we better do it before another norther hits."

Dud nodded. "In the morning."

When the Darst boys found out the next day they planned on burning brush along the Yegua, they asked to go along, but Dud refused. "The wind could shift, and I don't want you boys lost in a forest fire," he explained. "Stick around here or better yet, go to school. It will get your mind off things, and you might pick up some of the gossip going around town. Maybe somebody has heard something."

Dud asked Iris and Suzette to stay at the house. "Please don't go anywhere alone," he said. He hesitated, and added, "Somebody needs to stay with Zizi. Would you girls...." They both immediately offered to stay. Suzette, sitting near Iris, nodded. "I think I do not want to dance anymore," she said haltingly. "I will stay here too, if you will permit." Rashtah nodded and said, "Oui. Me too." Suzette looked at Jesse.

"I would like a few days to think, please," she said softly, almost pleadingly. "To see if I can fit in."

Jesse took a deep breath, surprise and pleasure suffusing his face. "Of course," he managed to mutter.

Dud took Iris's hands in his. "Iris," he said, and she looked up at him, eyes intense and waiting. "I know how you feel, but I need you. Will you stay away from the café and help me here for the time being? I'll talk to Ruby and Joe about it."

She lowered her eyes, bowing her head slightly. "Of course, Mr. Dud."

"Good girl," he said, patting her hair. "I knew I could count on you."

Dud had trouble with Ponder. He wanted to go, and Dud beseeched him to stay behind with the women and children. "Please, Uncle Ponder, they're upset and scared."

"All right, gol darn it," Ponder said. "Do you boys know what you are doing?"

"Uncle Ponder," Dud said, snapping. "I'm forty-some-thing years old."

"I didn't ask you how old you were," Ponder growled. "I asked you if you knew what you were doing."

Annabelle and Elizabeth slipped in before they left, and Boyd cautioned them about roaming the town alone. "We know," Elizabeth said. "Papa already warned us."

"You be careful," Annabelle said. "Me and Elizabeth like you a lot."

Once in town, they found more than the usual number of men loitering. Crowds filled the stables, and it took half an hour to get their horses. Stopping at the store, they bought cans of coal oil, but did not at either place hear any news that could throw light on the

murder. Felix had sent word to the sheriff, but told him
there were no suspects. Since killings happened routinely
in Tie Town, and there was no one to arrest, he did not
bother to come.

In the early morning hours before the wind came up,
the three men burned a semi-circular firebreak on one
side of the Yegua. At nine o'clock the wind began to blow
from the south.

"This is it, boys," Dud said. "We may be burning the
only chance we have of finding that treasure, but I reckon
we don't have a choice." He put his torch to the dry grass.

Each man set fire to strategic spots along the firebreak
and stood back to let the wind do the rest. As the heat
bore down, they roamed the firebreak to make sure the
licking flames did not leap across it. At the end of the day,
the yaupons, cedars, and cacti were gone; leaving the
larger oaks standing like sentinels in what appeared
nothing but ruin and destruction. In the spring, a carpet
of green grass would take over; the oaks would lose their
scorched appearance, and the land would look as if it had
been created that way thousands of years before, but for
now, it looked hideous.

The men returned home, charred and black with soot,
reeking with the smell of acrid smoke. When Dud
touched something, he left a streak of filth, and every time
Boyd and Jesse came near him, their odor nauseated him.
"I don't care if it's not Saturday night," Dud said. "I'm
taking a bath as soon as I finish supper. Do you think Iris
has cooked something?"

"Do you think the Pope is Catholic?" Boyd said, acting
as if just taking a breath was almost too much for him.
"All you have to do is point a finger at your mouth, and

Iris runs to the stove. I've never seen any human so spoiled in my whole life."

"I believe my sister has spoiled you and your old man worse than I've ever dreamed or hoped for," Dud snarled back.

"Shut up, both of you," Jesse said. "I'm sick of listening to you."

When they came into the house, they found Felix waiting for them with the others. Iris and Suzette gave them shocked looks, but said nothing as they put food on the table. Felix did not say much either, for a change, but glanced at them thoughtfully.

As soon as the three firemen had washed their hands and faces, they sat down to eat. Zizi refused to get up, lying immobile with grief on one of the cots in the bedroom. Ponder placed food on a plate and took it in to her, shutting the door behind him with his foot. No one said much of anything; the Darst boys ate with downward faces. Ponder came back in just as they were finishing. Iris rose to clear the table, but Ponder put a hand up to stop her, and she sat back down. He looked at Dud.

"Dud," he said. "It's time you told these people what is going on."

"I agree, Dud," Felix said. "Quit holding back on us."

Every face stared at Dud. He looked at Boyd and Jesse. They gave short nods, so Dud told the story, warts and all. He did not say he had slept with Mary, but Suzette and Iris would know he had. "I acted a fool," Dud said. "Everyone tried to warn me, but I wouldn't listen."

Frank's face turned white. "Is this Mary and Ev, are they the ones who killed my father?" He pounded his fist on the table. "I will slaughter them!"

"Hold on, boy," Dud said. "I'm not sure of anything. We're not even sure they were anywhere near your parents. Ev would stoop to murder, yes. But even though Mary is deceitful and cunning, I cannot see her standing by and letting him beat on your father and then shoot him."

"You were wrong about her once, Dud," Felix said.

Dud flushed, ashamed to admit in front of everyone how he had been taken. "That woman made a fool of me, yes, but I still don't believe she's that evil."

No one said anything. Ponder shook his head at Dud and looked away in disgust. Dud turned to look at Iris. She stared at him with wide, solemn eyes. He flushed and turned away, unable to face her. Suzette broke the silence. "What are you going to do?"

Dud took a deep breath. "We could walk away from this and never look back. But then we'd never know who killed Ugor. We'll try to find the sign leading us to the treasure, and as soon as we do, we'll lay a trap for whoever is behind all this."

Nods of agreement went around the table. Iris's face expressed nothing but trust, making Dud feel even more hellish.

"Felix, I don't have to warn you to keep your mouth shut. However," Dud said, pointing to Gabby who had climbed into Iris's lap. "Gabby, this is a secret. If I hear you even mention the word treasure before this is over, I'm going to tear your butt up."

Gabby, eyes wide, nodded. Frank gave the boy a hard look. "Don't worry; I will see to it Gabby stays quiet."

"I'm going to the barbershop and take a bath with as

much hot water as they can get in the tub," Dud announced.

"Mr. Dud, the boys might like a bath, too," Iris said. "And maybe haircuts?"

Dud breathed a sigh of relief, eager to do anything Iris might ask of him. He gave them a speculative look. "Frank could use a shave, too," he said.

While Frank turned a deep red, Iris said, "If you all put on fresh clothes, I'll wash what you have on now in the morning."

As the women took the dishes into the kitchen, Boyd leaned over to Dud and hissed, "Spoiled, spoiled, spoiled."

"Shut up," Dud said. "You're just mad because Elizabeth wouldn't dream of touching your crusty clothes."

Boyd turned away quickly, and Dud worried for a moment he had offended him. In five minutes time, however, Boyd was laughing and joking about something else. Dud almost wished he had—Boyd needed to give Elizabeth a long, hard look.

That night as they lay clean and shaven in their cots, Dud thought he detected a shift in the wind. He rose and went to the door. The wind blew hard from the east. He went back into the house, got a chair, and put it outside the door. He sat in it, and leaning against the wall, hooked his feet in the rungs while he watched the skyline of the Knobs hills. The night grew so cloudy; he could not see the moon, although it was near and full. To his thankfulness, soft patters of rain hit, and he was able to go in the house and sleep, knowing the wind would not whip up the ashes they left and set the whole countryside on fire.

Iris and Suzette rose early in the morning to prepare breakfast. Rashtah, even though she despised Lottie, went to her job cleaning the Gilded Lily. She told Suzette she wanted to save money to get married if she ever found a man who would have her; plus, it was a good place to pick up tidbits of gossip.

After breakfast, Dud announced the ground wet enough from the previous night's rain to explore the land at the Knobs. Iris and Suzette begged to ride along after Ponder surprised Dud by volunteering to stay with Zizi. "I don't think anyone will bother us in broad daylight," Iris pleaded.

"Gabby can ride with us." Suzette added, "It should be perfectly safe for us to go, Oncle Dud."

Dud relented, and as they were preparing to leave, Annabelle and Elizabeth stopped by. When learning that Iris and Suzette were going, Annabelle begged to ride, too.

Dud let out a heavy sigh. "This is not a picnic," he said.

"Oh, let her go, Uncle Dud," Boyd said.

Annabelle turned to Elizabeth. "Sissy, do you want to go, too?"

"No, I don't want to see some smelly old burnt out pasture," Elizabeth replied. She looked at Boyd, batting her eyelashes, and said, "Maybe a buggy ride some other day?"

Boyd paused. "Are you sure you don't want to go with us today, Miss Elizabeth?"

Elizabeth's eyes blazed in a green fire. She snapped a short "no."

Dud interjected before the sparks coming from her eyes could start another conflagration. "Miss Annabelle, you'd better get permission from your mother first."

Iris went with Annabelle to explain they only intended

to have a look around and did not plan on staying all day. Elizabeth stayed behind and tried to hide her anger with flirtatious banter directed at all three men. The girls returned, smiling and talking. Elizabeth wavered, looked about ready to get into the wagon with them, but in the end, flounced away without saying goodbye to anyone but Annabelle. Dud once again felt sorry for Elizabeth. He had watched other men try to tame women in various ways, but never with as much patience and fortitude as Boyd. He had to be driving Elizabeth stark raving crazy with his behavior.

Felix met them at the wagon yard and got in the back of the wagon without being asked.

"Anyone else like to go along?" Dud said, holding out his arms and looking around.

"Dud," Felix said, "put it in a little brown jug and put a cork in it."

The girls began to titter, and Dud shot Iris a hard look that made her giggle even more. She put her hand to her mouth and pressed her lips together, trying to control her amusement. Dud felt like grabbing her, throwing her on the ground and having his way with her. He just as quickly tried to rein that thought in.

"All right, let's go," he mumbled. His hands shook a little as he got on his horse. "Come on, Old Tom," he said.

Dud rode while Boyd drove the wagon with Jesse beside him. In a little while, Jesse told Annabelle to ride up front, and he took her place in the back next to Suzette. The rain had cleared the air, and as they approached the property, they could only see a few spots still smoldering.

"Not much to look at, is it?" Dud said, surveying the

335

blackened landscape. As his eyes scanned the terrain, his shoulders slumped. All he saw was charred stumps, blistered bark, and a few large rocks they had walked by and studied a hundred times before. "Nothing," he muttered. "Not a darn thing." Boyd and Jesse looked as unhappy as he felt.

"Look at that," Annabelle said, pointing her finger to one of the larger stones lying like a solitary boulder. "It looks just like a dead cow." She smiled. "You could call this place 'Dead Cow Ranch.'"

All three of them took a sharp intake of air and turned to stare at one another. Dud put his forefinger briefly to his lips. "It does look like that, doesn't it, Miss Annabelle, you sweet little thing."

Iris gasped. "Is this what—?"

Dud gave the barest shake of his head, and Iris stopped. He gulped and studied the rock formation. It was narrow on one side, gradually getting bigger until it looked like the hips of a cow lying on its side. Because of the brush, they had not seen its true shape. Old Tom went to it and lifted his leg. Dud dared a glance at Boyd and Jesse. Boyd said, "Hallelujah and praise the Lord," under his breath. Dud gulped again and said loudly, "Well, let's look around and see what else we see." He could hardly tear his eyes from the stone, marveling that it had been right in front of them the whole time.

They drove the horses and wagon around, pretending to be interested in others things, while their minds dwelt on the small boulder looking like a dead bull in a black pasture. When he could barely contain himself any longer, Dud said, "We'd better be getting back. Annabelle's mother will be looking for her."

Felix got out of the wagon in town. However, when they dropped Annabelle off at her house, Nellie Harrison insisted they come in for refreshments. Suzette, frightened, looked at Jesse, but he took her hand and led her into the house. If Nellie had any qualms about a girl who wiggled her behind in front of a crowd of love-starved men coming into her home, her face did not show it. They followed her into the parlor while casting glances at one another. Annabelle poured tea from her new set, and Elizabeth pattered innocently about inconsequential things, as if she had not been goaded almost beyond endurance by Boyd's standoffishness that afternoon.

"Suzette," Nellie said, and Dud suddenly knew why they had been invited. "Annabelle tells me you have quit the stage."

Suzette gave a nervous nod. "Yes," she said in voice barely above a whisper.

Jesse intervened. "I have asked Miss Suzette for her hand in marriage," he said. "She is considering it."

Nellie smiled benevolently. "I'm sure you will make the right decision, dear."

Felix, Dud suddenly thought. That would explain everything.

Now that Nellie had the lowdown straight from the horse's mouth, they were able to leave fairly quickly without seeming rude. Felix came by just as the boys were coming in from school. Iris prepared an early supper, and as they went to the table, Dud told Felix about the afternoon.

"I'd swear Nellie Harrison has heard all about Suzette's life from the time she was an infant," he said.

"Well, Dud, your voice does carry." Felix said. "Haven't

you heard? There's a whole group of men ready to ride to Oklahoma and tear up a certain saloon. The only thing stopping them is the hope that Suzette will turn Jesse down and pick one of them instead, now that she is considering taking up matrimony as a vocation."

They sat down at the table. Ponder loaded two plates with food and took them in to Zizi, insisting she eat something with him. Dud, in the middle of the group gathered around the table, waited until everyone had finished eating. He cleared his throat, and they looked at him expectantly.

"We are going to have to work together to pull this off," he began.

"We're going for the treasure tonight then?" Boyd asked.

"Yes. Annabelle unwittingly gave us the clue we were looking for," Dud said, explaining what he wanted the boys to do.

They nodded and Dud continued. "Ponder will stay here with Zizi and Gabby. We need to get out of town without being noticed by nosy bystanders. Iris, Suzette, if you are willing, I'd like for you to create a diversion in town."

Iris and Suzette quickly nodded. He continued. "It will require some very unladylike behavior on your part." He watched, and they nodded again. "You'll have to stage a catfight in front of the Gilded Lily just before dark. Pretend you are fighting over Jesse."

"Mr. Dud," Iris said, "I don't think anyone would believe that I'm after—"

Suzette poked her and interjected. "Don't worry, Oncle Dud; we will make it look good."

"You'll have to tear each other's clothes and roll around in the dirt," Dud warned.

"It is fine," Suzette said. "I know how to take the seams from our dresses and tack them so that when we pull, they will simply look torn." She raised her chin. "It will be my finest performance." Turning to Iris, she added, "We must practice the ugly things we will say to one another—just remember later they were pretend."

Iris nodded. "Okay. I'm game."

Iris was the gamiest woman he ever met, and Dud wanted to kiss her. Kris interrupted his thoughts.

"What about me?" he asked. "What am I to do?"

"I want you to stay near Miss Iris and Miss Suzette tonight. They may need you."

Kris protested and grew angry that he could not go with the men, but Dud remained adamant.

"When Miss Iris and Miss Suzette begin their scrape, you and Mr. Felix will spread the word that a catfight is about to happen. I want everyone in town to be watching that brawl and not see us slipping out to the Yegua."

THIRTY

"YOU GOL DANG BOSSY LITTLE HORNED TOAD," PONDER yelled. "I will too go if I want to."

Ponder sat on his horse, reins in hand, while Dud sat in the wagon. Grateful that the house on Pecan Street stood away from the rest of the homes and hoping none of the neighborhood ladies were hearing the cussing he was taking, Dud tried to calm his uncle down.

"Look, Uncle Ponder," he said finally. "If something happens to me and the boys, who is going to look after these women? Who is going to keep Iris from marrying another bastard? Who is going to keep Suzette from slipping back into prostitution? Who is going to keep Zizi and her sons from starving to death? Now use your fool old hard head."

Boyd and Jesse stood nearby, looking at the sky, the sunset, anything but their two squabbling uncles. Frank and Mike Darst sat in the wagon bed watching and listening with round eyes and solemn faces. Devoted to their mother, it was their wide eyes staring at Ponder that finally moved him to give in.

"All right, blast it to hell," Ponder said, getting off his horse. Jesse climbed in the wagon next to Dud while Boyd got on his horse. Dud turned and instructed the Darst boys to lie down and cover up well with the Navajo blanket. Felix walked outside with Kris to see them off. Felix looked worried and excited; Kris and Ponder gave them glum stares.

"Come on, Old Tom, let's go," Dud said, popping the reins. As he drove out of town, he could scarcely believe after all this time, they were finally going to dig for the treasure. As he controlled the reins, guiding the horses deeper into the land of the Yegua Knobs as the sun crept down the horizon, Dud felt another stab of regret over the death of Ugor Darst. That Zizi and the boys did not hold him responsible was something to be grateful for. The boys had listened carefully to his instructions at the house as he explained how they should dart and chunk rocks to cause a distraction without endangering themselves. "But only if we're in dire straits and can't get to our guns," Dud had admonished. "And stay out of our line of fire."

Earlier that afternoon, they had waited in the front room for the sun to go down, listening as the sounds of Iris and Suzette practicing their roles filtered in from the bedroom.

"You are nothing but a French whore, say that," Suzette commanded. Iris's mumbling could be heard, and Suzette said, "No! Don't be nice! Say it with feeling! Remember there are lives at stake! *Zut!* Look, Iris, pretend...," and she lowered her voice so they could not hear.

"I'm sick of you batting your eyelashes and wiggling your behind in his face!" Iris shouted. "If you rub your bosom on his arm one more time, I'm going to kill you!"

The men looked at one another in shock. "I wonder what she told her to pretend," Felix had muttered, and Dud had lamented he would not be there to see the show.

Darkness descended on them, the moon up and shining. As they neared a ravine lined with oaks and pecans, Dud said over his shoulder in a voice just above a whisper, "Remember boys, one owl call if you spot someone watching us, two owl calls if you see them about to approach us."

A muffled "yep" came through the blanket. Dud slowed the horses. He did not look back, but knew by the lightening of the wagon the boys had slithered out. He simply said, "Old Tom," in a soft tone so the dog would go with him. Without picking up speed, Dud allowed the team to slowly make their way to the shoulder-high stone Annabelle had pointed them to.

Dud turned the wagon in front of it, stopping as close as he could and still allow room for shoveling. Boyd dismounted while Dud and Jesse got wordlessly out of the wagon. Boyd reached in the wagon bed, taking out a lantern. Even with the moon so bright they felt as if they were almost in daylight, he lit it and set it on top of the stone at the high end. Dud removed the shovels and handed one to each of them. Next to the handle of the shovel he handed Boyd nestled a rifle. Boyd walked to the darkened end of the stone, crouched and looked at the ground. When he came back up, all he held was the shovel. Dud pushed his into the ground in front of the stone; Jesse went to the other end. Silently, they began to dig. Old Tom sniffed the ground around them and then got out of the way. Before he could disappear into the night, Dud commanded him to stay, and the dog went under the wagon to lie down.

Bathed in moonlight, they worked in a night so still, the leaves looked glued to the trees. The sandy soil made easy digging, the large grains making scraping noises against the metal of the shovels. The three of them began two-foot deep trenches, planning on meeting and then beginning on another two feet. For a long time, all that could be heard was the sound of heavy boots jabbing the shovels, sand and metal, and the plops the dirt made as they threw it beside them. They made a semicircle around the rock, and had started digging deeper in their troughs when Old Tom suddenly stood up and gave a couple of barks. "Indians, Tom," Dud said softly, and the dog grew stiffly quiet.

"Hoot," the sound of the owl came. They looked at one another without raising their heads and continued to dig, every nerve growing taunt. Dud felt so keyed up; at first he failed to realize he had hit something hard. He thumped it three times before it got through to him that he had struck metal. He began to dig around it. Boyd and Jesse paused, looking at him. Dud knew it was a strongbox even without seeing it clearly. Heart pounding, he got down on his knees and began to claw. Jesse reached down, and together they pulled the large box from its hiding place.

The fat, old-fashioned lock on it had rusted. Dud's blood pumped so fast the veins in his hands pulsated. He pulled out his pistol and stepping back, blew the lock off. The sound of it firing rang through the night, the smell of gun smoke replacing the odor of burnt grass. Dud swallowed; his mouth dry and gritty.

"Hoot! Hoot!" the owl called and a low growl came from Old Tom. Boyd did not hesitate, and using the wagon as cover, slipped to the back of the boulder. Dud and Jesse gave no indication Boyd was no longer beside them. Instead, Dud took a deep breath and bent down, opening the lid with stiff fingers. Keeping his right hand free, he took the lantern in his left hand and held it over the metal strongbox.

He and Jesse stared inside the box. In one slow motion, they turned and looked at one another.

"I think you should let us see, Dud," a voice several yards away called.

Dud shut his eyes briefly. Rising and turning, he said, "Hello, Ev." A woman dressed in a dark dress stood next to Ev, a heavy veiled thrown back from her face. Dud added, "Mary."

He could see the flash of Ev's white teeth, shining with the avarice of a greedy banker behind the heavy beard he had grown. Mary took a jerky step forward.

"Throw your guns down, Dud," Ev said. "We won't hurt you, and there'll be no hard feelings."

Dud stood still. "What about Ugor Darst, Ev?" he asked.

Ev shook his head. "I didn't do it, Dud," he said. "I slipped into town and got wind of what happened, but it wasn't us that did it."

Dud wanted to believe him, and opened his mouth to say more, but a movement behind Ev and Mary stopped him. Johnny stepped from the shadows, pistol in his hand.

"That's right, Washburn," Johnny said. "He didn't."

Ev started and Mary gasped as they whirled to face Johnny's Smith & Wesson.

"Surprised to see me, Washburn?" Johnny said a leer. "That was a nice little party your girlfriends threw in front of the Gilded Lily. Too bad I couldn't stay for the end of it." He waved the pistol. "Everybody, throw your weapons down," he said. "Now! You too, Washburn."

Reluctantly, Ev let his gun slide from his hand. He turned and looked at Dud as if they were now allies. From the shadows, two more figures emerged. This time, it was Lottie, and she held a knife to Kris's head, his hands tied and his eyes wide with fright.

"Do what he says, Dud," she said. "I won't kill the boy, but this knife might slip and cut off his whole ear instead of just a lobe."

Dud swallowed and slowly removed his pistol, throwing it on the ground in front of him. Jesse did the same.

Johnny took a step forward, waving the gun. "Bring the box over here, Washburn, and no tricks. You don't want the same fate as your friend Darst."

"Shut up, Johnny," Lottie warned. "And watch him, he's like a snake."

Dud looked at Jesse before bending down to the box. He paused—on the ground a curious yellow fog swirled at his feet.

"What is it, Washburn? Pick up the box," Johnny ordered. Dud picked it up, looking at Johnny as he did. Yellow mist swirled at his feet, too.

"What the hell!" Johnny yelled with a start when he saw it. In the next second, Dud saw twin flashes of polished metal and three dark figures behind Johnny.

"That was for my father!" Frank shouted. Dud dropped the box and lunged through the thick yellow mist for his gun. Finding it, he looked up and saw Johnny poised, back arched, still holding on to his pistol. A rifle exploded from behind Dud; Johnny went down, his gun firing as he fell. Ev, hit by the wild shot, grabbed his midsection and bent over. While Lottie and Mary screamed, Ponder grabbed Kris and jerked him away.

Dud, Jesse, and Boyd rushed forward. Mary stared at Dud, taking a step backward.

"It was all Ev's doing, Dud," she shrieked. "He forced me; he forced me to go in with him."

Ev raised his head to her. "You lying...," he said and crumpled, almost disappearing in the soupy putrid fog that enveloped the ground.

Mary shot Dud another frantic look before she turned and ran. Boyd made to go after her, but Dud put out his hand. "Let her go."

The knife had fallen from Lottie's hand, and she stood staring down at Johnny's inert body. "Johnny, Johnny," she mumbled. She looked up at Dud, fire leaping into her eyes, and she took a step forward.

Dud aimed his pistol at her. "Back, woman," he said.

"You killed him!" she screamed. "You murderer!"

"Don't give me that," Dud said while she stood smoldering. "His death is on your head, not ours. You could have had me when I was young. Even later, you could have had Felix or Thompson or any number of men, but instead you chose to lead this thug even further down a bad road. He didn't have the brains to think this up, you did!"

In answer, she spat at the ground, ever defiant. "Save the phony preaching for your little sugar baby, Dud. What are you going to do with me? Johnny killed Darst, I didn't."

Dud glanced at the Darst boys hovering around Ponder. They had untied Kris and were watching with gasping breaths. "Any of you boys got a pencil on you?"

Surprise suffused their faces, but Frank fumbled in his pocket until he found a pencil stub. He walked forward, giving it to Dud. As he walked back to his brothers, he gave a quick, frightened glance at Johnny's inert body, two knives and a bullet exit wound protruded from his back. Frank turned, burying his head on Ponder's shoulder, and began to weep.

"Get one of those bank notes, if you would, Boyd," Dud said, unwilling to keep his eyes off Lottie for that long.

Boyd leaned down to the box, and as he peered in it, he too paused. He looked up at Dud and Jesse, but wordlessly bent back down, peeling off one of the bills. He brought it to Dud, and Dud handed him the pencil.

"Write on it, 'I, Lottie, do hereby relinquish the ownership of the Gilded Lily Saloon to Felix O'Brien' and date it."

Boyd crouched near the lantern and used his leg to write upon. When he finished and rose, Dud said, "Hand it to her. Sign it, Lottie. Sign it leave this part of the country."

"You can't do this to me, Dud!" she screamed. "Everything I have is tied up in that saloon."

"Take the money, take the girls, take whatever upstairs furniture you can carry with you, but leave the downstairs bar alone. If you get vindictive and try to burn the place down, I'll have to come looking for you, and I don't want to do that. I don't ever want to see you again."

She grabbed the bill and the pencil from Boyd. Looking down at it, her eyes grew wide when she realized what she had in her hand. She scribbled her signature on it, and handing it back to Boyd, threw back her head and laughed.

"Oh this is sweet, Dud. This is so sweet. All the trouble you went through with your little poker playing poppet for this."

"Leave, Lottie," Dud said.

She shook her head laughing. "Adios, Dud," she said. She turned and faded into the darkness. In a minute, they heard the sound of a horse galloping away.

They stood still for several seconds, staring at one another. Suddenly, the Darst boys rushed forward and wrapped their arms around Dud. Boyd and Jesse came and put their hands on his shoulder.

They laughed and hugged one another. Frank let go and bent down to the strongbox. "What is this? It looks like paper bills, but it's not."

Dud squeezed Mike's arm and rumpled Kris's hair. "It's Confederate scrip. It's useless.'

"You mean there is no treasure?" Mike said, disappointed.

"Of course there is," Dud said. "The treasure is we didn't get our fool heads blown off. That's the real fortune."

Boyd and Jesse gave short laughs and nodded their heads in agreement.

"You might as well keep that money," Dud told them. "It will be something to show your grandchildren."

Boyd shut the lid, and picking up the box, placed it in the back of the wagon.

"What do we do with these two?" Jesse asked.

Dud looked at the bodies of Johnny and Ev. Who was going to miss them? "Bury them here, I guess."

Dud turned to Ponder. "Uncle Ponder!" he began, but his annoyance drained and he smiled instead. "Thank you. Thanks, Uncle Ponder."

By the light of the moon, he saw the corners of Ponder's lips curving upward. "Anytime, Dud," he replied. "Anytime."

"Look, Mr. Dud," Kris said, tugging at Dud's sleeve and pointing at the dog. "Old Tom smells something."

Old Tom, sniffing around the hole the strongbox came from, began digging in it, throwing out piles of dirt with his large paws. Dud drew closer, and hearing the dog's nails hit something, he looked down.

He stood up suddenly. "There's something else down there!" They all dropped to their knees, and pushing poor Tom aside, they dug with their hands.

"It's another box," Boyd said excitedly.

In a few seconds, he was proved right, and they heaved an even heftier chest out of the hole. Dud handed his pistol to Boyd. "Shoot the lock off. My hands are shaking."

Boyd fired, and after the lock shattered, they fell down. Gathering around the trunk on their knees, they looked at one another.

"Jess," Dud said. "Would you do the honors?"

Jesse nodded and leaning forward, opened the lid.

This time it was not paper. Dud pushed his hand in and drew out a fistful of gold coins. "Double eagles," he said. "Gold, but not Spanish gold."

They stared in wonder at the coffer brimming with coins. Dud continued, speaking almost to himself. "Probably somebody didn't know which way the war would go, so they covered all their bets by burying both currencies and died before they could come back for it."

Everyone began laughing at once. "How much is it?" Mike asked.

"Enough for all of us," Dud said, taking off his hat and running his fingers through his hair. "Even after we buy Old Tom the biggest ham bone in town."

THIRTY-ONE

FELIX MADE PLANS IMMEDIATELY TO SELL THE GILDED LILY.

"I found my true place, Dud," he said. "Losing that saloon was the best thing that ever happened to me, and getting it back was the second best. I'm much obliged to you." He grinned. "I knew you could do it, Washburn."

The Darst boys recovered from the trauma and excitement with the speed of youth. "I hope, Mr. Dud," Frank confided when they were alone; "I hope I never have to kill anyone ever again."

Suzette would not take any money. "I did nothing, Oncle Dud," she said. "Really, it was fun." However, she agreed to marry Jesse. They decided that after he took her home to meet his parents, they would leave so he could attend medical school.

"It's going to about kill me to lose you, boy," Dud said.

Jesse grinned. "Oh, I imagine I won't be too far away once I get my degree."

They held a council to decide the fate of the Darsts. Felix had left to look for a buyer, Suzette and Jesse to be alone together. The others gathered around the table. Dud sat on one end with Ponder and Boyd on each side. Iris sat at the other with Zizi. The boys stood near their mother.

"Frank," Dud began. "Did you and your brothers talk to your mother about going to live with us on our ranch?"

"Yes, Mr. Dud," Frank said, standing straighter and clearing his throat. "However," he began, trying to look as grownup as possible, "since our father's death, we are now the men of the family. It is our duty to find a suitable husband for our mother. It is our wish that before we go to your ranch, that she should marry Uncle Ponder."

Dud gaped as the other Darst boys stood nodding their heads in agreement. Zizi moved hers up and down and said, "Ponder, sure."

Surprised, Dud said with a short laugh, "Well now, look here boys, that's not the way we do things in this country."

Before they could answer, Ponder said, "Yes it is. I accept!" He removed the chaw of tobacco from his mouth and gave Zizi a pleased grin.

"Wait a minute!" Dud thundered. He stared at Ponder and back at Zizi and Iris. "Does she know he is seventy years old? Iris! Ask Zizi if she knows how old Ponder is."

Iris turned and whispered something to Zizi. She whispered something back. Iris turned to Dud. "She knows," she said, while Zizi and the boys continued to bob their heads. Zizi whispered something else in Iris's ear. Iris looked at Dud.

"She said her grandmother told her it was better to be an old man's princess than a young man's slave." Having repeated this, Iris pursed her lips and gave Dud a look that dared him to disagree. She knew the second half from experience. The boys stood waiting.

Dud turned to Ponder. "Uncle Ponder!"

His uncle looked at him kindly. "Dud, she and the boys need a new beginning in their life, and I need a happy ending in mine."

When Dud continued to stare at him in doubt, Ponder grew agitated. "I still got it, Dud," he bawled. "It may have been asleep for a while, but I still got it!"

"All right, all right!" Dud said. "Don't give me no details!" He turned to look at the others. "Fine by me then."

He took another deep breath and looked at Boyd. "I'd like to talk to you about Elizabeth, though, Boyd."

Boyd gave him a puzzled look. "What about her?"

Dud glanced at the others, embarrassed to discuss what he wanted to say in front of everyone, but Boyd appeared not to care. Dud cleared his throat. "Well, Boyd, I like Elizabeth just fine. But I don't think she's the right girl for you."

"I don't want to marry Elizabeth," Boyd said, acting as if Dud was touched in the head. "I want to marry Annabelle."

Dud's mouth dropped open for the second time. "But Boyd...," he began and stopped. Had Boyd ever once given Elizabeth a look or a word that said he wanted to court her?

Ponder slapped the table with the palm of his hand. "Excellent idea!" he said.

Dud shot him a murderous look. "Is your name Jesus?" he yelled, but his angry words rolled off Ponder. He turned back to Boyd. "Listen, son," he said. "I know

Annabelle is a luscious dish, but can you imagine what it would be like to be married to her twenty years from now? How her childlike ways would begin to grind on your nerves?"

"Uncle Dud," Boyd said firmly. "Annabelle has never been allowed to grow up. She's different with me. Even if she wasn't, I love her and I'm ready to risk it."

Feeling like the wind had been knocked out of him, Dud looked around the table. His eyes rested on Iris. She nodded her head. Dud turned to Boyd. "All right," he said. "Everything is all settled. We can leave in a few days."

He got up from the table to get another cup of coffee from the stove. From the corner of his eye he saw Iris lower her head. She glanced at the others around the table. Rising, she slipped out of the room.

She disappeared that afternoon and did not return. It seemed to Dud that everyone ignored him—or maybe they were just too wrapped up in their own lives. Dud finally asked about Iris, and Boyd told him she had gone back to the boardinghouse. "Is she feeling poorly?" Dud asked. It was not like Iris to leave without telling him goodbye.

"Maybe," Boyd answered. "Uncle Dud, I really need you and Uncle Ponder to talk to Mr. and Mrs. Harrison on my behalf."

Before Dud could answer, he pressed on. "You know me—I state things as raw as an onion. I need someone who can convince the Harrisons I'm right, especially Mrs. Harrison. With Uncle Ponder there to back you up, you can do it, Uncle Dud."

Dud stared down at his hands. He looked up, letting

his eyes roam before he answered Boyd. Finally, he looked back at him. "Do I have to wear a suit?"

Boyd grinned. "You look fine, Uncle Dud."

Nevertheless, they spruced up before facing the Harrisons. Later, as they stood waiting for their knock to be answered, Dud surveyed Boyd. He wore a new shirt and bandana and had slicked his unruly hair down with so much pomade; Nellie was bound to place a doily behind his head so he did not ruin her sofa. He looked stiff and uncomfortable, just as Dud felt. Only Ponder looked relaxed. Now that he could see a future with yet another wife, and a very sweet and pretty one to boot, fifteen years had dropped from his age.

"Why, hello there," Woody said, opening the door with a newspaper in hand. He gave them an astonished look, and then he grinned. An old pro at listening to awkward men and boys asking permission to marry his daughter, he bid them to come in. This time, Dud thought wryly when he entered the house, Woody was in for an even bigger shock than just seeing Boyd with his hair under control.

Woody told them to enter the parlor and sit down. He smiled again, placing himself in a chair in front of them while they perched on the sofa. "What can I do for you, boys?" he asked jovially.

"I want to marry your daughter," Boyd said without preliminaries.

Woody grinned again, "Well, Boyd, that's something—"

"I want to marry Annabelle," Boyd interrupted.

Dud heard gasps from behind the parlor door. They watched as a change came over Woody Harrison's face—first confusion, disbelief, and finally outrage. Dud spoke.

"Don't say anything, Harrison, until you hear us out." When Woody opened his mouth to protest, Dud stopped him. "Please, listen to us first."

Woody leaned back in his chair. He gave Dud a disgusted wave of a hand. "Only because you are a friend, Washburn."

Dud took a deep breath. "Boyd has spent a lot of time in Annabelle's company. Innocent time," he hastened to add. "He has come to the conclusion that Annabelle's problems have improved and will improve as time goes on as long as she is not held back by a family that is perhaps too protective of her."

Woody again opened his mouth to object, but Dud cut him off. "Harrison, you know as well as I do that Annabelle is starting to experience normal woman to man feelings. Now you can either let her marry Boyd, or run the risk of some unscrupulous man taking advantage of her innocence and naivety."

Woody threw down the newspaper and jumped up in anger. Dud bounded from the sofa to face him. They glared at one another for several seconds, but Dud stared him down. He had only voiced what Woody had begun to fear. Finally, Woody crumbled, sinking down in his chair.

"If I thought her truly backward," Dud added. "I would never mention it."

Woody rubbed his forehead for several seconds. He put his hand down and looked up. "I think my wife should listen to what you have to say."

Dud nodded, and Woody called for her to come into the room. She entered immediately; looking distressed, and sat on the edge of her husband's chair, taking his hand.

"Dear heart," Woody said, stroking her hand. "Dud has something he wants to discuss about Annabelle"

"I know," Nellie said, looking at Dud. "I heard part of it," she had the grace to confess.

Dud sat down and took a breath. "I'd like to tell you a little bit about Boyd first, if I may." The Harrisons nodded, grateful for a respite that would allow them marshal their thoughts and perhaps give them time to form a rebuttal.

Dud cleared his throat. "Boyd was six and Jesse four when their mother became ill. My brother-in-law took her to every doctor, every quack he could find. All his money and mine went to try to heal her. We tried every remedy anyone had to offer, but nothing worked. Finally, he asked me to go with them to a revival service where a preacher boasted he could lay hands on the sick and heal them. My brother-in-law carried my sister to the tent meeting in his arms, looking at me with tears in his eyes and saying, 'This is it, Dud; I don't know what else to do for her.'

"As we walked in, an old cowboy who used to work for us, who I thought had been dead for years, stopped us. He said, 'Mr. Dud, they say at the Big Bend of the Rio Bravo, there is a spring that will heal the sick.' I thanked him and looked at my brother-in-law. Going there would mean risking their lives to marauding Comanche and Apaches, and dodging Mexican banditos and Comancheros all the while. If they made it there, they'd probably never make it back.

"During the service, they went forward to the altar, but nothing happened. When he brought my sister back, my brother-in-law sat down a defeated man. He closed his eyes for a long time. When he opened them, he said,

'I'm going, Dud. I'm taking her. Will you and Ponder look after the boys for us? And you'll have to round up my cattle and herd them to market with yours; else won't none of us be eating this time next year.'

"I agreed, but I was wary of rounding up cattle with two little boys and taking them on a cattle drive for hundreds of miles. I swallowed my pride, and leaving Boyd and Jesse in a hotel room under the care of one of the maids, I went to my ex-wife and pleaded with her to help. She refused and took great pleasure in telling me quite a few things about myself I did not want to hear. When I got back to the hotel, Boyd was taking a lump of opium from Jesse's hand just before he stuck it in his mouth. I chewed that girl up one side of that hotel room and down the other, her just a looking at me and grinning foolishly from a dope-filled dream. I knew right then I couldn't leave them in anyone else's care and have a moment's peace.

"I parked Boyd's rear on an old bell mare with Jesse behind him and told him I'd whip his bottom if he let anything happen to his brother." Dud stopped to glance at Boyd. Boyd sat straight with his eyes on the floor.

"He never did," Dud continued. "He looked after his brother from here to Dodge City and back. Six months later, my brother-in-law brought my sister back with roses in her cheeks. They have four fine girls, and Boyd has looked after those girls just as well as he did his little brother on the back of an old horse on one of the most dangerous trips I've ever taken in my life."

Dud paused. Nellie and Woody were watching him with tears in their eyes—eyes that had lost some of their belligerence. Dud changed to a more matter-of-fact tone.

"Boyd will inherit his parents' ranch, as they do not want to break it up, with the condition that any one of the family, including me, could always live there if need be. Jesse will receive a comparable sum of money. The girls will also be provided for.

"Woody, you and Nellie are not going to live forever. Elizabeth has told me that she has every intention of taking care of her sister. But if you want Annabelle to live as much as a normal life as a woman can, you could not find a better man than my nephew Boyd to have her live it with."

Nellie began to weep. Woody rubbed her back and patted her shoulder. "Mother?" he asked.

Nellie shook her head, unable to speak. Woody kept staring at her until wiping her tears; she gave a short nod of her head. He turned to Dud and Boyd.

"I think Annabelle should make the final decision."

Dud nodded. He rose from sofa and went to the parlor door. When he opened it, he saw a stricken and solemn-faced Elizabeth. Annabelle stood looking surprised.

"Miss Annabelle, would you come in here a minute, please ma'am?"

She did and went to sit by her father. "Annabelle," Woody explained. "Boyd would like to marry you. It would mean living with him far away from mama and papa, and doing things like cooking and cleaning all on your own. Do you want to do that?"

Annabelle stared at Boyd and looked back to her parents. "Could you visit me?"

They looked at Boyd, and he said, "Yes. Yes, whenever you like as long as you like. You will always have a home with us."

Annabelle looked at Boyd again. She did not speak at first, but sat staring. Finally she asked, "Why me? Why do you want me and not Elizabeth? Elizabeth is prettier than I am. She has a bigger bosom than I do."

Boyd blushed. He looked down, at an uncharacteristic loss for words. Finally, he raised his head and said, "I love your sweet nature. I like the way you smile. I like the kindness you show to all God's creatures. I think you are beautiful—even more beautiful than Elizabeth."

"All right, I will," Annabelle agreed.

Her parents burst into tears. They heard footsteps running up the stairs and the sound of springs creaking as Elizabeth flung herself on her bed. Dud wiped his forehead with the back of his hand. He turned and looked at Ponder. Together they let out long breaths of relief.

When they finally made their leave, Woody told Dud, "Boyd is the only man I would ever give my consent to. You know that, don't you?"

Dud nodded. Boyd was the only man he would have ever recommended.

That night, it was as if the yellow mist of the Yegua Knobs had unleashed the hounds of hell. Coyotes yowled and yapped the entire night. The noise did not seem to bother anyone but Old Tom and Dud. The dog stood on the gallery barking, and none of Dud's threats made him stop his pacing back and forth, growling and howling in return.

The next morning when Iris did not come back, Dud, feeling miserable from his restless night, went to the boardinghouse to check on her.

Her landlady treated him even more like scum than usual, hollering up the stairs. "That bastard is here, Iris!"

Dud felt so out-of-joint, he did not even threaten to knock her down for calling him a bastard. She looked down her nose at him, murmured "animal," and left him standing alone with his hat in his hand.

Instead of bouncing happily down the stairs, Iris walked down with quiet, hesitant steps. Her hair was combed down, and she was barefoot, making her look even younger and more vulnerable. She stopped at the threshold and said, "Hello, Mr. Dud."

"Iris, are you sick?" Dud asked, but she shook her head. "Well, honey, are you getting your things together? We're leaving for South Texas just as soon as these weddings are over."

Iris swallowed. "I'm not going," she said in a tiny voice.

Dud stood flabbergasted. "What do you mean, you're not going?"

Iris shook her head. "I'm not going to with you," she said louder.

Dud stood with his mouth open, breathing heavily. He thought his heart had stopped. "What? I don't understand. I thought that's what you wanted all along, to find your brothers."

Her lips trembled, and with tears springing in her eyes, she shook her head, turned and ran back into the house and up the stairs.

The landlady returned, gave Dud a stony look, and slammed the door in his face.

Dud stood there with his mouth open, unable to believe what happened. Finally, he left the gallery, turned and looked back, but all that faced him was a shut door. He walked down the street in shock. Boyd and Jesse stood next to Ponder by the bench in front of the surveyor's office, watching him.

"She's not going with us," Dud muttered. He looked from Ponder to his nephews. "She said she's not going. I guess she doesn't want to leave the excitement of Tie Town."

"Dudford," Ponder said, "did it ever occur in that thick skull of yours that Iris is waiting for a proposal?"

"A proposal?" Dud asked, dumbfounded.

"Good God, chowder head! Where are your brains?" Ponder shouted.

Dud stood aghast. "I can't marry Iris! I'm too old for her," he said. "Besides, don't you remember me describing what a handsome brute her husband was? What mare would want to be with an old mustang after a young Clydesdale?"

Ponder, his face suffused in anger, shook his fist at Dud. "Don't lie to us," he roared. "And don't lie to yourself, either. You know darn good and well you don't have any intention of marrying Iris because it would interfere with your whoring ways."

"I…," Dud began.

"Oh shut up!" Ponder said. "For years I've listened to you moan and complain because your first old lady deserted you, using it as an excuse to run off and whoop it up with barroom floozies in different towns, playing the big man with money so whores would hang on you. I told you I'd kill you if you hurt Iris, and I'm just about there."

They stared at one another, breathing mutual rage.

"Uncle Dud," Jesse said quietly, "Iris has never had eyes for any man but you since the day we met her."

Deflated, Dud looked away, shutting his eyes. "I haven't got guts enough to propose to Iris."

Boyd and Jesse each took an arm and turned him in the direction of the boardinghouse. "Get going, Uncle Dud," Boyd said, giving him a shove. "Remember, God hates a coward."

Old Tom began trotting toward the boardinghouse, and Dud found his feet following.

Reaching the gallery, he wiped his mouth and ran his hand over his forehead. He banged on the door. A curtain flickered. Iris opened the door and stood without speaking.

"I am a divorced man," Dud began, hat in hand. "My first wife hated my guts and left me. She doesn't mean a thing to me now, and I don't mean a thing to her except as an embarrassment. My God is big enough to forgive people their mistakes, but some people don't see it that way and it bothers them."

Iris said nothing, but continued to watch him with her big eyes. He swallowed and confessed. "I think the main reason she left is because we didn't have children. She had one later with another man." He paused and added the rest, painful as it was. "I might not ever be able to give you children."

He stopped—everything he had hid from himself and the world so long spilled in anguish in front of a woman he loved more than his own life.

"Lon said it was my fault we didn't have children," Iris said. "I found out later..., well, I found out a lot of things after we were married. And I was about to leave him when he died."

"Well," Dud said. "You want to try again with me?"

Iris gulped and nodding her head, she urged him on. "You mean…?"

"Yes," Dud said, the last wall falling down. "Marry me, Iris."

Iris bounded into his arms, hugging his neck and pressing kisses all over his face. "I love you, daddy," she whispered. "I'm never going to love any man but you."

Dud knees went so weak, he almost fell down. He hugged Iris tightly to him, grateful she was even better at fishing than she was at playing cards.

THIRTY-TWO

THE HARRISONS AGREED TO LET FELIX PERFORM THE
ceremonies, but insisted he do it in their parlor, not the
saloon, which suited Iris. Suzette agreed. "Perhaps it is for
the best," she said. "We are all starting a new life, yes?"

Elizabeth, once her ego got over the shock, quickly
realized she was free to marry whomever she wished, and
she chose the surveyor. Dud left Felix in charge of the
house on Pecan Street, and as a wedding present, gave the
surveyor and Elizabeth one year's free rent. Although
Boyd tried to tell them there was no need, Elizabeth and
the Harrisons insisted on sharing Elizabeth's hope chest
with Annabelle. As they pulled away from the house with
a loaded wagon, they saw smoke coming from the kitchen
and heard Elizabeth's agonized wail.

"Elizabeth's burned another roast," Annabelle said.

Their wagons made a caravan, along with Rashtah,
who refused to be left behind. Stopping by Iris's previous
landlord because she wanted to pay the rent money she

felt she owed him, Dud succeeded in buying back her mother's rocker and china closet. As they stood outside, waiting for the storekeeper's wife to empty it of her things, Dud told Iris as they looked at the line of wagons behind them, "Remember when you said you intended to tell your husband you were running away to join the circus? I think you did."

To his surprise, Benjamin appeared carrying a saddle. He threw it in the back of the wagon and sat down. Dud said, "No drinking on the job, Benjamin," and the old Indian nodded his head. He looked past Dud to Boyd and Jesse as they stood talking with their wives. "You got them women," he pointed. "You get Benjamin woman, too," he said, tapping his chest.

Dud snorted. "She's in the back of the last wagon."

A smile crossed Benjamin's face, showing his five remaining teeth. He slapped Dud on the shoulder. "You all right, Boss," he grinned.

They were all anxious when they reached Dud's sister and brother-in-law's ranch. As before, the girls caught sight of them and ran squealing and calling to their parents. As the men helped the women from the wagons, the smiling family greeted them, looking inquisitively at the shy Darst boys and the young women who Boyd and Jesse had brought home.

As his sister and brother-in-law hugged their sons, Dud walked over to Clarissa. She stood gazing at the Darst boys with tears of wonder in her eyes. She turned to Dud. "Oh Uncle Dud, I can hardly believe it."

He patted her shoulder. "They are going to live with Uncle Ponder on the ranch for the time being," he said.

"But you'll get to see them every now and then. I promise you when the time is right, something will work out."

"Oh, Uncle Dud! Thank you."

"Now wipe those tears and remember your manners. Go over there and offer them a drink of water. Show them where they can put their things."

She nodded, wiping her eyes and smoothing her apron before leaving.

As Ponder introduced his new wife, Dud nervously read surprise on his sister's face, but she smiled and hugged Zizi, nevertheless. Iris hung back, and he was about to go to her when his sister walked forward.

She stood next to Dud and marveled at the group of people accompanying her sons. "Are they good women, Dud?" she asked.

He looked at them and nodded. "Yes, Sister, they're all good women."

She turned and noticed Iris. "Dud, who is this pretty girl?"

Dud grasped Iris by the hand and pulled her forward, placing his hands on her shoulders as he stood behind her. "Sister, this is the woman I've given my heart to. This is my wife, Iris."

A blank look came over his sister's face, the look that meant she could jump either way, and Dud squeezed Iris's shoulders as she tried to smile and say hello. His sister began to cry. "Oh my word!" she exclaimed. "Oh Dud, it's about time." She went to Iris with open arms, hugging her tightly.

As the two women smiled and embraced, Dud let out a breath he did not realize he had been holding. Suddenly, his sister caught sight of Old Tom digging in her flowerbed.

"Get away from there!" she screamed. "Dud, can't you do something with that dog?"

A LOOK AT: TESTIMONY

BY V.J. ROSE

When his old friend Rocky shows up at Jack's West Texas ranch to spend the summer, he brings along his sexy granddaughter, Toni. Thrilled at first, Jack begins to have doubts. Toni is hiding something even as she freely admits doing whatever it takes to keep Rocky and herself afloat. Jack finds himself so happy he doesn't care if he's being used; besides, he's hiding secrets of his own.

AVAILABLE NOW FROM V.J. ROSE AND WOLFPACK PUBLISHING